Also by

BRUCE ALEXANDER

Blind Justice

Murder in Grub Street

Watery Grave

Person or Persons Unknown

Jack, Knave and Fool

Death of a Colonial

THE COLOR OF DEATH

THE COLOR
OF DEATH

BRUCE ALEXANDER

G. P. PUTNAM'S SONS
NEW YORK

G. P. Putnam's Sons
Publishers Since 1838
a member of
Penguin Putnam Inc.
375 Hudson Street
New York, NY 10014

Library of Congress Cataloging-in-Publication Data

Alexander, Bruce, date.
The color of death / by Bruce Alexander.
p.   cm.
ISBN 0-399-14648-2
1. Fielding, John, Sir, 1721–1780—Fiction.   2. London (England)—History—18th century—Fiction   3. Judges—Fiction   4. Blind—Fiction.   I. Title.
PS3553.O55314 C65   2000   00-039014
813'.54—dc21

Printed in the United States of America

1   3   5   7   9   10   8   6   4   2

This book is printed on acid-free paper. ∞

For Harold Bordwell

ONE

*In which a letter
is delivered
and a shot fired*

✥

By the end of that day in 1772, a concatenation of events would have
begun which would alter considerably the circumstances of life there at
Number 4 Bow Street. We had no notion of that, however, as we sat
together like a proper family at breakfast. Annie, the cook, had baked a
fresh loaf, and we ate it warm with rashers of bacon and lumps of good
country butter. The mood was festive. It was seldom, after all, that the
five of us were together at the table so early in the day. More frequently, we came one by one, ate what was conveniently at hand, and
headed off along our separate paths. On that morning, however, Lady
Fielding was to attend a meeting of the board of the Magdalene Home
for Penitent Prostitutes, a charitable enterprise which she herself had
brought into being. Her preparations for this event had lasted well past
the usual hour of her departure for the Magdalene Home. Nevertheless, there was then time for her to converse with Sir John; to give the
day's orders to Annie and me; and to tease her secretary, Clarissa, the
orphan who Sir John had taken on as his ward that she might be saved
from the Lichfield poorhouse.

Rising, she took one last gulp of tea and waved to me to show that
she was ready to leave. It was my task, reader, to precede her down the
stairs to the street in order to make sure that a hackney coach would
be waiting at our door for her. And so I proceeded. Just as I left the
kitchen, however, I heard Clarissa ask what she was to do during the
rest of the day.

Lady Fielding did then reply: "Why, the duchess will have luncheon
following the meeting, you may be sure of it, and who knows what will

follow that! In short, I may be gone the entire day, and so you may spend it as you like. It is yours, my dear Clarissa."

I heard no more, but what I had caught thus far was quite enough, thank you. I knew full well that though given the day's freedom, Clarissa would be expected to enjoy it in my care. At thirteen, she was considered by Lady Fielding far too young to walk the streets of London, even in the daylight hours.

And so it proved to be. Returning, I was hailed by Sir John and asked to sit down. I reluctantly took a place beside him, fearing the worst.

"You saw Lady Fielding off in a hackney?"

"Oh, I did, sir."

"But she gave you no specific idea of the time she might return?"

"No sir, I'm not at all sure that she knows, Sir John."

He sighed. "Probably not."

I had the feeling that he was temporizing, simply marking time until he found the opportunity to address a topic he would as soon not discuss.

"I wish there were a way she could inform us when she was ready to return. Then I might send you to fetch her back." He paused. I wondered if he wished some comment from me. But no, he pressed onward: "Simply put, I wish that the streets were safer."

"Yet," I objected, "Mr. Bailey and all the constables have made all but a few corners quite safe at night."

"That's just it, you see, Jeremy. I suspect that in some quarters it has become riskier by day than at night. Robberies in daylight have become a particular problem. I have included in the new budget a request for two extra constables. If I'm refused, then I fear I shall have to transfer two of the night men forward to days."

"Is it truly so bad, Sir John?"

"Bad enough," said he, "that I must ask you to watch over Clarissa on this, her day of liberty."

Ah, there it was, thought I. And I could not but admire how skillfully he had maneuvered me to the point where his request seemed both reasonable and necessary. Well, no doubt it was. That, however, did not persuade me to like better the task of playing nursemaid to one who seemed by nature discourteous, cantankerous, and more generally disagreeable than anyone else in my circle of acquaintance. That she was intelligent and clever I would not dispute. Nevertheless, her intelligence and cleverness seemed most often to be used to prove me wrong and embarrass me.

"Your silence tells me that you are less than delighted by my request."

Though blind he may have been, Sir John saw more with his other four senses than I could with my own keen eyes. How could he learn so much from a moment's pause, a mere hitch in time?

Sir John Fielding had been magistrate of the Bow Street Court for near twenty years and had gained a reputation among Covent Garden greengrocers as a fair and just arbitrator of their disputes; even criminals of the district seemed to think him evenhanded. So I could hardly say that I was then surprised when he undertook to set things right with me. I believe that in effect he wished to persuade me now to volunteer for the task for which I had just been drafted. He would do this by convincing me that what in any case had to be done was just and noble and at the same time quite generous of me.

"You know," said he in a quiet, reasoning tone, "she thinks quite highly of you. You seem to be something of a model to her."

"Clarissa? Surely not, sir!"

"Indeed it's true, Jeremy. She greatly admires the single-minded way that you have applied yourself to the study of law."

"Oh?" said I, making a question of it as I considered the claim. I knew that Sir John would not lie regarding such a matter, and so I accepted it that Clarissa had praised me. But even better was it to realize that she could only have formed her opinion from what she had heard from him. *He* must first have spoken well of me.

"Now, I admit that she is a willful girl," said he (which did surprise me somewhat). "She will express her opinion on every matter and argue beyond reason that hers is the right one. Yet, I believe you might teach her to be different."

"But sir," I protested, "I have tried—and often. I reason with her, and it does little good."

"Put in another way, you argue with her. You attempt to correct her, to point out her errors. Is that not so?"

"Well . . . yes."

"Then leave off that in the future. Try teaching not by precept but by example. Behave toward her as you would have her behave toward others. You must try to be an elder brother to her."

"An elder brother?" I echoed his words in what, I fear, was a rather dubious manner.

"Why yes," said Sir John. "Should that be so difficult to imagine?"

"Perhaps not if I apply myself to the task."

Thus, it came about that not much more than half an hour later, Clarissa Roundtree and I, Jeremy Proctor, both of us dressed in our best, were on our way to call upon Samuel Johnson. When Clarissa learned that sometime that day I was to deliver a letter to that distinguished personage (actually no more than an invitation in the form of a note, which I had penned for Sir John the day before), she immediately forsook any plans she may have had and asked if she might accompany me. Indeed she asked so politely that I wondered if perhaps Sir John had not had a few words with her as he had with me. Whether or not this were so I never discovered.

If I seemed especially hostile to Clarissa at this time, when earlier we two had apparently reached a reconciliation of sorts, it was because she had only recently dismayed and angered me with what I must admit was not much more than a prank. Ever since she had come to stay at Number 4 Bow Street she had been in close company with Lady Fielding—companion and "secretary" to her. I have permitted myself the use of upside-down commas, for I had always been dubious as to the nature and extent of the secretarial help which she provided.

It must have been considerable, however, for Lady Fielding declared she had no notion of how she had managed earlier without her; in particular she praised her skill as an organizer. Further proof had come on a Sunday not long before when, with nobody about below on the main floor, Clarissa took it upon herself to alter thoroughly the filing system which Mr. Marsden, the court clerk, used. (It should be made clear that though he may have used the system, he did not invent it; his predecessor, Mr. Brogden, had done that.) Next day there was no little confusion as the court clerk attempted to fathom what had been done, yet when Clarissa confessed and explained the principle upon which she had reorganized the files (names, and not dates alone), Mr. Marsden declared her system superior and applauded her efforts.

However, he regretted that he had not the time to learn it thoroughly, and so he put me forward to Sir John as file clerk. That came as an additional duty—one in addition, that is, to serving Sir John as amanuensis, doing the buying for the household each day in Covent Garden, and running every conceivable errand for the court. When, I wondered, was I to find time to read for the bar? Besides, tending the files was not merely onerous, it was also slightly embarrassing. What healthy young lad would wish to be a file clerk? When I expressed myself in this regard to Clarissa, she did little more than snigger—hence, my hostility toward her.

Yet as we two tramped along in silence, I thought once again of what Sir John had said about acting as an elder brother to Clarissa. I thought I knew what he meant by that, but I was not absolutely sure. In my experience, elder brothers were as often cruel to younger sisters as they were kind. But Sir John, of course, was urging me to be protective, instructive, and friendly to her. All that, I suppose, was within my power. Still, if he were suggesting that I offer her brotherly love, then that surely would be quite beyond me. Why, even if she were to—

"Where was it that you said he lived?" Clarissa asked, interrupting my ponderings as she had often enough done before.

"Johnson's Court," said I.

"Just imagine, having the street where you live named after you. That would indeed be fame."

"So it would be, but I fear it is a distinction that Mr. Johnson has not yet achieved."

"What do you mean?"

"Johnson's Court it was called before he moved there, and so it will be known when he departs."

"Are you sure?"

"Of course I am," said I a bit smugly. "I would not make such a statement unless I were certain of my facts."

She gave me a hard look but said nothing. Our destination lay just off Fleet Street. We made our way there along the Strand. The crowd in the walkway, men and women on their way to their day's labor, bumped and jostled us so that we could not move much faster than a shuffle.

Pressed toward me, she asked in something more than a whisper, "Have you been there often?"

"Where?"

"You know where! To see Mr. Johnson."

"Often enough."

"What is he like?"

"Why . . . that is . . . well . . ." How could one describe Samuel Johnson? He was, perhaps, unique, but . . . "Well, you know, in his manner he is not unlike Sir John—that is, in his deliberate style of speech, and their voices, too, are somewhat alike."

"Deep?"

"Johnson's is the deeper."

Then did I laugh, startled by the picture that flashed before my inner eye. It was quite like that of Mr. Johnson, yet it was one of a man a bit younger, and even more corpulent. The laugh was one of surprise only, for that face brought with it the deepest associations of unhappiness.

With all this I had received a frown from Clarissa. "What has struck you as funny?" she asked.

"No, not funny—nothing of the kind. For an instant, I saw a face from the past resembling Johnson—a deacon in my village named Kercheval. When my father . . ." I hesitated. "When my father died, Mr. Kercheval came for me to take me to the magistrate who would determine my future."

"Your future was the parish workhouse," said she. "You may be sure of that."

"I must have supposed it, for at my first opportunity I broke away from Mr. Kercheval and ran away fast as ever I could."

"And where did you go?"

"Why, here. To London."

"And how did you come to meet Sir John?"

I had never told her the tale of my arrival in London: how I had been duped by a thief-taker and brought, falsely accused, before the magistrate's court at Number 4 Bow Street, and how Sir John Fielding saw through this cruel deception and sent the conspirators on their way. Why had I withheld this from her? Was I too proud? Did I feel it would lower me somehow if the truth were known?

Well, whatever the reason, since we had by then passed along the Strand with Temple Bar in sight, and Johnson's Court lay not so distant, I decided it was time to tell. The version she heard as we moved on, still buffeted by the crowd, was somewhat abbreviated—a summary, more or less—but the important facts were there. And by chance, when I had concluded, the turn for Johnson's Court lay just ahead.

"Why then," said she, having heard all, "you came to Bow Street much as I did."

"Indeed," said I. "Had you thought otherwise?" I eased her round the corner into the quiet of the Court.

"I don't know what I thought. You seemed so well settled that I—"

When Clarissa failed to finish the sentence, I pointed toward Mr. Johnson's door and guided her in that direction. "We're here," said I.

"What? Oh, I . . . yes, of course."

I gave three stout thumps upon the door, and we did not wait long, for almost immediately came the sound of footsteps beyond. The door opened, and for a long moment I said not a word. Expecting to see Miss Williams or one of the other members of the household staff, I was surprised—taken aback, one might say—to see the face of a black man: young, smiling, and quite confident. He looked at me encouragingly, nodded, and waited for me to speak.

Clarissa stepped in then, saving me from further embarrassment. "We have come to see Mr. Johnson," said she.

"Ah, well, is he expecting you?" His voice was pleasant enough and authentically that of a Londoner. But was there, perhaps, the hint of the island lilt to it that I heard from time to time in Mr. Burnham's speech? Perhaps, and perhaps not.

"No, but I have with me a letter for Mr. Johnson from Sir John Fielding, magistrate of the Bow Street Court," said I.

"I'd be happy to give it to him. You may leave it with me and consider it delivered."

Would this be another contest of the wills of the kind which took place each time I delivered a letter to the Lord Chief Justice? I hoped not, indeed I did.

"I should be happy to do that," said I to him, "but Sir John would like it read, and an immediate answer given—if at all possible."

"Oh, it is possible," said he, throwing open the door, "but you must wait a bit, for he is not long risen. Come in, come in, both of you, and we shall sit together and talk. I would like to make your acquaintance."

Clarissa and I exchanged glances, and then, smiling, we entered. He led us into a small sitting room where I had previously waited upon occasion for the great man. Indicating a place for us on the settee, he took a chair by the door and asked our names. He introduced himself to us as Francis Barber.

"However," said he, "you may call me Frank."

"We have not met before," said I. "Have you recently joined Mr. Johnson's household?"

"No, it would be better said, I recently *re*joined the household. I've been away at school, you see."

"Which school?" I asked, half expecting that I might be told that it was Oxford or Cambridge, for he was of a proper age. But would a black man attend one of the great universities? I thought not.

"It is a school run by a Monsieur Desmoulins, who is a Frenchman."

Clarissa leaned forward eagerly. "And did you learn French from him? I should like to learn that language. It is a most beautiful tongue."

"Oh, it is, right enough, and I did learn a bit of it, but I fear I had my hands full with Latin. And I must say, Greek was quite beyond me. They seemed useless to me. When would I meet an ancient Roman or Greek whom I might speak with?"

Clarissa and I, both autodidacts, agreed most emphatically, for such as we were, utility was all. (While I cannot speak for Clarissa, I know that today I would be less likely to dismiss those dead languages as useless.) But when he went further and declared all education "beyond plain reading, writing, and sums" to be excessive and unnecessary, then we were forced to demur.

We argued with him on that point quite heatedly for some minutes; he maintained that the six years that he had spent under the tutelage of Monsieur Desmoulins was not much more than time wasted, and we maintained that it was not. Clarissa said that Frank Barber himself was proof of the efficaciousness of Monsieur Desmoulins's schooling. She declared him as gentlemanly as any fellow one might meet in St. James Park.

Then, did he reveal himself to me as somewhat vain. He preened a bit, striking a pose with his head tilted just slightly toward the light. "Oh," said he, "do you really think so?"

"Of course we do."

"Well, thank you for saying so." His self-conceit, such as it was, seemed quite childishly innocent.

At that, and with a great bustle of authority, a stout-figured woman, well-known to me, appeared of a sudden in the doorway, scowling down at Frank—on the occasions I had encountered her here before, she seemed always to look displeased.

"Mr. Johnson would like to see you, Frank," said she. "He is now come down for breakfast." Then, having delivered her summons, she turned about and left as noisily as she had come.

Rising, he waited until he had heard the last of her, and said, at not much above a whisper, "That's Miss Williams. She doesn't like me—no, not at all." He himself started from the room, but turned back to us and declared, "I'll tell him you're waiting to see him."

As soon as we were alone, Clarissa began muttering to me about Francis Barber. She asked who he was and what was his relation to Mr. Johnson. I assured her that I had neither met nor heard of the fellow before. Rather insistently, she rephrased her question, and I rephrased my answer. We might have gone on so for the rest of the morning, had not the subject of our lame discussion swiftly returned and bade us come along with him that we might see Mr. Johnson. Following obediently, we were conducted down a short hall to a room just off the kitchen where I had met Johnson at breakfast on one previous occasion. Frank introduced us, and, with a cheerful goodbye to all, took his leave.

Mr. Johnson looked from me to Clarissa and back again to me. "Well," said he, "you, young sir, have been here before. We are somewhat acquainted, and I understand there is a letter for me from Sir John Fielding, but is it of such heavy matter that it took two of you to carry it?"

Clarissa, never at a loss for words, spoke up fearlessly as ever: "By no means, sir. I came along that I might meet you and gaze upon your face."

"If that was your purpose, child, you must be sorely disappointed," said he in response. "This face of mine frightens some—but gives others cause for merriment." He took a prodigious gulp of tea and smiled upon her.

"We have things in common," said she.

"Oh? Tell me then, by all means."

"Well, we are both natives of Lichfield."

"And we have proven ourselves wiser than its entire population by leaving the place when we could."

"You are the son of a bookseller," said she, "and I am the grand-daughter of one. My mother did often tend the shop for him."

"What was the name of the shop?"

"Gladden's. Perhaps you remember it?"

"I thought I might—but no. It has been many years since I left." He seemed to be attempting a polite withdrawal from his conversation with her.

But Clarissa, not in the least mindful of this, pressed on with what she had so boldly begun. "Finally," said she, "we have in common the vocation of literature."

He looked at her slyly. "Ah, could one so young as you be an author?"

"Not yet, but I am preparing myself for a career similar to your own."

"Well, in that case, I have two bits of advice for you. First, do not neglect your Latin, for there is nothing quite so good for style as famil-iarity with that language and its grammar. My second piece of advice is more practical: If you are truly serious about writing, then you must choose a pen name of the masculine sort, for as a female you will greatly limit your chances of acceptance—by editors as well as by the general public."

She found this quite unacceptable. "There I must disagree with you," she began.

Yet she never finished, for Mr. Johnson turned from Clarissa to me, chastising her by ignoring her obviously and completely. "Now," he said rather pointedly to me (and not to Clarissa), "what of this letter from Sir John? I do hope he is not communicating to me in his official capacity."

"Nothing of the kind, sir," said I, as Clarissa at last fell silent. "It is naught but an invitation."

Again that sly look from him. "Are you then in the habit of reading the missives you deliver?"

I produced the letter in question and handed it to him. He wiped his hands thoroughly on his napkin, preparing to read it.

"No sir, I am not in the habit of reading them. I am, however, in the habit of taking them in dictation."

He chuckled approvingly at my response and pulled open the letter at the seal. So poor was Johnson's eyesight that he was forced to hold whatever he wished to read at no more than three inches from his face. Thus it was that he perused the contents of the letter. I had seen all this before and was not in the least surprised, but when I glanced over at Clarissa, I noted the look of consternation upon her face. I feared in that instant she might make some unwanted exclamation of sympathy, but, catching her eye, I shook my head, and she kept silent.

"Well and good," said Mr. Johnson as he put down the letter. "I should be happy to come at the date and hour which he has specified. Ten days hence—that should give me time and opportunity to do any rearranging that need be done." Then did he pause, or perhaps hesitate, as if taking a moment to reach a decision. "You do not have an invitation for that fellow Boswell, do you?"

"Nooo," said I, "but one might be written for him if you wished it so."

"On the contrary," said he, "I would *not* wish it so. As it happens, he is down from Edinburgh, and he manages to beg invitations to every dinner to which I'm invited. It seems that no matter where I go he is there, asking questions, drawing me out on every conceivable question. It is most annoying. Do ask Sir John not to invite the fellow, will you?"

I gave a proper little bow. "Very good, sir."

"Shall I write out a reply to Sir John's letter?"

"Oh no, Mr. Johnson, I shall convey your response to him." I paused but a moment. "And so, with your permission, we shall take our leave of you."

"Good day to you, young sir. And to you, young lady," said he to Clarissa, "I shall repeat my advice. First, work at your Latin, and second, adopt a male pen name."

Would she insist on pressing her argument? I turned and saw her performing a careful curtsey. Reassured, I took her arm and guided her from the breakfast room and down the hall to the door. It was not Frank Barber but Miss Williams who was there to see us out. That she did with a curt "good day," pausing not an instant to wave us out to Fleet Street.

"I went too far, didn't I?" The words were out of Clarissa's mouth the moment that the door slammed shut behind us.

"Well . . ." Was I to tell her the truth? Was I to say that she had embarrassed me, irritated Mr. Johnson, and disgraced herself—and managed it all with just a minute or two of idle talk? No, I could hardly say that, could I? And so all I said was: "I think perhaps you failed to keep in mind who it was you were speaking to."

"I think you're right. Oh, Jeremy, what am I to do? To have the ear of Mr. Johnson and then simply to prattle on about what I had in common with him—as if he cared for a moment—and then to try to engage him in argument on the question of a pen name. What could I have been thinking? Samuel Johnson, after all!"

"Dictionary Johnson," said I, as we turned back on to Fleet Street and there joined the tide of humanity on the move toward Temple Bar.

"Yes, so they call him. Just imagine what it would be to be the author of a dictionary of the English language!"

"Well, he had assistants—six, I believe."

"But Samuel Johnson *is* generally recognized as its author."

"Insofar as a dictionary can be said to have an author—yes, I suppose so."

"But of course! Every book has an author. And poor Mr. Johnson ruined his sight in the great effort to produce his dictionary. Why, he is near as blind as Sir John."

"Perhaps, but I've heard it said he had an infection of the eyes when he was a child, as a mere babe. That may be why he must read with his nose in the pages."

"Whatever the reason, my heart goes out to the man." Clarissa walked along in silence for a bit. I waited, sensing that she had left something unsaid. Then at last she spoke: "Jeremy, the next time it becomes obvious to you that I should hold my tongue, I would like you to let me know. Give me a pinch or squeeze my hand, or . . . do something, anyway, to pass a signal to me that I must stop."

"You say the next time? What about the time after that?"

"Then, too—and the time after that, and so on, until I've mastered my tongue."

"That may take quite some time," said I, merely meaning to tease. "Your arm may be blue from all the pinching."

"So be it," said she. And, having taken what between us amounted to an oath, she set her face in such a way that she seemed much older than her years, and marched resolutely forward.

Clarissa kept up the pace for quite some time, but eventually she slowed somewhat. Yet still, she said nothing. She seemed to be giving thought to a particularly troubling matter.

After we had walked thus for a good, long way, she turned to me and sought my opinion. "Do you suppose," said she, "that the study of Latin would truly improve my writing style?"

Late that evening—after Clarissa had exhausted me through the day with her questions and comments, and following Lady Fielding's tardy return from her board meeting, slightly tipsy from the duchess's wine served at the luncheon—late that evening (to repeat) I was summoned down from my eyrie to the kitchen where Sir John awaited.

"We must be gone, Jeremy," said he. "Robbery and murder have been perpetrated in St. James Street. Mr. Baker brought the news only moments past." In fact, just then I could hear his footsteps descending the stairs.

"St. James Street!" It came from me as an exclamation. "Surely not Mr. Bilbo's residence?"

"No—but close by. Pull on your coat and grab your hat. We are to meet Mr. Bailey there. The new constable, Will Patley, was first on the scene, and I fear that he may forget all that he was taught about protecting the premises against intruders, the curious, even against the victims of the robbery themselves."

"There are some who never seem to learn those lessons," said I.

"All too true, I fear."

We went down the stairs together, he with his hand upon my shoulder, the two of us in close step. (He had recently taken a tumble and had become quite distrustful of even the most familiar stairway.) Mr. Baker waited near the door, in his hands a brace of pistols, holstered and mounted on a belt. I took them from him and buckled them on under my coat. Mr. Baker claimed it was foolish to go out in the streets unarmed at any time near midnight or after; and I, as Sir John's companion on these late-night rambles, had the responsibility of defending him, so I wore the pistols. For his part, Sir John disapproved on principle of all but his constables bearing firearms, so he said nothing. (It was a blind man's way of looking in the other direction.) As a result of all this, not a word passed among the three of us until I was satisfactorily armed.

Only then did Mr. Baker speak up: "There's a hackney at the door. I whistled him down from the corner and told him to wait on pain of death."

"On pain of death, Mr. Baker?"

"Well, Sir John, sometimes I exaggerate a little just to keep their attention."

"And your threats work well enough?"

"I ain't had to kill any yet."

"And thank God for it," said Sir John with a chuckle. "It would indeed be a black mark against the Magistrate's Court."

With that, we departed Number 4 Bow Street and climbed into the waiting coach. I had so often walked to the Bilbo residence in St. James Street and knew the way so well, that I thought of it as only a short distance away. In reality it was not, but the time it took to get to St. James was barely sufficient for Sir John to tell what he knew of the robbery. He knew little of the murder; we would learn more of that upon our arrival.

To summarize: At about ten in the evening, a gang of well-armed men tricked their way into the home of Lord Lilley of Perth. As it happened, Lord and Lady Lilley were absent that evening, attending a dinner at the residence of the Dutch ambassador. The robbers herded the entire household staff into the kitchen below the stairs, put a guard upon them, and then proceeded to strip the place of everything of value—Lady Lilley's jewels, paintings, statuary, silver plates, the odd piece of furniture, et cetera. So much was taken that it must have been necessary to cart it away in a wagon; evidently one was waiting at the rear of the mansion. It took less than an hour to empty the house of its treasures. The homicide was most peculiar: One of the staff, a footman, was taken from the company in the kitchen and summarily shot. Even more peculiar was the fact that the raiding party was made up entirely of black men.

When the hackney driver pulled up at the number on St. James Street which he had been given, I spied Constable Brede standing guard at the door. I passed word of this on to Sir John. He seemed quite pleased to hear it.

"That means," said he, "that Constable Bailey is inside. He will have heard something from every witness in the house and will be able to inform us just who of them is worth talking to and which may be passed over. This need not take as long as I feared. I, for one, Jeremy, was quite ready to retire when word came of this outrage."

"But you've always said, sir, that the most important work in any investigation is done at the first visit to the scene of the crime and that there was no point in rushing through it."

"Have I always said that?" He sighed. "Probably I have. How unkind of you to remind me."

Mr. Brede passed us through, saying little, as was his way. And once inside we soon discovered that Mr. Bailey had arranged things as Sir John predicted. The magistrate's chief constable may not have been greatly talented as an interrogator, but long experience had taught him the sort of thing Sir John would be interested in; it had also taught him how to recognize one who was withholding information, equivocating, or just plain lying.

According to Benjamin Bailey, though he had not quite finished talking to all the potential witnesses, it seemed to him that only a few would be worth the magistrate's attention.

"I thought you might want to talk to the butler first," said he to Sir John.

"Always a good place to start."

"He it was who opened the door to that murderous crew."

"Ah yes, but the mention of the murder reminds me, Constable Bailey, has Mr. Donnelly been sent for?"

"Yes sir, indeed he has. I sent Will Patley for him soon as I arrived. Just like you told us, sir, if there's a killing or even a wounding, we send for the medical examiner—right away—ain't that right?"

"Quite right. But now, if you will just put me with the butler . . ."

"Certainly, sir—right over here."

The butler, a Mr. Collier, was a slight man of not much more than forty years with a bloodied bump on his forehead. He stood in a corner of the great entry hall, somewhat apart from the rest of the servants gathered there. His small hands were clasped before him in such a way that if his eyes had been shut or his lips moving, I should have sworn that he was praying. Indeed he looked like a man in need of prayer. Never, I think, have I seen a man appear so obviously overcome by worry. Sir John did not add to his burden. He questioned him as gently as I had ever known him to question any witness.

He did not, for example, ask Mr. Collier directly how it had come about that he had opened the door to the robbers; rather, he took a circuitous route and first solicited the opinion of the butler on a variety of matters related to the invasion of Lord Lilley's residence.

Sir John asked, for instance, how many there were in the raiding party. Mr. Collier's reply: "That is difficult to say, sir, for in the beginning they seemed not so many, but I'm sure there were more of them there at the end."

"All of them were black men?"

"All that I saw."

"And did they speak as black men would speak?"

In forming his answer to this question, Mr. Collier paused; he seemed troubled. "Well, that was where I was deceived, you see," said the butler. "I wouldn't have opened the door to a black man at any time of the day or night, no matter what his tale of woe. But whoever it was talked through the door — I'd say he was probably the leader — and he talked just as any Londoner would. He made a fool of me for fair — and now I fear for my position. I shall be blamed for this."

Only then did Sir John ask the question that must have interested him most: "What was it that he said which persuaded you to open the door to him?"

Realizing that he had come at last to the matter he wished sincerely to avoid, the butler hesitated long enough to clear his throat, then plunged ahead: "He described a most terrible carriage accident which he said had taken place nearby in St. James Street. 'Was there a doctor who lived hereabouts?' he asked through the door, for there was, he said, a woman pinned in the wreckage who could not be freed unless the carriage were set right. Footmen would be needed, or porters. Could any be spared? 'The poor woman was near crushed,' he declared. 'She might die if she weren't soon helped.' "

The butler continued: "All this, mind, was said in tone and manner just as one might hear the same said in Covent Garden or any street in London — except there was terrible urgency in his voice. He seemed quite overcome with worry and fear. To this moment I find it difficult to believe that he was shamming." At that point, Mr. Collier took a deep breath, as if fortifying himself for what lay ahead. "Well, what can I say in my defense? Convinced by the sound of his voice, I opened the door out of kindhearted concern, sympathy, and, well, curiosity, too, must have played a part."

"But indeed you did open the door," said Sir John.

"I did, sir."

"What then occurred?"

"I had no sooner heaved back the night bolt and opened the door a crack when it was slammed against me. I fell unconscious there in the hall, probably only for a minute or less, for next thing I knew I was dragged down the hall and then down the back stairs to the kitchen. It was not until all the rest of the staff had been moved into the kitchen that I was fully conscious."

"How many men entered by way of the front door?"

"I would have no way of saying exactly, for I was unconscious most of that time, but probably no more than three."

"And were all of them black?"

"I could only say that the face I glimpsed ever so briefly as I opened the door was that of an African. I was told by others of the household staff, however, that all who entered, including some who were seen to enter through the rear door of the house, were unmistakably of the black race."

"And what do you know of the murdered man, Mr. Collier?"

"Very little," said the butler. "Walter Travis had not been long on staff. I hired him three months past to replace a porter who'd fallen mortally ill with the pox. Lord Lilley didn't want one who was ill in such a way under his roof. Travis brought with him a good character from his last employer. I have no notion why anyone should have been killed, nor why they chose him."

"Hmmm," said Sir John, "it does indeed seem strange." He mused a moment upon the matter, and then spoke up again. "You may go, Mr. Collier. By the bye, if Lord Lilley blames you, as you say he will, I should be happy to reason with him on the matter. I take it that he has been sent for?"

"He has, yes sir. Oh, thank you, sir. I am greatly obliged to you, sir."

All the while the butler said this, he was backing away and bobbing his head like some puppet. I no longer pitied him as I had at first. He cared a bit too much for himself, it seemed to me, without caring much for others. What had happened, for example, to the poor fellow dying of the pox? Collier seemed not to care. Why did he say he would, under no circumstances, open the door of Lord Lilley's residence to a black man at any hour, night or day? And why did he feel so unfairly deceived simply because one who proved to be black spoke as any white Londoner might speak? Had I not, that very morning at Dr. Johnson's, met Frank Barber and heard him talk as any proper fellow from Fleet Street might? Not all those who look as Africans speak as Africans, after all.

By then it seemed to me that Sir John had been entirely *too* gentle with the butler. I was just putting together a well-reasoned complaint to the magistrate when he rumbled something deep under his breath.

"What was that, sir?"

"I said, 'I never dealt before with such a lickspittle.' "

"But . . . but . . . you encouraged him, Sir John. You were a good deal nicer to him than was necessary."

"I may need him a bit later."

Just then Constable Bailey appeared with a woman—hardly more than a girl—in tow. She had quite a saucy manner and seemed rather to enjoy the attention given her. She regarded the captain of the Bow Street Runners rather flirtatiously. For his part, Mr. Bailey's attitude toward her was one of stony indifference. He delivered her to Sir John with a curt "Mary Pinkham, personal maid to Lady Lilley, sir. She may have something to say which you'd be interested in." And having said that, he departed, returning to the task he had assigned himself.

"Well, Mistress Pinkham," said Sir John, "what is it you have to tell?"

"Naught that would interest you, Your Magistrate, 'cept—"

"You seem to have me confused with the king," said Sir John. "And while that is most flattering, the proper form of address when speaking to me would simply be 'sir.' "

"Yes sir," said she, and gave a proper curtsey. "Well, as I was sayin', sir, the onliest thing you might be interested in is that I was the last one caught."

" 'Caught'? I don't quite understand."

"Simple enough, sir. When the robbers come in, they caught most of the servants below stairs where they'd just finished eatin', and Mr. Collier they caught when they come in. I was the onliest one was upstairs. I was in her ladyship's bedroom, straightening up for when she comes back, laying out her nightgown and all."

"I see," said the magistrate, "and when were you aware that something was amiss downstairs?"

"Oh, I could tell. There was of a sudden a terrible lot of shouting and noise, and I could tell there was something wrong. I didn't want no part of it."

"And how did you react?"

She looked at him blankly. Clearly, the word was not in her vocabulary. " 'React,' sir?"

"What did you do then?"

"I hid myself in Lady Lilley's closet, the one with all her frocks and all in it. She has so many clothes, sir. Really, you've no idea."

"I'm sure she has," said Sir John, somewhat annoyed at her, "but let us stick to the matter at hand. Now, as you were hidden away in the closet amongst all those frocks, were you able to hear the robbers as they went from room to room?"

"Oh, yes sir, I surely was, sir. They was yellin' and shoutin' about, goin' all around the house. Why, they scared me half to death, they did."

"Now, Mistress Pinkham, I ask you to give some thought to this next question." He paused to give weight to what followed: "Would you say that these men who came to rob the house knew their way around it? Would you think it likely that they had a map of the interior to show them where things were located?"

She did give the matter some thought, but her answer, when it came, may have disappointed Sir John. "No sir," said she, "I don't think they was ever in the house before, and I don't think they had a map. The reason is, when they come upstairs, I could hear them very plain, and they were saying, 'Where is it?' and, 'Which is the room where the duchess sleeps?' They were searchin' through the whole upstairs for the room where I was hidin'."

"And eventually they found it," he put in.

"They did, sir, but it took them a while, and if they'd had a map of the house, or as you say, known their way around, then they coulda gone right to it."

Sir John sighed. "I see your point, and I must admit it has a certain validity."

"Sir?"

"Oh, never mind. Of course all this searching about was not done in an effort to find you."

"No, sir. They just opened the closet door, and there I was."

"They were after something quite different."

"They was, sir, and it was m'lady's jewels."

"And they found them."

"Yes sir, I told the robbers where they was hid." Neither in her face nor in her voice was there any hint of shame or embarrassment as she made her confession. She even wore a slight smile as one might while engaged in any sort of polite conversation.

"Told them, did you?" He seemed more amused than shocked at her audacious revelation.

"I did, sir, and you would, too, if you'd had a knife stickin' up your nose. They offered to slit it proper if I didn't tell." She shrugged, as if the choice she'd made had been the only reasonable one. "And so I told them."

Sir John laughed out loud at that. "Your logic," he said, "is altogether unassailable. I mean to say, you may be certain that you did the right thing. However,"—and here he lowered his voice—"I would not tell it to your Lord or Lady Lilley as you told it to me. Tell them that you fought and screamed and so on, and that one of the robbers happened upon the jewels just as they were about to begin torturing you in earnest. Now, doesn't that sound better?"

"Oh, much, sir, I'll practice it, I will."

"You do that, Mistress Pinkham." And having said that, he dismissed her. But then did a second thought persuade him to call her back again. "I have but one more matter to mention to you, and that has to do with the manner of speech used by the robbers."

"Sir?"

"The way they talked. I have been told that all were black men—Africans. Is that correct?"

"All I seen were."

"And did they talk as black men would talk?"

"That I wouldn't know, sir. I never talked to no black man before. They just sounded regular."

"Thank you, that will be all."

And off she went, pausing only to curtsey and blurt out a thank-you.

"Well, Jeremy," said Sir John, turning in my general direction, "what did you think of her?"

"I would say, sir, that what she lacked in valor she made up in good sense."

"Well put," said he, "but tell me, is Mr. Bailey about? Now that I've talked to a couple of them, I feel as though I'd like to talk to more—just getting into the spirit of it, so to speak."

"Yes sir, Mr. Bailey is just across the room." In fact he had been talking for quite some time with a man nearly as large as he.

"Beckon him here, will you?"

That I did, and Mr. Bailey came, bringing the big man along with him. "Sir John," said he, "I've someone with me here who can tell you a bit about the murdered man."

"Ah, at last," said Sir John. "I was hoping you'd find one such. The butler hired him but claims to know nothing about him."

"Well, I know something, don't know all," said the newcomer.

"Your something will be most welcome, Mr. . . . Mr. . . . What is your name, sir?"

"Burley," said he. "Tom Burley in full. Walter Travis and me were porters together. We did all the furniture moving, the heavy lifting and loading—just the two of us."

"Then you must have been well-acquainted with the man."

Tom Burley sighed and shook his head. "Nobody got *too* well-acquainted with him. He was a hard man to get to know."

"Well, there are those, of course. But perhaps you could tell me, Mr. Burley, something of his background. Where was he from, for instance?"

"Right here in London, as near as I can tell. He never talked about anyplace else, anyways. Certain things he said made me think he'd put in some time in prison."

"Debtors prison? The Fleet? Bridewell?"

"No, I think he'd seen the inside of Newgate. I don't know for what, or for how long, but he got to talking about it once, told of the nasty little tricks played by the warders on the inmates, and he told it in such a way, it seemed pretty certain to me he knew from experience."

"Hmmm," said Sir John, musing for a moment, "yet he was hired. The butler said he'd been given a good character by his last employer."

"Aw, that meant nothing, sir. He counterfeited it, made it all up hisself, then handed it over to a scrivener to get it Englished proper and make it look as such should look."

"You know this for certain, Mr. Burley?"

"I know he told me that's what he did. And if you're wondering why I didn't snitch, I'd have to say it ain't my nature to do so. As long as he did his share of the work—and he did—I'll keep mum on the matter."

"Why do you suppose he was singled out to be killed? Was it done as a warning to the rest of you there in the kitchen—a threat?"

"Oh, perhaps something of that sort. Something was said. A threat was made. It was just when they were getting ready to leave, they took him along. But that wasn't the reason—not to my mind."

"Then why was he taken? Why was he killed?"

"I've something in mind about that," said Burley. "I think it might be he was in on the sacking of the house—told them when to come and what was where, and so he expected to leave with them. He didn't seem overly worried when he went up those steps. Shoot him down, and you've got one less when you divvy the whack."

Sir John nodded thoughtfully, considering at length what had been said. "Did you view the body?" he asked at last.

"Oh yes. We'd all heard the shot fired out back, so we had a pretty good idea where to look. Travis was shot in the back of the head—by surprise, I'd say. Poor cull never knew what hit him."

"I wonder if you—"

"Beg pardon, Sir John." It was Constable Bailey. Usually a model of well-mannered propriety, he would not think of interrupting his chief unless there were a matter of some urgency.

"Yes, Mr. Bailey, what is it?"

"Constable Patley has just returned with Mr. Donnelly, and Mr. Donnelly would like to know where is the body?"

"Show him, won't you, Mr. Bailey? Or if you don't know, take Burley here with you. He can show you."

"As you say, Sir John." This was delivered with a salute. He did a quick turn and went off to fetch Mr. Donnelly.

"All of which leaves us," said Sir John to me, "without Mr. Patley. Do you see him about?"

I looked round the room—but looked in vain. He was nowhere to be seen. "No sir," said I. "Shall I check outside with Constable Brede?"

"No . . . well, perhaps. But first let me try this. *Constable Patley!*" he bellowed. *"Come at once."* At that all heads in the great entry hall (and most of the household staff were there, milling about) turned his way, surprised at his intemperate shouting. I, too, was surprised, for I had never known him to employ such methods before. Ah well, he was full of surprises.

"Tell me, Jeremy," said he mildly, "do you see him now?"

"I'm afraid not, Sir John." Ah, but I had spoken a bit too early, for there he was, pulling himself away from the flirtatious Mistress Pinkham. They had just stepped from behind the wide, winding staircase which so dominated the room; they had thus been hidden from view. "No, I was wrong, sir. I see him now. He's coming this way."

Constable Patley presented himself at attention and brought a stiff hand to his brow in a military salute. (He was said to have been a soldier in the colonies.) "Here I am, sir!"

"Constable Patley, is it?"

"Yes sir!"

"I have a few questions for you."

"And I am pleased to answer them, sir."

"That is gratifying," said Sir John. "Now tell me, Mr. Patley, where were you when you were notified of this felonious invasion of the Lilley residence?"

"Quite close by, sir, walking the Pall Mall, I was."

"And who was it approached you? Which of the servants?"

"Why, I don't remember his name, but he come running up to me, and he said there'd been a terrible robbery and murder at Lord Lilley's. I sent him on to Bow Street and come here myself. Did I do right?"

"You did right enough, but I wanted to talk with whomever it was brought word to Bow Street. Do you see him here?"

Mr. Patley, a reasonably tall fellow to begin with, went up on his tiptoes to survey the faces of those in the room. There must have been more than a dozen there in the entry hall, but most of them were women—upstairs maids, downstairs maids, cooks, kitchen slaveys, et cetera. After studying them carefully, he came down to our level, shaking his head in a negative manner.

"No sir," said he, "I don't see him anywheres."

"Well, next time, when such a crime is committed, you must at least get the name of him who reports it."

"I promise to do it that way in the future," said Mr. Patley.

"See that you do, sir, for you will need names and facts for the report that you must write."

"Report, sir? What report?"

"The one that you will write and give to Mr. Marsden, the court clerk, in the morning. Didn't Mr. Bailey tell you that when you are first on the scene of any serious crime, then you must write a report on it?"

"He said something about that, sir."

"Well, it seems your turn has come, does it not?"

"As you say, sir."

"Oh, and by the bye, you must have in it some estimate of the value of the goods stolen. It need not be absolutely accurate; it can later be raised or lowered. That you can probably get from the butler, Mr. Collier. If not, then tell him I said that we must have it. Is all that understood?"

Constable Will Patley sighed a deep, unhappy sigh. "All understood, sir," said he.

"Is there some part of this you wish to discuss?"

"No sir, it's just . . . I didn't realize there'd be such a lot of pen work to be done. I ain't very good with a pen."

"Well, do as well as you can. Mr. Marsden will evaluate it in the morning."

"Just like school, sir?" There seemed to me to be a bit more than a hint of impudence in that.

"No, not quite." Sir John paused and rubbed his chin in thought before proceeding: "Mr. Patley, you have not been with us long. You are not yet accustomed to our procedures, but once you are, I believe you will understand their usefulness." Then, with a nod: "That will be all."

The constable saluted in the same military fashion as before and barked out a "Yes sir" before turning and marching off, more sober-faced than when he had come. He attracted a good deal of attention to himself with these exaggerated movements. Mistress Pinkham, for one, stared with such intensity at him that she seemed almost to consume him with her eyes. Only then did it occur to me that women, especially young women like her, would no doubt find him quite handsome—"a rum cod," as Jimmie Bunkins would have it—"dashing," as you might say.

Then did Sir John bend toward me and whisper: "Did he salute me again?"

"Twice, sir," said I, "once at arrival and once at departure."

"I wish he wouldn't do that. Perhaps you could mention it to him. Tell him that something more . . . oh, I don't know . . . *informal* might be better."

"Well," said I, "I'll try."

"Jeremy . . ."

"Yes, Sir John?"

"Let us leave here. I am suddenly grown weary."

"Did you not wish to wait for Lord Lilley?"

"No, there is no telling when he will return. He is, as I have heard, socially timid, and he might consider it too great an insult to the Dutch ambassador if he and Lady Lilley were to leave early. He may be prepared to wait, no matter what disaster may befall his house."

"Then by all means, let's be gone," said I.

"By all means, let's," said he.

Sir John left word with Mr. Brede, nevertheless, that when Lord and Lady Lilley were to return, he was to tell them that Sir John would come tomorrow in the morning that he might discuss with them details of the crimes committed in their home. In the meantime, Sir John requested that none of the household staff be discharged or penalized, for he had not finished his examination of them. As we left, the constable instructed us to walk to Pall Mall if we wished to engage a hackney.

"A hackney," said Sir John, "by all means."

And so we set out, the two of us, at an easy pace for Pall Mall. Though visible to me down at the end of the street, it was, as I well knew, some considerable distance away; I offered to run down to the corner and bring back a hackney coach.

"They come by with great frequency," said I. "Indeed, I shouldn't be but a few minutes gone."

"No," said he, "I find the night air rather refreshing. It has restored me somewhat."

And so we continued along St. James Street, and as we went I looked left and right at the great houses. Even in the moonlight they looked impressive—or perhaps especially then, for the night shadows seemed to cover over the imperfections and worn spots that were visible during the day. (Not all the houses in this district were in the same excellent state of repair.)

As we approached Mr. Bilbo's residence, I saw that lights burned in a number of the windows. It was indeed one of the grandest in this street, having formerly belonged to Lord Goodhope. Mr. Bilbo, the owner and operator of one of London's most popular gaming houses, took the house in settlement of the nobleman's gambling debt. Since then, I had been there often, for my friend, Jimmie Bunkins, had been taken by Mr. Bilbo as his ward; and through my intercession our cook, Annie, had been accepted as a scholar by Bunkins's tutor, Mr. Burn-ham. All in all, I was well-known there, though no better than Sir John himself, who maintained a curious relationship with the head of the house, Mr. Bilbo. As a gambler and the proprietor of a gambling estab-lishment, he could never be accepted as a respectable gentleman in London society. There were those who tut-tutted at Sir John's friend-ship with such a man. To them, the magistrate would say gruffly, "I like the man, and there's an end to it."

As we passed the house in question, I mentioned it to him and noted the smile spread across his face.

"Ah yes," said he, "it is here on the same street as the Lilley resi-dence. I'd nearly forgotten. I daresay Black Jack is counting chips at his club at this moment."

"There are a few lights lit," said I. "Bunkins and Mr. Burnham, no doubt."

"No doubt. It is quite late, though. Why, it must be well past mid-night." We walked on in silence, past the neighbors to the Bilbo resi-dence; Pall Mall was then much closer—or so it seemed.

"I wonder what Mr. Bilbo will do when he hears a house on his street has been robbed," said I.

Sir John thought about that a moment, and then chuckled, "He will probably distribute pistols and cutlasses to all in the house. Or perhaps construct a redoubt before the front door. Or both."

We laughed together at that. The idea of fortifications built in St. James Street seemed especially rich. What would the neighbors say? Indeed what must they have said when Mr. Bilbo moved in, followed by those persistent rumors that he had made his first fortune as a pirate in the Spanish waters of the New World.

But to me it seemed that there were more urgent matters to discuss: "Tell me, though, sir, what did you think of those you questioned?"

"In truth," said he, "I did not think much of them. The butler seemed interested only in defending himself. The maid—well, she did well enough, I suppose, and I certainly would not have had her get her nose slit to protect those jewels, but . . . Oh well, they offered something—the porter was actually quite shrewd and helpful, but . . . but . . . oh, damnation! It just never ends! Too many robberies! Too many killings!"

I had not meant to cause him such annoyance. It was just that I had not realized the depth of his frustration. These ironical jokes of his, which now seemed to come with greater frequency, were his way of dealing with his discouragement. That very morning he had bared his true feelings when he had said that he wished the streets were safer. Why had I not then taken him more in earnest?

All this might have been said to him, but none of it was. I simply grasped at the most convenient response. (Nor, as you shall see, would it have mattered much what I attempted to say at that particular moment.) What I managed was no more than this: "Well, perhaps tomorrow's visit will prove more fruitful."

"I suppose it may," said he. "After all, we—"

He had my attention as he spoke, and so it was that by the light of the streetlamp, I caught a flash of strong movement from the corner of my eye. I turned, looked, and saw that little more than twelve feet away a man stood before us, his feet planted firmly, his arm straightened, and in his hand, a pistol.

At once I pushed Sir John to the pavement and struggled to throw back my coat that I might draw forth one of my pistols from its holster. As it came free, the man before me fired. I raised the pistol, cocking it, and fired back at him. Had I but taken a moment more I would have hit my target at such a short distance, but my shot went wide. I pulled the left-side pistol from its place and raised it for another try. But by this time our assailant had taken to his heels, fast disappearing down a walkway which ran along the side of one of St. James Street's grand houses. I went after him, hoping for a better shot. And then, of a sudden, I stopped.

Good God, Sir John! I could not go chasing assassins, thus leaving him alone. Nor could I discharge the pistol, for there might be others of the gang about.

I ran back to Sir John, expecting to find him up and about, ready to pursue his attacker on his own, calling down heaven's wrath upon the villain. But no, he lay crumpled where I had pushed him, apparently unable to pull himself to his feet. Was he hit? Was he dead? I had not even considered such a possibility.

Kneeling down beside him, I saw that he was breathing—shallowly, yet breathing nevertheless.

"Sir John," I whispered urgently, "you are wounded. Can you tell me where you were hit?"

"Shoulder," said he, panting, "in the shoulder."

Gingerly, I pulled back his coat and saw the blood spread upon his white linen shirt. "I must get you to Mr. Donnelly."

"To Mr. Bilbo. Take me there." He seemed now to be gathering strength. "Jeremy," said Sir John, "what did the fellow look like?"

"I . . . I'm not sure, sir." And indeed I wasn't, for all had happened so very quickly. But I concentrated upon the picture I held in my mind. And then I had something—to me, a quite unexpected something— that I might report.

"Sir, I believe he was a black man."

TWO

*In which Sir John
appoints me to an
interim position*

Of all that happened following this astonishing and frightening event, I shall speak only briefly and in summary.

After having made my declaration to Sir John, I heard running footsteps from the direction whence we had come. I cocked the loaded pistol and made ready to shoot, should it be another assassin come to finish the work of the first. But no, it was Mr. Brede, who, having heard shots fired, had come in all haste. Together, we carried him to Mr. Bilbo's house, which was not so far away. Mr. Burnham came in answer to Mr. Brede's urgent thumping upon the door. I responded to the challenge issued from inside and told what had happened. The door swung open, revealing Mr. Burnham, pistol in hand, looking, somehow, as if he had just come in. I noted the constable's surprise at the tutor's dark face. As soon as we had Sir John lying comfortably upon a sofa, Mr. Brede ran off to fetch Gabriel Donnelly, the medical examiner for Westminster who was, luckily, still nearby at Lord Lilley's performing his official duties.

Through it all, Sir John had remained conscious. In fact, by the time we laid him down upon the sofa, he was more responsive, more talkative, than when we had picked him up from the pavement of St. James Street. He had kept up a steady stream of cautions and warnings. In spite of his wound—and as yet we knew not whether or not it be serious—he was truly still in command.

Mr. Donnelly, who had only a few years past been a ship's surgeon in the Royal Navy, had in his day treated many (did he say hundreds?) of such gunshot wounds. After boiling his instruments—Jimmie Bunkins

wakened the cook, who saw to this—he removed the bullet and bound
the wound. By this time Sir John was dutifully drunk from Mr. Bilbo's
best brandy. When the surgeon had done, he pronounced the wound
"serious enough, though by no means mortal." He did caution, however,
that the wound must be kept clean and the dressing changed once a
day. (Hardly necessary in my case, for I had seen in Mr. Cowley an
example of what might happen when one was irresponsible in caring
for a wound; a gangrenous state, which led to the amputation of his
left leg.)

"And where will you be?" he asked the magistrate.

"Where will I be? What a question!" Sir John, still drunk, slurred
these words considerably so that they were barely comprehensible,
even to me. "I'll be at Number 4 Bow Street, where I belong."

"No he won't. He'll be right here." It was Mr. Bilbo, thumping into
the room, loud as he liked, as befit the proper master of the house.
Bunkins had gone off to the gaming establishment to fetch his master
that he might know of his friend's misfortune.

"I'll go home if I wish . . . wish to." Indeed, it was barely possible to
understand him.

"You will not. You're too drunk to go home." Indeed Mr. Bilbo had
made a good point. Even if Sir John had not been shot and lost a considerable amount of blood, I doubted that his legs would carry him to
the coach, be it a hackney or Mr. Bilbo's own.

Black Jack Bilbo they called him, partly in respect of the dark beard
he wore, though perhaps also for the dark moods which came upon
him all of a sudden. Now, with his thick legs planted wide and his fists
upon his hips, he appeared as a bull might, fuming and snorting, and
about to charge. Just to see him in that threatening posture would
have frightened most men.

Even had he been able to see him so, Sir John, of course, would
have remained unmoved; his friend did not frighten him, nor could he.
Nevertheless, as a magistrate and as a man, he was ever one to admit
the truth when he heard it, and after a moment's consideration of the
matter, he said in a manner of surprise, "Am I drunk? Jeremy, are you
here? Would you say that I am drunk?"

"I fear so," said I.

"You," said Mr. Bilbo, "are disgustingly drunk. Would you wish to
go home in such a state?"

He thought upon that for a good long while. For a moment, I thought he might have drifted off to sleep. But no. "P'r'aps not. S'pose I'll stay. But you Jeremy, you go home and tell Kate where I be when she wakes. S'clear?"

"Most clear, Sir John."

"S'good. Now I think I'll sleep." Which he did—off in an instant.

Black Jack Bilbo assured Mr. Donnelly that Sir John would be well cared for. He then offered us a return to our separate abodes in his coach. We gladly accepted and rode in style to the humbler streets surrounding Covent Garden. After I had returned the brace of pistols to Mr. Baker and told him of the evening's events, I struggled up the stairs to the kitchen—but I got no farther than that. Having settled down to the table with a glass of milk and a chunk of bread, I thought to satisfy the raging hunger that had attacked me of a sudden. Next morning Annie found me asleep at the table, the bread half eaten and the milk half drunk.

First Annie, and then Clarissa, tried to rouse me—yet without success. Only Lady Fielding, when she woke to find herself alone in bed and saw I had returned without Sir John, managed to separate me from the arms of Morpheus, though it was not easy.

She shouted at me: "Jeremy! Jeremy! You must tell me what has happened!"

She pummeled me with her fists. "Get up! Wake up, you wicked boy! What have you done with my Jack?"

That, I think, was what brought me to my senses. It was not the screams in my ear, nor was it even the blows she rained upon my head and shoulders; but to hear myself so unjustly accused by one so close to me—that demanded immediate redress. What had I done with her Jack? What indeed!

Jumping to my feet, I defended myself vigorously. "Lady Fielding," said I, "if he is your Jack, he is also mine. I have done naught *with* him. What was done last night was done *to* him by an armed assailant. In short, Sir John was shot at close range and wounded."

"Shot!" exclaimed Lady Fielding. "Wounded?"

Annie and Clarissa, who stood behind her, echoed her concern.

I then told them in detail all that had happened, nor did I, in the telling, scant my efforts to defend him and see him safe to Black Jack Bilbo's. I did also quote Mr. Donnelly on the extent of Sir John's wounding, "serious enough, though by no means mortal."

"Oh, thank God," said Lady Fielding.

"He will require care," said I. "His dressing must be changed each day."

"Oh, we shall see to it," said she. Then, looking behind her for confirmation, she added, "Won't we, ladies?"

"Of course," said Annie.

"You may be sure of it," said Clarissa.

And so it was soon settled: All three would travel with me to Mr. Bilbo's residence after breakfast—Lady Fielding and Clarissa to check upon Sir John's condition, and Annie to her daily reading lesson with Mr. Burnham. (Our cook had now had near two years of instruction in letters; and as she was bright and eager to learn, she could now read and comprehend all but texts so dense they would give a challenge to all but Oxford scholars.) And I? Well, I would naturally do whatever Sir John asked of me to help keep alive the investigation begun the night before. He would also surely want me to take a letter asking that for the foreseeable future all cases ordinarily tried by the Bow Street Court be brought instead before the magistrate for Outer London and its environs, Saunders Welch. Mr. Welch might complain bitterly, but I could see no other way to handle it.

Breakfast was quite generous, though not as leisurely, as the day before. Even so, it was near nine before Lady Fielding and the other "ladies" (as she called them) had reached that stage of readiness when a hackney might be summoned and set to wait at the door for them. And so it fell to me to go down to fetch the coach.

Yet it happened that I was stopped on my way by Mr. Marsden, the court clerk, who sought to know something of Sir John's condition. I spoke reassuringly and again quoted Mr. Donnelly—serious but not mortal.

"Constable Brede brought the news," said Mr. Marsden. "I was quite overcome, I was, when I heard the news. I been workin' for the gent near twenty years now, and I've seen him in some tight places, but he never took a bullet before."

To hear such made me most uncomfortable. After all, had I not been Sir John's guardian? Was he not my responsibility?

"I . . . I'm afraid I hadn't my pistol out quick enough. I was armed, you know. Constable Baker saw to that."

"Oh, think not upon it, Jeremy," said Mr. Marsden. "From what I heard from Mr. Brede, you acquitted yourself right well. Tried to push Sir John out of the line of fire, you did, and returned fire."

"And missed!" That, reader, came not from me but from just behind me in a deeper voice which was most familiar. "Or so *I* heard."

I turned round and faced him. "You heard correct, Mr. Fuller. And when I sought to pull my second pistol from its holster, he turned and ran from me."

"As well he might. Even a blackie's got more sense than to stand there and let you have another shot at him. He *was* a blackie, wasn't he?"

"As I remember it," said I, "yes he was."

At that Mr. Marsden gave a long whistle. "You don't mean it," said he in wonder. "I'd not heard that."

"Well, now you have," said Mr. Fuller as he turned sharply on his heel and walked away.

Mr. Marsden stared after him, perplexed, for a long moment. Then, coming to himself, he said, "Ah, Jeremy, I almost forgot. I've something here for you."

"What is that, sir?"

"It was left with me by the new fellow, Constable Patley. He'd heard about Sir John, so he thought I should give it to you instead." So saying, he pulled a folded and somewhat wrinkled sheet of paper from his coat pocket and offered it to me. "He says it's his report on the robbery at Lord Lilley's residence."

I took it from him and glanced at it. There seemed little for me there, and so I tucked it away. "I'll look at it later," said I.

"I got little from it for the file," said Mr. Marsden. "A name, and not much more."

"I'll read it to Sir John when he's ready for it. But right now I'd better find a hackney. We're off to see him at Black Jack Bilbo's."

Then, with a wave, I left him and proceeded out the door to Bow Street.

It was Mr. Burnham who answered my knock upon the door to Mr. Bilbo's residence. My first glimpse of him told me that though he had been up quite as late as I, he appeared to be far better rested. Smiling, he threw the door wide and beheld the four of us standing on the porch. When his eye fixed upon Lady Fielding, the smile vanished from his face and was replaced by a look of alarm. And it seemed to me that when he stepped aside to admit us, he did so only after a considerable hesitation; indeed one might say that he showed a certain reluctance in allowing us into the house at all. I could not but wonder why.

Beginning with Lady Fielding, he greeted us each one by name there in the entrance hall. He then looked about as if in hopes of finding someone to whom he might pass us on—but there was no one about.

Lady Fielding thrust herself forward and said in a voice at once insistent and confidential, "Mr. Burnham, you must tell us, how is he?"

"Uh, you mean Sir John, of course?"

"Indeed! Yes! Of course!"

"I believe he does as well as anyone might expect. Perhaps better. Though I must confess that I have not looked in on him this morning."

Lady Fielding stepped back and regarded Mr. Burnham thoughtfully, perhaps wondering at his odd behavior. "But of course you would not have seen him this morning, for you, sir, are a tutor and therein your responsibilities lie. You are not here to nurse Sir John, but we are. We have come this long way from Bow Street to do just that. We shall gladly take responsibility for his care."

"Yes, certainly. I quite understand."

She looked at him rather sharply. "Do you?"

"Yes . . . quite . . ." But then a thought struck him: "Ah, but no doubt you ladies would like first to refresh yourselves. Right this way—in here, *please*!"

He threw open the door to the little room just off the entrance hall; once a sewing room, it now served as the classroom in which Mr. Burnham drilled Jimmie Bunkins and Annie in their lessons. Bunkins, in fact, was inside, looking up from the book he had in hand, apparently startled by the intrusion.

"There is a water closet just through that other door," Mr. Burnham continued, "and a mirror of good size."

"A water closet!" cried Clarissa. "Oh, do let me see. Do you pull the chain to make it work?"

"Come along," said Annie. "I'll show you how it's done." Though Annie could not have known the specific nature of Mr. Burnham's difficulty, I surmised that she understood that something was amiss, and that he wished to create a delay. (That much was obvious even to me.) Annie grasped Clarissa by the arm and whisked her away through the door that had been pointed out to them.

Lady Fielding stood in the middle of the room, frowning. The curiosity with which she regarded Mr. Burnham now seemed to have given way to suspicion.

I myself started into the room, thinking to greet my friend Bunkins, but in mid-step I felt myself held back firmly. Looking round me, I saw that it was Mr. Burnham that had a firm grip on my shoulder. Then he bowed slightly to whisper, softly but earnestly, into my ear.

"Jeremy, go upstairs now—second door on the right. You will see what must be done."

With that, he gave me a firm slap upon my back and sent me on my way. I jog-trotted to the stairway and took the steps two at a time. I felt thus obliged by the great urgency I sensed in what he had said.

Nevertheless, my mind raced faster than my feet. Clearly, Sir John had been moved. I had left him the night before lying upon the sofa in that same little room below. And there could be little doubt, surely, that he had been moved into the room that lay behind the second door on the right. But what should I see that *must* be done? What could be wrong with Sir John? When I had left him there, he seemed able to resist any lingering effects of the gunshot wound. And certainly Mr. Donnelly, with all his doctor's art, was capable of treating such a hurt. Had he not said that he had treated hundreds like it during his time as surgeon in the Royal Navy? (But perhaps I should have asked him how many survived his ministrations.)

With my mind thus preoccupied, I found I had walked past the second door and had reached the third. In fact, I was about to knock upon it when I realized my error. I hastened back and, dispensing with all formality, I did not trouble to knock but threw open the door and burst into the room.

It would be no exaggeration, reader, to say that I had never before, nor have I since, experienced such a moment of shocking surprise as I did then and there. For in the bed, which took up much of the space in this modest-sized bedroom, I found Sir John contentedly ensconced beneath a comforter; he was resting as well as anyone could hope. This was as I had expected it. But beside him, sleeping just as soundly, was a woman, young and comely. In fact I recognized her: Her name was Nancy Plummer, and she was a hostess at Mr. Bilbo's gaming establishment. She made her home at the Bilbo residence, as did a number of his other employees. I knew her to be a pleasant and obliging person. I

hoped dearly that she would be pleasant and obliging enough to understand why I must now rout her out of bed and move her someplace
else—at least for the length of Lady Fielding's visit.

I reached over and gave her shoulder a sound shake. (I noted that
the shoulder was bare and thought that a bad sign.) Her response was
simply to turn away from me and move even closer to Sir John. This, I
thought, wouldn't do at all.

"Nancy!" I said, giving her another shake, "Nancy, you must awake
and be quickly out of bed."

But I was too timid, not near loud enough. I would have to shout full
in her ear if I were to have even a chance of waking her. I glanced
uneasily at the door, fearing that were it open, I might be heard downstairs. But it was shut tight, and I was free to shout loud at her.

"Wake up! Wake up! Wake up!"

But that she absolutely refused to do. All that I could get from her
were a few groans, a sniffle, and a cough. What was I to do? Again I
shook her, and again it did naught. The situation seemed to be growing
worse as each minute passed.

At that instant the door opened and Jimmie Bunkins rushed into the
room. He looked as agitated as I felt, though not near as desperate.

"I can't get her awake," said I to him. "Nothing seems to work."

"Never surrender to circumstance," said Bunkins. "That's what Mr.
Burnham always says. I'm here to lend a hand, chum. Nancy always
was a sound sleeper."

"That's missing it by half."

"I'm also come to warn you that Mr. Burnham can't hold them much
longer. They'll be up here any minute."

"What'll we do?"

Bunkins took a moment to think, then nodded with a sudden assurance that I found quite inspiring. "Let's pull her out of bed," he said. "If
we can get this blowen on her two feet, she has to wake up, don't she?"

"We can try it," said I.

And try it we did. Bunkins threw back the comforter, revealing a
good deal more of her than I was prepared for. I stood for a moment in
an awkward state, paralyzed by embarrassment.

"What's the matter with you?" Bunkins demanded as he took a firm
grip on her feet. "Grab her, and let's get on with it."

"Grab her? Where?"

"Anywhere you want, but let's get her out of bed and upright."

Yet still I hesitated, taxing Bunkins's patience still further.

"Listen," said he, "don't look if it bothers you all that much. But come now, together, you and me, Jeremy, let's . . . *lift!*"

I grasped her at her armpits and tugged as Bunkins hauled her feet out of bed and put them down on the floor; then he grabbed her arms and pulled her up and toward him just so. Tugging, pulling, and lifting, we did manage to put her in a vertical position, more or less on her own two feet. Bunkins and I looked hopefully, one at the other. He nodded; I moved back, and he stepped away. But oughtn't her eyes to open? I looked closely at her. Perhaps her eyelids were beginning to flutter just a little. Of a sudden I was aware of the beating of my heart. But just when it appeared that we were succeeding, she collapsed without warning upon the bed, first in a sitting position, then tumbling down onto her side into the horizontal. Bear in mind, reader, that through all this she had not spoken a word, nor could I claim that she had truly opened her eyes. Just as amazing, however, was the fact that Sir John himself had slept through it all. I was certain of that, for all during my unsuccessful efforts to rouse Nancy he had snored as loudly and constantly as some amateur on the bass viol, sawing away on the same two notes. Zoom-zoom, zoom-zoom, zoom-zoom . . .

"I got one last idea," said Bunkins. "If this don't work, we'll—"

As with so many other things in life, that too was lost, for as Jimmie Bunkins was offering to confide his "one last idea," the door behind him which led to the hall opened very quietly and Lady Fielding came in on tiptoe. Hers was, after all, a sickroom visit. Would Sir John be awake? Would he be in pain?

As she soon learned, he was neither. He slept most contentedly with a naked woman beside him. Her eyes accommodated this; it took her mind a moment longer to take it all in, and that was when she screamed. It was, reader, a fine, full-throated scream, one of the sort which, as they say, "could awaken the dead." While there is no proof that any such miracle was accomplished, it seems likely that it woke all who slept in the Bilbo house.

Sir John flung off his bedclothes and bounded out of bed, revealing himself in his white linen underbreeches. Unable to see either the reason for the scream, or its origin, he shouted out a warning against the Spanish and flailed the air with an imaginary sword. It occurred to me later that in his dream he had returned to the siege of Cartagena.

Nancy, for her part, reacted contrariwise. Finding herself bare, she covered her body with the comforter, jerking it up to her chin. She looked angrily at Bunkins and me, no doubt suspicioning the worst. Yet she saved her greatest scorn for Lady Fielding, whom she rightly fixed as the source of the loud noise that had roused her.

"Who're you and what're you doing in my bedroom?" she demanded.

"Who're you and what are you doing sleeping naked with my husband?" countered Lady Fielding.

"How I sleeps is none of your affair. And what do you mean, I slept with your husband? I am very particular who I sleeps with, and I'm sure I wouldn't sleep with nobody married to you."

"Well then, look upon him and tell me if he comes up to your high standard."

Wherewith Lady Fielding pointed rather dramatically at Sir John. (He had by then emerged from his dream state and at that moment appeared somewhat dazed as he attempted to orient himself.)

"Kate," said he in a small voice, "is that you I hear? I . . . I've a terrible headache."

"Quiet, please, Jack," said she. "We'll discuss this later."

Nancy laughed in spite of herself. "Why, it's the Beak, so it is! Though he does look right fetchin' in his kickseys, I'd never be so bold as to try to lead him astray. Wouldn't even try."

"Then how did he get into your bed?"

"How should I know?"

The two simply glared one at the other as the small crowd that had gathered just outside the door grew larger. In the beginning, it was no more than three: Mr. Burnham, Annie, and Clarissa. Now, however, there were four or five more. Then did another appear, one dressed in a richly embroidered dressing gown, though otherwise rather disheveled and rumpled; his beard was matted, and hair (what there was of it) stood in spikes. It was the cove of the ken, Black Jack Bilbo. He seemed to have grasped the situation immediately as he came into the room.

"Ah, Lady Fielding," said he, playing the peacemaker, "let me assure you that Nancy ain't to blame"—then did he cast a quick disapproving glance at his employee—"except perhaps for her sauciness and disrespect."

"Then who is, Mr. Bilbo?"

"I fear that I am, m'lady," said he. "Y'see, just after the surgeon left, your husband got a terrible chill, he did. He was shivering, and his teeth were chattering away. Mr. Burnham, who is more learned than I am, knew not what was to be done, did you, Mr. Burnham?"

"Oh, no sir, I did not," said the tutor.

"But I, being a practical man and having some experience in such matters, decided he should be put in beside Nancy Plummer, who had then been asleep for some time. Now, what you must know is that when Nancy sleeps, she sleeps as sound as no other in this world. So she could neither object, nor could she trouble Sir John. All she could do was lend him, unbeknownst, the heat of her body. It seems to have had a beneficial effect upon him, gunshot wound or not."

"Do you expect me to believe that?" She asked that in a manner less bold than the words may indicate. Her manner of speech was uncertain. She looked to him for reassurance. There could be no doubt that Mr. Bilbo had swayed her.

"I expect only that you believe the simple truth, and that I have just told you," said he. "I myself was cured of a mortal chill in just such a way by a princess of the Siboney tribe."

There was naught but silence between them for a considerable space of time. But then did Sir John speak up in a voice which resounded with a bit of his old strength and authority.

"That is all very well, Mr. Bilbo, but what did you do with my breeches? I shall need them for the trip home."

It took near an hour of preparations before Sir John was able to make that journey back to Bow Street. Not only was it necessary to fetch him his breeches, but he was also in need of a new shirt, for Mr. Donnelly had ripped the old one quite to shreds in the process of removing the bullet from his shoulder and treating the wound. It was finally decided that the shirt offered by Mr. Bilbo would do, even though the sleeves were much too long. Sir John wore his blood-stained coat home as a matter of pride, though Lady Fielding claimed that she was greatly embarrassed by it.

Once the matter of dress had been settled, Sir John held conferences in the music room—two of them. The first was with Lady Fielding. Though I sat near the door, waiting to have a word with Sir John, I heard nothing of what was said between them. Their conversation was conducted in low tones for their ears alone. Sitting there, I happened to remember the report on last night's robbery written by Constable Patley, and passed on to me by Mr. Marsden just before we had left for Mr. Bilbo's residence. I pulled it from my coat pocket, smoothed it out upon my knee (as it was given to me wrinkled, and had become further wrinkled in my pocket), and, with some difficulty, read as follows:

I was woken palmal wen a felo cum doun from St. James Street an tol me Lord Lili's hous was robd an it was the blaks did it. I tol him to go to Bow Street an tel Sir Jon whilst I wen to whar he cum frum. He sed his nam was Wiyam Wotrs. I tuk charch at the Lords hous. I found out ther was a man kilt too but I dint git his nam.

Clearly, reader, Constable Patley's strength was not orthography. Once I had puzzled it through, I remembered Mr. Marsden's complaint to the effect that all he had gotten from Patley's report was a single name. Indeed he may well have fared better than I, for I could not, with any exactitude, puzzle out the name contained in this report, so-called. What could it be? William Waters was the most obvious possibility, but it could just as well be William Walters, or even William Walker—allowing for Patley's faulty memory, or his inability to express such a name in letters. Did it matter? Probably it did not. But I, word-proud as I was, felt offended by such ignorance. After all, Sir John had stipulated that all constables who comprise the group known as the Bow Street Runners must have letters and numbers; they must know writing as well as reading. Had he been tested? No doubt Chief Constable Bailey had taken Patley's word that he was literate—and in a way he was. I had, of course, gotten the sense of his message. I admitted that he had learned at least so far. The question was, whether or no he could be taught more. Would Mr. Burnham take him on as a scholar? Would Patley agree to it?

Out came Sir John and Lady Fielding from the music room. The skin round her eyes was flushed pink; her eyes glistened. She had been weeping. Beneath the black silk band he wore, I knew that Sir John's eyes were quite destroyed; he could not weep, nor would he. His jaw was set, however, and his mouth turned down in such a way that his face had a stern appearance.

I bobbed up from the chair in which I had been sitting and approached him, hoping to detain him for some minutes longer, that I might have a few words with him. But again he worked one of his wonders of sightless seeing.

"Is that you, Jeremy?"

"Yes, it is, Sir John. If you have the time and the strength, I should like to talk with you. It should not take long."

"Of course," said he. Then did he turn to Lady Fielding: "Kate, my dear, find Clarissa and prepare to leave. We shall all go off to Bow Street together."

She murmured her assent and, much subdued, went down the hall in search of her young charge. Sir John waved me to the door and took my arm.

"Put me in a chair," said he. "I'm unsure of myself in this room. I can't seem to find my way around in it."

I did as he asked, kicking shut the door behind us. I found a comfortably padded chair for him and pulled over one of a plain design for me.

"What will you then, Jeremy?"

"I've two matters to discuss, sir. First of all, I would think it wise if you were to dictate a letter to Mr. Saunders Welch, asking him to take all your cases until such time as you are able to resume your duties. He has no doubt heard of last night's event."

"No doubt," said Sir John in a manner somewhat abstracted.

"If we are to persuade him to take over today, we should probably get the letter to him immediately. I could take it in dictation right here, sir."

Oddly, he said nothing, simply sat.

"Uh . . . I don't see how he could refuse, sir."

Again, nothing for a moment. Then: "That is not the question, lad. It seems to me that whoever it was shot me is not absolutely certain if I am alive or dead. I think it of the utmost importance that I present myself in the Bow Street Court as usual today to prove that I am alive."

"But might he not try again?"

"To shoot me? Oh, there is a chance, I suppose. But I think that highly unlikely. There is but the one street exit, and there will be armed men about."

"Mr. Fuller?"

"Mr. Marsden, too. I'll see to it he wears a brace of pistols—perhaps you, too, eh? Above all, Jeremy, it is important to demonstrate that wounding a magistrate will in no wise stop or even interrupt the dispensation of justice at Bow Street."

"As you will then, Sir John."

"And I will that there be no letter to Mr. Saunders Welch. Now what was the other matter you wished to talk about?"

"About last night's investigation," said I.

"Well, what about it?"

"You wished to talk to him who reported the robbery and murder to Mr. Baker."

"Yes, and I was more than a little disappointed that our Constable Patley could not present him to us for interrogation. In fact, he could not even supply the fellow's name."

"He must have gotten it from the butler there at the Lilley residence then, for he provided it in the written report he left with Mr. Marsden."

"Indeed? And what was the name?"

"Waters—or possibly Walters, something like that. It was a little difficult making it out."

"This fellow, Patley, writes a poor hand I assume?"

"You might say so, yes sir, but would you like me to interrogate Waters, or Walters, or whatever his name be?"

Sir John gave that some thought. "I would," said he. "Indeed I would. To be truthful, Jeremy, if I am to sit the court each day, as I intend to do, I'm quite sure it will take all the energy that I can muster. If we are to continue the investigation—as we must—then I fear the conduct of it falls upon you. I leave it in your hands. You may come to me for advice—consultation, if you will. In fact, I rather hope you will, but you will have to do the actual labor of interrogation, fact-gathering, and such."

I knew not quite what to say, so overcome was I by the evidence of trust shown in this generous act—yet I felt that I must say something. "I shall try my utmost to . . ." I fumbled, "to justify the faith you put in me."

"Well, that much is understood."

"Thank you, Sir John."

"See if you can still thank me when you've done with it. But off with you, Jeremy. Go down to the Lilley residence and put the fear of God into them. Talk to whomever you must need talk to. Don't be shy. Be rude, if you must, but don't be shy."

To my surprise, my knock at the door of the Lilley residence was answered not by the butler, Mr. Collier, but rather by the porter, Mr. Burley, who had told us a good deal about the murdered man. Far more surprising was the attitude he showed toward me. I was greeted by a frown. When I attempted to speak, he shook his head severely and made to shut the door in my face. That, I would not allow.

"Take your foot out of the door," said he.

"You remember me, don't you?"

"I do. You was here last night with the blind magistrate from Bow Street who was asking all the questions."

"Right you are," said I. "And as you may or may not know, that blind magistrate from Bow Street was shot, just down the street from here. He has appointed me to continue the investigation in his stead. I've been granted full powers."

"You're talking pretty powerful for one so young. How old are you?"

"That matters not one jot," I declared quite snappishly. "Whatever he had the power to do, I now can do." (Perhaps I was a bit carried away by my new authority.) "I can bring a swarm of constables here this very night to force answers for my questions. How would you like that?"

"A sight more than I would having a swarm of soldiers underfoot."

That I did not understand. "What do you mean?"

He sighed and grudgingly opened the door just wide enough for me to slip through. "Come into the hall here," said he. "I'll explain the situation to you."

As I stepped inside, he closed the door carefully and noiselessly behind me. Then did he speak in a tone hardly louder than a whisper.

"When Lord Lilley come home last night, he went room to room counting his losses. You can tell when he gets angriest 'cause that's when he gets quietest. And when he'd finished his tour of the house, he and the Lady went right upstairs. He's a very cold man, he is.

"Today, early this morning, he gathers us all together and announces who all gets sacked and who stays."

"But Sir John left a request that none of the staff be discharged until he —"

"I know. I heard about that. But there's Lord Lilley's answer to your chief. As for the rest of us—the ones he's not throwing out in the cold—he told us under no circumstances was we to talk to Sir John or his constables, or help in the investigation. So you can see I'm taking a great chance here just talking to you."

"But that's nonsense. How are we to—"

"True, true, I know. The master's gone off to the Tower to demand soldiers to patrol St. James Street. He says Bow Street can't deal with the crime no more."

"But . . . but that's not true. I mean, Sir John—that is . . . Is there any chance that Lord Lilley will have his way?"

"I don't know, p'rhaps. He's a duke, ain't he?"

"But I have special need to talk to one of the household staff who was evidently absent during our visit last evening—a William Waters."

The porter looked at me blankly. "There's no one of such a name here," said he.

"Well, then, perhaps it would be William Walters."

"No, sorry."

"William Walker?"

He shook his head in the negative rather solemnly.

"Is there no one by a name even remotely like it?"

"No, lad, there's no William at all. And as for family names with a 'W,' we've got only a Wiggins, but first name's Elizabeth. She's the cook."

I stood there quite dumbfounded, rendered mute by my frustration. It seemed to me that I should have this confirmed by the butler. He was, after all, the chief of the household staff. "Could I speak with Mr. Collier?"

"No, 'fraid not. He's been sacked. That's why I'm tending the door. I s'pose I will be till they hire a proper butler."

"And Pinkham?"

"Sacked."

"Anyone else?"

"Piper and Albertson—kitchen slaveys."

"What was their offense? I mean, the last two."

"They complained about the sacking of the first two—and Lord Lilley overheard. But now you must go, young man, for I've no wish to follow them out into the street."

"I understand. And I have but one more question; it is this: Who was it carried the news of the robbery to Bow Street?"

Burley thought a moment upon it. "I'm not rightly sure anyone did," said he. "But you'd have to ask Mr. Collier about that to be sure of it."

I stood, arms folded, a scowl upon my face and a pistol at either side. I was placed prominently before the public entry to the Bow Street Court, inside the courtroom itself. The usual crowd of spectators paid little heed to me and to the similarly well-armed Mr. Fuller at the other door; Sir John and Mr. Marsden paid none at all. The business of the court was carried on as usual.

I had been armed and assigned my place by Mr. Marsden upon my return to Bow Street from the Lilley residence. He, the court clerk, sat beside the magistrate, a large, old cavalry pistol prominently displayed on the table before him. This show of arms was, of course, meant to discourage any further attempt upon Sir John's life. I, for one, doubted there would be any such attack in a place so public. There was, after all, not a single black face among the many in the courtroom, and I knew quite well that his assailant of the night before had been an African.

In any case, Sir John's session had gone routinely well that day. No shots were fired, and there were no disturbances of any sort. For his part, the magistrate sent a pickpocket off to a term of sixty days in prison; fined two brawlers for disturbing the peace in Bedford Street; and settled commercial disagreements between two Covent Garden greengrocers and their customer. An average day it was, perhaps a bit lighter than some. Even so, by the time Sir John had heard the last case, he was visibly exhausted. I saw him rise from his place, then did I notice that his left arm, bent at the elbow, was suspended in a narrow cloth sling. I turned away, giving my attention to the last of the spectators as they filed past me and out the door. When next I turned my attention back to him, I was shocked to see him collapsing to the floor before my very eyes. Fortunately Mr. Marsden was close by, and reaching out to him, he managed at least to ease his passage down. I hastened to them, hoping that I might be of some help.

"Mr. Marsden," I called out before I had quite arrived, "what is wrong?"

"What indeed!" he wailed. "I could do naught to prevent his fall."

Sir John, I saw, had slipped to a sitting position there on the floor and was fully conscious. "There is nothing wrong with me but a brief bout of lightheadedness. Why, it could happen to anyone." Grousing and grumbling he was as one might, having slipped upon the stairs.

"But the truth of it, Sir John, is that it happened to you," said Mr. Marsden, obviously distressed. "We must have you looked after." Then, turning to me: "Jeremy, go tell Mr. Fuller to come at once. Then you must run and fetch the doctor—the Irishman in Drury Lane."

I did as he said, sending Mr. Fuller back into the courtroom whence he had just come, and then ran at full speed for Mr. Donnelly. Luckily, I found him in his surgery and quite ready to match me stride for stride as we raced back to Bow Street.

We found Sir John still in the courtroom, sitting in the chair from which he had presided over the day's session. Mr. Marsden hovered nearby. Mr. Fuller, having aided to the extent to which he was capable, had excused himself and was no doubt preparing his single prisoner (the pickpocket) for his journey to jail.

"Well," said Mr. Donnelly, looking down upon Sir John most severely, "and what did I prescribe for you last night just before I left Mr. Bilbo's residence?"

"I've no idea," said Sir John, "I was drunk at the time—as you well know."

"Jeremy," said the surgeon, turning to me, "what was it that I prescribed?"

"Bed rest," said I in a manner most emphatic.

"Exactly," said he. "And here you are paying the price for your disobedience. But let me examine you, so that I may see if you have done irreparable damage to yourself."

And without further ado, he pushed aside Sir John's coat, pulled up his shirt and listened to the patient's heart with a kind of ear trumpet which he had pulled from his bag. Satisfied, he removed the dressing he had applied the night before and examined the wound itself. "You're coming along," said he.

" 'Coming along'? What does that mean?"

"It means, Sir John, that if you take care of yourself in the manner I have prescribed, then you may well make a swift recovery. If you do not, then you may find yourself chronically ill with the effects of the gunshot wound—not dying, you understand, but never fully recovering."

Sir John was silent for some time, considering the choice that he had been offered. "All right," said he, "I'll go upstairs to my bed and hope for the best."

"But," said the surgeon, "not before I've put a new dressing on that wound."

Sir John offered no argument, and Mr. Donnelly accomplished his task with his usual efficiency. As for the ascent to the floor above, when the surgeon suggested that he be carried up the stairs, Sir John refused utterly to allow it, declaring that I, Jeremy, would precede him in the usual way; and that Messrs. Marsden and Donnelly should trail him closely that they might catch him in the event that he should fall backward.

Thus we proceeded without mishap. Sir John's hand was firm upon my shoulder, and his step was much more sure than I had anticipated. When I opened the door to the kitchen, I found Annie seated at the table, reading in the book given her that day by Mr. Burnham. Seeing that it was Sir John who accompanied me, she was out of her chair in a trice and at his side.

"Sir," said she in a manner most solicitous, "what may I do for you?"

"Ah, it's Annie, is it? They are about to put me to bed—and I must admit that I am quite tired. But I wonder, dear girl, could you provide something for me to eat? I've had naught since dinner. Some cold meat, bread, and tea would do me nicely."

"Make it bread and broth and nothing more," said Mr. Donnelly. "Let us see how well he holds it down."

Annie looked uncertainly from one to the other, but in another moment we were gone—up that shorter flight of stairs and into the bedroom which Sir John shared with Lady Kate. Here he needed no help: He was most familiar with the room. He sat down upon the bed and removed first his right shoe and then his left.

"Mr. Marsden, and you, Mr. Donnelly, I fear I must ask you both to leave now. Jeremy will ready me for bed. I thank you both for your concern and your assistance. I shall see you again soon, I'm sure." This was said, reader, with great authority.

Court clerk and surgeon looked one at the other, shrugged, and with meek goodbyes, departed the room.

Sir John sat upon the bed, listening to their footsteps down the stairs and across the kitchen. He turned my way then and said, "Help me out of my coat and breeches, Jeremy, and tell me what you learned at the Lilley residence."

I did as he requested, though it pained me to inform him of Lord Lilley's actions and my consequent inability to gather further information from there. I felt myself a failure in this.

Sir John, however, took the matter with equanimity and, as he settled down beneath the bedcovers, he said to me, "Don't worry upon it. Lord Lilley has for some time wished the army to take part in the policing of the streets. There would be little to be gained by it—and anyone with a penny's worth of sense knows that. I would like you to see if you can locate the butler, however. I don't know that we need search out Pinkham, or the two others. Nasty . . . fellow that . . . Lord Lilley . . . don't you think?"

"Oh, I do, sir."

I am not sure, in all truth, that he heard me, for by that time his head had sunk to the pillow, and as he had concluded that last speech, his voice had grown fainter and the words slower to come. I spoke his name quietly and got no response but his heavy, rhythmic breathing. I was satisfied that he was asleep. I tiptoed from the room and met Annie on the stairs; she moved carefully, carrying the tray of food that Sir John had requested (meat had won out over broth).

"Is he asleep?" she whispered.

I nodded.

"Ah, well," said she. "I can't say as I'm surprised. Come down, and we'll drink the tea. I'll just put the rest away. None of it will go to waste."

I followed her suggestion, and only minutes later we two were at the kitchen table sipping the tea she had brewed for Sir John. I, too, could have done with a bit of a nap, and so the tea was most welcome as a stimulant, though a cup of coffee would have been far more welcome. Nevertheless, my mind began properly to work once more, and as the cobwebs cleared, I found myself telling Annie all I had heard that morning from Burley, the porter and butler pro-tem. It seemed I had good reason to do so.

"Annie," said I, once I had told the tale, "Sir John wishes me to persist and find the butler to question him further."

"Look for the lady's maid, as well," said she. "Now that she's out of their employ she may have more to say."

"That's just the problem, you see. How would I go about looking for them? Where would I find them now that they've been cast out? I thought you might know. You were in service once yourself, after all."

"I thought I was still," said she, with a curious smile.

"Well . . . yes, I suppose you are — and I am, too, of course — but I mean those who work in the great houses. Where do they go once they've been given the sack? Where should I look?"

At that, she threw back her head and gazed up at the ceiling, as if she hoped to find the answer to my question written there. She held that pose, thinking hard upon the matter for quite some time. Then did she take a sip of tea, still frowning, and give me a most direct sort of look. "You should go to the great houses up and down St. James Street and ask after them at the door. Those in service there keep well in contact. Remember that I worked in St. James Street myself. I remember that's how it was there then. But you must convince them that you mean no harm to the butler — or to the maid. Only then will it be likely that they will pass you on to those you are looking for."

I found the butler, Mr. Collier, three houses up from Lilley's in the residence of a Mr. Zondervan, a rich Dutch merchant. He had not found a place on the household staff (nor was he likely to), but his friends in the Zondervan kitchen beneath the stairs had gathered round him to give him their support and their advice on where he might go to find a new place of employment. This I had learned from the butler of the house, who admitted me only after I convinced him that I did truly represent Sir John Fielding of the Bow Street Court, and that Sir John was greatly displeased that Lord Lilley had closed his door to the investigation.

"He had specifically asked that Lord Lilley take no action until his investigation was complete," I had said to the Zondervan butler. "He thought Mr. Collier and Mistress Pinkham quite without guilt in the matter. He felt that the facts would exonerate them from all blame."

That last bit, I concede, was a little far from the truth. Nevertheless, it helped me gain entry into the house, for I concluded with a request that if he were to know Mr. Collier's whereabouts, would he then please convey my need to speak with him.

The butler, a tall man, looked at me rather closely, as if assessing my worth (which in a sense was exactly what he was doing). Then did he say to me, "You may tell him that yourself, if you like. Right this way, young man."

He lectured me, as we walked to the back stairs, on how fortunate I was to have come when I did. Was that because Mr. Collier had only lately arrived and would not stay long? No, it seemed that I was lucky that I had come when Mr. Zondervan ("the master," as he was called) had just left on a quick visit to the Continent. "If he were not," said he, "I could not possibly allow you inside."

I divined from this that Mr. Collier was also fortunate in having come when he did. He did not, however, appear as one who judged himself so. On the contrary, at first glimpse he seemed, if anything, more agitated and troubled than he had when Sir John had interrogated him the night before. He sat at the far end of the long kitchen table surrounded by no less than four of his cronies from the Zondervan staff. With him I spied an older woman of a rather slovenly appearance (surely the cook) and a man in rough twill who toyed with a great, high horsewhip (undoubtedly the coach driver) and two male servants of undefined position. Mr. Collier held the attention of all as he railed against the perfidy—nay, the treachery—of employers. There was general agreement amongst his listeners at that. He inhaled deeply and made ready to fire another broadside, but just then I managed to catch his eye. He said nothing at all for a moment as he stared at me, frowning, unable quite to place me.

"Here now," said he, "I know you, don't I?"

"Yes sir, you do," said I. "When Sir John Fielding asked questions of you last night I was there at his side."

"So you were, so you were."

"He has sent me to ask a few more questions of you."

Mr. Collier said nothing for a moment, evidently considering the matter I had put before him. Then, of a sudden, did he lash out at me: "Oh, he did, did he? Well, he did precious little to help my cause with Lord Lilley; why should I help him now?"

His personal disaster had made him bold—far bolder than he had been before. That he now had the opportunity to perform before an audience must also have given him encouragement. His four listeners had become eager participants in the show. They murmured praise for his last outburst as I sought the proper words with which to soothe his anger. Something must be said—that much was certain.

"You must know that he left a message for Lord Lilley with one of the constables. He asked that none of the household staff be discharged or penalized," said I.

"I know he *said* he would make such an appeal, but why did he not come this morning and present an argument on our behalf to the master?"

"Because, my good sir, he was shot down by one of the robbers right here in St. James Street in a dastardly attack. He, who nearly lost his life, is far more the victim of those villains than you, sir, who lost only your employment!"

Was this how I hoped to soothe the feelings of this testy little man? Not likely, I fear. After all, I reminded myself, the purpose of this visit was to get this fellow to answer some questions and not to scold him. And yet, I again reminded myself, when he sent me out to perform this task, Sir John had instructed me not to be shy—to be rude if I must— but not to be shy.

Yet when Mr. Collier next spoke the nature of his response surprised me with its sudden change in tone and temper.

"Yes," said he, "well . . . I . . . uh . . . did hear something about that. How is he? I hope . . . he—"

"He will survive," said I.

"I am greatly relieved to hear it."

Looking round me, I saw that the audience, which had grown by one or two, was now similarly overcome with pious sympathy. Their faces had lengthened; their heads were bowed. But why not? These were servants, were they not?—as indeed so also was Mr. Collier. If I had spoken rudely because of my feelings for Sir John, then I had also spoken to him with the voice of authority. And he, as a servant, responded best to expressions of authority.

I took a step forward and leaned over him in a manner somewhat threatening. "I have questions for you," said I to Mr. Collier. "Will you answer them?"

"Absolutely, young sir, to the best of my ability."

"Very well. Had you anyone on the household staff by the name of William Waters?"

"Nooo, no indeed we had not."

"William Walters? William Walker?"

"Nothing like that. No one by any such name was employed at Lord Lilley's."

Having had Burley's information confirmed, I went on to the next question: "As butler of the Lilley residence, you presided over the staff. When you knew that the robbers had gone, who did you send to summon help? To bring a constable? To notify the magistrate?"

Mr. Collier looked at me, blinked a couple of times and said, "Why, I'm not sure."

"Give it some thought."

That he did quite visibly, screwing his face into a mask of concentration, shutting his eyes to exclude all distractions. He held this pose for a minute or more, quite impressing me with the intensity of his concentration. Only then did he relax sufficiently to say: "I did not send anyone."

"You're sure of that?"

"Well . . . yes. I was dealt such a blow to my head when the robbers came through the door that I was incapable of collecting my thoughts when they had gone. It . . . it must have been someone else sent for help."

"Or someone had taken it into his head to go."

"Yes, I suppose that could be, too."

"Mr. Collier," said I, "you gave Sir John quite a detailed report regarding what happened prior to the entry of the robbers—and I'm sure quite an accurate one, as well. I wonder if you would now put your mind to what happened afterward."

"Afterward? But . . . as I said, the blow to my head from the door left me a bit addled, I fear."

"I know, but I fear you must try."

He did try, no doubt to the best of his ability. First he told how he had been dragged through the house, then taken down the back stairs and dumped upon the kitchen floor. That, in any case, was where he came fully conscious. The staff—all except for Pinkham (who was later to join them) and the coachmen (who awaited Lord and Lady Lilley at the ambassador's residence)—had been gathered together in the kitchen, where they were held prisoner by a threatening black man with a ring in his ear, a pistol at his side, and a cutlass in his hand. Mr. Collier then explained that from that point on, all that he could glean of the robbers' activities within the house had come to him through his ears. He heard the footsteps of more men above them as they entered through the rear of the house. How many? He could not be sure; perhaps three in addition to those who had come through the front—perhaps more. In any case, the robbers were very well organized, for they did not stay long. How long? Only minutes—as many as fifteen, though perhaps ten would be more accurate.

"And in that time," I put it to him, "when was it Pinkham joined the rest in the kitchen?"

"Only toward the end," said Mr. Collier. "That would have been in the last few minutes."

"How *many* minutes?"

He seemed to take offense at my persistent questioning. "I have a timepiece, but I did not consult it. I can be no more accurate than I have been."

"We shall let it stand then at a *few* minutes."

Something had occurred to him. That was evident from the vague expression that of a sudden appeared in his eyes.

"What is it?" I asked. "What are you now thinking?"

"I am now thinking that perhaps I can say with some certainty that it was just at the very end that she was brought down to the kitchen, for he who brought her had a conversation in whispers with him who had been standing guard over us."

"Have you no idea what was discussed?" I pressed him thusly.

"Oh yes, indeed I have, for it was then that they selected Walter Travis out and took him away."

"Walter Travis?" I knew I should know the name, but . . .

"The man they murdered."

"Ah yes," said I. (Glad I was that Sir John had not been present to hear me make such an error.) "Was he simply grabbed out of the crowd and taken away? Was nothing said?"

"Yes, there was a good deal said. A great threat was made by the one who brought Pinkham down. He said that they were leaving and none should follow. And if we was to do that, he would kill this fellow who was now their hostage, as well as any who followed. Now, I can't swear to it, because all these blackies look alike to me, but from the sound of his voice I'd say he was the same one tricked me into opening the front door for him and his fellows."

"Are you saying then, Mr. Collier, that Walter Travis was slain because some of those in the kitchen trailed the robbers out the back?"

"No, no such thing," said he with great certainty, "because just as soon as they were upstairs and out the back, we heard the shot, and we knew somehow that poor Travis had been killed. For some time afterward, we waited there in the kitchen. Burley, the other porter, was the only one of us who showed any eagerness to get upstairs. He got on well with Travis. You might even say as how they were friends. I cautioned Burley, held him back till there was no point holding him back further. And then he was first one up the stairs. He found the body where we expected it would be — right there in the back garden."

"And you saw it there yourself?" I asked.

"Well, yes, eventually. First thing I did was go through the house room by room to see all that was missing. I got to credit those black boys. They stole a lot in a very short time."

"How much did they steal? What sort of cash value could you put upon it?"

"That would be difficult to say, but with the paintings, the silver plates, the Chinese vases, and all, I'd guess it at thousands of pounds — maybe close to ten. God knows what the jewels were worth — perhaps an equal amount, but likely more. I made up a list for my master — or former master."

Mr. Collier's listeners were brought somewhat aback by these estimates of his. There was a groan of appreciation, a whistle, and eyebrows shot up right and left.

He then added: "I suppose it was because I was so deeply involved in assessing the extent of Lord Lilley's loss that I failed to send out for a constable. Just all of a sudden, not long after the robbers left, there was a constable at the door. I suppose that you know the rest."

I supposed that I did, for I had not then learned a tenet held by all interrogators: No matter how many times a turnip has been squeezed dry, you can always get more water from it. And so, upon ascertaining that I might reach him again through the staff of the Zondervan residence ("I'll make sure they always know where I'm at"), I took my leave of them all, thanking Mr. Collier for his cooperation.

My patient waiting paid handsomely when word came from Lady Fielding that Sir John was at last awake, and that upon waking he had asked to see me. As the three women puttered joyfully about the kitchen preparing a dinner tray for him who had not eaten for twelve hours or more, I hurried up the stairs to his bedroom, eager to tell him all.

Yet before I could begin, he questioned me closely on the matter of food.

"Did they give you any idea how long it would be? I'm altogether famished, you know."

"No sir, they did not," said I. "But all three were working at it. You should not have long to wait."

"There was none of this nonsense about clear broth, was there?"

"I did not discuss it with them, sir, but I know it as fact that Annie went especially to Mr. Tolliver's in Covent Garden for a beef chop. I happened to glimpse it sir, and it's monstrous large."

He smacked his lips as a child might. " 'Monstrous large,' you say? Couldn't suit me better. But quickly, if you can, dear boy, tell me if you've made progress in the Lilley matter. Give me your report."

Quickly was indeed how I told it. Because I knew I had much to tell, I had organized it well during the time that he slept. First I told of finding Mr. Collier at the Zondervan residence through Annie's help and of the interrogation that followed. I made no effort to repeat question and answer through the entire session, but rather offered what I thought to be the most important items to emerge from my discussion with the butler.

For instance, this: "Mr. Collier estimated the worth of all things stolen at up to twenty thousand pounds."

"So much?" Sir John groaned. "Oh, dear God! What more?"

"Well, there was this, sir: According to Mr. Collier's recollection of the time he spent in the kitchen with the rest, awaiting the robbers' departure, the lady's maid, Mistress Pinkham, did not join her fellow servants until the house had been sacked. Not until they left was she put with the others in the kitchen."

"Hmmm," said he, "that was not the impression she created when she talked to us, was it?"

"No sir, it was not. There may be cause for suspicion."

"There *may* be. Continue to look for her. We must talk with her again. What else did you turn up?"

"Not much worth mentioning from Mr. Collier. However, I interviewed Constable Patley as he was coming on duty this evening."

"And what did you discover?"

"I discovered that the supposed servant from the Lilley residence who notified Constable Patley of the grand robbery was more or less fictitious."

" 'More or less'? What does that mean?"

"It means, sir, that while we must credit it that Mr. Patley was approached by someone and told of the robbery, we do not know the identity of that someone. The name given by the constable in the rather crude document which pretends to be his written report of the crime corresponds to that of no one on the household staff of the Lilley residence. Nor does Mr. Collier recall sending anyone forth to report the crimes of theft and murder; he said that he was too busy tallying up the cash value of the objects stolen to remember to do what needed to be done."

"And so," said Sir John, "where does that leave us?"

"In a rather awkward place," said I.

"And what place is that, Jeremy?"

"Sir, I explained all this to Constable Patley—well, you might say that I confronted him with it."

"With what result?"

"He admitted that he had made up the name."

Sir John popped up in his bed to something near a seated position. For a moment he was speechless—but only for a moment, for he bellowed loud and deep, *"He what?"*

"That's right, sir. He was, in the end, quite apologetic, but at first he insisted that it could make no difference anyway, since the information given was quite accurate. After all, there had been a robbery at the Lilley residence, hadn't there? That sort of thing. He couldn't, for the life of him, understand why you had to have the name of him who had brought the report. But since you had to have a name, he supposed that William Waters would do as well as any. The truth was, he admitted at last, that he had not asked the messenger his name, but simply given him directions to Bow Street."

"Shall we discharge the fellow now, do you think, or wait until he does serious harm to person or property?"

"I think it best to wait, Sir John, as you will, too, once you have overcome your anger. Yet I have still more to tell."

He sighed. "Go ahead then. I would have it all."

"Well and good," said I. "The mysterious messenger went on, as we know, and arrived here at Bow Street. He knocked upon the door, and Mr. Baker came to answer it. The fellow, whoever he was, gave him the particulars in a great rush and said that he must get back to the Lilley residence, for he would be needed there. Mr. Baker asked only that his informant wait while he might fetch paper and pencil and jot down the important details. Yet the man refused to remain and ran off, shouting the number of the Lilley house in St. James Street. Constable Bailey happened to be bringing in a prisoner, and so he went off to St. James and collected Mr. Brede along the way. And, as you know, Mr. Baker—"

"Came upstairs and informed me of what had happened," said Sir John, completing the sentence. He thought a moment upon it, then said, "And so I doubt Mr. Baker managed to get his name, either. Was there any sort of description of the fellow?"

"About all they could agree upon was that the man was uncommonly tall. But Sir John, I do not believe that it would have mattered had either Mr. Patley or Mr. Baker managed to get his name, for it would probably have been a false name, in any case."

Suddenly alert to possibilities, Sir John mused aloud: "I believe I follow your train of thought. It had occurred to me, after all, that if no one from the Lilley residence went out for help, only those who had caused the trouble—which is to say, the robbers themselves—could have delivered the news. The point is, why should they have wished to do so? Were they so proud of their work that they wanted to invite the constables and the magistrate to come and admire it? I think not, Jeremy."

"I have an idea, sir," said I. "By turning in a report on so great a crime as this—robbery on such a grand scale and murder, too—they could indeed be certain that you would be summoned. In fact, they went to some pains to be sure you were." At that moment I paused for effect, took a deep breath, and continued: "Could it be, Sir John, that all that happened at the Lilley's was an elaborate trap which, baited, was set to bring you—specifically *you*—out where you would present an easy target?"

"A conspiracy?"

"Something of the sort, yes."

It was then that Lady Katherine entered, bearing his dinner upon a tray. It was more than a mere dinner — a sumptuous feast, rather.

"There now, Jeremy," said she, "you've had him long enough. I've brought him something should take his mind from those dreary court matters."

He whispered to me: "We shall speak of this later — tomorrow perhaps. But go now, lad. You've done a good day's work."

THREE

*In which the investigation
proceeds and another
house is sacked*

Next morning early I set off for Covent Garden. The greengrocers
were freshening their stock to make it look like it had come in new
from the market gardens. A few drunken blades staggered out of Car-
penter's coffee house, ending their night of revels in sullen silence; I
passed them warily on my diagonal route across the piazza. My goal
was prominent from almost any point in the Garden—not for its size
nor garish decoration (it was neither large nor colorfully painted), but
simply because it was the only one of its kind this side of Smithfield
Market.

Mr. Tolliver was a butcher, one who had violated tradition and perhaps broken a long-forgotten rule or two by opening his stall in one
corner of London's grandest vegetable market. There he had pros-
pered. And if not always so popular with his neighboring stall-keepers,
who envied him his customers, he was nevertheless well-liked as a man
and well-respected for the quality of his meat by those who bought
from him. And not least in that matter of liking and respecting him
were we who lived at Number 4 Bow Street.

He was a big man, as are so many who take up the butchering trade,
and he had a big voice of a strength and volume which would carry it
clear across Covent Garden, as he demonstrated that morning.

"Hi, Jeremy," came the shout. "And what brings you out so early?"

I waved in answer, knowing that my voice would not carry so far.
But once I judged myself near enough, I called out, "I've come for
another beef chop!"

At that, the heads of hungry men and women around me turned; they were laborers in the green market who had no more than heard tell of such cuts of meat. Not wishing to draw envious attention to myself, I was somewhat chagrined at that. I vowed to say no more until I reached him. When I did, I spoke at little more than a whisper, for Sir John was the subject of our discussion.

"Was it Annie chose the last?" I asked. "It was a great success with him who ate it."

"No, it was Lady Kate herself," said Mr. Tolliver. "She had me pick it and cut it, as she's always done in the past."

"Then I'll do the same."

Hearing that, he hauled a whole rib section of beef from the locker and tossed it on the chopping block. He took a moment to check it over, then selected a cut somewhere near the middle. With a cleaver and an unerring eye, he broke the bone in two places, then took out his saw and began cutting away. "How is he?" he asked. "Kate said he'd collapsed yesterday after his court session."

"True enough, but he seemed much improved even *before* he ate your chop."

"Well, there's nothing like beef for putting blood back into a man. He must've lost a good bit."

"Oh, he did. The ball taken from his shoulder must have been forty caliber or better."

"I'd assume then that he'll need more time in bed. He better not try to hold court every day. No telling what could happen."

"We're quite in agreement on that, sir. I've a plan. I *may* be able to persuade him."

"Well, good luck to you on it. Once he gets his mind made up, he's a hard man to get to change—as we both know." Then, having finished, he held the chop high. "There, Jeremy, what do you think of that?"

Returning, I found that Annie had prepared a breakfast tray and was ready to depart for her reading lesson at the Bilbo residence.

"He's awake," said she. "I heard him stirring and coughing, and then he started calling for his breakfast."

"And what did you tell him?"

"I said that it would be there directly. It's ready for him now. You can take it up to him, the way you wanted."

"Thank you, Annie. Go along now."

And with a nod, she took her leave.

I carried the tray up to his bedroom, where I found him on the chamber pot, purging himself of his night water. When he had done, he stood, dropping his nightshirt, and collapsed back into bed.

"Did you sleep well, Sir John?" I asked.

"I suppose I did," he replied rather impatiently. "For one in my condition it is sometimes difficult to tell."

"Oh? How is that, sir?"

"Without sight, how can one be absolutely certain whether one is dreaming, or having conscious thoughts?"

I mulled that in my mind as I set the tray down and proceeded to adjust his pillows so that he might comfortably sit up in bed.

"Is it so difficult to distinguish between the two?" I asked.

"Sometimes it is," said he.

I waited, expecting him to elaborate upon that statement (which to this day puzzles me), yet he did not. So I lifted up the tray table and placed it before him. Upon it, I placed the document which I had drafted and written the night before.

"What is that which you have put there?" He reached out and touched it suspiciously. "Am I now reduced to eating paper?"

"No sir." I laughed in spite of myself. "It is a letter written in your style. I should like you to sign it, sir."

"And only then may I have my breakfast?"

"Of course not, Sir John. Here, I'll put the tray before you now — bread, butter, four rashers of bacon, tea."

"No, wait," said he in a manner rather sharp. "Am I allowed to know the contents of this letter?"

"Certainly. It is a letter from you to Mr. Saunders Welch —"

"Perhaps," he said, interrupting, "you had best read it to me."

And that I did, clearing my throat and reading aloud. "Dear Mr. Welch: As you may have heard, during the discharge of my duties, I suffered a gunshot wound in the shoulder night before last. Yesternoon I conducted my magistrate's court as usual, but was warned against continuing this by the attending physician, Gabriel Donnelly. And so I fear it is necessary once again to request your help. I ask only that you hear the criminal cases that would ordinarily be heard by me. The rest I shall simply delay until such time as I am once again in possession of my full strength and can resume my duties. Please give your answer in the space below. I remain yours, et cetera, et cetera."

"Well," said he, "this is interesting, is it not? I had mentioned my occasional difficulty in distinguishing between the waking and sleeping states. But there are always clews that help me to know. For instance, now that you have read this letter to me, I know that I am dreaming."

"What's that, sir?" Was this one of his tricks?

"Indeed, dreaming! For I know very well that in my waking hours I told you just yesterday that I would continue to hear cases at the Bow Street Court. I remember declaring to you the importance of demonstrating to him who shot me that what he did will in no wise interrupt the dispensation of justice. I thought I put that rather well, didn't you?"

"Why, yes, but—"

"Now, I know, Jeremy, that you are far too bright a lad to forget what you are told from one day to the next—ergo, I must be dreaming! Only in a dream could circumstances be altered so radically."

He was making light of me, playing me for a fool. In my boyish way I resented that. Yet far more did I resent his reckless treatment of himself. Did he not know how important he was to us all? What would we do without him? How could London spare him?

"Yes," said I, "you made that speech about not interrupting the dispensation of justice, then you went to your courtroom, heard a few cases, then promptly collapsed."

"I did *not* collapse," he replied. "I merely suffered a passing spell of lightheadedness, as I made clear at the time."

"But why *not* allow Mr. Welch to take your cases? It is his duty to do so. He should have come to you yesterday and made the offer."

"Why not indeed! I'll tell you why. He is, first of all, a bad judge, a poor magistrate, and no more than a few hairs short of corrupt. He would rather fine a murderer than free an innocent man, for there might be money to be squeezed from the innocent." I had never heard him talk about another in such strong language, certainly neither judge nor magistrate. But there was more: "And as for your last point, Jeremy, you are correct—he should have made the offer. But he did *not*, which shows us what sort of man he is. That gives me another very good reason to continue to hear cases at Bow Street."

"And what is that?" By this time the two of us were fair shouting one at the other.

"It should be obvious: Because he did *not* volunteer, it would be completely inappropriate for me to ask it of him. I will not beg from one such as he."

"But . . . but . . . but . . ." I sputtered and fumed, yet there was no more to be said. I, at least, could think of naught. "All right," said I. "Consider the letter withdrawn. The matter is closed."

With that, I picked up the tray and delivered it to Sir John. "Your breakfast," said I as I slammed it down before him.

"Would you pour my tea, please?" said he, apparently once more as unperturbed as when I first entered the room.

I mumbled some sort of assent and did as he asked. Once I had done, I set about buttering his bread.

"It was well writ," said he.

"Pardon? What was?"

"The letter to that fellow, Welch."

"What? Oh . . . that . . . well . . . thank you."

"My objections had to do solely with its content."

"Yes, of course, I understand."

"Well, I hope you do. I do hope I've made my reasons clear. But sit down, won't you, Jeremy?"

I grabbed a chair and pulled it over to beside the bed. As I seated myself, I noted that he had begun to munch upon his breakfast, a chunk of buttered bread in one hand and a rasher of bacon in the other. I waited until he had swallowed. Only then did he speak.

"First of all," said he, "about that theory which you voiced last evening."

"Yes sir?"

"Interesting, truly interesting, but I believe you are but half right. Where you err, I think, is suggesting that that huge theft was planned and executed solely—or even chiefly—to bring me forth as a target. Their haul from Lord Lilley's was far too rich to be considered a mere exercise for such a purpose.

"But to me, it seems," he continued, "that you are quite right about the rest. Which is to say, whoever organized this robbery—and there is something familiar about the manner of it—was certainly eager to use it to bring me there. I agree that he who reported it was probably sent there specifically to make sure I came. Well, I did come, and we know the result. And so I must ask you to stand again, pistols by your sides, through today's court session."

"I will. I'll be there."

"And what had you planned in the way of furthering the investigation?"

What indeed? I had given some thought to it—though perhaps not sufficient, so intent was I upon dissuading Sir John from sitting his court as usual. But I put before him what had occurred to me.

"Well, sir," said I, "two avenues of investigation seemed possible, but I fear I know not how to pursue them—not in any practical way, that is. The first would be to find out what I can about Walter Travis, the man who was left dead by the robbers. If he had a criminal past, as Mr. Burley suspected, then knowing more of him might lead us to those who killed him—and perhaps tell us why."

"A reasonable assumption," said he. "I'd talk to Mr. Marsden about that. Though Travis is no doubt an alias, Marsden may have heard some stories about who left criminal pursuits for a life in service. The novelty of that would assure that it would be circulated up and down Bedford Street. A good story is long remembered. Oh, and talk to Mr. Bailey, too," added Sir John. "He got a look at the fellow, did he not?"

"He did, sir—and I'll do all that you suggest. But about that second avenue I mentioned . . ."

"Yes, oh yes, what is it, Jeremy?"

"It also occurred to me that if we could find the booty, we could also very likely find those who had stolen it. But beyond looking at those known to be fences up in Field Lane, I know not where to inquire, nor to whom."

"Yes, well, to search in Field Lane you would need someone who knew the stolen items by sight—the butler would do if you can locate him again. Didn't he make up some sort of list of stolen items?"

"I believe he did."

"But in truth," he continued, "I am not sure that you are likely to turn up anything in Field Lane. A theft of such enormity could hardly be handled by any one of the fences there—nor even perhaps all of them together. They are at best rather small enterprises. Disposing of

Lady Lilley's jewels, for instance, would be quite beyond them. Jewels are rather special."

With that he paused a goodly pause, leaned his head back on the pillow, and gave prolonged thought to the matter. Only thereafter did he resume.

"This may surprise you, Jeremy, but regarding the jewels, you might best talk with Mr. Moses Martinez."

"The *accountant*?"

"Ah well, he is that among other things—sometimes an investor and sometimes a banker, and sometimes a financial adviser. But with all else, he is a Jew, and the Jews do largely control the market for precious stones in Amsterdam. I mean in no wise to implicate Mr. Martinez in the theft, nor in the fencing of what was stolen, but he has contacts there in the diamond district and if he were to make some discreet inquiries . . ."

"I see. Indeed I shall do that, sir."

"And as for the rest of the goods taken the other night, why not go to Lloyd's Coffee House and ask Mr. Humber about them?"

"Mr. Alfred Humber? Truly? What would he know about such matters as this?"

"Mr. Humber knows a good deal about many things," said Sir John somewhat mysteriously. "Just try him and see if he has anything to offer. That should keep you busy, eh, lad?"

I agreed that it would and rose from my chair to depart.

"Just one more matter," said he, holding me there at his bedside. "Are you absolutely certain that the man who shot at me there in St. James Street was *black*?"

"Well," said I, somewhat at a loss, "as sure as I can be about most things. That is to say, we were beneath the streetlamp, and he was not. And when he appeared I was greatly distracted, trying to push you out of the way while also attempting to get a shot off at him. Nevertheless, in spite of all that, I retain a picture of him, and that picture is of a black man—an African."

"All right," said he, "I accept what you say—I must. Yet I cannot think for the life of me what black man I might so have offended that he would wish to kill me." He sighed; the matter did truly trouble him. "But on your way now. Report to me when you have something to report. And not before."

. . .

Thus the day passed rather quickly. In no more than a few minutes, I had been given much to do: at least a day's work, and more likely two or three. I liked it well that he had left the execution of the tasks to me. As soon as Annie returned at mid-morning, I set off at quick march to the office of Moses Martinez in Leadenhall Street in the City of London. The only difficulty I experienced there was that which I had foreseen, and Sir John had more or less foretold. I well recall the incredulous and hurt expression Mr. Martinez wore upon his face as I told him that Sir John hoped he might be of some aid in tracing jewels of Lady Lilley's, stolen from the Lilley residence the night before last.

"Surely he does not believe that I had something—anything at all— to do with that monstrous robbery!"

"Indeed he does not," said I, in what I meant to be a most reassuring tone. "He values your friendship highly, and I myself have heard him commend you to others as the most honest of men."

At that, Mr. Martinez seemed appropriately relieved. "Very well then," said he. "What might I do for you?"

"Sir John thought only that perhaps through your contacts with those in the gem trade in Amsterdam, you might be of some help in this matter."

"Ah, indeed, perhaps I might. What is the value of these jewels?"

"Upwards to ten thousand pounds."

"Indeed? Well, in that case, they would almost *have* to be sold off in Amsterdam. Give me a few days, young man—enough time to make some inquiries—and perhaps I shall have some information for you and good Sir John." With that, I said a polite goodbye and ran toward the river for Lloyd's Coffee House.

My business there with Mr. Alfred Humber was even more quickly executed. I found him seated at his usual table in the room, which even at that early hour was dense with tobacco smoke. His hands were folded over his protuberant middle, and his eyes were heavy-lidded in such a way that he seemed to be napping as a fat old tabby would do. George, his ever-present assistant, sat at the table with him; he had grown from the rag-tag errand boy I had first met to a sleek young underwriter who showed only disdain for lads like me. No matter; we ignored one another as I sat down and sought Mr. Humber's attention.

"Well," said he to me, rousing himself from his somnolent pose, "what will you with me today, young Mr. Proctor?"

"Information, Mr. Humber. Sir John suggested that I come to you in this matter of a great theft which occurred night before last. All manner of valuables were taken: paintings, silver settings, plates, even jewels. There is some question of where these goods might be disposed of. He suggested you might have some idea."

"He *did*? I wonder how he might have come by such a notion as that!" Then light did flicker in those sleepy eyes and a smile spread cross those hanging jowls. "But wait," said he, "perhaps I do have an idea or two about that—something I discussed some time ago with Jack. Dear God, he does have a long memory."

I leaned forward eagerly, wishing to miss none of what was to follow. Yet, there was nothing to miss.

"Yes, indeed," said he, "but I fear you'll have to wait. It will take a day or two at least to talk with everyone. And to be sure, I must talk to them all. Come tomorrow—or perhaps the day after would be better."

I sighed. "Whatever you say, sir." With which I rose, offered my thanks, and took my leave. Only then did I receive so much as a glance from George. I replied with a sneer.

And so I managed to return to Number 4 Bow Street, just in time to strap on the brace of pistols and take my place at the courtroom door as Sir John rapped upon the table and called his magistrate's court to order. Again, what followed was more or less uneventful, and I praised God for that. The session did, however, go on a bit longer than the usual; by the end of it he was visibly depleted, his face pale with exhaustion. He waited until the last of the spectators had left. I shut the door on them and barred it, and then did I come forward to assist Mr. Marsden in bringing the magistrate to his feet. He rose easily enough and kept his feet solid beneath him, but when he walked toward the door and on to the stairs, he moved at a slow, plodding pace. Joined there at the stairway by Mr. Fuller, we undertook to move him to the quarters up above in the same manner we had employed the day before: I moving ahead of Sir John, who trailed me with his hand on my shoulder; Mr. Marsden and Mr. Fuller brought up the rear, ready to catch him should he fall.

Thus we brought him as far as his bedroom, where we sat him upon his bed and helped him out of his coat. Kicking off his shoes, he threw his feet upon the bed and, in breeches and waistcoat, eased himself back upon the two pillows that I had prepared for him. I nodded at the two men who had helped bring him to his bed, and they backed silently out the door. There, a moment later, Annie appeared.

"Can I bring you something, Sir John?" she asked. "Anything at all?"

"Annie? Why yes, child. A nice, hot cup of tea would suit me well."

"You'll have it, sir, in no time at all."

As she left, Sir John turned to where he knew me to be and asked for my help in getting out of his clothes and under the comforter. "And by all means, hang my things out of sight. I'll not have another lecture from Mr. Donnelly on the harm I do myself by daring to venture out of bed."

"Yes sir," said I.

"And should he ask you—or Annie—if I have been obedient to his rule, you must assure him that I have indeed been."

"Surely you would not have us lie!" said I, hoping that the impudent smile on my face could not be detected in my voice.

"I would have you do as I tell you," said he sternly. "All medicos are tyrants, and as tyrants they deserve to be lied to."

"As you say, Sir John."

"Now away with you, Jeremy. And tell Annie that if she does not hurry with that cup of tea, I shall likely be asleep by the time that it arrives."

I told Annie no such thing, for just as I made to go, she was there at the door, a large, steaming cup on a saucer in her hand. A wink from me and a nod from her, and I was on my way.

I returned to the Zondervan residence in St. James Street in search of Mr. Collier, formerly of Lord Lilley's household staff. I found him where I should least have expected to find him. The butler, who introduced himself to me as Mr. Hill, said that Mr. Collier had asked to see Mr. Zondervan's collection of paintings, and he was in the room which was set aside as a kind of picture gallery.

"He fancies himself an expert," said Mr. Hill in such a way as to make it plain he thought Mr. Collier nothing of the kind. "If you but follow, I shall take you to him."

I was ushered down the long central hall to a room just opposite the kitchen stairs and the servants' quarters. Then did he surprise me by producing a key and inserting it in a keyhole just below the door handle.

"You've locked him inside?" said I, mildly shocked at this disclosure.

"This door is always locked, except when the master is inside. That is as he would have it."

Then, throwing it open, he revealed Mr. Collier at the other side of the room, his back turned toward us, studying a painting with an intensity it hardly seemed to deserve. It was no more than a picture of dancing peasants—colorful, yes, but scattered, difficult to fix with the eye, poorly composed (or so it seemed to me). Mr. Collier turned toward us and nodded. Mr. Hill and I took places on either side of him and gave it our attention, as well.

"It is very pretty, is it not?" said Mr. Hill in a rather airy manner.

"Beautiful," said Mr. Collier. "It's a Brueghel," he added, as if that explained all.

"It must be very old," said I.

"It is over a hundred and fifty years old," said Mr. Collier, "but how could you tell?" He turned to me, waiting for my answer.

"People don't dress like that anymore."

He sighed, signaling his disappointment. "No, they don't."

I waited as he continued to stare at the picture. There were others hung about the room, a good many others which I liked better. I wondered why he didn't look at them.

After clearing my throat twice to gain his attention, I suggested that he come with me to inspect the pawnshops in Field Lane, which were known to operate as fences.

"Fences?" said he. "I do not quite understand the term."

"They are places which accept stolen goods from the thieves who took them and resell them to the public at less than their true worth."

"I did not know such places existed. Why are they not shut down? Why are those who operate them not punished?"

"They have protection from the law," I explained, "so long as they can show that pawn tickets were filled out for the stolen items and the operator of the fence will swear they were presented to him as the personal property of him who pawned them."

"Hmmm," said he. "The law is indeed strange."

"At times it may seem so," I agreed. "But if you accompany me and identify any items we see as Lord Lilley's property, they can be seized as stolen goods and returned to him. It might indeed move him to invite you back into his service."

He drew himself up to his full height, thrust out his chin, and said, "I would not accept such an invitation if it were offered."

"Nevertheless, Mr. Collier, you are in a unique position to aid in the investigation. Since you made a survey of what had been stolen and drew up a list, then you probably know what is missing better even than Lord Lilley."

"Ha! I'm sure I do. Most of what he had he ignored. It was only when he had paid an exorbitant amount that he took any notice of an object at all."

"Well, then . . ." said I.

"Harry," said Mr. Hill to Mr. Collier, "I believe what the lad is trying to tell you is that you *must* assist him, whether it pleases you or not."

Mr. Collier turned sharply to me. "Is this true?"

"Well . . ."

"Oh, all right then, why not? It would do me good to get out for a bit, so long as you, Charles," he spoke pointedly to Mr. Hill, "let me finish in here another time."

"Tomorrow, I promise," said Mr. Hill. He was most reassuring.

"Well, enough then, young man," said Mr. Collier to me. "Let me get my hat, and we'll be on our way."

And so, in a short time we were in a hackney and on our journey to Field Lane. If it was far enough to justify a coach ride, the distance was even greater from St. James Street if measured in guineas, crowns, and shillings. We went from high to low in no more than a few miles, from luxury to misery. When at last the ride was done, Mr. Collier stepped down from the coach, looked around him, and shuddered.

"Is this what awaits me?" he moaned. Not knowing the answer, nor even what, precisely, he had meant by that, I said nothing.

In most ways, perhaps, it looked like any other street in London's poorer districts—that is to say, no worse than most. (It was said that there were far more squalorous locations across the river.) Nevertheless, an air of desperation seemed to brood over the length of it, foul as the smell that rose from the Fleet River—a veritable sewer—nearby. Those who walked it up and down, men and women both, went with stooped shoulders and bowed heads; even the children in the street played listlessly, never raising their voices nor laughing. The four pawnshops stood scattered along the narrow way, two on the east side and two on the west side. Why they should be gathered there so closely, I have no idea. Yet there they were, and we were bound to visit each of them, and search them all through. We stood on Holborn Hill; I indicated the direction, and we set off to perform the task for which we had come.

The contents of pawnshops do not charm me, and neither do the shops themselves, except in rare instances, interest me. I had, by the time of that visit, taken a sufficient number of robbery victims through Field Lane, so that I know, and was known by sight by, each of the four proprietors. There was no need for me to display the warrant I carried in my coat pocket. I went unchallenged. They said nothing but simply fell back and allowed me and my companion to prowl through the shop as long as we liked. Mr. Collier was, indeed, thorough. He went slowly through each pile, dug into every corner, and sorted through the contents of drawers and compartments. There was no need for me to call to his attention any area that he had neglected because he neglected none. I helped simply by knowing the plan of each of the shops and introducing him to storage areas he might not otherwise have known about.

Thus we went through all four of the shops. We then went back to Holborn Hill where I waved down a hackney coach. As we boarded, I said to Mr. Collier, "There is but one more shop that I should like you to go through. It is on our way back to St. James Street."

"I have no objection," said he, "though I hope it is not near so sad as that last street you took me to."

"Bedford Street," I called up to the driver.

"That's said to be a dangerous place."

"After dark, perhaps, though not at this hour."

He lapsed into silence as we began our journey. He had traveled just as quietly to Field Lane.

Our destination, of course, was the shop that had formerly belonged to George Bradbury, who served as fence to Covent Garden's most skilled and dedicated thieves. Mr. Bradbury died for his sins, and his widow sold the pawnshop, lock and stock, when she emigrated to the North American colonies. Since then I had called there perhaps two or three times to make the sort of search I had done more often up in Field Lane. The new owner, a man by the name of Garland, was too honest or perhaps too timid to engage in the sort of backdoor enterprise in which the former owners had engaged so eagerly.

In any case, the trip did not take a great deal of time, and we were deposited right in the middle of Bedford Street, which put us directly before Mr. Garland's shop.

"Here we are," said I to my companion. I climbed down and paid off the driver.

"Well," said Mr. Collier, emerging into the light and looking the street up and down, "it doesn't look so bad."

"It is, as I said, a street like most in London until night falls and the villains and scamps come and claim the ale houses and dives as their own."

At just that moment, a drunken wretch came hurtling through the open door of a low place next to the pawnshop; he landed in the gutter nearby. The innkeeper leaned out the door and snarled a few curses at the poor fellow before retiring into the darkness of the gin shop.

Mr. Collier watched the offender attempt vainly to push himself up to his feet. He turned to me. "You say it's worse than this after dark?"

"Oh, much," said I.

Pointing to the pawnshop door, I herded him forward and inside. The proprietor of the place, Mr. Garland, was there immediately to meet us.

"We should like to take a look around," said I. "The magistrate has sent me."

"I know who you are. I remembers you from your last visit," said he.

Mr. Collier had already begun his inspection, looking at clocks and vases and other bits and pieces standing about the front of the shop. It did not take long. He simply shook his head in the negative and turned toward the door, presuming that we were done.

"We shall be looking in the back room, as well," said I to the shopkeeper.

"Well and good," said he, striving to contain his anger, "but I told you once I do not engage in such illegal trade. Why will you not believe me?"

"In a word, Mr. Garland, because he who preceded you had a long history of it. And his widow, from whom you bought the shop, put her very heart into such dealings. Of that I can speak from some personal knowledge."

"I'll not ask what that knowledge is. I've heard enough about her — murdered her husband, she did, or so they say. Heard about it a hundred times, at least." He shrugged and waved a hand dismissively. "All I know is she gave me a good price on the place, and the stock. And that's all I need to know."

As we went thus at each other, Mr. Collier slipped past us and into the rear room, which I knew from my earlier searches contained most of the ticketed items in the shop. We followed him. And I noted immediately that Mr. Garland had done a great deal of work putting to order the chaotic jumble that earlier prevailed in the large rear room. That made Mr. Collier's work much easier. He went swiftly through the room just as he had those in Field Lane. He lingered only at the two stacks of paintings mounted in their frames piled upright against the wall. Yet he did not linger long. He was done as quickly as I might have hoped. Mr. Garland was glad to see us go and said as much.

It took little to persuade Mr. Collier to continue the rest of the way on foot. We were soon away from Bedford Street, and out on the Strand, and into the swarm of humanity. Crowded it may have been, yet it looked a bit better and smelled better than what we had left behind. I know that my companion noticed the improvement, for he commented upon it.

"Ah," said he, "how good it is to be getting back to my part of town."

"*Your* part of town, sir?"

"Why, indeed! I may be but a humble butler, but all of my employment has been in that area in which you found me—St. James Street, St. James Square, Great Jermyn Street, the best addresses in London. There are few who would differ with me on that."

"Well, no doubt they are very good addresses, Mr. Collier, but would it be fair to say that they were *your* addresses? After all, sir, to take the most convenient example, Lord and Lady Lilley no doubt would contest your claim."

"Oh, no doubt they would."

"They would say it was their address."

"Ah, but I lived there, too, and *I* ran the house."

"Does that give you the right to claim it as your own?"

He considered my question. "Not the whole house, perhaps." Then did he puff up a bit; his chin went up, and his chest came out, attracting curious glances from the passersby. "But the address was as much mine as it was that of the duke and duchess."

"That much I'll grant, but—"

"You seem an intelligent lad," said he, interrupting. "Let me tell you that I've been doing some thinking since I was thrown out so coldly from that house in St. James Street. I believe I shall avail you of a bit of it." He paused but briefly, then plunged on: "I despise myself as I was there—far too eager to please, far too fearful of giving offense. I was an arse-kisser—or to put it less vulgarly, a toady, a sycophant, a . . . a . . ."

"A lickspittle?"

"Precisely! And why did I play such a role? Why, to curry favor, to seek recognition from my employer that I might be liked, well-treated, given greater responsibility. And, let us ask, who was my employer? One who was, in every way but two, my inferior. Which is to say, first of all, that he had a title, and secondly, that he had great wealth, more than he could ever spend in his lifetime."

"I do not understand," said I. "Since he has a title and great wealth, how can you claim to be superior to him in every other way? It may not be just, but that is how the world measures greatness. What other ways are there?"

"Well . . . well . . ." he sputtered, "taste for one thing. I believe I told you, young sir, that Lord Lilley valued his possessions purely according to what he had paid for them. Nor is he alone in that. There is not one duke or earl in the realm who can claim to possess even a modicum of personal taste. If it were not for Italians and Frenchmen here in London, and an occasional word from a butler"—he did then give a mischievous wink—"their houses would go unfurnished and their walls empty. They are so utterly without taste that, left on their own, they would not know what to buy."

His long rant put me somewhat on the defensive. After all, I was well aware that our quarters at Number 4 Bow Street were rather bare of adornment. We had not a single picture on the wall, nor one piece of statuary, and the rooms were furnished with odds and ends left behind after brother Henry's departure for Portugal (and his subsequent death). What use had a blind man for such? And Lady Fielding, for all her pretensions, was quite indifferent to the decorative or visual arts. In short, we lived well enough without taste.

"How can it be so important?" I asked in a manner which I meant to seem dismissive. (I began at this point to peer ahead, searching for a place where I might conveniently part company with this pouter-pigeon of a fellow.)

"Important? My dear boy, taste is more than important! *Le bon goût c'est tout!*" he declared, making a neat little French rhyme of it—then translating helpfully, "Good taste is all—everything!"

We had come to the end of the Strand and the beginning of Charing Cross Road, a perfectly suitable sort of place for me to send Mr. Collier on his way, a smile on my face as I delivered a firm pat to him on his back. I had more than begun the goodbye ritual, in fact had even delivered that final pat on the back, when he looked me in the eye and declared: "Young man, I am disappointed in you."

"I'm sorry to hear that, sir."

"No more than I am sorry to tell you. I thought, when I noted your eye roaming o'er the Vermeers and the Rubens in Mr. Zondervan's gallery, 'Now, there is a lad who may not know much but who perhaps could be taught.' But unfortunately . . ."

"I really must be going," said I, "but you'll be all right from here on."

"Of course I will. But let us consider Mr. Zondervan. Now, the man has taste, no doubt of that—I should be the last to dispute it. Nevertheless, to keep his artistic treasures hidden away as he does and under lock and key, that truly seems most unfortunate. Who is he hiding them from?"

"Mr. Collier, I thank you for your cooperation, but now I must return to Bow Street." I said it quite firmly. "Goodbye."

"What? Oh, I suppose so. Yes, goodbye."

With that, I turned round and left him where he stood, separate lines of pedestrians flowing on either side of him. Yet after a few steps I turned back for another look. I caught sight of him, moving along now, gesturing with his hands so that I was sure that he was still talking, even though I was no longer with him to listen. But then the crowd swallowed him up; he had quite disappeared.

He seemed perhaps a bit mad, pushed into that state by his rude dismissal. He had annoyed me, it was true, but far more than annoyance, I felt pity for the old man (he must have been forty or more).

I had a great desire to talk about him with someone. But with whom? It did not seem proper to discuss him with Sir John or Lady Katherine. Annie, it struck me, would have little interest in him. That left only Clarissa. Well, why not? She, at least, would see the drama in it. I wondered vaguely what she might have to say.

So you see, reader, the first day of my investigation may have gone quickly, as I said, yet it was not particularly fruitful. I vowed when I took myself up to bed that night that tomorrow I would do better.

Though I could only guess at what time of night it may have been, footsteps upon the stairs to my room brought me wide awake out of a deep sleep.

"Who is there?" I challenged the intruder.

"It is I, Jeremy." The voice was Lady Fielding's. She came to the open door of my room and leaned inside, no more than a light form against the darkness of the hall.

I rose up in bed to show that I was fully awake. "What is it?" I asked. "Is Sir John well?"

"Oh yes, but one of the constables has come with word of another great robbery. Jack cannot go, he simply cannot."

"I agree."

"I would not even wake him to tell him. I fear you will have to go and act in his stead."

"It will take me no time at all to be ready. If anyone is waiting downstairs, you may tell him that I shall be there in minutes."

And, indeed, I was. Fully dressed but with shoes in hand, I descended the stairs. At the bedchamber of Sir John and Lady Fielding I paused a moment to hear his steady breathing. As I did, she appeared and whispered, "Take care, Jeremy." Then did she surprise me with a motherly kiss upon the cheek. And I continued upon my way.

Below, none other than Constable Patley awaited me. Mr. Baker, for his part, stood ready for me, holding two pistols in holsters, prepared to buckle them about my waist. As he did this, he cautioned me to hold my fire as long as possible, and aim carefully at the trunk. It sounded like good advice. I only hoped that in the event I should have the presence of mind to follow it. But, having been readied for the worst, I could now depart. After I thanked Mr. Baker, we set off into the night.

Constable Patley was my companion and my guide. As we made our way, he recounted to me all that he knew of the crime. It seemed that Mr. Bailey, the captain of the Bow Street Runners, had been his companion this night when again they were approached by someone, a servant of a house in Little Jermyn Street, that had just been sacked by a band of black men. Were there any injuries? Yes, a man lay dead, though he had not, strictly speaking, been murdered. In the course of the robbery one of the household staff had been taken by an attack of some sort—apoplexy or a sudden stoppage of the heart—and it had put him in such a state that he could not be revived.

Having heard this much, I asked the question which I was sure Sir John would have asked in my place. To wit: "Has the doctor been sent for?"

"He has, yes," said Mr. Patley. "Soon as Bailey and me arrived, he took a look at the body where it was lying and sent the stable boy off on a horse to fetch the doctor."

"Gabriel Donnelly in Drury Lane?"

"I b'lieve that was the same as before." He was silent for a moment. "Yes, that was it." He had grown a bit sullen.

"And you went to Bow Street to fetch . . ."

"Well, not exactly you—not you alone, anyways. I thought—and maybe Mr. Bailey thought, too—that the magistrate would be well enough to come."

"But he's not," said I with great certainty. "He has sent me in his stead."

"You know how to do all that asking questions and all?" He seemed rather dubious.

"Yes." That seemed sufficient. I could see no need to convince him of my qualifications.

He was silent for a good long space of time. We must have crossed a number of streets before he spoke up again. Then, of a sudden, he burst out with something quite unexpected; it was as if he had thought long upon it yet held it back.

"I want to ask you something," said he.

"Ask me anything you like."

"How old are you, anyways?"

"How old am I? Why should that matter?"

"You said I could ask you anything."

"But I didn't say I'd answer." I hesitated but a moment and thought better of what I had said. "Oh, all right," said I. "I am seventeen years of age."

"Well, let me tell you something, mister damn-near-a-magistrate, seventeen is how old I was when I took the King's shilling. And I then had as fine an opinion of myself as you seem to have of your own self."

Having heard that, I was about to interrupt with a counterattack before he had even properly begun. However, curiosity persuaded me to hold my tongue.

"Yet we differed in one partic'lar," he continued. "And that was in respect of our elders. I soon found out that if I cared to live out the length of my enlistment, it was important for me to pay attention to what those who'd been in the regiment a while might have to say, and not go trying to tell them how *I* thought *they* ought to do things. I had much to be grateful for to them.

"Now, I know you had a bad opinion of that report I wrote out on that first big robbery in St. James Street. That much I heard from that man Marsden, the magistrate's clerk."

Finally, reader, I could hold my tongue no longer. "Mr. Marsden had a bad opinion of it, too," said I, "and so would Sir John have had if he had sufficient sight to read it. Well, he couldn't have read it—none could—not the way the words were spelled. You authored something unique! It seemed another language entirely. Not to mention the near total absence of facts and details."

"Well," said he, "I'm working on those reports—with Mr. Bailey. He's showing me how to write them the way Sir John wants."

"Can he teach you how to spell correctly?" It was, I blush to say, a question intended less to elicit a reasonable response than to antagonize. And antagonize it did.

"You ain't going to leave me alone on that, are you? You would scorn me as a man for no more than some words ain't spelled to your liking. Well, all right, young sir, you may discover there's more to judge a man by than that. I'm not saying I'll be the one to teach you, but I can damn near guaranty you'll find out from somebody sometime, and it'll probably be sooner 'stead of later."

I had offended him, which was bad enough, though to make things worse, I had offended him by intention. Of a sudden I saw this, which is to say, I had a clear picture of myself as an arrogant young puppy. The picture appalled me, and I might well have set about to make amends (which would have been proper) had he not grabbed my arm and jerked me to a halt. Instinctively my arms came up, and my hands formed into fists. If it came to it, I was ready to defend myself.

But no. Mr. Patley pointed somewhat behind me and to my right. "We're here," said he. "This is the house."

I turned and looked at it, frowning. Why, I knew the place, and I knew it well. I had delivered many a letter there, and even been inside a number of times. "This is the Trezavant house, isn't it?"

"Yes," he said, "that's the name." It occurred to me that it might indeed have been better if Sir John had come, for Mr. Trezavant was the coroner for the city of Westminster. There were political considerations, matters of precedence, which I hardly felt competent to deal with. Nevertheless, I would deal with them as best I could.

"Come along then, Mr. Patley. Let us do what must be done."

FOUR

The door was opened to us by a big man in his shirtsleeves — a porter, no doubt, or perhaps a footman (I've no skill in telling them apart). In any case, we were warned by him to step carefully as we made our way inside. Immediately the door shut behind us and I saw the cause for caution.

The body of him described by Mr. Patley as having died from apoplexy or a stoppage of the heart lay on the floor of the hall just beyond the door. I was somewhat taken aback by the sight.

"The master told us not to move him until the doctor had a look at him," said the big fellow.

"Quite," said I. "So I take it the doctor has not yet arrived?"

"No, young sir, he ain't."

I knelt beside the black-clothed body and called for light. Given a single candle in a holder, I examined the face of the dead man and found that he was, as I had feared, the Trezavant butler, a sweet-natured old man who had shown me only kindness on my frequent visits to the house.

"The butler," said I, rather superfluously.

"So it is, and a good man he was, too," said he who had opened the door. "His heart had been giving him trouble the last year or two. I wager that's what done him in."

If so, a stoppage of the heart must have been more painful than ever I had supposed, for the features of his face, frozen by death, bore an expression of great pain. His had not been a peaceful passage.

I rose and handed back the candle. I inquired as to the whereabouts of Mr. Trezavant. (I was sufficiently aware of the rules of etiquette governing the situation to know that it was the master of the house to whom I must speak first.) And I was directed to his study, where I had always found him in the past. I made ready to go there, but first I addressed Mr. Patley in what I hoped would seem the proper note of polite authority: "Constable, perhaps you will find Mr. Bailey now. Tell him I am here and ready to talk with any whom he deems worth questioning."

"Certainly," said he—a proper response.

Assuring the porter (or again, perhaps he was a footman) that I knew the way, I set off down the hall for the study. When I arrived, I paused a moment before the door, taking time to organize my thoughts and prepare myself for what lay ahead.

I was quite unprepared for what I found beyond the door. I knocked upon it and was invited to enter. Was there something strange about the voice? The manner of speech? Perhaps, but I threw open the door and marched inside, eager to find out what I could which might aid materially in the capture of this crew of ruthless robbers.

Mr. Trezavant was at his desk, as he always seemed to be, his great weight and huge girth quite obscuring the chair upon which he sat. His head hung low, and as I came close I saw that his jaw had gone slack; his mouth hung open.

He was drunk. I had seen drunken men—and women—in sufficient numbers on the streets of London to know the look well. When he raised his eyes and regarded me, they carried a familiar dazed expression. And then the proof: Nearly, though not quite, hidden behind a considerable pile of ledgers on his desk, I spied the brandy bottle from which he had imbibed.

He squinted at me, probably seeking to fix my image in focus. "Who're you?" he asked at last.

"Jeremy Proctor, I came when—"

"Oh yes, I . . . Now I reco'nize you. You . . . you . . . Sir John . . ."

"Yes sir, I am Sir John's assistant."

"Whar's he?"

"I fear he was unable to come. He was wounded two nights past in the discharge of his duties. I have come in his place."

"You?" He laughed. "You're . . . you're . . . but a . . ."

"A lad? Indeed that is true, sir, but I have been well-prepared by Sir John, and with your permission, I shall question you and members of your household staff to gather information for our investigation."

"All I can tell you . . ." And at this point came the longest pause of all; near a minute passed by, perhaps more, as I waited. But eventually, my patience was rewarded. "All I can say is . . . they were a crew of cruel black buggers."

"Yes sir," said I. "I'll make a note of that." I could see there would be little of use that I would get from him. "But tell me, sir, is Mrs. Trezavant here? Would she be available for questioning?"

"My wife," said he, "is where she b'longs." He seemed to feel that he had explained all.

"And where is that, sir?"

"In . . . at home."

"Here?"

That seemed to anger him somewhat. He glared at me. Was he annoyed at me for asking, or at his wife for some unexplained offense?

"No . . . in Sussex, and she took the coach . . . the coach and four this morning."

"Well, thank you, sir," said I, backing toward the door, "I'll not bother you further."

"No bother . . . a pleasure . . . Always were a most p'lite lad. My best to Sir John. . . . Talk to anyone you like."

I had reached the door. I felt behind my back for the doorknob. "Thank you, sir," said I.

"I b'lieve I'll just take a nap," said he.

And so saying, folded his arms upon the desk and laid his great head, rather like a baby's, down upon them.

Not waiting another moment, I made a quiet exit from the room and into the hall. And there, waiting for me, I found Mr. Benjamin Bailey who, as chief constable, directed the quotidian operations of the Bow Street Runners. Perhaps, to put it more clearly, he was regimental sergeant major to Sir John's colonel. That arrangement seemed to satisfy him.

He walked me a bit down the empty hall to a point removed from Mr. Trezavant's study so that we might talk more freely.

"Did you get anything from the coroner?" he asked.

"Nothing at all. He was quite besotten."

"Drunk?"

"Completely." I looked at him then, no doubt as hopefully as I felt. "What about the servants? Are there some worth talking to?"

"Oh, I suppose so," said he. "Yes, you should talk to a few of them, but you're going to find that this robbery was just like the last, except for one or two details."

"And what are they?"

"You'll find out, Jeremy. It wouldn't do for me to draw conclusions for you."

I sighed. It seemed that even my old friend, Mr. Bailey, intended to put me to the test. Ah well, I could hardly have expected it to be otherwise.

"Lead the way," said I to him. "Find me a room, and bring them to me one at a time." I meant that as a challenge.

The first particular in which this robbery differed from the earlier was in the crucial matter of gaining entrance. Mr. Collier, Lord Lilley's former butler, had been duped into opening the door by an individual, evidently a black man, who told a sad tale of a terrible coach accident—and, what is more, told the tale in the tone and style of a native Londoner; there were no African inflections, not even the flat and now quite familiar accent of the North American colonies.

But there at the Trezavant residence, the butler could not tell us what was said, how it was said, nor for what reason it was decided to unlock and open the door. No, the butler could not tell us, but, as it happened, there was a witness to the event—and he could.

Mr. Bailey brought to me a John Mossman who, as it turned out, was the selfsame fellow who had admitted Mr. Patley and me to the Trezavant residence. He said that he and the butler, whose name was Arthur Robb, had been discussing in the hall what they might do with the master. There I halted him and asked what was meant by that. Why, after all, need anything be "done" with Mr. Trezavant?

"Well, the way of it was this, young sir," said the porter. "The master'd been drinking through a good bit of the day, and quite steady after dinner. He had collapsed at his desk—quite unconscious he was. So Arthur and me, we was discussing just how we might get him up to his bed on the floor above, the master bein' so big and all."

He went on to explain that he was the only porter on the household staff and that those who might have helped—the footmen, the coach driver—had taken Mrs. Trezavant off to the country home in Sussex and would not return until the morrow. Arthur, he was just too old and frail to be of much use carrying a big load like that. All of which was quite interesting, and perhaps later would prove relevant, but I urged Mr. Mossman to get on with his story that I might learn how the robbers had gained entry.

"We was some distance back in the hall," said he, "but we both heard the knockin' on the door real plain. It was loud and you might say right frantic. So we hastened to the door, and Arthur calls out his 'Who is there?'—for it was well past the hour when you might open the door to anybody who knocks upon it. Then in response we heard this terrible wail, a cry for help it was, and the voice that did the crying was a woman's voice."

"A woman's voice?" I exclaimed. "You're sure of that?"

"As sure as I'm here before you now. She said she'd been attacked in St. James Street, which is only a little ways over, and that she was bein' chased. Oh, she sounded terrible frightened. Well, Arthur and me, we looked one at the other. All I could do was shrug, saying it was up to him, like. But Arthur, he didn't give it but a moment's thought. He was damned if he'd have some poor soul raped on our doorstep, so he starts pulling the bolts. And once that was done, he moved the door back—he couldn't have had it open much more than an inch when it came open just like it'd been flung. It hit Arthur hard in the head, but I was behind him and managed to jump back out of the way. Then all of a sudden, there was four black men swarming through the open door with pistols and knives in their hands, and poor Arthur was reelin' about holding his head where the door hit him. Before you knew it, he was clutchin' at his heart and not his head, and, well, he just collapsed there by the door where you saw him. I couldn't even ease his way down because by that time one of the blackies had a pistol stickin' in my face."

"Did you get a look at the woman who knocked upon the door?"

He thought about that a moment, as if for the first time. "No, I can't say I did. They hustled me downstairs to the kitchen far too quick."

"Could the woman's voice you heard have been mimicked by a man?"

"You mean makin' his voice sound like a woman's? No, I don't think so. I don't see how it could've been a man."

Except for fixing the time of the assault ("Not long after ten," said he, "but not yet half past the hour"), the porter and I had finished our business. Mr. Bailey brought into the room (barely a corner cupboard, really, beneath the stairs, and just off the kitchen) one of the maids, a sort of assistant to Mrs. Trezavant's personal maid. She had more or less come forward as a volunteer, according to Mr. Bailey, for she wished to make a few things clear—or so she said.

"What is it you wish to make clear?" I thought it likely she sought to be interviewed purely for the attention that it would bring her. Therefore I had determined to spend as little time with her as possible.

"I wish to make clear it wasn't me responsible for telling the robbers what happened to the lady's jewels," said she. A bold girl, not much more than my own age, she was attractive in a saucy way.

"If it wasn't you," said I, hoping to move her along, "then who was it? They're gone, I take it."

"It wasn't nobody," said she with firm conviction. "They're gone, but wasn't ever stolen."

"Then who has them?"

"Mrs. Trezavant has them. I saw her take them along when she left for the country. Her maid packed the dresses and frocks, but she took the jewel case along in her own hand. I saw her take it my own self."

This was more interesting than I had at first realized. I wondered where, with a few more questions, it might lead.

"Didn't Mr. Trezavant see the jewel case in her hand when he bade her goodbye?"

"He never said goodbye. He just stayed where he was and sulked. See, they had a terrible row in the morning, and she was gone not much after."

"What was the row about?"

"About money—what it always is with them. I prob'ly shouldn't say so, but you'd hear it from one of the other servants, I'm sure."

"Did she object that Mr. Trezavant did not give her sufficient money to run the house?"

(I was out of my element completely here, reader. I had merely heard that this was often so in marriages.)

"Oh no," said she, plainly amused at my error. "She's richer than he is—or her family is. She's got money—rents and such—he can't touch, and that drives him quite mad, it does. He wants her father to trust him with a big loan, but she won't beg for it as he wants her to do."

"So she took the jewels with her," I ruminated aloud. "Now, why did she do that?"

"Prob'ly she was afraid he'd sell them, or pawn them. She doesn't trust him, and I can't say as I blame her."

"You don't seem to like him much," said I.

"Who would after he put the robbers on me?"

"And what do you mean by that?"

"I mean when they went in to force him to tell where the jewels was, he told them he didn't know, but I would."

"That was not very gallant of him, was it?"

"I daresay."

"How did you manage to convince them that the jewels were gone from the house?"

"It wasn't easy," said she. "First thing they did, they put a stiletto up my nose and threatened to slit it." I remembered the same threat had been made to Mistress Pinkham at the Lilley house. "See? Right here you can see where they cut a little." She tilted her head back and pointed to a bloody scab that had formed at the tip of one nostril. It was not large; nevertheless, it was impressive. "How did I convince them? She echoed my question. "I told him the truth. I showed them where the missus had them hid and swore I saw her take the jewel box 'way with her so as to keep what was inside from her husband."

"And they accepted what you said?"

"They had to. It was the truth." Then did she reconsider. "Well, it wasn't simple as all that. One of them was all for cutting my nose off right then and there. But the other one, he said, 'No, I b'lieve her.' He said it just like that, and then he gives me a wink." She grinned. "Proper Southwark fella. I could tell from the way he talked. That's where I'm from myself."

"You could tell he was from Southwark?"

"Di'nt I just say so?"

"Not an African then?"

"Well, he was *sort of* an African, I s'pose."

"What do you mean by that?"

"I mean that if he wants to go round with his face painted black so he looks like an African, then that makes him *sort of* an African, doesn't it?" It was evident that she strongly suspected that one of the robbers, at least, was no true African, but an imposter.

She added: "The other one—the cruel one—he was a bit more genuine."

I took a moment to consider that, and then put to her another question: "Were there but two? Mr. Mossman said that four had come through the door."

"Oh, there was more than that by the time they were all together. They came in the front and the back. For all I know, they come in the windows, too. And they were yellin' back and forth, pickin' up the paintings right off the wall, gathering in the vases and dishes, even furniture. They were a busy lot—whilst they were here."

"And how long was that?"

"Oh, ten minutes, no more than fifteen."

"And they were all black?"

"Well, that's the way they looked, anyways." That was said with a wink.

"Where were you while this was going on?"

"I was upstairs with the two of them. They pulled me out of the kitchen where I was with all the rest of the help."

"And that," said I, "was because Mr. Trezavant had told them you knew where the jewels were hid—was it not?"

"It was so," she agreed. Then, oddly, she averted her face as she might if seeking to hide tears—though she had not till that moment seemed in the least tearful. "Now he says I told them where they were, and I had a duty not to—as if I'd risk my nose for him!"

"Oh," said I, sufficiently moved just then to give her a pat upon the shoulder, "he was drunk and will no doubt feel differently in the morning."

"Only if the missus comes back with the jewel case."

I had taken a few notes through the interview. As I was about to tuck away my pencil, I realized I had not yet taken her name. I asked it.

"My name is Jenny," said she, looking up suddenly, a winsome smile upon her face (causing me to wonder at her quick recovery). "Thought you'd never ask."

But ask I had, and as was often said in those days, in for a penny, in for a pound. "And what is your family name, Jenny?"

"Crocker," said she, right pertly.

"I may have need to question you further."

"Well . . ." she sighed. "Sunday is my day free. P'rhaps if you dropped by early in the afternoon . . ."

"Or in the morning?"

"I've an engagement."

"The early afternoon then." I gave a little bow. "That will be all. You may leave with my thanks."

And that she did, casting one last smile over her shoulder just at the doorway as I waited patiently for her to disappear. I thought it time to seek Mr. Bailey that I might learn if he had another whom I should interview. I heard a door close and assumed (quite rightly) that Mistress Crocker had vacated the kitchen. I stepped out of the little cupboard room, looked about and, seeing no one, went up the stairs to search for Mr. Bailey.

The prospect of seeing Mistress Crocker once again was not in itself at all unattractive, and I was sure that I would find enough questions to ask to justify a stroll with her in the park. Nevertheless, what interested me most was her *morning* engagement. Who might she be seeing then? I wondered about that as I ascended the back stairs. I could not say what it was had made me curious—a fleeting, odd, furtive expression, some subtle change in her demeanor. Yet curious I most certainly was.

Once at the top of the stairs, I rounded the corner, which put me at the foot of the long central hall. From there I could tell by the babble of voices and the small crowd that had gathered at the far end of the hall that some great event had taken place. I went swiftly to join the crowd that I might learn what had happened.

The first thing I noticed when I joined the outer circle of onlookers was that, so far as I could tell, all were members of the household staff. Then did I spy Mr. Donnelly in the midst of the crowd, kneeling over an inert figure—the butler, Arthur, of course. The two constables peered over his shoulder; each wore a look of concern upon his face. Then did Mr. Donnelly look up and his eyes went directly to me.

"Jeremy!" he called, silencing the buzz of the spectators. "Come forward to me here."

I did as he directed, squeezing between Mr. Mossman—the porter— and a large woman who must have been the cook. I knelt across from Mr. Donnelly and looked down at the butler, not quite knowing what to expect.

"This man is alive," said Mr. Donnelly to me.

He certainly did not appear to be. His eyes were still shut and the corners of his mouth were pulled back in the same grimace I had seen before. In fact, in every particular he appeared just as he had earlier.

"I know he does not seem so, but you must take my word for it. I've held a looking glass to his mouth, and each time I've done so, it's been clouded."

"Not a heart stoppage then?"

"No, no, apoplexy rather. I must get him to St. Bartholomew's. Now, I have just learned that the Trezavant's coach and four is at their country home in Sussex. Could you go quickly to the Bilbo residence and ask the loan of their coach and team, driver and all? Explain the situation and put it to them that it would be a great favor to Sir John."

"They will not hesitate, I'm sure."

"Then go swiftly," said the surgeon.

"Like the wind," said I, jumping to my feet. Then I pushed my way to the door, and a moment later I was in Little Jermyn Street, running for St. James.

Indeed they did not hesitate at the Bilbo house. Mr. Burnham answered my knock on the door again and, as he had before, looked as if he had just returned from a long outing. He brought me inside and to the coachmen who were witting about in the kitchen, drinking tea. I made my appeal to them, and the driver rose, declaring that they had over an hour before they were to collect Mr. Bilbo. "Why not do a good turn for some good soul?"

"The horses need a proper run, anyways," said the footman.

And so, reader, the horses had their run. At a gallop, they delivered poor Arthur to the hospital, as Mr. Donnelly and I held on to him, steadying him as the coach rocked back and forth on the cobblestones.

Mr. Donnelly remained at St. Bartholomew's in order to discuss what might be done for the patient in the way of treatment (apparently very little). But I was whisked off to Bow Street, riding atop the coach by invitation, holding on for dear life yet enjoying the journey far more than earlier.

Next morning, having eaten my own breakfast, I took the tray Annie had prepared for Sir John up to his bedroom. I thought to wake him with a cup of hot tea, but when I entered the room, I found him awake and sitting up in bed. How long had he been so?

"Ah," said he as I crossed the threshold, "Jeremy, is it? Come in, come in. I've been waiting for you."

"Oh? How long have you been awake?"

"I've no idea, really. But I understand from Kate that there was another robbery last night of the kind that took place at Lord Lilley's, and that you answered her call and went out in my place."

"That's correct, sir." Setting down the tray before him, I busied myself pouring the cup full of tea from the small clay pot that Annie had supplied. I put it in his hands and waited as he sipped from it. Then I found for him an empty spot on the tray that he might set the cup down.

"I wish I had been there," said he, "for as you know, there is much to be learned at the scene of the crime when memories are fresh. Nevertheless, I trust you, and you have otherwise been proceeding with the investigation, have you not?"

"I have, sir. If you wish me to tell you how it progresses —"

"No, no," said he, waving me to silence, "report only when you are ready. I do, however, need a few details regarding last night's robbery. First of all, who was it that was robbed?"

"The home of Mr. Thomas Trezavant."

"The coroner? Oh, dear God. I'll be hearing much about this, I'm sure. Was he present? Did he meet the robbers?"

"Yes sir, he met them and said they were cruel black buggers, which indicated to me that he had been tortured in some way. I saw no evidence of this, however, and I must say he was quite drunk when he said it."

"He was, was he? To what purpose did they torture him—if indeed he was tortured?"

"Probably to force him to reveal where his wife's jewels were hidden."

"She was not present?"

"No, Sir John, she had left much earlier after a considerable row, and she took the jewels with her that Mr. Trezavant might not sell or pawn them."

"She—*what*? Jeremy, this seems a bit more complicated then I had supposed. I think you had better tell it to me right from the beginning.

Leave nothing out. Let me be the judge of what details may be dispensed with."

And that was indeed what I did. It took the better part of an hour to tell the story complete, and even then I omitted the altercation between Mr. Patley and me. During a good bit of the time, Sir John ate happily away at his breakfast, munching his bread and butter and crunching his bacon. Breakfast aside, he gave me his full attention.

When I had concluded, he nodded but said not a word for some time. He seemed to be considering all that I had told him. At last he spoke forth: "And so to sum up, Jeremy, the assault upon the Trezavant residence was quite like the one upon Lord Lilley's, except that a woman pled that the door be opened, rather than the male who, a couple of days before, described the terrible carriage wreck in St. James Street."

"That would seem to be so, sir."

"Yet you only managed to talk with three at the house: the porter, who had been there when the robbers battered their way inside; the upstairs maid, who told you tales of the connubial difficulties of her master and mistress; and finally, Mr. Trezavant himself, who could tell you little because of his drunken state. Am I correct?"

When it was put thus, I had to admit that it sounded rather like I had wasted my time there. I hadn't felt so at the time. "Well, Sir John, I thought it significant that Mistress Crocker gave it as her opinion that at least one of the Africans was not truly what he seemed to be. In a way, I thought *that* the most important matter to come out of my interrogations. You yourself asked those you talked to at the Lilley residence if the robbers seemed truly to be what they seemed."

"And all of them," said Sir John, "agreed that the black men did indeed seem to be black. Only she—your Mistress Crocker—gave it as her opinion that one of them was not. And after all, Jeremy, it was only an *opinion*."

"True enough," said I, "but all those who agreed that the robbers were indeed black were likewise giving that only as their opinion."

"Hmmm." The expression which appeared on Sir John's face was one of exasperation. "I fear that this discussion could be carried on ad infinitum, and there is really no need to prolong it since there is no way to prove one of us right and the other wrong. But I have an idea." And there, reader, he halted, somehow giving the impression that he believed that having said this much he had said enough.

I sighed. "And what is the idea, Sir John?"

"I shall consult with Mr. Burnham."

His reply puzzled me somewhat. "I don't quite follow, sir," I confessed.

"Why, it's simple enough. Why are we at such a disadvantage—not to say a loss—with this case?" It was merely a rhetorical question. He plunged on: "Because, Jeremy lad, we know next to nothing about the black population of our city. We know not their number, nor their customs and habits, nor their tendencies toward criminality—as I said, we know next to nothing. Yet we do know one who is a member of that group by virtue of the color of his skin. That one, of course, is Robert Burnham, teacher to your friend Bunkins, and to our own Annie. I should like you to go to Mr. Burnham this morning and invite him here. Persuade him to come to us for a visit."

"I doubt he will come until he has finished his morning reading session with his two scholars," said I. "Shall I bring him up here to your bedroom?"

"Oh, by no means. I'm feeling stronger today. I shall remain downstairs after my court session and simply wait for him in my chambers and receive him there. That would be far more proper, don't you think? He, as I recall, is one who likes to see the proprieties given strict observance."

And so it was that I set out for Black Jack Bilbo's residence at mid-morning, after having washed up and scrubbed down our quarters above the stairs. My last task of the morning was to give Sir John any assistance he might require in dressing (which was not much); when he retired at night, his clothes for the next day were laid out in strict order by Lady Fielding so that he might dress himself in the morning. Occasionally his shirt or his waistcoat was buttoned crooked or his hose needed hitching. When I was not about to provide these finishing touches, Mr. Marsden attended to them. Once a few adjustments had been made, Sir John and I descended the stairs together. I left him with his clerk as they began their daily discussion of the court docket.

There was yet time enough left so that there was no need to hurry to St. James Street, and indeed I did not hurry. The great early morning rush of workers to their work had ended some time before. And while one could hardly say that the streets were empty of pedestrians (the streets of London were *never* empty), it was nevertheless possible to amble the distance without fear of being buffeted and bumped from either side, or having one's heels trod upon.

My pace had slowed because I was deep in thought. I frowned and fretted as I went, trying to think of what step might next be taken in the investigation. While I was not yet at an impasse, it seemed to me I was somewhat limited. I must wait until Mr. Martinez and Mr. Humber had information for me—if indeed they would have information to give. I had, however, done nothing to explore one avenue of investigation: I saw that I must learn something of Walter Travis, the porter who had been murdered during the raid upon the Lilley residence. But what *could* be learned—and how? I gave some thought to that, and promised myself to give it more once things had quietened down a bit—but would they ever? I began to appreciate the utility of those long hours that Sir John spent alone and in the dark in that little room off his bedroom which he called his study. There, I realized, was where he conducted his investigations; that was where he fit the pieces of the puzzle together.

Thus did my thoughts run as I made my way to the Bilbo residence. There were shops at one end of St. James Street—and beyond them the grand houses, of which Black Jack's was indeed one of the grandest. It was, however, not the best kept, for as he did not employ a butler, neither did he keep a gardener on his household staff. He thought both unnecessary. A fellow who worked in St. James Park came by from time to time to trim the bushes and do what needed to be done in the back garden. Mr. Bilbo dispensed with a butler easily enough by ruling that anyone in the house who heard a knock upon the street door was obliged to answer it.

As it happened, my good friend Jimmie Bunkins was nearest when I rapped hard upon the door with the brass clapper. It was his face that appeared as the heavy door swung open. That meant that class was done for the morning, which in turn justified the timing of my visit.

"Ah, chum," said he, "shove your trunk inside. Come! Come! Come! Let me be the first to ask ye. How's your cove fare?"

"Sir John? Oh, he's right as rain. Moves his smiter well now."

(Be not intimidated, reader, for if some of the words recalled and quoted above seem unfamiliar, they are no more than bits and pieces of "flash," the cant of the London underworld. Indeed, Bunkins had been a member in good standing of Covent Garden's great legion of thieves until Mr. Bilbo took him in and bettered his lot. Bunkins simply invited me in and inquired after Sir John's condition. I replied that he was doing well and could move his arm without difficulty now.)

Then did I hear the harpsichord jangling from the drawing room, and a moment later Annie's voice joining in. It was another Handel oratorio. She had been humming something like it around the house for the past few days. Now, however, with Mr. Burnham's accompaniment and her voice at full, I was given some true idea of the sound of the anthem as it would be heard with full chorus at the Academy of Ancient Music. I was most favorably impressed.

"Keeps gettin' better, don't she?" said Bunkins with an approving nod. "That moll can really lip a chaunt."

"She can," I agreed. "Will they be much longer?"

"Don't think so. They been at it a while already."

"Well then," said I, "I've something to jaw with you proper."

"And what might that be, chum?"

"I need to know if in those days when you were a scamp you came across a fellow named Walter Travis."

Bunkins frowned a moment in thought, then gave a firm shake of his head. "No, I can't say as I did."

"That might not be his true name."

"Well, then it could be just any cod."

"I know, but listen. He was about ten years older than you and me, a big man, six feet or more, and he was on the scamp himself. He'd put in a spell at Newgate."

"Well, that brings it down to a few hundred."

"All right, this may help. Travis came out of the clink and went into service."

"You mean like a butler?"

"Not so grand as that—just a porter—but at a big house belonging to a lord, no less."

"Would this be the cod who got himself killed at Lord Lilley's the other night?"

"The very same."

Bunkins scratched his jaw. "Now you've given me something to work with," said he. "A scamp workin' for a duke—I'd say that's rare. That'll give me something to go to my old partners in crime and jaw about—sort of thing they'd remember. With him dead and gone, they'd have no reason to keep a dubber mum. What do you want to know about him?"

"Well, his proper name, for one thing, and if he was in on the sacking of the duke's down the street. And if you can get that, maybe you can also get the names of those who did the sacking."

"Oh, I doubt I can get their names. I don't know no snitches, and if I did, I got nothing to trade, if you follow me."

"Yes, I follow. If you can get anything at all I'll be grateful."

And there we left it. No further discussion of Walter Travis (whatever his true identity) was needful. And besides, the sound of the harpsichord had ceased, and Annie's sweet voice had stilled. There was naught but the murmur of voices in conversation coming from the room down the hall.

"They're done," said Bunkins. "Want to take Annie back with you?"

"Probably," said I, "if she wishes to come. But I've a message from Sir John for Mr. Burnham."

"Come along then, chum. No time to deliver it like the present."

Following Bunkins down the hall, I sought the proper words to use to present Sir John's invitation. I realized that if I were to offer it in a casual manner, he might choose to come at his leisure—hours later, a day later—or, knowing Mr. Burnham, perhaps not at all. On the other hand, if I put the matter to him with too great a sense of urgency, he might shy away, thinking perhaps that Sir John held him suspect as one of the robbery crew. Mr. Martinez, whom Sir John has known for years, leaped to a similar conclusion, and probably because of the crude manner in which I put the matter to him. You must be discreet, I instructed myself, yet not too discreet—direct but not blunt.

In short, I instructed myself well. The question I asked myself later was why I had not followed my instructions.

"Uh, Mr. Burnham," said I, approaching him with a smile upon my face, "I have an invitation to extend to you from Sir John."

"Why, what a pleasant surprise," said he, returning my smile. "What is the nature of the invitation? Is it for dinner? For supper?"

"Neither, I fear. He wishes you to come to him after his court session is done."

"To ask me a few questions?"

"Well . . . yes. I suppose he will do that."

"About the recent robberies which were supposedly done by men of my color?"

"Uh . . . some questions about that, and some questions about other matters of a more general nature."

"Hmmm," said Mr. Burnham, considering the matter. "Have I a choice?"

"Of course," said I. "You may come or not, as you wish. But Sir John wishes earnestly to speak with you, and since, because of his wound, he cannot come to you, he hoped you might come to him."

"If that is the case, then I should be most happy to come." He said it with a great dazzling smile, thus relieving me considerably.

Of our return to Bow Street, there is but one event worthy of report. It so happened that we chose a route which led us down Little Jermyn Street and past the Trezavant residence. Was it my thought to do so? I hope it was not, for had we but taken another route, we should have thereby avoided a good deal of trouble and a bit of suffering, as well.

We went down the broad walkway, the three of us — Mr. Burnham to the outside, I to the inside, and Annie between us. As I recall, we talked of a number of matters along the way, and I believe that as it happened we were discussing the robbery which had taken place on that very street. I noted that just ahead of us a hackney was stopped before the Trezavant house. I called the attention of my companions to this circumstance, and we fell silent as we approached the place. And it was a good thing that we did so, for just as we were about to pass, the door to the house opened and out came Mr. Thomas Trezavant. He moved ponderously down the stairs, shifting his great weight with care from one step to the next until he reached the bottom. There he planted his feet firmly and looked at us as we walked by. In my haste I have written that he looked at "us." Not so. He stared openly and in a most hostile manner at Mr. Burnham and at him alone. Even when I attempted to divert Mr. Trezavant's attention by greeting him in a bright and friendly way, he stared on, acknowledging me only with a grunt.

Not a word passed among the three of us until we were well out of earshot. But then Annie broke the silence, saying, "Did you ever see such a look as he gave you, Mr. Burnham? If looks could kill, you'd be lying dead before his front door."

"Indeed," said Mr. Burnham. "He seems to have blamed the entire race for his misfortune."

We talked of it a bit more as we walked on, but by the time we reached St. James Square, we were on to more pleasant matters. Though I cannot speak for the other two, I had quite forgotten the incident by the time we reached Number 4 Bow Street. There Annie left us, climbing the stairs to the kitchen as we continued on to meet Sir John in his chambers. Mr. Burnham was openly interested in the area named by Sir John the "backstage" of his court—and particularly was he fascinated by the strong room. He scrutinized the two prisoners inside in such a way that he seemed to be wondering what felony they might have committed to have brought them to such a place. I greeted Mr. Marsden, the clerk, and Mr. Fuller, the jailer, politely and with a smile. Mr. Marsden returned it in kind; Mr. Fuller, who seemed to have cultivated a dislike for me, merely scowled.

Sir John was standing behind his desk when we passed through the open door to his chambers. He extended his right hand in a gesture of friendship.

"Ah, Mr. Burnham, is it you?" said he as the tutor took his hand and shook it warmly.

"It is I, Sir John, right enough," said Mr. Burnham. "And quite flattered I am at your invitation. How may I help you?"

"Do sit down." He gestured at the chair which he knew very well was placed just opposite him beyond the desk. Delaying a moment, he settled into his own chair, leaned forward, and said in a serious manner, "You may help me, sir, by answering a few questions."

"As you like, Sir John, anything at all."

"Mr. Burnham, I have a friend named Moses Martinez, who is a Jew. When I have questions regarding the Jews, individual or in the aggregate, I ask him. But as you know, I have now had a troubling matter involving those of the African race put before me. Since I know no one but you of that race, I'm afraid I must turn to you for such information as I need."

"That seems quite reasonable."

The two men made an interesting study in contrasts. Sir John, straining forward, his fingers intertwined; and Robert Burnham, relaxed, almost casual, as he leaned back in his chair and waited for the magistrate's questions. It struck me then that perhaps Mr. Burnham was not taking the occasion with sufficient gravity.

"How has it come to pass that there are suddenly so many Africans here in London? Oh, and by the bye, how many are here? Have you any idea?"

"I have it on good authority that there are roughly fourteen thousand of us in England, and surely, most are in London."

"Oh, so many? But no doubt you're right," Sir John agreed. "And London is probably where most are."

"Still," said Mr. Burnham, "I would take exception to your use of the word 'suddenly.' I would wager there have been black faces here ever since English ships began sailing around Africa to reach the Orient. Two centuries, at least."

"Yes, but there is a contradiction even in the presence of Africans in England. They are, or were, slaves, and slavery has been banned in England since the thirteenth century."

Mr. Burnham jumped forward in his chair, eager to make his point: "Exactly! A contradiction! And it is on that contradiction that the argument rests for the freedom of them all. It is on that contradiction that I argued my own claim of freedom to my father."

"Oh? That's a story I must hear," said Sir John. "That is, sir, if you've no objection to telling it."

"None at all, for it is in itself a good example of certain aspects of this confused situation."

"Pray proceed."

"I came to London as many, or perhaps most, of those of my color have come in this century. Which is to say, we were brought here by our white masters. I was different from all but a few in that my master was my father, and he raised me as a son and not as a slave. I was as well-educated as anyone could be in Jamaica, and when my father married an English widow with children of her own, I served as their tutor. I had them all reading by the age of seven."

That last he said quite proudly, and there he paused, a smile upon his face, as if reflecting upon his first days as a teacher.

"And then?" prompted Sir John.

"And then," said Mr. Burnham, "we all traveled together from Jamaica to London. My father's business was to secure a loan with which to expand his holdings in the Caribbean. He had become a rich man and wished to become richer. He had no difficulty securing the loan, but in the course of my stay here I became acquainted with the contradiction we have been discussing. I went to my father and informed him that since we were in a land in which one human being's right to own another was not recognized, I would be within my rights to demand my freedom. He was taken aback and a bit hurt to learn that I wished my freedom in London—and not in Kingston, as he offered. But once he became convinced that this was my desire, he had a document of manumission written out by a lawyer and settled a not inconsiderable sum upon me."

"You are fortunate to have such a father," said Sir John.

"Indeed I know that—and he knows I know, for we write once a month, exchanging news and our views upon the great matters of the world. It may interest you to know that, in principle at least, he is opposed to slavery."

"It interests me, but it does not surprise me. Many of those who engage in immoral practices justify themselves saying that it is naught but economic necessity forces them to do so. They often declare that, given their preference, they would be in a more respectable line of endeavor."

This was said by Sir John in a rather cool manner. Mr. Burnham had no immediate response. He threw a glance in my direction, the first he had given me since he had begun his talk with Sir John. I had seen him previously in profile, and now for the first time in full-face; he did not look happy.

"My father is a moral man," said he at last.

"Oh, I've no doubt of it. But you also said he was a rich man, did you not? I believe your phrase was, 'he was a rich man who wished to become richer'—and I'm sure he has. But not so rich as to free all his slaves."

"Perhaps someday he will," Mr. Burnham said suddenly, in an almost defiant voice. But he continued in a more reasonable tone, "I used my own story simply as an example, Sir John. Others of my color have claimed their freedom as I did, and have been shipped back to Jamaica in irons, or have been sold outright to another master, right here in England. Still others, knowing their ambiguous legal situation, have simply kept silent and run away at the first opportunity."

"Yes, and there have been cases before our courts which have treated aspects of this . . . this contradiction we have been discussing. There is, in fact, a case before the Lord Chief Justice that—"

"As I well know," interrupted Mr. Burnham eagerly. "The Somerset case* may indeed put an end to slavery here and in the colonies."

I sensed the excitement in him regarding this matter of law. He was not alone in this. All London was talking of it during that spring of 1772.

The two had sometime earlier exchanged their conversational attitudes. Mr. Burnham now sat forward in his chair, fully absorbed in the matters they discussed. Though similarly absorbed, Sir John had adopted a more relaxed style; leaning as far back as he might, rubbing his chin in a considering manner.

Far down the hall, I heard the door to the street slam shut. Had someone departed? Entered?

"It may be so, as you say, that this trial will determine a great deal," said Sir John. "But knowing Lord Mansfield as well as I do, it may well be that it is decided narrowly upon the facts of the case. He does not believe in deciding great social and political issues in a court of law."

There were heavy footsteps down the hall. Though the Lord Chief Justice often made his entrance in just such a way, the pace of the footsteps—slow and deliberate—was not his. Sir John frowned at the anticipated interruption.

Mr. Burnham, also frowning, spoke up in response: "Well, sir, all I can say is that I hope that you are wrong."

Then did Mr. Marsden's voice come to us as he attempted to intervene. He offered to announce the unknown guest. Yet the footsteps continued plodding heavily toward the magistrate's chambers.

At last the visitor appeared, barging through the door as he pushed aside Mr. Marsden, squeezing in. It was a figure of great proportions. Indeed it was Mr. Trezavant, dressed just as he was when we had passed him earlier, yet a good deal more florid in the face, breathing heavily as he stood for a moment, surveying the room.

"Sir John," he began—but got little further.

"Mr. Trezavant, is it you? What have you to discuss that is of such importance that it cannot wait for my clerk, Mr. Marsden, to announce you?"

---

*More of this later, reader.

That should have intimidated him, but it did not. He held his ground, and he continued in a loud voice, near shouting at us across the room: "I came here to tell you that I saw your young assistant consorting with a criminal, but now I understand better. He has brought the fellow to you, has he not? Has an arrest been made? Are you interrogating the culprit?"

"Sir, you make no sense at all. I have no notion of what you mean — no, not the slightest."

"Why, I saw these two in company with a young woman as they passed by my home in Little Jermyn Street. I could hardly believe my eyes."

"Please make yourself clear."

"This man, the African, him it was who led the band of thieves who robbed my home of its treasures, assaulted me, and caused my butler to collapse in an apoplectic attack."

Having made the accusation, he pointed across the room at Mr. Burnham, just so there should be no mistake. "I demand that he be held and bound over for trial. I will see this man hanged, or know the why and wherefore of it. Sir John," he said, fairly shouting it out, "I leave this up to you."

FIVE

*In which Mr.
Burnham tells an
unconvincing story*

After he had quite stunned us all, Mr. Trezavant turned round and stamped out of the magistrate's chambers (thus exhibiting a sense of the dramatic that I had not known he possessed). In his haste, he bumped Mr. Marsden aside once again. The clerk stared after him in a most puzzled manner.

"Sorry about that, sir," said he. "I just couldn't hold him back."

"Think nothing of it," said Sir John. "That fellow has been a trial to me from the moment I met him."

As the clerk disappeared, Mr. Burnham rose from his chair in a manner I could only describe as cautious and addressed Sir John: "And what about me? Shall I, too, think nothing of it?"

"Well, perhaps a bit more than nothing—but not a great deal more. I presume you know where you were last night?"

"Yes—yes, of course I do."

"And where was that, sir?"

"Why . . ." He hesitated—not so long as to make one suspicious, but long enough to cause notice. "Why, I remained in the house all evening. I was reading in my room, so I was. That's what I was doing until Jeremy here knocked upon the door, looking for the loan of Mr. Bilbo's coach."

"When was that, Jeremy?" Sir John asked of me.

"It must have been near midnight," said I. "Near it but not yet upon it."

"But by then," said he, "the robbers had come and gone, the constables had been notified, and Patley had gone to fetch you. Is that not so?"

"Well . . . yes sir."

"Perhaps you could find one or two others who could vouch for your presence in the house during the evening, Mr. Burnham."

"Oh, I'm sure I can." It was said with certainty. "Master Bunkins? The coachmen?"

"They would do very well, sir," said the magistrate. "I shall send Jeremy by the residence to talk with them."

"And in the meantime?"

"In the meantime, what? I do not understand, sir."

"Am I to be detained?"

"By no means, Mr. Burnham. Jeremy here made it clear that Mr. Trezavant was quite drunk, both during and after his home was invaded by that band of brigands. My chief constable, Mr. Bailey, seconded that in his written report. I doubt that in such a state he could retain the memory of his assailants. And quite frankly, even believing a sober Mr. Trezavant would call for a greater leap of faith than I am capable of. You are free to go, sir."

Though Sir John could not see the bow Mr. Burnham made him, it was a pretty one; no mere bob of the head. Bending at the waist, the tutor dropped down quite low, and in this curious posture he spoke: "I thank you for your trust in me." Then, straightening to his considerable height, he turned and started for the door.

"Oh, but Mr. Burnham, one last matter. I was about to pose a group of questions to you when we were interrupted so rudely."

Stopping, turning, the tall Jamaican gave the magistrate his full attention. "So? What have you then, Sir John?"

"Are you acquainted with others of your color here in London?"

"I am. Though I have not sought them out, there are so many about that it was inevitable that I should meet a few. One or two of them I call friend and see from time to time."

"How are they employed?"

"Most are in domestic service, though you may find them in many different trades and occupations."

"Even thievery?"

"Perhaps," said Mr. Burnham, "for with such a number of us in this city, there are bound to be a few lawbreakers among us."

"Do you know of any who have that reputation?"

"No, not even those who are but rumored to have turned to villainy.

Let me say, Sir John, that it may well be that there are fewer Africans who have turned to crime than with other comparable groups."

"Oh? And why is that?"

"Because, sir, if a black man commits an act of violence or a brazen theft, he will immediately be identified as a black man and be thus much easier to discover and arrest. Since this is no suppositional matter, and the particular Africans you have in mind are those who entered and robbed the homes of Lord Lilley and that man, Trezavant, then I would say that if they were *truly* men of color, I believe they would have been far better advised to disguise themselves in whiteface."

"Are you suggesting . . . ?"

"I suggest nothing at all, Sir John. I merely offer an opinion."

With that, Mr. Burnham turned once again and made for the door. He was through it, and down the hall in no time at all. We listened to his footsteps beat a quick rhythm to the door.

Then was he gone with the bang of that same door out into Bow Street.

"Shall I catch him up, Sir John?" I asked him. "I might have the opportunity to talk with Bunkins before their afternoon class begins."

"No," said he, "let him have time to talk with your friend, Bunkins, the coachmen, and anyone else he might get to lie for him."

"Sir? I don't quite understand."

"He is not telling the truth. That much is plain. Yet it is often the case that we can only get to the truth by listening carefully to the lies that we are told."

"In what particulars do you think that he is lying, sir?"

"Why, I mean with regard to where he was last night. Oh, yes, indeed. But that does not mean that I believe, along with Mr. Trezavant, that Mr. Burnham is the captain of that crew of robbers."

"How is it that you came to those conclusions, Sir John?"

"Well, I fear it's little more than a feeling on my part. But my feelings in these matters usually prove out. In fact, they always do."

"Indeed," said I, puffing up a bit, "I, too, had a feeling about Mr. Burnham. Twice, sir, on those occasions upon which I visited Mr. Bilbo's residence following the robberies, Mr. Burnham answered the door, and I had the distinct feeling that he had just returned to the house. He was perspiring, and he seemed somewhat out of breath."

"So you share the feeling that he spent those evenings away from home?"

"I do, yes, sir."

"Do you then believe that Mr. Trezavant has him properly identified?"

"Not at all, sir."

"Good. Then we are in agreement. Go out and talk to them all. Listen to them carefully, and perhaps you can detect the holes in the tales that you are told; through them we may be able to wriggle our way to the truth."

And so, having helped Sir John upstairs and into his bed, I set off upon a path that had become all too familiar to me over the past few days. I decided to alter it a bit, walking by way of the Hay Market and Piccadilly, and in this way I entered St. James Street from above. Had I not chosen to go by this roundabout route, I should not have come to the corner of St. James at Little Jermyn Street, where I encountered a familiar face and figure. It was none but John Mossman, the porter who had been present when the robbers made their spectacular entrance into the Trezavant house. He saw me, just as I saw him, and gave me a wave and a great "hallooo," as he hurried to the place where I awaited him. It was a fortuitous meeting; he had news to impart—quite a lot of it, as it turned out.

"Fancy I should meet you here," said he, upon arriving. "I was going on to Bow Street later today to seek you out."

"Oh? Had you something to add to what you told me last night?"

"Not I, but another. The cook, an old girl named Maudie Bleeker, asked to see you, to give you a bit of information. It ain't so easy for a cook to get away during the day, y'know, so I told her I'd go by the magistrate's and put you on notice, so's you could come and see her."

I gave a bit of thought to that. I was eager to talk with anyone who might add to the flimsy bits of information I had gathered last night; nevertheless, there was a difficulty.

"Mr. Mossman," said I, "I should like nothing better than to talk with the lady, but truth to tell, I wish to avoid meeting your master because of a recent misunderstanding."

"Ah," said he, "well then you're in luck, lad, for this very morning he went off to Sussex on the post coach."

"But I saw him earlier boarding a hackney."

"It was to take him to the post-coach house. Well I know it, for he asked me, would I go up there and have the coach come by here to pick him up. When I told him they wouldn't do that, he was quite miffy, he was. That's when he asked me to summon him a hackney coach that he might get to the coach house."

"He was off to inform his wife of the robbery, I suppose."

"Off to plead with her to come back, is more like it." He grinned in open amusement at his master's troubles. "I'm going now to haul back a grand vase of the kind his wife collects. It's to take the place of the one the robbers stole." He ended with a laugh.

"Well, since he is away, I will indeed visit Mistress Bleeker."

"You do that," said Mr. Mossman. "She'll be glad to see you, and maybe what she's got to tell will really help you some. She kept mum to me, wouldn't say what it was."

I thanked him and began moving a step or two down Little Jermyn Street, but he waved me back.

"One more thing," said he. "What do you know of poor Arthur? Is he still with us?"

"Is he alive? Well, he was when last I saw him. All that can be done for him at St. Bart's will be done."

"Which ain't much, I fear."

"No, not much, according to Mr. Donnelly."

"A great shame it is, for Arthur was a grand fellow. Never had a bad word for anybody. I don't know what you'll think of the new one."

"New one? You mean he already has a replacement?"

"You might say so. A fellow come to the door this morning and said he'd heard of our misfortune, and could he see the master. He was already dressed up in butler's livery and ready for work. I can't say whether he has the position permanent or not."

"No doubt that depends upon Arthur's recovery. Hmmm," said I, again imitating Sir John, "interesting, very interesting. Goodbye to you then, Mr. Mossman. I'm quite glad we met."

We parted. I hurried on to the Trezavant residence, and as I went, I attempted to arrange my expectations in some pattern with what was already known. What would Maudie Bleeker have to say? Would it change much—or even possibly all? I promised myself that I would visit St. Bartholomew's Hospital and see for myself how Arthur Robb was getting on; perhaps he might have regained the power of speech.

I rapped smartly upon the door with the brass knocker that was placed approximately in its middle. There followed a pause, and then came the repeated click of heels across the hardwood floor. From within came the voice of a man: "Who is there? Please state your business." There was indeed something familiar about it—yet I could not immediately place it.

"Jeremy Proctor," said I, raising my voice to near a shout, "from the magistrate's office. I am come to continue my investigation."

The door swung open, revealing Mr. Collier, who was, until a few nights past, the butler to Lord Lilley of Perth. I exclaimed at this, voicing my surprise at discovering him in this new position.

"No more surprised than I am to see you, young sir," said he.

"How did you know to come here?" I asked.

"The word went out this morning regarding what happened here last night. It traveled all round the St. James area. I heard that the butler—I believe his name was Mr. Robb—was seized by an apoplectic fit and delivered to St. Bartholomew's Hospital. I understood immediately that they would be needing a butler, if only temporarily. And so I simply came here and offered my services to Mr. Trezavant. He seemed delighted to accept them."

"Did you tell him how your last employment had ended?" I asked him, perhaps a bit unkindly.

"Oh, indeed I did. He would have heard of it in any case. His only response to what I told him was to ask me if I had learned a lesson from the experience. I assured him that I had. That seemed to satisfy him. Such a nice man."

"Well," said I, "you're a fortunate man, Mr. Collier."

"More than you know, young sir, for Mr. Zondervan, the master of the house where you visited me, has sent word that he will return on this very day. And hospitable as were my friends on the household staff, they would not have allowed me to stay beyond this morning." He beamed at me then, happy to share his good news. There could be no doubt that he was a man altogether changed from the one I had met earlier. He was buoyant, ebullient, and probably once again something of a lickspittle.

"But come in, come in," said he, stepping back from the door and flourishing a hand in invitation. "How may I serve you, young sir?"

Stepping inside, I waited until he had closed the door to the street. Then lowering my voice, I said, "I wish to continue interviewing the staff."

"Of course," said he. "To whom do you wish to speak?"

For some reason, I was reluctant to be specific. "Why not bring me below stairs, and I shall talk to them as they become available."

"Why, that sounds like a splendid way to accomplish your purpose. Right this way, if you will."

As I followed him down the long central hall, I imagined poor old Arthur lying mute upon some bed in St. Bart's. What was his future? Had he any? Even if he were to recover completely, it was unlikely that he would be able to reclaim his position in the Trezavant household. Mr. Collier would surely not allow it; he meant to stay.

We descended the narrow staircase and emerged into the kitchen. I looked about me and found three at the big communal table. One of them, an ample-bodied woman of about forty years of age, gave me a rather sharp look but offered nothing in the way of a greeting. Conversation stopped among them.

I turned to Mr. Collier. "This will do very well," said I to him. "I thank you for your help, sir."

"You're sure then?" He smiled left and right, receiving nothing in return from those at the table—but undaunted, he smiled on. "I'm certain you'll get everything you need from these good folk. I'll leave you with them." (It was clear to me that he had not yet learned their names.)

So saying, he left me, thumping noisily up the steps, as if announcing his departure in a loud voice—a little too loud, it seemed to me. A picture formed in my mind of Mr. Collier standing at the top of the stairs, his ear turned to us below in the kitchen. I remembered how smartly his shoes had sounded only moments before on the hardwood floor of the hall; no such noise had followed the heavy footsteps on the stairs.

"Who're you?"

The woman whom I had supposed to be the cook had broken the silence with a loud challenge. In response, I put my forefinger to my lips in a call for quiet. Immediately the three at the table leaned forward, their attention engaged, their interest aroused.

I went to the little group and said to the woman in a low tone (though not a whisper), "Are you Maude Bleeker?"

"I am—so what would you with me?" She had suitably quietened her own voice.

I beckoned her. She rose from her place and obeyed my signal, following me to the pantry room in which I had interviewed Mr. Mossman and Mistress Crocker. The others turned to watch us, unable quite to fathom what transpired, yet not so curious as to remain. They began shuffling out as I shut the door behind us.

Once inside the small pantry room, I felt we might speak in an ordinary tone. That, in any case, was the manner in which I addressed her when I said: "I am Jeremy Proctor, here from the Bow Street Court. I understand you have something to tell me regarding the robbery."

"You cert'ny made it here quick. Mossie didn't leave more than ten minutes ago."

"I happened to meet him at the corner of St. James Street," said I.

"Did you now? Well, ain't that a happy accident—near as happy as that butler comin' along without an invitation to take poor Arthur's place."

"Do you not believe I am who I say?"

"Oh . . . I suppose I do. Yes, I do. I seen you in bad light last night talkin' to Crocker and Mossie. You're the same one. It's just this fella Collier comin' along after Arthur's job when he ain't even dead yet, that's set us all off a bit, I daresay. Something strange about it."

"It may seem so," said I. "But I can tell you that I first met him at Lord Lilley's in St. James Street. He lost his position in Lord Lilley's household because he let in the robbers in much the same way that Arthur did."

"I know, so he said. Still, it don't seem right. I notice you took some precautions yourself—or ain't we talkin' where he can't hear us?"

"True enough; I have a few doubts, as well. But please, Mistress Bleeker, let us stop all this fencing about and get on to why I have come. Mr. Mossman said you had something to tell me."

"Shhh! If it's truly him, and he were to know that I'd reco'nized him, then I'd be a dead one indeed."

"All right, Maude," said I, "just tell me what you have to tell me and be done with it."

Clearly, she did not like being rushed. Her eyes flashed angrily at me, yet only for an instant. She regained control of herself, nodded, and proceeded: "All right, it is this way then. I'll tell you what I know and what I think, and I won't mix the one with the other." She paused, unable for a moment to continue. "But where to begin?"

It did not take her long to decide, and the story she told began down in Sussex where, as she said, she learned all her cooking from her mother, who cooked for Squire Leonard, father of Justine (the future Mrs. Trezavant). He was the richest man in that part of the county, noble or commoner.

By the time Maude was twenty, she had learned all her mother had to teach her, and in fact excelled her in some particulars. There being no place in Sussex where she might exercise her prodigious powers as a cook, she determined to seek employment in London. Her widowed mother allowed her unwed daughter to go up to the great city, though truth to tell, she had great misgivings—and well she might. There was little employment in London, particularly not in the great houses where Maude sought employment. She had naught but a letter recommending her skill in the kitchen and her good character from a provincial squire, and that meant little to the lords and ladies—and even less to their butlers. She was, in fact, ready to return home in defeat, when, at the inn where she stayed, The Key by name, there occurred a great row between the innkeeper and the cook in his kitchen, which resulted in the departure of the cook, an Irishman of no great culinary talents. Maude Bleeker, who happened to be present in the eating room during the worst of the row, immediately volunteered to take the Irishman's place in the kitchen. And the innkeeper, having little choice, installed her at once. From that day forth, she was a great success at The Key. Her skill as a baker was especially famed; tarts and scones from her oven became known across the city. It was not long until The Key, which was known, if at all, as an inn where travelers might take a meal if they'd no better place to go, soon became celebrated as quite the best public dining room in that part of London, which incidentally also had rooms upstairs to let for travelers.

Now, The Key was located hard by Covent Garden at Chandos Street and Half Moon Passage. Since much of Maude's work in the kitchen was done in the small hours of the morning, and since she was at heart a rather adventurous sort of girl, she came to make it a habit to trip over to Tom King's notorious coffee house in the Garden at the time most of those in the great city were arising. Most of them, let it be said, though not all—for the streets around Covent Garden were home to a great number of thieves, gamblers, whores, and villains of every sort; and Tom King's coffee house was their last gathering place of an evening.

At first she came as a mere observer, and indeed there was much to observe. Though the show put on by the patrons was far more entertaining than many seen at Drury Lane, it was sure to be a bit bawdier than any that could be presented there. As she went to Tom King's so often (and it became known that she was the cook who had changed the fortunes of The Key), she was soon drawn into their games and diversions, known as "Maudie, the girl from Sussex." And, eventually, she met a young man there and formed an attachment of sorts. He did not properly court her, but he teased her in an affectionate way, told her jokes and wild tales, and took to accompanying her on her walks from the coffee house back to The Key. There were days and nights, sometimes whole weeks, when he disappeared without notice, but he would reappear without explanation; and each time she would welcome him back unquestioningly, for he brightened her dull life considerably.

Then, one day, it all ended quite without notice. During one of his periodic absences, a regular there at Tom King's, a clever little thief, who had adopted the name Tollibon Lucy, offered her sympathy to Maudie. When asked why sympathy should be due her, it was explained that her Johnny Skylark, which was the name by which she knew the young man, had been apprehended by the "Beakrunners," and would be going up that day before the "Blind Beak of Bow Street." But why? What had he done? "Didn't you know your Johnny-boy was a thief?" asked Lucy. "And he ain't *just* a thief, but a proper village hustler, a regular prince among thieves!"

That day, she left her assistant in charge of the kitchen and went off to the Bow Street Court, that she might be present at the appointed hour to see her Johnny-boy go before the solemn magistrate to be bound over for trial in the criminal court at Old Bailey. She learned a number of things about him that day. First of all, she heard his true name read out by the court clerk: It was John Abernathy. Then did she learn the extent of his known crimes: They were many, and varied, and included every sort of theft from burglary to highway robbery; most, however, were the sort in which Johnny Skylark would lead a band of armed men into the house of a rich man or a noble and steal all that could be quickly gathered up. There were, however, no charges of murder against him, and for that she was especially grateful. But finally, too, she found out that she was not the only one who had for him a special fondness: There was, in fact, a whole chorus of female sympathizers who wept bitterly to see him in chains and applauded him bravely when he was sent before the magistrate. Young Mr. Abernathy seemed, however, greatly angered at the poor blind magistrate, and seemed to blame him for all his troubles. In fact, he made some sort of threat when he was sent off to Newgate Gaol to await trial.

Maude Bleeker was quite devastated by the experience, for at heart, even with years in London, she was still a country girl, provincial, and rather simple. She returned to The Key and offered her notice; days later she went back to her mother at Squire Leonard's great house outside Robertsbridge. She arrived just in time to take part in preparations for the wedding of Justine Leonard, the squire's only child, to Thomas Trezavant. (It was a step up for Justine, for though not himself a noble, her groom had close ties to a noble family; Squire Leonard paid dearly for that rise—and would continue paying.) For the most part, Maude's contribution to the grand occasion was in the form of a great outpouring of her famous scones and tarts. Mr. Trezavant, though not nearly so large as he became, was well on his way. The man had a sweet tooth, and he declared Maude's baked sweets the best he had ever tasted. When he heard that she was presently at liberty and was given a fine character by the squire, he hired her instanter, and she followed the bride and groom to their new residence in Little Jermyn Street.

And so, some years after her first journey to London, Maude Bleeker got what she had previously sought: a position as cook in one of the great houses. This, of course, pleased her, but there was bitterness, too, in her return, for there would be no Johnny Skylark there to welcome her back. She was saddened by that, but at the same time she felt betrayed by him: the extent and nature of his known crimes shocked and frightened her; the women who had shouted their sympathy so loudly to him had intimidated her. Maude wanted only to put him out of her mind. She never went to Tom King's coffee house to ask what had become of her Johnny Skylark. She assumed, quite reasonably, that he had been hanged at Tyburn, and was never given any reason to think differently until the night before.

"And among the robbers you recognized the man you knew as Johnny Skylark?" I interrupted, thinking to urge her forward.

But she was not to be hurried. She took a deep breath and continued her story, telling how upon that night she had, of a sudden, heard a great thunder of footsteps on the ground floor above and could not suppose what was happening above stairs. Then, starting up the steps to find out what she could, she was nearly knocked over by a half-dozen of the staff chased by two black men who prodded them down at cutlass-point. Her two kitchen slaveys were routed out of bed to join the rest. Then came another of the robbers from up above and delivered a little speech to all those who had been packed into the little kitchen, assuring them that all would be safe if they kept quiet and be patient "whilst me and my fellows go about our business." If, on the other hand, any on the household staff attempted to resist or escape, they would surely be murdered on the spot.

"*Was that him?*" I demanded—indeed, I fairly shouted.

"Who?"

"Why, Johnny Skylark—John Abernathy, whatever you wish to call him," said I. "It's of him you've been talking the last quarter hour, is it not?"

"Course it is," said she, "and course it was him. I just wanted you to know how I came to reco'nize him after all those years."

"How many years was it?"

"Over ten. Was it so long?" She reflected, looking back upon her life, searching for milestones. "No, longer—it was close on twelve years past."

"How did you recognize him? What was it convinced you?"

"Well, I b'lieve it was his voice," said she. "I've a good memory for them, and when he first started speakin', I was lookin' off in some other direction, and when I heard the first word or two, I said to myself, 'Here now, I know that voice.' And just as anyone might, I turned to it to see who it belonged to. It took me a moment because of the way he had changed, but I'm sure it was him, for you see, I came to know him well."

"The way he had changed?" I repeated. "In which way had he changed?"

"Well, course he was older, and that may account for all else. But he looked cold to me, cruel—and that was never him before. He was a warm person, a lovely, funny sort of man."

"I see." There was something specific I wished to hear from her, yet I knew not how to get it, short of putting words in her mouth. And I knew, having heard Sir John interrogate so many, that such would never do. As she had told her story, a number of approaches had occurred to me—but I had rejected all. At last, I decided to put it to her in the plainest manner possible: "Mistress Bleeker, would you tell me please if John Abernathy, who was known to you as Johnny Skylark, was a white man or a black man?"

Reader, she gave me the queerest look ever had been sent my way, as if she thought me just escaped from Bedlam. Then, surprisingly, she started to laugh. "Now I know what you mean," said she, once she had calmed down a bit. "It's that silly dark paint he wore that you're talkin' about, now ain't it?"

"Yes, I suppose it is."

"Well, that didn't fool me, not one bit. Once you know someone well as I knew my Johnny, then a bit of paint ain't going to fool you. No, he was white, all right—white as you or me. Mossman, the porter, he said that all of that crew—least all he'd seen—were got up in that same way and may not have been real black men at all. But Crocker, she thinks the one cut her nose was a true African."

So it seemed that the household staff had discussed the matter in detail amongst themselves. That, I feared, could be dangerous to Maude Bleeker, and perhaps to Crocker as well.

"You were standing quite close to him, I take it."

"Close enough to reco'nize him. Near as close as I am to you right now."

"Do you suppose you were close enough that he might have recognized *you*?"

She took that under consideration. I could do naught but wait. At last she did shake her head indicating the negative. "No," said she, "there was no sign of reco'nition from him. I doubt he even saw me, though I was right in front of him. Even if he had . . ." She lowered her gaze. "I'm much stouter than I was twelve years ago. Two or three stone can make a great difference in a person's appearance."

"Even so," said I, "it would be wrong to bandy his name about.

Indeed, I would not discuss it further with members of the staff. The robbers have murdered once, you know."

That ended my interrogation, such as it was. I told her that I, or perhaps Sir John, might return to ask more questions of her. Or, on the other hand, she might be invited to Bow Street.

Yet there was something more. I spoke up just as she was leaving, and she turned back to me in the doorway to the pantry.

"May I ask one last question?"

"Ask it," said she.

"You may have helped us considerably in the investigation with what you've told me," said I. "Why did you do it?"

"I ain't thought about that too much," said she. "But it seemed like the only thing to do. When I heard what Johnny had done—all the stealing, and now the killing—well, I didn't see how I could hold nothing back."

"Thank you," said I, "but do be careful."

I was let out the back door, five steps up from the kitchen to the garden. To me it was apparent that Maude's friends wished to keep Mr. Collier ignorant of my comings and goings. They were suspicious of him. Perhaps I should have been, too, but that afternoon I had spent in his company was sufficient to convince me that he was no real danger to me or to any of the staff. He seemed at worst simply a nosey old fellow of forty: envious, fearful, ineffectual. Wrong he may have been to make such unseemly haste in applying for Arthur's position, but I knew him to be desperate, despite the bold words he had spoken when last we had met. He knew no other way of earning his bread except butlering, and so when the opportunity came, he grabbed for it, not giving damn-all for Arthur, nor for anyone else. I supposed that I could not greatly blame him for it.

Marching on to Mr. Bilbo's residence in St. James Street, I reviewed my purpose in going there. Deep down, I felt I had been sent by Sir John on a fool's errand. If Bunkins and the coachmen were certain to lie to me, what then was the purpose of asking them at all about Mr. Burnham's activities the night before? According to Sir John, by closely examining their lies we might reach the truth. That seemed a dubious premise to me.

I allowed myself these rebellious thoughts, for I felt that my questioning of Maude Bleeker had yielded the most important facts yet uncovered in the investigation. I was quite filled with my own success as an interrogator, never considering that I hardly had any right to claim it. After all, I had been sent by the porter to hear what she had to say, had I not? It had been her wish to tell me what she had experienced, and what she had seen, was it not? And why had I been summoned, why had I been told so much? I had sense enough not to believe the reason she had given. It was far less likely that she should have been prompted by that great list of crimes of which he had presumably been guilty, than that she was inspired by a desire for revenge against her betrayer. Yet, whatever her motive, she had made us a great gift. That was the truth of it; nevertheless, I had convinced myself that I had drawn the information from her most cleverly, that I had managed somehow to trick it out of her.

And so did I come to that house in St. James Street, which I had known by an odd set of circumstances* since my first days in London. I hopped up the three steps to the oaken door, as beautifully paneled as any in St. James, grasped the heavy knocker, and rapped four times. Waiting, I heard steps beyond the door; then they ceased, but contrary to my expectations, the door did not swing open. Still I waited. I rapped again and again, and again heard the shuffle of feet on the other side.

Then came a cry of annoyance: "Awright, awright, give me but a moment, and I'll have the door open. I'm puttin' on m'hat." The voice was female, and again there was something about it which suggested I should know its owner. No, it was not Nancy Plummer, nor did I believe it was Mr. Bilbo's cook. Had he taken a new paramour?

At last the heavy door moved, ever so slowly at first, then more swiftly until a young lady of about twenty was revealed; she was dressed for the street.

"Who are you, and who do you wish to see?" She blurted it forth breathlessly and quite indifferently. Yet she took note of me of a sudden, as I did of her. She stared, and I stared back.

"I knows you," said she, frowning. "You're . . . you're . . ."

"And you," said I, "you're—now I have it. You're Mistress Pinkham."

*These circumstances are described in the first of my memoirs of the investigations of Sir John Fielding, which was titled *Blind Justice*.

"So I am. And you're the lad was with the Blind Beak when he asked me all those questions, ain't you?"

"Why, indeed I am. Jeremy Proctor is my name. Sir John and I were both most indignant when we heard that Lord Lilley had discharged you, along with the butler. Sir John particularly requested that no action against you be taken until he had the opportunity to talk with you again."

"Lot of good that did."

"Where have you been? I searched St. James up and down looking for you and Mr. Collier that we might have our talk."

"Well, I been right here. Nancy Plummer and me been friends for years, we have."

"Has Mr. Bilbo taken you on here?"

"Onto his household staff, you mean? Oh no, he has so few, and I'm more of a lady's maid, anyways. I just been stayin' here in one of the spare beds."

"I never thought of asking after you here," I admitted. "I come here so often I was sure I would have heard it from Mr. Burnham or Jimmie Bunkins or from Mr. Bilbo himself."

"Well, this is where I been. But it ain't where I'll be much longer."

"Oh? How is that?"

"I been looking for employment, and it seems like I found something at last."

"Excellent, Mistress Pinkham. Would that be in London, or . . ."

"Cert'ny in London. I couldn't live long nowhere else," said she with great certainty. "Might be some stayin' in a great house in the country, though. Can't say as I'd mind that."

"Oh, indeed not!" said I, presenting her with a cheerful smile.

She, for her part, returned the smile. There followed an awkward pause. "I must be going. I've an appointment with my new employer," said she, starting forward, expecting me to step aside.

I held my ground and would not let her round me. "Where may we reach you, Mistress Pinkham? Here? Or perhaps at your new place of employment? We must have that talk, I fear."

"Well . . ." She looked left and right, obviously eager to be gone.

"I could meet with you here, or perhaps at your new employer's. Who is the new master, by the bye?"

"Uh . . . it ain't certain yet that I got employment."

"I'm sorry. I must have misunderstood," said I. "But where would that be? Where will you be employed—*if* you are employed?"

She sighed. "Bloomsbury Square."

"And your employer will be . . . ?"

"Lord Mansfield."

"Thank you. I shall be some time here, and I expect that you will be back here long before dinnertime. We shall have our talk when you return."

She looked at me rather queerly then, as she might if I were a rabbit blocking her path and snarling menacingly when she sought to pass. I, however, made no further move to block her way. I stepped aside and allowed her by; more, I even offered a slight bow as she passed.

Once inside the house, I closed the heavy door after myself. Standing there in the hall, I felt quite like an intruder. I was not there by invitation, nor would I be entirely welcome if my purpose were known. Still, I had a task to perform, and fool's errand or no, perform it I would as well as I could.

I was near enough to the closed door of the classroom so that I could hear Mr. Burnham's voice intoning some lesson in geography to Bunkins. (Where was Van Diemen's Land? I had no idea.) I would not, could not, interrupt them. It would be best for me to go direct to Mr. Bilbo, in order to inform him of my presence in his house, and state bluntly just why I had come. It would not do to go tiptoeing about the house, asking questions behind his back. Thus, having made a firm decision, I set off down the long hall to look for Mr. Bilbo where he most likely would be found.

What had been the library in Lord Goodhope's day was now Black Jack Bilbo's study. Because he had been a seafaring man, the place was handsomely decorated with seascapes, paintings of ships in harbor, and pictures of exotic locations. In one corner was a maritime compass, and standing beneath the room's high windows stood a ship's helm. There were maps on the walls, and all manner of keepsakes—pistols, shells, arrowheads—scattered on shelves that had previously contained Lord Goodhope's books. If Sir John's retreat between the bedrooms was a bit small to be called a study, then Mr. Bilbo's was a bit too large. Yet that fitted the man well. He was in every way a large figure—in every way, that is, except measureable height. Though not a tall man, he was deep-chested and great-bellied; each of his thighs would have matched the size of an ordinary man's waist; his beard was big and black; and his heart was as large as that of any man in London.

I had but to knock upon the door frame and stick my head within to be waved forward.

"Jeremy, me boy, come in, won't you?"

I came inside and took the chair opposite his desk, which he pointed to rather grandly (he was also fond of large gestures).

"Always happy to see you," said he to me, "though I can't say that this visit is entirely unexpected."

"Mr. Burnham told you what came to pass during his interview with Sir John."

"He did. He told me all about it—or as nearly all as he knew."

"How that huge fellow marched right in and pointed him out as the leader of the band of robbers?"

"Trezavant is his name, I understand."

"The coroner of Westminster."

"Ah!" said Mr. Bilbo, rolling his eyes at the information I had given. "*That's* why Sir John dared not send him packing."

"Yes, oh yes," said I. "Mr. Trezavant is a friend of the Prime Minister's and was appointed to his position by the Lord Chief Justice."

"Ah, politics." He shook his head in dismay. "I understand he's a near neighbor of ours."

"That's right—on Little Jermyn Street."

"Mr. Burnham suspects you of taking him down that particular street so that fellow Trezavant might get a good look at him and make certain identification."

I jumped indignantly to my feet. "Why, that's not true!" My voice was loud, certainly, but under control. "That was pure happenstance. I would never do such a thing, nor would Sir John ever ask me to."

"That's what I told him. Sit down, Jeremy. I have a point to make."

I did as he said. He waited to speak until I was once more situated across the desk from him. He then did lean across it, his big hands clasped before him, his dark eyes staring into mine.

"I told Mr. Burnham that I had known the both of you, Sir John and you, Jeremy, long and well enough to be certain that you would not play such low tricks as he describes. And I tell you now, lad, that I've known Mr. Burnham long and well enough to be sure that he would not commit theft and murder, as this man Trezavant says he has. When you do truly know a man, in the way I've known him and you and Sir John, then you know what they're capable of and what they're not. Black man or white man, I'd take his word for it. But of course if it's Mr. Burnham's word against the coroner of Westminster, then that complicates things considerably."

"There is another complication, Mr. Bilbo."

"And what is that, lad?"

"Neither Sir John nor I believe that Mr. Burnham is guilty, as Mr. Trezavant charges. Yet, Sir John — and I too, I must confess — does not believe that he spent his time quietly at home last evening, as he says he did. That is why Sir John sent me here to attempt to confirm his story from the comments and testimony of those who were here at the time."

"To confirm it or put the lie to it?"

"However it turns out, I suppose." I hesitated at that point, but then decided to be altogether frank with Mr. Bilbo. "Sir John expects that I shall be lied to, but he says that even the lies may be of some value, for they may lead us to the truth. I have yet to divine how this may be so."

"He's a clever one, ain't he? Only he could devise a way how lies would lead to the truth." He laughed at that, clapped his hands, and laughed some more. Then the laughter suddenly stopped. "But let me tell you, Jeremy," said he, "Sir John was dead right about one thing, and that's that you'll be lied to. In fact, I'll tell you now that I stayed less than an hour at my gaming club, and all the time I was here — that is, up to about 10:30 — Mr. Burnham was also here, and I'm absolutely sure of it."

"Is that the truth, Mr. Bilbo?"

"I'm willing to swear to it, Jeremy."

And that was not at all, in this instance, the same as telling the truth.

"It would be my word against Mr. Trezavant's, and though I'm a gambler, there's many a duke and earl willing to swear that I run the finest and most honest gaming club in all London. They wouldn't keep coming to me if it were not so."

With a nod of his head, he indicated that there was nothing more to say.

I rose from my chair. "Then I have your permission to talk to all who were about your residence last night?"

"Of course," said he. "You never need my permission to come into this house and talk with anyone."

"Thank you, sir," said I.

Then did I turn and walk the length of the study. Only at the door did I pause and turn back to Mr. Bilbo.

"Sir," said I, "on the way in I happened to meet a Mistress Pinkham whom I had earlier met at Lord Lilley's. Do you know much about her?"

He sighed. "No, I don't. She's an old chum of Nancy Plummer's, she is. We sometimes take in orphans who got no place else to go — not just anyone off the street, you understand. They got to be vouched for, and Nancy vouched for her. Beyond that, you'd have to ask Plummer."

"All right then, I'll begin with Bunkins, if they're through with class for the day."

And that I did. I shall not linger over my interview with Jimmie Bunkins — our acute embarrassment, his inability to provide details — nor shall I detain you long, reader, by reporting directly on what was said between me and the coach driver and the footman. It was all a great waste of their time and mine — or so it seemed to me. And of course it earned me their resentment, and perhaps also Mr. Burnham's enmity.

They all told exactly the same story with exactly the same details. According to each and all, Mr. Burnham had retired to the drawing room to read. What was he reading? A book. What was the title of the book? The vicar of someplace or other. Who wrote the book? No idea. Then how could you be sure that this was the particular book he was reading? Because he kept running out to read aloud parts of it he specially enjoyed. (There was some intentional irony in Mr. Burnham's choice of the book he purported to be reading that night, for it was my copy of *The Vicar of Wakefield*, by Oliver Goldsmith, which I had lent him.) According to them, Mr. Burnham would make regular rounds from the drawing room to the kitchen below, where the coachmen sat at the table, then up to Bunkins's room, every quarter hour or less; that was how they were all so sure he had been present through the entire evening and had not slipped out, robbed a house around the corner with his crew of black villains, and then slipped back in so that no one had noticed.

All of that struck me as a bit ludicrous, I fear.

As it happened, I talked to the coachmen in the stable behind the house. In all truth, they paid me little heed as I questioned them, for they were occupied in hitching up the team and otherwise readying the coach for a trip up the river to Richmond, where Mr. Bilbo had an appointment with the duke, no less. Indeed they left me behind, though not alone, for as I stood in the great, wide door, watching them go, I was joined there by the stable boy, a young country fellow of about fourteen who had not worked there long; whilst the coachmen had hitched the horses, he had labored at cleaning out the stalls. He smelled rather strongly at that moment, yet I stayed close, for just as I was about to leave he started talking. I was keenly interested in what he had to say.

"Can't figure why Mr. Bilbo don't take that trip on his saddle horse. That gray mare is just the prettiest and the best I ever did see. It's a shame the master don't ride her."

I attempted to explain to him that seamen like Mr. Bilbo are often poor horsemen and shy about exhibiting their lack of skill. The boy, however, seemed not to listen to what I had said. He continued in the manner in which he had begun.

"If it wasn't for Mr. Burnham, that mare wouldn't get no riding at all," said he. "He sits well in the saddle, I'd say. Wonder where he learned."

"Does he take the horse out often?" I asked.

"Oh, not often, I wouldn't say—two or three times a week, four at the most. Always on Sunday."

"Did he have her out last evening?"

"Oh, didn't he, though! He didn't get in till near half after eleven and kept me up till near midnight, rubbin' her down, coolin' her off. Must've taken her on a pretty long ride." The boy paused, reflecting upon that. "Well, if he didn't, nobody would."

I thanked him and, with a wave, walked slowly away. What I might have done instead was grab the young fellow and kiss him on both cheeks in the French style, then turn a couple of cartwheels, for he had turned my fool's errand into a rewarding investigation. I could hardly contain myself as I returned to the house.

Yet I was not so excited by what had transpired that I failed to notice a familiar figure descending the stairs. It was none but Nancy Plummer, of whom I had recently seen a great deal. I hastened to overtake her, ere she disappeared. I hailed her by name. She turned and frowned when she recognized me.

"I've a few questions regarding Mary Pinkham," said I.

"Well, I've a few questions for you regardin' what you said to her."

"What do you mean?"

"I mean that soon as ever you talked to her, she come back to me, askin' about you. And that she did whilst she was throwin' everything she owned into her portmanteau. She left," Nancy declared. "She left just like that, cursin' your name, she was."

SIX

*In which Frank
Barber makes a
surprise appearance*

It often seemed that Sir John Fielding responded rather poorly to news
of the sort that a lad of seventeen would deem of the utmost importance.
One such instance occurred upon my return to Number 4 Bow Street. I
burst into the kitchen, thinking to travel through it up to his bedroom.
But I found upon my entry that he was seated at the table, half-clothed,
as Mr. Donnelly dressed his wound. As chance would have it, I had not
been present previously during such an exercise. This was my first
glimpse beneath the bandages since they had first been applied. To me
the wound appeared rather ugly—red and puckered and scabbed
over—but the surgeon seemed well-pleased with its condition.

Having first made certain that Annie was not within earshot, I
blurted out the story of my visit to Mr. Bilbo's residence: I told of the
strange and quite unacceptably complex manner that had been devised
to convince us that Mr. Burnham had been present in the house all
through the evening; of the stable boy who, without malice and unin-
tentionally, revealed that Mr. Burnham had been gone all through the
early part of the night; and finally did I tell of my odd encounter with
Mistress Pinkham and her hasty departure thereafter.

Sir John listened closely, as only Sir John could, squeezing his
lower lip gently, stroking his chin. Nevertheless, when I had concluded
that part of my report, his only comment came as something of a disappointment.

"Hmmm, yes, well, that is most interesting, isn't it?"

Yet I was too excited and eager to impart what more I had to tell to
be greatly discouraged. So I then launched into the remainder of my

tale. I began by telling of my chance meeting with Mossman, the porter, and how he had informed me that Mr. Trezavant had departed to bring back his wife from the family manse in Sussex.

This information seemed to stir Sir John rather more than anything I had brought back from Mr. Bilbo's residence. He was moved to comment, "Ah, yes, that gives us a day or two in any case."

And I was moved to wonder, a day or two for what? Yet I said nothing and continued directly to the news of Mr. Collier's sudden appearance as butler in the Trezavant house, and the tale told me by Maude Bleeker. I recall that I told the latter in great detail, though not, I'm happy to say, in such great detail as Maude Bleeker had given it to me. Attempting to inject a bit of drama into it, I concluded, "And she discovered that the man's true name was John Abernathy when he appeared before you in the Bow Street Court below."

"And he was the man she recognized among the robbers?"

"He was the man she had known as Johnny Skylark, yes sir."

"She's sure of that, is she? After all, the fellow she spied for a minute, or perhaps a little more, in the kitchen, had a black skin and not white."

"True, but—"

"And it does seem to me, Jeremy, that even given the possibility that he wore blackface as a disguise, his face might well have changed greatly under that dark paint in twelve years' time."

"All I can say, sir, is that she seemed quite sure."

"Yes, well . . . perhaps." He lapsed into silence, but I said nothing, for it seemed quite certain that he would have more to add. "The fact is," he resumed (confirming my supposition), "I do remember this fellow John Abernathy. I remember his voice as he called curses upon me. He was angry at me because of the case I had assembled against him. I had a number of his robbery victims from years past right there in magistrate's court. One after the next, they identified him as the thief who had robbed them at sword-point, at pistol-point, whatever. The case against him was as sure as any that ever I sent on to Old Bailey. I've no idea what happened to him there, however. I was on to other things. He could have been sentenced to transportation, rather than the rope, I suppose." He tested that in his mind for a moment. Then did he add: "Not really very likely, though."

"Perhaps I might invite Maude Bleeker here, sir," I suggested, "and you might hear her story for yourself."

"No! no! no!" He flapped his hand irritably. "It would do no good, or very little, unless we knew what had become of Mr. Abernathy — how he had been sentenced, et cetera. And Jeremy, I fear I must ask you to find that information for me. It will be in the file. If the cook is correct, and all this happened twelve years past, then you shall have to look for it in the cellar."

My heart sank. I greatly disliked digging through the files in the best of circumstances. But what to me was quite the worst was searching through those dusty files in the cellar; I had no idea how I might go about it, now that Clarissa had rearranged them.

As if reading my mind, Sir John remarked, "It will give you an opportunity to learn the new filing system. I'll urge Clarissa to help."

Through it all, Mr. Donnelly had stood and listened, apparently quite fascinated, to my report to Sir John and the discussion that followed. Sir John had stated his intention to sit up and have dinner with "the family." The surgeon had consented, and in celebration Annie had made a special trip to Covent Garden that she might get from our butcher, Mr. Tolliver, a piece of meat worthy of the occasion. And so, I buttoned Sir John's shirt and helped him gingerly into his coat.

Mr. Donnelly asked the magistrate's permission to take me downstairs with him. "I have," he said, "a few things to discuss with Jeremy."

Sir John, assuming those few things would have to do with his treatment, granted permission indifferently, though he warned the surgeon he would not likely take any of the cures that were prescribed. "Food and drink are all I shall allow inside me," said he. "I saw what the learned doctors did to my poor Kitty."

(He referred, reader, to his dear first wife, who had died of a tumor four years before; she was grossly mistreated by a series of doctors with potions and medicaments until Mr. Donnelly came along and properly diagnosed her malady, yet was too late to do more than ease her passing.)

"I shall keep that in mind, Sir John," said the surgeon. "In the meantime, do you wish to be assisted up to your bed for a rest before dinner?"

"No, I shall take my rest here at the table. Annie should be along soon to keep me company."

And thus did I accompany Mr. Donnelly down the stairs and to the door to Bow Street. It was there at the door, in the dim light provided by the small window above the lintel, that we had our discussion.

"I called you down," said he, "because I have two matters that I wished to talk to you about."

"By all means, let us talk, sir."

"The first matter has to do with Mr. Robb."

"Robb?" Oddly, the name meant little to me, spoken thus by him. Yet it took but a moment to puzzle my way to the proper answer. "Ah," said I, "you mean the butler at the Trezavant residence. I knew him as Arthur."

"Yes, he is the one. I saw him earlier today at St. Bart's, and I must say I was not pleased by his condition. He speaks and is occasionally conscious, though perhaps not fully. I'm told by the caretakers at the hospital that these periods, short at best, are becoming rarer and, well, shorter. I believe that he is slipping into a coma state—a deep sleep from which he will never waken. Death will soon follow."

"There is nothing that can be done to save him?"

"I know not what it would be. He is old—I have no idea how old. His brain has had a great shock. He has only taken a bit of water since his arrival in St. Bart's, and if he goes into a coma, he will not be able even to take that. Without water, without nourishment, he will surely die of thirst or hunger."

"How terrible," said I.

"Yes, it is, but I do not tell you simply to draw sympathy from you. I know that you have questions for him. My advice to you is to go to him at the hospital and put them to him during one of his intervals of consciousness—that is, if you can catch him during one of these."

"I shall," I promised. "I'll go tomorrow."

"Tomorrow may be too late."

"Oh . . . well, do they allow visitors at night?"

"I foresaw this," said he, as he removed a letter from his pocket, "and wrote out a kind of pass for you which should enable you to visit Mr. Robb at any time of the day or night."

Taking the letter as it was offered, I thanked him and promised to get to St. Bartholomew's as soon as ever I could. "But," I added, "you heard of my duties of this evening."

"I did, yes, and that brings me to the second matter I wished to speak to you about. When I found you there at the Trezavant house, doing the sort of work always done in the past by Sir John, I thought, Indeed, why not? Sir John could not go. Jeremy has always been with him on these visits to the setting of the crime and knows which questions to ask; and I'm sure you did a good, workmanlike job there."

"Well, I tried, but—"

"Let me finish. That was my impression then, but as I listened to your report to Sir John, I was struck by what you had accomplished with your investigation. You'd made it your own. You brought important information to him. He knows it, and will use it, though he would not let you see that."

"But why?" I interjected. "Why is he so guarded with me? Why will he show no enthusiasm—no satisfaction even—for what I bring him? No matter what it may be, he always gives me the feeling that somehow I have fallen short. Wasn't it so today?"

He conceded it was so. But then he continued: "I had a teacher at the University of Vienna, a teacher of anatomy, which for one who wishes to be a surgeon, is probably the body of knowledge most important of all. His name was Gräbermann, which translates roughly as gravedigger, if I'm not mistaken. In any case, I was quite certain that he was digging my grave for me. Though I tried to please him, studied tirelessly for his lectures, and answered all his questions correctly, I was constantly exposed to the bite of his sarcasm. He never accepted what I had to say without some belittling comment, and sometimes such were tossed out quite gratuitously. His object? Well, I never could quite grasp what was his object. And so, you can imagine my surprise when I heard from one of my friends, also a medical student, that he had heard our Professor Gräbermann commending me to another member of the medical faculty as 'the most knowledgeable and promising of all his students.' I was astonished, so much so that when his course of lectures in anatomy was done, I went to him and asked him how I might reconcile his treatment of me with his opinion of me. He thought that very bold and said so, but because it was bold he responded. 'My dear young fellow,' said he to me, 'I kept returning to you for answers to my questions for I could be sure that you would give me the right answers. Yet I could tell that you wished most of all to please me with the answers. You sought my approval, where as my personal approval had nothing to do with the subject of anatomy, nothing at all. And so, Herr Donnelly, I derided you, made sport of you before the class so that you might understand that anatomy was all-important and my approval, nothing.' "

He peered at me. There was something challenging in his look.

I said to him, "I think I understand, sir."

"Do you? Well, let me put it plain. I think you are more interested in pleasing Sir John than you should be, or you need to be. Sir John, on the other hand, has noted this, and he seems to withhold his approval for just that reason. He wants you to—"

Just then the door did interrupt us. Annie was on the other side, pushing against it, returning from Mr. Tolliver's stall in Covent Garden with a cut of meat judged worthy. Having bumped us out of the way with the door, she begged pardon and hurried past. Something seemed to be troubling her.

Mr. Donnelly and I did not resume our talk. With Annie gone, he held the door open for himself and smiled a goodbye smile at me. "Well, I've talked quite enough," said he in farewell. "Let us leave it that you're doing well, very well. Don't worry that Sir John may not be pleased. Please yourself."

And having said what he had intended, he departed, leaving me to reflect upon it.

The dinner, which was intended as something of a celebration, seemed hardly that, for Annie was ominously quiet throughout. She had cooked with her usual skill, no doubt of that—the beef roast that she had selected was perfectly prepared, with abundant dripping for the potatoes and carrots. Yet our group, which Sir John called his "family," was such that when one member was downcast or out of sorts he (or in this case, she) could bring down the rest. Not even the bottle of claret that Sir John had opened helped much to enliven the feast.

When we were done, Annie cleared the table and volunteered to do the washing up. Though Lady Fielding at first offered objections— ("She's done enough cooking the meal, don't you think?")—Sir John overrode them and sent Clarissa and me down to the cellar in search of John Abernathy.

"Who *is* this fellow, Abernathy?" she asked, eager to hear the worst. "How many did he murder?"

"Perhaps none, or so he claimed. Yet he was a dedicated and most active thief; what Bunkins would call 'a village hustler,' always on the scamp."

"Ah, that's flash-talk, surely. You must teach it me."

Just then I threw open the door to the cellar. The profound darkness before us was rather intimidating, even to me; it inspired a wail of dismay from her.

"Oh, Jeremy," said she, "must we? I had forgotten how frightening it can be down there. There are rats—or some such creatures that patter about in the dark."

"Well, you must have been down there quite some time—long enough to change the files around, as I understand."

"Yes, but I was with Annie most of the time—no insult to you intended, Jeremy—and she propped the door open."

"Well, I can do that," said I, and set about to do so. "And I've got a lighted candle. Here, I'll light yours for you. That should give us as much as we need."

And so, thus equipped, we descended the stairs, I in the lead, Clarissa behind, and each of us bearing candles burning bright; the open door also shed a bit of light below, but only a bit, for darkness had long since fallen on London.

Clarissa's improvement of the filing system used by the Bow Street Court was simple enough, though there could be no doubt that it had made it much easier to find specific cases. Previously, individual cases were simply filed under the date upon which they were heard. Clarissa's innovation was simply to list under the date the names of all those whose cases were inside the date folder; it was no longer necessary to look inside each folder to see which cases had been heard upon that day. It was a wonder to me that the files had not been changed in this way long before. That suggested to me what I had long suspected: that the files were very seldom consulted; for the most part, they were stored and forgotten.

In this way, Clarissa and I were able to go quickly through the files for 1760, the year designated by Maude Bleeker as the one in which her Johnny Skylark appeared before Sir John Fielding, magistrate of the Bow Street Court.

"What did you say this fellow's name was?" Clarissa called to me from one end of the year's files.

"John Abernathy."

"I have it here," said she, "—tried on September 27th."

"Really? Why, that was indeed quickly done." Working from the beginning of the year 1760, I had myself only reached the middle of March.

"Shall I remove the case file from the folder?"

"No, I think not. We—*what happened*?"

What happened was this: Either I had not propped the door properly, or someone had, out of ignorance or malice, kicked away the brick that I had used. The door shut of a sudden with a great bang, thus creating a great draft which swept down the stairs and blew out our candles, plunging the cellar into complete darkness.

A scream rose in her throat, which she barely managed to stifle. She made her way across the few steps that separated us. "Yes," said she, "what did happen?"

I started to explain when a sudden scurrying of tiny animal feet sounded quite near to us. Just as sudden I ended my explanation, that I might better listen. Clarissa, on the other hand, let forth the scream she had only moments before stifled. She stood so close and screamed so loud that I was near deafened. Then did she throw her arms about me, pressing herself to me tight, squeezing me with all her strength, which was considerable. (She was no longer the frail little runaway from the Lichfield poorhouse.)

"Come along," said I, "let go, and we shall find the stairway."

"I'm afraid," said she. "I do so hate those things."

"Come along," I repeated.

And holding her firmly about the waist, I took us to the stairs.

The location was well-fixed in my mind. I murmured to her encouragingly and got her up the first step and then the second, and so on, up to the very top. And when we reached it, I found the door was locked. Well, thought I, so much for the possibility of any *accidental* removal of the door prop.

I beat loudly and lustily upon the door. I raised my voice in repeated shouts to "open!" And Clarissa joined her voice with mine.

It was not long before I heard footsteps and then the sound of the key turning in the lock. The door swung open, revealing a surprised Mr. Baker. He stepped aside.

"Well, what are you doing in there, Jeremy? Or maybe I should say, how'd you manage to get yourself locked in?"

"I've no idea," said I, though I immediately excused Mr. Baker from blame. We had always been on the best of terms.

"You all right, Mistress Roundtree?"

"Well, I got a bit of a fright."

"I've no doubt of it," said he. Then he turned and smiled at me. It was a most peculiar half-smile which communicated doubt, amused indulgence, and a certain manly understanding between him and me. He winked. Only then did I grasp that he believed that Clarissa and I were engaged in some adolescent version of the game of male and female—in short, that we were trysting for such purpose.

"We were searching for a file. When the door came shut—you see? I used this brick to prop it open—that blew our candles out." I wanted all this understood.

"Ah, well, no harm done," said he, and with a nod, he left us standing there at the door to the cellar.

"Do you know what he thinks?" said I rather hotly to Clarissa. Then did I notice the expression upon her face; it was quite like the odd smile given me by Mr. Baker. I was most surprised at that, and perhaps a bit shocked.

"Oh, I can guess," said she. "But as he put it, 'No harm done.' "

"Well, I hope you managed to bring the file with you. Didn't drop it in your great fright, did you?"

"No, I didn't," said she rather coldly. "If I had, I should only have had to go back and retrieve it. And I have no intention of going down there ever again. Certainly not with you." She ended her speech with a sniff.

"Well and good," said I. "But let me see that file on John Abernathy, will you?"

Without a word, she handed over the thick folder. I had no difficulty finding the Abernathy file, and I knew that what I wished to know would be on the very last page of the many which made up his file. There it was: "The prisoner, John Abernathy, was sentenced by Justice Francis Seward to transportation to the colony of Jamaica, where he would be sold to labor for the term of his natural life. He was sent out in chains on the HMS *Avenger* on October 11, 1760." So it was. Maude Bleeker's Johnny Skylark was not hanged: The possibility did exist that she had seen him, just as she claimed.

"Take this, the whole folder, and present it to Sir John," I said to her. "He may want you to read it to him—or perhaps not. In any case, tell him I wished you to read to him the note on sentencing on the last page of the file."

She was suddenly curious. "Well, all right, but what about you? Where will you be?"

"At St. Bartholomew's Hospital," said I. "I must visit a sick friend."

That sick friend, of course, was Arthur Robb. I hiked across London town to see him, weighted down somewhat by the two pistols that I carried in my coat pockets. I had requested them from Mr. Baker, the armorer and night jailer. When he heard where I was going, he thought it quite wise for me to go armed and otherwise prepared for trouble.

The part of the city in which St. Bartholomew's was located was not so much dangerous as it was dark and deserted at this time of night. It stood hard by Smithfield. The market would be full of customers—and most active—in a few hours' time; but just now it was empty of all but stock to be slaughtered. I should have to choose my route to St. Bart's carefully, taking the wider, better-lit streets and avoiding the narrow, dark streets which surrounded the hospital in such plenty.

Most of the above I have paraphrased from what I remember of the advice Mr. Baker had given me as he checked over the two weapons and loaded them.

"Are you sure you don't want them in holsters on a belt, the way you usually wear them?" he asked.

"No, I'll be going into the hospital proper, and I daresay they wouldn't want me walking amongst their patients with pistols in plain view."

"That makes good sense."

I fell silent for a moment as I considered whether I should bring the next matter up for discussion. And though I hesitated, curiosity won out.

"Mr. Baker, have you any idea who might have kicked the door shut and locked us in the cellar?"

"Well 'tweren't me." He was very emphatic.

"Oh, I know that. That's why I'm asking you."

He looked me full in the face, scratched his head, and grimaced in thought.

"Well now, let me see. I didn't know you were down there, you two, so you must've gone down at the end of Fuller's watch."

"I suppose we did." Now there was a thought, for after all, I did not get along well with Mr. Fuller and had not for some time.

"Was anyone else around?"

"Oh, let me think. Yes, Bailey and Perkins got called up to talk with Sir John. They didn't stay long. That new fellow—what's his name? Pat-something."

"Patley," said I.

"That's it, Patley. He waited down here and left with the other two. But truth to tell, Jeremy, I don't know why you're letting this bother you at all. Didn't hurt anyone. 'Twasn't much more than a prank, was it?"

"No, I suppose not. I'll put it behind me."

"It's best you do."

I was, however, not as good as my word. I worried away at the matter for over half my journey to St. Bart's. Mr. Baker was right, of course. It was hardly more than a prank, and a mean-spirited one at that. And it was true, as well, that Mr. Fuller delighted in such tricks; he was notorious for the indignities, large and small, that he forced upon prisoners. Nevertheless, Constable Patley seemed a likelier candidate—though I could not specifically say why that should be. Was it simply because he had been a soldier, and the "prank" seemed to me to be the sort of jest that might enliven boring evenings in the barracks room? Or was it something deeper? It was true, I admitted, that I had acted rather arrogantly toward him on our march to the Trezavant residence—though not altogether without reason. Was this simply his way of getting back at me? Or did my suspicion go deeper still?

I gave all this greater thought than it deserved; mulling it about in my mind; posing Mr. Fuller against Mr. Patley; attempting to articulate to myself the basis of my uneasiness around Mr. Patley, the vague hostility that I felt toward him—to no avail.

At last, finding no answer in what, after all, was mere speculation, I dropped the matter and urged myself to think about something else— anything else. Then did I turn past Old Bailey and start up Gilt Spur Street—not within sight (and smell) of Smithfield yard. And there, quite unbidden, Clarissa Roundtree popped into mind. What a strange one she was! More often than not, she was bold as brass—just as she had been with Samuel Johnson, and as she so often was evenings at table. She seemed to wish all to believe her as capable as any man. Yet would a man scream, and clasp me to him, as she had when the candles were blown out and a rat began scurrying nearby? Indeed, I think not. And what, after all, could she have meant by that sly look that she gave me, and her own comment upon Mr. Baker's comment? What, I asked myself, was she thinking of? Well, that was quite enough about Mistress Roundtree, was it not?

I put her out of my mind, and there she stayed for a minute or two — until (again, quite unbidden) I happened to remember how she had felt when she had flown into my arms there in the darkened cellar. As I may have observed elsewhere, she was rather tall for her age and much better, well, better . . . *developed* than she had been when she first took her place in the household a year past. The point is, she fitted me rather well for one her age. But was I even sure of her age? I had thought her about twelve when first I saw her; that would make her thirteen, would it not? Perhaps she was older than that. She certainly *felt* older.

Thus, with such foolish thoughts as this circling through my brain, I arrived at St. Bartholomew's Hospital, oldest and largest in London. I chastised myself for not thinking more seriously while on this most solemn occasion. Arthur's life would soon end — Mr. Donnelly had attested to that — and I surely owed him more decorous notions than those I had just had regarding Clarissa. Perhaps he would wish me to pray with him — but what prayers did I know? What could I say in comfort to him?

I passed through the great stone gate and glimpsed above it the statue of King Henry VIII as I went under it. Then did I go straight to the office in which Mr. Donnelly had signed the papers of admission as I and the footman held Arthur between us, doing what we could to make him tolerably comfortable. I rapped hard upon the door and waited but a moment until a loud voice came from beyond it.

"Who is there?"

"I am come from the Bow Street Court to question one of your patients."

Apparently I had said the right thing, for a key turned the lock, and the door came open.

"You should of come earlier," said the sharp-faced fellow who barred my way. "You need permission from a doctor to come in after six."

"I have that." I fetched out the letter given me by Mr. Donnelly and handed it over to him.

The fellow stepped back and beckoned me inside. I entered as he took the letter over to a candelabrum that he might read it.

Two candles lit the room which, though of medium size, was crammed full with file drawers and bundled piles of what I supposed to be medical records. It wasn't until I had been in the place near a minute that some movement in one dark corner followed by a cough brought another man into view. He was a burly sort of man, older and stouter than he who had answered my knock at the door.

"All right, I keep this," said the letter-reader as he waved the missive at me. "You're free to go up to talk to your man, Robb, for as long as you can get anything out of him. Been here before? You know the way?"

"No," said I, "no, I don't."

"In that case, Will here will take you there. Ain't that right, Will?"

"I'll do it if I must," said Will from his dark corner. "Come along, lad."

Though short-legged as men of his size and shape often are, he moved so swiftly that I was forced to follow along at something close to a jog-trot just to keep up with him. He led me across a large courtyard to the building at the farthest side. Looking up at the dark walls all round me, I was reminded of Newgate Gaol, which I knew to be nearby; yet St. Bart's was even larger, darker still, and altogether more forbidding than that most notorious prison.

Burly Will fair flew up the steps and through the door and quite left me behind as he took the stairway to the next floor. Yet he waited for me there as I arrived somewhat out of breath. He had a little speech to make.

"Now, young sir," said he in a low voice, "I would give you a bit of advice."

"And what is that, sir?"

"I and another conveyed your Mr. Robb to this floor when he was brought in last night. Now, I've worked here more years than I would care to say, and I've seen many hundred come and go, so that I've a sense of who's going out on their feet and who's going out in a box. Mr. Robb is one who'll soon go, and 'twon't be on his own. If he's alive now, he ain't likely to make it till morning."

"So I've heard," said I. "The doctor who brought him in said that I should talk to him now, for I might not get another opportunity."

And it was precisely for that reason that I wished to see the old man immediately. I wanted this fellow Will to take me to Arthur's bed. I shuffled my feet, seeking to impart to him my eagerness to get on with it.

Yet he talked on: "He's one of those who is sometimes awake and sometimes not. You must catch him awake if you want him to answer you proper. Now, the way to get him awake—" He paused and peered at me closely. "Do you have a knife with you?"

"No, why?"

"Well, a knife is best, you see—just a quick jab with the point of it, not deep, don't want to hurt him none, just enough to cause some pain. It's pain that wakes 'em up, quicker an' surer than anything. But you ain't got a knife, so that won't do. Next best thing is a good, sharp pinch. On his arse is the best place—maybe the only place with one so skinny as he is. Now, mind what I say, lad, for this is the only way you're likely to get anything from one so far gone." He gave me a sharp nod. "Come along," said he, and went off at the same fast pace as before without so much as a look back at me.

I ran to catch up as he passed first one door and then another. Finally, he turned in at the third, pausing an instant before he disappeared to beckon me inside. The ward was barely lit by candles at either end. Yet it was not difficult to make out the full figure of my guide standing at the foot of a bed about halfway down the aisle.

"Here's your man," said Will. "Is there somethin' else you need?"

I looked about but failed to see the item I sought.

"Would there be a chair? Something I could sit on? I may be here quite some time."

"I'll see what I can do." And off he marched, looking left and right into the spaces between beds to fulfill my request. Not far away he found a plain straight-backed chair. He brought it to me and accepted my thanks with a mock salute. Then he was gone.

My attention went at last to Arthur Robb. True, he breathed still, but lightly, shallowly, and somewhat irregularly, as one might if he were losing the knack. I bent over him, and in the dim light satisfied myself that he showed no signs of waking. His eyes were shut, but his face was far from relaxed; he wore the same pained grimace I remembered from the night before.

I touched him lightly on the shoulder nearest me—with no result; his eyelids gave not the slightest flutter and his breathing continued as before.

"Arthur," said I in a quiet voice, "wake up. I have some questions for you."

There was no response. I gave him a good sound shake—and there was still no response. No, not so much as a blink or a word spoken.

By this time, I was well-reminded of my fruitless efforts to waken Nancy Plummer. I could not waken him with a scream, as Lady Fielding had wakened Nancy, for I had not such a scream in me. And even if I found one deep down in my throat and brought it forth, I would likely waken the entire ward, perhaps the entire floor, along with Arthur. I sank down in the chair and considered the matter at some length.

Though it was not late, all those in their beds seemed to be asleep. The sound of steady breathing was all that I heard about me. Only Arthur, of them all, gave signs of great labor in his efforts. What could I do? It was evident that time was short. Mr. Donnelly's grim prognosis had been seconded by Will. There was little could be hoped for him beyond this night.

I tried shaking him again—without result. I left off for a minute or two, then did I jump from the chair in which I sat, grabbed the all but lifeless form on the bed by both shoulders, and gave it a great prolonged rattling, up and down, down and up. Had I seen another behave so cruelly with the old man's frail and helpless form, I would have leaped in to stop him. Yet little good it did me to treat him so. The only sign of change in him was a sustained "ahhhh" that came from deep in his throat. Yet it signified nothing, for once I left off shaking the poor old man, he lapsed into the same pattern of labored, shallow breathing. I sat back down in the chair, a feeling of defeat heavy upon me.

I sat thus for what seemed a good long time, and as I did, a voice within me began asking, repeating: "Would it be crueller to pinch him, as burly Will instructed, than to continue shaking Arthur as I had been doing?" When first I heard his advice, I thought it unspeakably brutal. I knew that I would not consider jabbing poor Arthur with a knife point nor pinching his arse—under any circumstances. Yet there I was, considering it. Would it be crueller? No. Was it then worth an attempt? Reluctantly, I decided that it was.

I slipped a hand under the thin blanket which covered his frail body, found his lean buttocks with my forefinger and thumb, and twisted as hard as ever I could—and then I twisted a bit harder.

"Ow! Ohh! Ohh!"

It was Arthur, indeed. I had hurt the poor fellow awake.

"What are you doing to me?" he wailed in a manner most indistinct. It was as if he had little control of his tongue. What he said was much more like, "Wh'doong muh?"

Assured at last that he could respond by forming words and making himself understood, I left off torturing the old man, came forward, and addressed him as quietly and gently as ever I could.

"Forgive me, Arthur, but I was desperate to wake you. I must ask you some questions."

"Questions . . . why?" He seemed to be fading already. "Thirsty."

I looked about quickly and found a cup and a pot of water on the little table beside the bed. I filled the cup, propped him up and held him as he drank his fill. Indeed, it was not much that he took in—less than half the contents of the cup. But when he indicated he had had his fill, I lowered him to the bed and put the cup aside.

"Arthur," said I, "do you remember just before the Africans came through the door, a woman called through the door, begging you to open it, for she was fleeing an attacker." At that I paused, hoping for some sign from him that he had understood.

Yet all he managed to do was repeat the word "woman."

"Did you recognize her voice?"

He answered in a surprisingly forthright manner, with what sounded quite like, "King's Carabineers."

"What?" said I, quite in confusion. "Would you repeat that?"

And that he did—but slowly and with great effort. I felt again that I was losing him.

"Would you like more water?" I asked. Then, not waiting for a reply in the affirmative or the negative, I grabbed the cup of water and propped him up that he might drink again. Yet he took in even less than before. He seemed well-satisfied, however, and a smile spread across his face, quite transforming his features. Then did he speak but one word, a name.

"Crocker," said he, as he slipped from my grasp back to the bed.

I attempted to rouse him again. Indeed, I tried all short of pinching him. I would not, could not, do that again, for I felt that I had gotten from him all that he had to give. Perhaps a little later I would manage to bring him back with the offer of another drink of water. Yet for now I was content to consider what he had said and what, if anything, it might have meant.

Mulling it over again and again, I came to the conclusion that it may all have meant very little. "Crocker" was perhaps promising. It could have meant that when he opened the door he had caught a glimpse of Jenny Crocker, the upstairs maid, before the robbers rushed in. Having left the Trezavant residence from the kitchen by the back door on my last visit, I knew that it would have been quite possible for her to have run from the front door to the back and re-entered the house without being missed. But had she done so? The indistinct manner in which he had spoken—something like "Cwockuh"—caused some doubt that he had even said her name; I knew I could not swear to it. And I knew it would be difficult to reconcile the smile on Arthur's face as he said her name with what followed his putative glimpse of her— the rude entry of that thieving crew, the knocking of the butler to the floor, and the apoplectic insult to his brain that followed. Such elements did not fit together.

Then there was the matter of the "King's Carabineers"—that made no sense whatever. I tried to think what he might have seen when he opened the door to have inspired that quick and distinct response to my question. I strained so to find some answer to this that I exhausted my poor brain. I fell unintended into a sound sleep.

I was shaken awake by burly Will. The morning light poured in from windows I had not earlier even noticed. I stretched to drive off my morning stiffness. Then I turned in time to see the blanket pulled up over Arthur's sagging, lifeless face. Though I was fairly certain of the matter, I nevertheless requested confirmation from Will: "Does that mean he's . . ."

"Dead." He finished the sentence for me. "Yes, it does, young sir. Dead is what he is, and dead is what I said he'd be by morning."

There was a great flurry of activity among the patients in the ward. All, or nearly all, seemed to be dressing themselves, preparing for departure. Were all to be turned out? I asked Will where they would be going so early.

"To Sunday services," said he. "And them that don't go, I must look them over and say they're sick enough to remain abed. And if I say they ain't, then they get no dinner this evening."

That seemed to me harsh treatment, and I was about to say so when I realized with great consternation the import of what I had just been told.

"Is it Sunday?" I asked, rather flustered.

"That's when Sunday services is generally held, so it is."

"Do you happen to know the time of day?"

"Well, I know it's near eight, for soon as I get this lot off to the chapel, I'm off for the day. The Lord's Day is my day off."

I made to go, setting my hat to my head and pulling up my baggy hose. At last ready for the hike to Bow Street, I thanked burly Will and started for the door.

"Hi there, young sir," he called after me, "did you get anythin' from the old man here?"

"Something," said I, "but I know not yet what."

"Did you do like I said?"

"I'm sorry to say I did."

"Aw, don't take it on your conscience, young sir. The dead don't care."

What did he mean by that? That Arthur was certain to die so it didn't really matter? Or that he was already dead? (The latter was manifestly untrue.) In any case, I liked it not. Someone in the past had said something similar. Who was it?

I gave burly Will an indifferent wave and started my journey homeward.

My alarm in discovering the day of the week had to do with my Sunday appointment with Mistress Crocker. It had originally been set with the intention of asking her further questions. I admit, however, that at the time the appointment was made, I had little notion of what questions I might ask her. Now, however, there was much that I wished to know, yet still I wondered what questions I might ask. How was I to explore the hints I had taken from Arthur's pronouncement of her name?

My thoughts were on this problem when I entered Number 4 Bow Street and marched up the stairs, went into the kitchen, and found all but Sir John there at table eating breakfast. In all truth, I was quite unprepared for the abusive reception I received from Lady Fielding. She was quite angry at me, and I could not suppose why; she was intemperate, vituperative. Was it all because I had failed to rise and start the fire for Annie?

No, as it turned out, it was because I had remained away from home all through the night. It was, so far as I could remember, the first such occasion, and it seemed to me that I had good and just cause to have been gone so long—that is, if the cause had been made clear to Lady Fielding.

I turned to Clarissa. "Did you not tell her where I was?"

"You told me to tell Sir John—and I did."

"Where were you?" Lady Fielding demanded. "At some drunken party with your friend Bunkins, no doubt."

"No, I was at St. Bartholomew's Hospital, attempting to interrogate a dying man."

"Dying man indeed! How could you be sure he was dying?"

"Because he died."

Lady Fielding's attack faltered. Her anger suddenly exhausted, all she could apparently think of in rejoinder was, "Oh, how sad."

"*Well, did you get anything from him?*"

There was no mistaking that voice. Indeed, it was Sir John's fierce courtroom voice, the one with which he silenced unruly crowds and called them to order. He stood in his nightshirt at the top of the stairs, his hands upon his hips in a most pugnacious attitude.

"I got something," said I, calling back to him, "but not much."

"Well, come up here and give me your report."

With that, he disappeared into his bedroom.

I bowed to those at the table (no doubt overplaying it a bit). "Now, if you ladies will excuse me . . ." said I.

"Now, Jeremy," said Lady Fielding, "there is no need to carry on so. If I was sharp with you, it was because I was most terribly worried about you. After all, though you may not agree, you are but a lad still."

"I shall try to keep that in mind, my Lady."

Then did I glance in Clarissa's direction, perhaps expecting, or at least hoping, for something like an apology from her, as well. Nothing was forthcoming, however.

"Then," said I, "I shall join Sir John."

And with a nod, I left them.

Of my report to Sir John, I have little to say. He listened carefully to what I had to tell him as he sat up in bed, hands folded across his middle. When I had done, he offered no interpretation of Arthur's curious remarks, nor, having none, did I offer any ideas of my own. It was thus a rather brief interview. I stood up from the chair at his bedside and prepared to go.

"Now, as I recall," said he, "you had arranged to ask more questions of this young woman whom the butler mentioned. Is that correct?"

"It is, Sir John."

"Well and good," said he. "Get what you can from her. Use your manly charms, if you must."

"*Manly charms!*" I repeated, laughing. "I hadn't known that I had any."

"Of course you do. Flirt with her—that sort of thing. Oh, and one more matter. Try to find out from her—or from anyone else in the Trezavant household—when the master will be returning from Sussex."

I agreed to find out what I could and took my leave of him.

I include this account of my experience upon returning to Number 4 Bow Street for a selfish purpose. And that is, reader, to demonstrate how freely I was tossed about in my own household between "you are but a lad still," on the one hand, and "use your manly charms," on the other. There could be little doubt that Sir John and Lady Katherine held distinctly different views of me—that is, of the degree of maturity which I had achieved; nor could there be any doubt that I much preferred Sir John's to his wife's. After all, *I* regarded myself as a man and saw no reason why the rest of the world should not.

I presented myself at the door of the Trezavant residence a bit earlier than Jenny Crocker might have expected—all part of my plan. This way I might see who it was had engaged her for the morning. I had shaved closely and carefully, cleaned my shoes properly, and worn my bottle-green coat, all of which I hoped would add to my manly charms.

Mr. Mossman, the porter, answered the door rather than Mr. Collier, and I thought that curious enough to comment upon it.

"Ah, well, he went off someplace, he did," said Mossman. "Most of the staff has gone for the day or some part of it. The master was plannin' to return tonight, or tomorrow noon at the latest—or so he said when he left. I guess they all decided they would get in their visitin' whilst he was away. Usually he keeps half-staff on Sundays."

"So all of them went out, leaving you alone?"

"Me and cook is all that's here."

"Well," I said with a proper long face, "I've bad news for you. Arthur died during the night."

"Ah well," said Mossman, "none of us expected he would last long, even in the hospital—maybe especially not there. St. Bart's got a bad reputation, you know."

"No, I didn't."

"Few comes out alive." He stared glumly down at his shoes. "Were you there with him when he passed on?"

"Well, I was, and I wasn't," said I. "The doctor who put him in the hospital told me to go if I wished to ask Arthur questions. I asked a few of him. But then, as I sat beside his bed and pondered his answers, sleep overcame me. I fear I slept through his last moments here on earth."

"Ah, but at least he knew there was somebody cared enough to sit beside him in that darkest hour. That must have been a comfort."

"Hmmm, well, perhaps."

Oddly enough, Mr. Mossman and I had been strolling the long hall as we talked. I thought perhaps he was leading me to the back stairs—but no. Once we reached them, he turned me about, and we proceeded together along the way we had come.

"Arthur mentioned something rather odd," I said. "He was not fully conscious, and so it may not have meant anything at all, but I wanted to ask you, was he ever in the army?"

He stopped for just a moment, turned, and looked at me rather oddly. "Why, indeed he was. What was it he said?"

Not wishing to be too explicit, "The name of a particular regiment came up, popped out of his mouth, as it were."

"Was it the King's Carabineers?"

"Why, so it was," said I. "What do you know of it?"

"That was his old regiment. You might not've thought it of him—old and frail-looking as he was—but he soldiered a good long while back in the forties. He was first in Europe, France, and that, and then up against the Pretender."

"And all of it with the King's Carabineers?"

"That's right. It was a mounted regiment, you know."

"No, I didn't."

"Yes, and old Arthur, he could still sit a horse. I remember him showing off one morning down at the great house in Sussex. We was all amazed."

"Did he often see his former mates — go out and drink with them, et cetera?"

"No," said Mossman a bit regretfully, "when you work on household staff as we do, you're not really free to do much of that. But each year they had a regimental reunion. He wouldn't've missed that for any price."

"So he did keep in contact with some?"

"Must have."

I thought upon that until we had reached the door to the street whence we had started. Before he could turn me round and start back down the hall again, I planted my foot and put a hand upon the doorknob.

"I'll trust you to pass the word on Arthur to Mistress Bleeker and the rest of the staff," said I to him.

"Oh, I will," he promised. "You can be certain of it. They'll be sad to hear he's gone, but they'd all want to know."

I made to open the door, but it was much heavier than I had anticipated; I tugged without result.

"Here, let me do that," said Mr. Mossman, easing me gently to one side. "There's a bit of a trick to it."

He gave the knob a great twist, pushed the door out, and only then pulled it back. It slid open quite easily.

"Oh, by the bye," said I, "is Crocker about? I've a question or two for her."

He looked at me then in mild surprise. "No, she went out for a stroll with a fella, but I thought you knew that."

"You did? Why?"

"Why, because he's one of yours."

"One of *mine*? I don't understand." He did truly have me puzzled.

"No, no," said he, "I meant that he was a constable. In fact, he's the one arrived with you the night of the robbery."

Constable Patley, of course! He kept turning up, didn't he? What had he to do with Jenny Crocker? "Ah, well," said I, making an effort not to divulge the surprise I felt through the expression on my face, "he does not tell all."

"Few do," said the porter, ever so philosophically.

"When did they leave?" I asked.

"Oh, hours ago."

"In that case, they should be back soon. I believe I shall wait in front for their return."

"You can wait here in the sitting room, if you've a mind to."

"No, I think not," said I, "for I've a message for the constable. But thanks to you anyway."

With that I departed, though I walked no farther than the last of the three steps that led from the door to the walkway. And there I remained, waiting. In spite of what I had said about having a message to deliver to Mr. Patley, I had no wish to engage him in talk. I simply wanted to be visibly there so that I might embarrass him—if, indeed, that were possible.

Indeed, I had not long to wait. Nevertheless, if I truly hoped to inflict upon Patley some degree of chagrin, I was to be disappointed, for when Crocker came, she came alone. As I watched her approach, moving along at a swift pace and looking the very picture of amused contentment, I realized there would be no confrontation, and I confess that I felt some degree of relief at that. I stepped out to meet her. She looked up in surprise.

"Well," said she, "ain't you early!"

"Not really," said I. "You said the afternoon. I believe it's now just about noon."

"So it's *very* early afternoon." She shrugged. "Well, right enough. I'm sure I don't mind."

As we set off together, I mentioned my plan: "If you've a mind, I thought we might go to the Globe and Anchor on the Strand. It's a very respectable inn with an excellent eating place within. I thought you might care for coffee and cakes."

"Ooh, coffee! It does make me tingle. But I'm for it so long as this place is truly respectable."

"Oh, it is."

"Right enough then. A girl can't be seen comin' out of a place that ain't."

"Oh, indeed. I quite understand."

And thus, chatting away like a pair of happy magpies, we made our way to the Globe and Anchor. She was prettier than I remembered — or perhaps I should say, *even* prettier. I recalled the full lips, the tilted nose, the curls, and the blue eyes with accuracy. But memory had not done justice to the rest of her — that is to say, to that part below her pretty neck. In particular was I struck by her shapely and abundant bosom. It was quite developed for one of her youth; as I judged her, she could not have been more than a year my senior. I was quite gratified when, somewhere along Pall Mall, she did slip her arm tight into mine in such a way so that my elbow was cushioned quite generously by her. I recall that we were talking of my last, recent visit to the Trezavant residence.

"I was quite disappointed," said she, "when I learned you'd come by and not searched me out."

"Ah well," said I, "I was not there long. I was on my way to a house nearby."

"But you were there long enough to talk to Cook."

"Oh, so I was."

"What in the world would she have to say? She's such a stout old cow — eats too much of her own cooking, she does."

"What did she have to say? Oh, nothing much, really. For the most part, she told me what you had already said."

"What was that?" she inquired with surprising sharpness.

"It had to do with Mr. and Mrs. Trezavant, their rows, and all the rest. It seems that she grew up in the house that your Mrs. T. did, and wanted me to know all about her and her father and this matter of money between her and Mr. Trezavant."

"Oh, well, I told you all about that," said she rather airily.

"That's as I said."

"Yes, so you did. Sorry."

(I realize, reader, that what I told Crocker would be understood as a lie by most. Nevertheless, since I had cautioned Maude Bleeker against telling others her tale of Johnny Skylark, it seemed that the least I could do was follow the advice I myself had given her.)

"And how are your inquiries goin'? Do you expect you'll catch the robbers?"

"Perhaps eventually," said I. "At this point, however, we've not got much information — not near enough, anyway."

"More's the pity," said she.

"But for the time being, I should like to put those matters out of my mind and give my full attention to you—for you deserve it."

"La, sir, you flatter me so! You're such a gallant!"

(I could hardly believe that I should mouth such inanities, reader, but this surely was what Sir John meant by flirting—for it did, after all, seem to be working upon her.)

We walked on. I could not but notice how those whom we passed on Pall Mall walk looked upon us. We must have made a handsome couple, I in my bottle green coat and she—well, I have done my best to describe her. She herself seemed aware of the impression she made. She seemed to walk even more confidently. Her pace picked up as she listened to further extravagancies from me; remembering such now causes me such embarrassment that I prefer to say nothing more of them.

So came we, in any case, to the Globe and Anchor. It was, and no doubt still is, the finest hostelry on the Strand, and its dining room was renowned all over London. During the day—and on Sunday in partic-ular—those from the better parts of Westminster could visit the dining room in couples for coffee and cakes. Yet it was not so well-known then as to be overcrowded so early in the afternoon. We were welcomed and brought swiftly to a table private enough for confidential conversation, yet not so isolated that I might suspect that we had been tucked away out of sight. No, we fitted in as well as any. The coffee and cakes were as good as could be gotten at Lloyd's itself. Jenny Crocker seemed well-pleased by the place and my attentions. She admitted this was her first visit to the Globe and Anchor.

"No," said she, "I never been here before. Though I passed it many times on errands and that. Do you come here often?"

"Well," said I with a shrug, "not often perhaps, though I have been here before." Which was not, strictly speaking, a lie.

In general, I seemed to be succeeding in convincing her that, in spite of my apparent youth, I was a proper gentleman, or as she might have it, a "gallant." Playing that role, I ordered our refreshments and, when they came, listened as she cooed and giggled with excitement describ-ing the effect of the coffee upon her; she showed her appreciation of the Globe and Anchor's cakes by eating more of them in five minutes' time than I could have done in an hour. The burden of maintaining our conversation was upon me. I might have continued bestowing praise upon her, yet in truth, I could think of no more to give. With her silently chewing, the moment seemed ripe for me to introduce the subject for which I had been preparing her. However, just as I was about to do so, she said something through her mouthful of cake, which I understood so ill that I asked her to repeat it.

"Do you—" said she, then laboriously swallowed the last bit of cake in her mouth, "do you think you might sometime leave your line of work?"

The question took me so completely unaware that I burst out laughing. "Why? What's wrong with the work I do?"

"Well, there's ways of makin' more money, ain't there?"

"I suppose so."

"You're sort of a constable, right? Or kind of an assistant magistrate?"

"That's right, but now that you mentioned it, I am studying to be a barrister. That may pay more, depending on how well I do."

"But it's still the law, ain't it?"

"Certainly it is. What's wrong with the law?"

"Oh, nothing, I suppose, though you'll not get rich."

She did then go into a sulk. She fell silent and thrust out her lower lip until she discovered how difficult it was to chew with a drooping lip. I decided that now was the time to bring up the matter I had been about to broach a few moments before, though I had not yet thought of the proper angle of approach. That being the case, I decided to meet it head-on.

"Arthur died last night," said I.

Her response to the news was much stronger than I should ever have expected. Tears formed in the corners of her eyes. Her chin trembled. I whipped out my kerchief, which was fair unused and handed it to her. She dabbed and blew almost noiselessly into it.

"He was a *dear* man, old Arthur was."

"I was with him at the time."

"You was—er, were? Did he say anythin' before he passed on?"

"Yes, he did," said I. "He said your name."

"*My* name?"

This time the tears did indeed fall; they simply brimmed over and coursed down her pretty cheeks in a great flood. She wiped at them but could do little to stanch their flow. Blowing her nose seemed to help. Indeed, she seemed to be gaining control of herself—that is, until I made a fundamental error.

"And when he said your name," I added, "the pleasantest, happiest smile you could imagine appeared upon his face."

With that, she seemed to lose control completely. She threw her head back and let out a tortured wail which seemed to ring through the room. Then more tears, more sniffling, more blowing. Those at the table nearest us looked at us rather disapprovingly. The server came and asked rather pointedly if there were anything he could do. I took that as a hint that he would be happy to see us depart. Flustered and intimidated, I told him we were just leaving and threw three shillings down upon the table, overpaying shamefully. I had Mistress Crocker up and on her feet, then out the door in a trice. Out in the Strand, she managed to calm herself quickly enough. One last great blow was followed by a few dabs at her eyes with a dry corner of the kerchief. She offered it back to me, and I urged her to keep it lest she have need again. She assured me she would not and insisted I accept it. With a shrug, I took the kerchief. Clearly, I had put aside the role of the gallant.

We walked along in silence for quite some distance. I noted those we met did now look upon us quite differently. If they noticed us at all, they seemed only to glance at us in a manner that conveyed a certain patronizing attitude, then did they look swiftly beyond us. We left Pall Mall and wandered a bit in St. James Park. To me, at least, Mistress Crocker seemed to have recovered completely from her attack of lachrymosity: She walked with a quicker step and even ventured a smile at me. I thought it possible at last to proceed.

"Mistress Crocker . . . Jenny, I was wondering if you could account for this."

"How do you mean?" she asked, looking up at me quite innocently.

"How indeed. Well, I was referring to the fact that your name was his last utterance, and it was said with a smile. Why was that? What was your relationship to him?"

"Oh, I had a very good relationship with good ol' Arthur." She said it in such a way that she implied a good deal more than she had actually said.

"Really," said I, "can't you be more specific?"

"Well, I suppose it's all right to talk about it, Arthur bein' dead and all, but I must say it *is* a bit embarrassin' to me."

I said nothing, but simply waited for her to continue, a device I had seen Sir John use countless times. Silence, he had said, can be a powerful weapon in the hands of the interrogator.

She had stopped in one of the paths which ran through the park. This one ran parallel to Pall Mall and afforded some degree of privacy in that we could see if others approached. She looked up the path and down and, satisfied that there were no listeners about, began her explanation.

"I noticed, Mr. Proctor," said she, "that you look often at my bosom."

I was quite taken aback. Had I stared? Had my attention been so obvious? "Why . . . why, no . . . er, well," I stammered, "perhaps once or twice. I—"

"Oh, think nothin' of it," said she, dismissing my chagrin with a wave of her hand. "It pleasures you so, and that pleasures me. It seems perfec'ly natural that it should. My point is, you see, that Arthur liked them, too. Oh, didn't he though! Many's the time I caught him starin' at my bubs, and one time when I was tryin' to get some time off so's I might visit m'mum, I caught him glancin' down as you was doin', and I said to him, 'Arthur, I see you keep lookin' at my bubs. If you'll give me the time off I want, I'll give you a real good look at them.' So he thinks that over, and he gives me a nod, and he says, 'Done!' And I unbuttoned and showed him right then and there.

"So it became a kind of game with us, it did," said she, continuing. "Whenever I wanted somethin' extra out of good ol' Arthur, I'd let him have a look. But him being a man, it wasn't long till he wanted to touch what he saw. Ah, but I wouldn't allow that—not unless it was something *very* special I wanted, like St. Stephen's Day off as well as Christmas. But that wasn't often, and Arthur was always a gentleman about it."

I was simply speechless. This was no questioner's device to get her to tell more. On the contrary, I thought she had told me quite enough. I was amazed she had told me so much.

She looked at me, studied my face, and came to quite a reasonable conclusion: "I ain't shocked you, have I?"

I denied it, of course. "Why, no, of course not." Yet I'm sure I did not convince her.

Indeed not, for she went on then to justify herself: "Well, if you are, you shouldn't be, for I've heard it that there's a good many places in this world where the women don't wear nothin' at all up there on top. Arthur told me so himself."

I had not only heard from her a great deal about herself, she had also told me more than I would ever have dreamed about Arthur Robb. He had never been more to me than the friendliest—certainly the gentlest—of all the butlers with whom I came in contact on my usual rounds about the city delivering letters and messages for Sir John. I thought some comment upon Arthur might be appropriate, and I believed I was sufficiently recovered from the surprise she had given me to make it.

"Uh, well, I daresay Arthur was a far livelier fellow than I had realized," said I. "A soldier he was, and a . . . a—"

"Ah, he was lively, all right," she broke in, rescuing me. "He had a great sense of fun, he did."

"And how did he demonstrate it?" I had not noticed that in him.

"He was a great tickler, for one thing. Oh, Gawd, the man was merciless! All he need to do was come at me or the kitchen slaveys with his fingers out like he meant to tickle us and we would laugh and giggle and he ain't even touched us yet. And just let the master and his missus be out the house of an evening, and he'd be sneakin' about, tryin' to creep up behind us to tickle us near to death. Oh, he was a fright, he was." Fittingly, she ended her recollection with a giggle.

We began walking once more and soon found our way back to Pall Mall, and from there thence to St. James Street and Little Jermyn Street. We talked little on our way back to the Trezavant residence, for most of what might be said had been said. But not quite all.

"I understand that your master and his mistress will be returning this evening or tomorrow morning at the latest."

"So I hear," said Jenny Crocker. "The new butler got word today."

"Then Mr. Trezavant must have sent it off as soon as he arrived. Does that mean he patched things up immediately?"

"Not likely," said she. "It probably means they called a truce, and she's coming back to count up all that the robbers took."

I laughed at that, though I should not have. Mr. Trezavant had caused far too much mischief in the last few days to be considered in any way amusing.

"I have one last question, Mistress Crocker," said I to her as we entered Little Jermyn Street with our destination in view.

"And what is that?"

"Where were you when that band of robbers entered by the front door?"

"I was talkin' with Cook, which I'd been doin' for half an hour or more. You can ask her yourself, and she'll tell you the same."

That satisfied me. I might indeed ask for confirmation from Mistress Bleeker, but Crocker would not lie when she could be found out so easily.

"This was all just to find out if I was the woman told poor Arthur the tale and got him to open the door, wasn't it?" She put it to me as a sort of challenge.

"Why, no, I—"

She interrupted me: "Because if it was, you'd no need. You could of asked me the other night, and I would of told you the same."

"I know, but then I—"

"But then you'd not heard old Arthur speak my name, had you?" she said, speaking over my words. She sighed. "Well, I'm grateful you told me. That I could of given that good ol' fella such pleasure just rememberin' me whilst he was dyin' is something I'll remember till my own dyin' day."

We had arrived at the Trezavant residence, and I was more than happy for it. I had hoped for a casual parting and was quite unprepared for this. I'd no idea what to say to her. It seemed, however, that I need say nothing, for she had not stopped talking.

"Thank you for the coffee and cakes. It was a nice place you took me, though I doubt I shall ever return there. I'm sorry if I gave you some embarrassment when we left."

With that, she thrust her hand out at me with such speed and force that I thought at first she meant to hit me. But no, she wished me to shake it; that I did, rather limply, I fear. It was a gesture, on her part, of finality. She turned and marched up the few stairs to the door. She beat upon it with her fist, rather than use the knocker. I turned and left her there.

In my confusion I turned toward St. James Street, which took me a bit out of my way. It was not until I reached it that I turned and looked back the way I had come. I saw that she was no longer there before the door and assumed that she had been let in. Turning down St. James, I walked, head down, my thought fixed upon where and how I had done wrong. Indeed, it was certain that I had done wrong—I had no need to be told by Sir John nor any other.

So completely was my mind fixed upon what had transpired during the past hour and a half that I failed to hear the racket behind me until the crowd was quite close. When I did, I turned, looked, and saw them moving swiftly toward me. Running they were, a dozen or more men and a few women trailing well behind. All were in pursuit of one poor individual who was hard-pressed to keep ahead of them. They shouted after him, waved sticks, their fists, a horsewhip, whatever they might have handy. Why would they be after him? What could he have done?

Then, as the victim of this wild pursuit came closer, I saw he was a black man, and in another instant I recognized him. It was Frank Barber, Samuel Johnson's young fellow, whom I had met but days before. I must act, I told myself—and do what I could to help him.

"Frank," I shouted. "Frank! Frank! *Frank!*"

He turned. He saw me, and in a moment more he recognized me, beckoning to him. But what could he do? If he were to slow down to discover what I could do to help, the mob would catch him up and perhaps tear him apart. And so, I decided, I would come to him. I ran out into the street to head him off; and while I failed to do that, I was able to run alongside, matching him stride for stride—in spite of the heavy weight I carried in each pocket. Only then, as I ran beside Frank, did I realize what it was I was carrying in the capacious pockets of my bottle green coat. What indeed, but the two pistols entrusted to me by Mr. Baker the evening before. I had returned too late from my night at St. Bart's to return them to him this morning, and I had been loath to leave loaded pistols in my attic room, so I had simply shoved them in my pockets, where they now bounced dangerously. I shoved my hands down into my pockets to steady them, and as I did I took a look to the rear and noticed that our pursuers had fallen somewhat behind us—yet they came on steadily, and I was not sure that Frank would last much longer at the pace he had set for himself.

I pulled out the pistol from my right pocket and pointed the way with it to one side of the street. Perhaps Frank thought I was threatening him, for his eyes widened at the sight of the pistol. In any case, he did as I wished him to, running to one side of the street with me and taking a place on the walkway before one of the grand houses. We took our place before a sturdy, iron-barred fence. My original plan had been to seek shelter at Mr. Bilbo's, but Frank was already past it when I joined him running from the mob; I had a sort of plan, and it would work as well here as anyplace else in St. James Street.

The leaders of the mob (if, indeed, there were any leaders) were disturbed by this development—so unexpected was it—that they slowed of a sudden and stopped. They saw the pistol in my hand and liked it not.

"Frank Barber, get behind me. Put your back to the fence, and remain there, no matter what."

He did as I told him. His breathing was tortured. Could he speak with me?

"How long have they been chasing you?" I asked him.

"From ... St. James's Square ... all the way." His words were punctuated by panting gasps for air.

"But why? What did you do?"

"I did ... nothing ... *nothing!* ... I delivered ... a letter ... to a ... house in the ... square."

Though I was not then satisfied with Frank's answer, I soon found that he told naught but the truth.

His pursuers moved forward stealthily as if they hoped that by gradual encroachment they might overwhelm us without our having noticed.

"That's far enough."

I yelled at two of them who were shuffling ahead of the rest as a kind of advance guard; they were slender, wiry chaps, not much older than I, and each carried sticks thick enough to be called clubs, which they attempted to conceal behind them. They were no more than twelve or fifteen feet away.

"I said, that's far enough."

And to convince them forcefully, I leveled the pistol and aimed at a point above—though not too far above—their heads. I pulled back the hammer and then the trigger and thanked God and Mr. Baker for the answering report—something between a *crack* and a *boom*.

The effect was immediate and was just as I had expected: The two scrambled back to the shelter of the mob behind them; in his haste, one fell to the cobblestones, losing his stick as he fell, but he made it back before his partner. The entire mob, men and a few women, shifted back a good five feet. Through it all there was shouting and yelling, warnings and recriminations. Yet they did not scatter as I'd hoped they might.

The two I had sent into a wild retreat turned round and began haranguing those behind them.

"Here, now," shouted one, "he hadn't got but one ball in that pistol, and now he's fired it off."

"Come, let's grab that black boy!"

Each took a step—no more—toward us. I let them come no closer. Pulling out the second pistol somewhat ostentatiously, I aimed it without cocking it at the nearest of them.

"I'll kill the first of you who comes close." I said it loudly and most confidently; I half-believed it myself.

Again they fell back. Yet still the mob showed no signs of dispersing. Somewhat to the contrary, a crowd of onlookers had gathered on the other side of the street. They seemed neutral in their sympathies, but rather amused and entertained by what had happened thus far. Laughing and pointing they were, altogether indifferent as to whether I, or Frank Barber, or one of the mob were killed, so long as it were done in a sufficiently diverting manner.

Then was I surprised when one of those well behind the first row of Frank's pursuers came forward, a man of near forty he was, stout of figure and dignified in his bearing; he seemed not to belong with the rest of them at all. He waved his hand at me, as one might at school, to get the teacher's attention.

"May I speak?"

I aimed the pistol at him.

"You may."

"I believe you misjudge our intentions," said he. "We are here to see justice done. That blackie you are protecting is one of that gang of thieves that's been robbing the homes of the gentry and the nobles hereabouts. We who are here are in service to houses in St. James

Square. We saw this black fellow who stands behind you now lurking about the houses there, and he was recognized as one of the thieves."

"Recognized by whom?"

"That matters little. He is the right color, and we all agreed that he is one of them. Our intention is to bring him to justice."

"Well, you are all most fortunate," said I, "for I am an assistant to Sir John Fielding, magistrate of the Bow Street Court, and if you are correct, then Sir John will certainly wish to question him. And so I shall take charge of him. You have my thanks for bringing him to me."

"But—"

"And now," said I, interrupting, refusing to be intimidated by this pompous individual (who was surely a butler), "I must now command all of you to leave, disperse, and be gone." Is this what Sir John would have said? Something sterner perhaps in final rebuke: "You have together created a mob, and mob action will not be tolerated in the city of Westminster." There, I thought, that should do it.

And it might have, for those who constituted the mob began talking uncertainly amongst themselves, one or two began drifting away, and their well-appointed spokesman seemed, for the moment at least, at a loss for words. But just at that decisive moment, a big woman pushed through from the rear to the very front. She was indeed large in every way—tall, broad, and weighty—and biggest of all was her mouth.

"What's the matter with all of you?" she shouted out at her companions. "Are you goin'ta let this young pint of piss turn you round and send you back home? How do we know he's from Bow Street, like he says he is? I daresay his intention may be to take this nigger round the corner and turn him loose with a pat on his black arse. No, by Gawd, we'll make an example of that African like we started out to do. Follow me! He'll not dare to shoot a woman."

(Alas, reader, she had correctly perceived the limits of my ruthless intentions. Indeed, I would not, could not, shoot a woman. Perhaps I might shoot to wound a man—in fact, had done so—but I had never shot to kill anyone and dearly hoped I never would. As may have been plain to you, I was bluffing—playing brag with the mob.)

She turned back to me, anger and contempt writ upon her face. What could I do? Threaten her with an even graver warning? What could I *do*?

But as she started toward me, help came from a most unexpected source. Who should come bursting through the crowd of onlookers but Constable Patley? He ran forward, halting the woman, not so much in fear as in astonishment. Bending, he grabbed up the stick-club dropped by one of the two bold lads who had first challenged me. Without a word, he went directly to her and gave her a sharp thwack on her backside.

The audience on the far side of the street, gallants and their ladies, made great merriment of this, laughing lustily as they might at some jolly street fair.

"The lad is what he says he is," said Mr. Patley, "and I am a Bow Street constable. If all of you do as he says and disperse, leaving this place as quick as ever you can, then you'll have no more trouble from us. But if you stay, I'll knock you down one by one." And then he spoke direct to the big woman whom he had insulted with his stick: "And you, you foul-mouthed slut, I'll bring you in for inciting to riot. Have I made myself clear?"

There then issued from her a great stream of obscenity and profanity such as I had not heard in one dose in any of the lowest dives in Bedford Street. But reluctantly, grudgingly, she turned round, as did all the rest of the mob, and trailed out in the general direction of the square.

The audience did truly applaud, which amazed me, though it seemed altogether in keeping with the attitude of those pleasure-seekers from Pall Mall. Moreover, Mr. Patley bowed in response, which amazed me more.

"Jeremy," came the voice behind me. "Could you let me out, please? I am quite squashed here between you and the iron fence."

"Good God," said I, stepping quickly away. "Frank! Do forgive me! I'd completely forgotten."

"I rather thought you had," said Frank somewhat dryly. "Must I now go with you to be questioned by Sir John?" He looked at me rather dubiously.

"Oh, perhaps it might be best, since that is what I told them. You should, in any case, give him your account of what happened—the mob chasing you and all. Credit Constable Patley for saving us both. I must thank him myself."

Then did I look about me. The street had emptied quickly. There were but four or five scattered here and there, and Mr. Patley was not among them. He had simply disappeared—yet he could not have gone far. Where were we in St. James Street? The Bilbo house was not far, nor for that matter was Lord Lilley's; but closer, and between the two, stood the Zondervan mansion. Could he have gone in there? Who might he know inside? Could I ask him? Would he tell me?

I sighed. "Well, come along, Frank. Mr. Johnson will be wondering what's become of you."

SEVEN

*In which Sir John
begins interrogating
Mr. Burnham*

✦

Though he had done with his Magistrate's Court a couple of hours
before, Sir John was still up and about when I arrived with Frank Barber at Number 4 Bow Street. For the most part, Frank had been rather
quiet during our walk back; therefore was I mildly surprised when,
upon entering the "backstage area" of the Bow Street Court (strongroom, clerk's alcove, magistrate's chambers, et cetera), he became of a
sudden quite loquacious in Sir John's presence. He did not wait for me
to introduce him or present him, but rather went right to where the
magistrate stood conversing with Mr. Marsden, and offered himself as
an old friend.

"Sir John," said he, "it is I, Francis Barber. We met on a number of
occasions when I was much younger at the home of Mr. Johnson in
Gough Square. That was before I was sent off for schooling, from
which I have lately returned."

He offered his hand to Sir John—nay, more than offered, for he
thrust it at him, grasped the magistrate's own, and shook it vigorously.

"Ah yes," said Sir John, "I believe I recall you now. What brings
you here, young man? Have you a letter for me from Mr. Johnson?"

"No sir, as it happens, I do not. Yet, curiously enough, it was in a
way a letter from Mr. Johnson, one which I delivered to a house in St.
James Square, that brings me to you now."

Wherewith Frank Barber told his tale, much of which I heard for
the first time. He had, it seemed, done no more than deliver the letter to
a Sir Edward Talcott, resident of the square, when a crowd gathered

round him. Those in the crowd demanded to know what he did there, yet would not listen to his response. Instead they accused him of being one of that gang of robbers that had been raiding the grand houses thereabouts, and would not listen to his vigorous denials. They, it seemed, were household staff members in various residences around the square. As they pushed poor Frank about, threatening him, buffeting him, he saw that what had been a crowd was now a mob. They meant to harm him (he saw a horsewhip in the hands of one of them), perhaps kill him (another brandished a length of rope), and so, seeing an opportunity to break loose from them, he took it. He ran fast as ever he could, leading them once around the square and out of it, into St. James Street.

"And there," said he, "I managed, with the help of your assistant Jeremy Proctor, to elude them completely."

With that he concluded, quite astonishing me and frustrating me, as well. Was that all there was to it? Had I not stood off a dozen (fifteen? twenty?) with a single pistol? Had I not protected him with my very body? And what about Mr. Patley? Had he not demonstrated rare courage by intimidating the mob armed only with a stick? Had he not saved both Frank and me?

I opened my mouth, thinking to correct Frank's version; then almost immediately I shut it. For as I looked at Frank and noted the innocent expression on his face, I realized that he truly believed that this was how it had happened: He had done all with but a bit of help from me. There was naught for me to say which would not sound self-serving. Even to describe Mr. Patley's part in it—his dramatic entrance, et cetera—required first a description of the calamitous situation in which I found myself. And so, reader, I said nothing.

Yet Sir John, having heard all, must have suspected that something was amiss, for he said to Frank, "Tell me, young sir, how did you manage to elude the mob once you were in St. James Street?"

"Ah well," said he, "that was rather a complicated matter. No doubt Jeremy could explain it better." Though he sounded assured and confident in his manner of speech, the look in his eyes was uncertain, almost fearful.

"Jeremy?"

"If it's exactitude you seek, sir, it may take a while to work it out."

"Later, perhaps."

"If you don't mind."

Then did Sir John return to Frank Barber. "And how did those in this crowd, which became a mob, come to suspect you to be one of the robbers?"

"Why, it was a matter of color, sir. As I understand it, this gang of thieves present themselves as Africans."

"You doubt that they are?"

"I am not convinced of it." There was, in his manner of speech as he spoke these words, something almost arrogant. It was as if he were putting the burden of proof upon Sir John.

"Leaving that aside, you *are* convinced that it was only because of your color that you were abused and pursued by the mob?"

"Well . . ." He hesitated. "There may have been something else. There was something I said did not please them well."

"And what was that?"

He cleared his throat, took a deep breath, and plunged ahead. "When one of them, I forget which, referred to me as an African, I told them that I was no African but as much an Englishman as any one of them."

"Indeed that might not sit well with them," said Sir John dryly.

"They grew angry at that. And when I asked them which of them had served in the Royal Navy, as I had, they grew angrier."

In spite of himself, Sir John fell to chuckling at that. "My service in the Royal Navy never won me much respect."

The two might have gone on in this way for quite some time, for they had begun to warm one to the other. But then the door to Bow Street opened, and in came a surprise. It was Robert Burnham in the company of Mr. Fuller. I knew that as the day man and jailer, Mr. Fuller was the only constable Sir John had at his disposal, and so he was sent out from time to time to bring in prisoners, or those wanted for interrogation who might resist or come only reluctantly. It seemed, oddly, that one or the other might be the case in this instance, for while Mr. Burnham was not in chains, Constable Fuller did indeed have a firm grip upon his arm. And Fuller wore, as he always did, a brace of pistols.

"Mr. Fuller, is that you?"

"It is, sir," came the response.

"You have Mr. Burnham with you, I can tell. Did he give you any difficulty?"

"A bit. He was about to ride off somewheres, and I had to convince him that talking with you was more important than going for a ride of a Sunday."

"Nothing violent, I hope."

"Nossir, I just had to speak to him right sharp, is all."

"Mr. Burnham?" It was the first time he had addressed him directly.

"Yes, Sir John?"

"Is Mr. Fuller accurate in what he says? You were not hurt, or treated roughly? And you came, more or less, of your own volition?"

"I'm here. I'm not hurt. I'm not in chains."

"Good. Then you'll be in good fettle for a little tête-à-tête."

I happened just then to glance at Frank Barber, who stood quite close to me. The look of shocked astonishment upon his face was quite striking, for it expressed something personal—disappointment so profound that it was as if he were looking upon his fallen captain. I had not known, nor had I any reason to suspect, that Frank and Mr. Burnham were even acquainted, but obviously they were.

"Mr. Fuller, I must ask you to place Mr. Burnham in the strongroom while you and I talk briefly."

"Gladly, Sir John."

If Mr. Fuller was thus pleased by this, Mr. Burnham certainly was not. He did not physically resist, but his eyes shouted a loud protest as the great key was turned in the lock.

"Jeremy!" Sir John, who stood in the doorway to his chambers, called back to me. "I should like you in here, too."

As I trailed Mr. Fuller to where Sir John waited, I wondered at Mr. Burnham's status. If he were a prisoner, he was certainly being treated with deference by the magistrate. And if he had been brought in merely to be questioned further, then why was it necessary to lock him in the strongroom?

I glanced back at that wooden-barred cage as I entered Sir John's chambers and saw Frank already deep in whispered conversation with Mr. Burnham.

"Come along, Jeremy."

"Yes sir," said I, and took my usual place in the chair opposite Sir John with his desk between us. Mr. Fuller preferred to remain on his feet. He stood a space away, wearing his usual frown, his arms folded across his chest.

"I really haven't much to say," declared Sir John in a low voice, "but I wish to create the impression in Mr. Burnham's mind that we have a good deal of new information to discuss, so we need not hurry through this. If you have any questions, by all means ask them. If you have anything to add, by all means add it. You first, Mr. Fuller. Tell us, if you will, just what transpired when you visited the Bilbo residence and collected Mr. Burnham."

Constable Fuller utterly lacked all power of abridgement. His tendency in making any sort of report ran exactly counter to that of tight-lipped Constable Brede. Where details had to be drawn out of Mr. Brede, they flowed endlessly abounding from Mr. Fuller. While this suited Sir John well, particularly in the circumstances he described, it might indeed try the reader's patience if I were to attempt a literal copy of the constable's remarks. To put it another way: Since he refused to abridge, I feel obliged to do so in what follows.

Mr. Fuller had been shown through the house by Jimmie Bunkins, for whom the constable has a special dislike stemming from Bunkins's days as a young thief. He was fairly certain that an alarum was passed on to Mr. Burnham, who vacated the house while it was searched. What neither Bunkins, nor any of the rest expected, however, was that Fuller would have some knowledge of the place (given him by Constable Bailey, chief of the Bow Street Runners) — enough to know where the stable was located and how to reach it. He sought it out on his own, and found Mr. Burnham trying to saddle the mare without the aid of the stable boy, who happened to be visiting home that day. Burnham had it near done by the time the constable arrived, so that he made a brave attempt to mount the horse and ride out of the stable. But alas, because he was seldom called upon to saddle his own horse, he hadn't pulled the saddle-girth quite tight enough, and in the act of mounting, saddle and all came down upon him as he fell upon his backside. Though Mr. Fuller helped him to his feet, he was unkind enough to laugh at him as he did it. This provoked an angry exchange between the two men: Mr. Burnham demanded that the constable help him saddle up again, and was told that he had no need to do so, for he was going to Number 4 Bow Street to see Sir John Fielding. Mr. Burnham then said that he was far more eager to see what awaited him at the end of the ride than he ever would be to see Sir John. And on and on they went, the matter between them never resolved, until Mr. Fuller simply ordered Mr. Burnham to return the horse to her stall and come along with him to Bow Street. He emphasized his directive by toying with the grip of one of the pistols he wore, though he swore that he never actually took it from his holster. Without further ado, the horse was tended to, and the two men set off together to see the magistrate.

To tell that story to Sir John—complete with details and digressive excursions—took near ten minutes. Even Sir John, who had an apparently inexhaustible hunger for minutiae of every sort, was a bit overwhelmed by this, so that when he turned to me, he had but a question to be answered.

"Jeremy," said he, "what precisely was it that the stable boy told you with regard to the frequency of these trips? Was it every Sunday that Mr. Burnham rode out to this secret destination?"

I thought back that I might be precise in my response. "What he said, sir, was two or three times a week, four at the most, but always on Sunday."

"Hmmm," said Sir John, giving the matter some consideration, "that is rather a lot, isn't it? Did he say how long this had been going on?"

"Not in so many words, no, but the implication seemed to be that it was quite a long time—months, I should think. After all, when you say '*always* on Sunday' . . ."

"Well, yes, I see your point." He quietened down for a good long time, giving himself completely to thought. At last, he said, "A *woman*! That is it. That must be it. He is paying court to a woman some distance away. But how can we know who she is unless he tells us?"

We pondered that between us. Perhaps Mr. Fuller may even have given it a thought or two, but in the end there was naught said and no suggestion made. Sir John was, I believe, ready to adjourn our meeting when I decided to seek from him the answer to the question that had earlier troubled me.

"Sir," said I, "can you tell me, what is the legal status of Mr. Burnham? Is he a prisoner? Is he here for questioning?"

He smiled rather crookedly at that. "Well you might wonder, Jeremy. You'll find his status defined in no law book I know of. Let me say that as it stands now, there are but two matters against him. The first is the accusation made by Mr. Trezavant. Ordinarily, it would not in itself be sufficient to send him to the gallows, for we know that at the time he was visited by the robbers, the man was drunk. *Nevertheless*, Mr. Trezavant is the coroner of the city of Westminster, and his testimony as a witness cannot simply be dismissed; it is not good for the magistrate and the coroner to be at odds. Furthermore, he received his appointment as coroner because he is friend to the prime minister, and it is not good for the London magistrate and the prime minister to be at odds.

"But sir," said I, emboldened by my relation to him as scholar to teacher, "would you not say that those are political considerations, rather than legal?"

"Of course they are," said he, "but like it or not, Jeremy, much of life is determined by just such political considerations—as you will learn, my boy, as you will learn."

"Yes sir," said I, somewhat chastened. "Then I take it that Mr. Burnham is a prisoner."

"No, not quite, for putting aside the politics of the situation, there really isn't a strong case against him. But still, he must answer the charge made against him, and he must answer it with a verifiable alibi. So far he has refused to do that, for you found that he had lied with regard to his whereabouts on the nights in question. He cannot simply refuse to respond or lie, as he has done—and that, to return to what I said in the beginning, is the second matter against him. He must be made to treat this matter seriously, or I shall have to bind him for criminal trial in Old Bailey, and with the Somerset case now before the Lord Chief Justice, it is not a good time for any black man to present himself for trial.

"Now, as to Mr. Burnham's present situation," continued Sir John, "I would put it that he is here for interrogation, but we shall do all we can to create the notion that he is already a prisoner. I have instructed Mr. Fuller to dispense with the usual courtesies extended to one who is brought in for questioning. I wish to impress upon him the precariousness of his situation. I shall interrogate him in a most severe manner."

He paused then a good long pause, perhaps pondering what he might say to Mr. Burnham. But, rousing himself, he rose swiftly from his chair and said, "I think we've kept him waiting long enough, don't you? Bring him to me, Mr. Fuller," he said. "And Jeremy, go upstairs and fetch my sling, will you? Mr. Donnelly will soon be here and I do not wish to have him take me to task in this matter of my wound."

Upon leaving Sir John's chambers, I was surprised to see Frank Barber still at the bars of the strongroom, yet they could hardly be said to be conversing. Mr. Burnham was talking at Frank passionately, almost angrily. Though he spoke in tones too low to be understood, I could tell by the set of his body and the look on his face that he was most upset.

"Oh, Jeremy, I'd a word with you, if you don't mind." It was Mr. Fuller, catching me up with a tap upon the shoulder. He was remarkably respectful. I knew not quite what to expect.

"Yes? What is it, Mr. Fuller?"

"To tell the truth, I feel a bit foolish about this, but Mr. Baker mentioned to me that you took my little joke to heart."

"Your little joke?" What he referred to was now so far behind me that I was honestly in confusion as to just what he might be referring to.

"Well . . . I seen you go down to the cellar with that girl who helps out Lady Kate. And just for a joke, I shut the door and locked it." He looked away, obviously embarrassed. That quite astonished me. "Yes, it was me did it, but I meant nothin' by it, just as you might do with one of your mates. But Mr. Baker said you got out right enough."

"That's true," said I, letting the matter pass. "No harm done, though the girl was somewhat upset."

"They get so. Give her my apology. But as you say, 'No harm done.' "

With that, we parted company, and as we did, he offered me a little two-fingered salute, as one might give to a superior. That quite amazed me. Yet before I could consider what it might have meant, a row suddenly broke out between Frank and Mr. Burnham. I did not hear what set them off, but Frank yelled at the other not so much in anger as in a tone of pleading; nevertheless he terminated his discourse with a shout: "Don't be a fool!" Then did he turn and stalk away.

Robert Burnham shouted after him in an angry voice I had not heard from him before, "Do not dare cross me in this, Frank Barber!"

It appeared, however, that Frank had no intention of heeding Mr. Burnham, for he did not turn and look back but went directly out the door to Bow Street. As the door slammed, Mr. Burnham responded by pounding the wooden bars of the strongroom in apparent frustration. By the time I reached the strongroom, Mr. Fuller had gone off to fetch the keys, and I was left alone for a moment with this prisoner (who was not quite a prisoner). He was turned away, his head bowed, and a frown upon his face.

I considered the possibility of simply walking on to the stairs, which in a way I should have preferred. Nevertheless, I felt obliged to show him that my sympathies lay with him. Would it matter to him? Perhaps all he needed was a bit of personal encouragement to push him toward Sir John's purpose.

"Mr. Burnham," I called to him, "how do you now?"

"You see me here as I am, and you can ask such a question?" said he. "I daresay you are not the keen lad I thought you to be."

That stung a bit. Still, I was not to be so easily put off.

"I fear that was a bit callous, sir," said I. "Forgive me. But . . . well, if you will but aid Sir John in his inquiries, then there would be no need for you to remain where you are."

"You, as well? Tell me, did you instruct Frank Barber in his arguments? Or did he you? Of a sudden, all those I counted as friends seem to be against me."

I knew not how to respond to that, and further did I hear Mr. Fuller rattling his keys behind me. There seemed little to do but take my leave.

"I beg you to believe that I am not against you. I wish you only well, sir."

With a nod and a wave of my hand, I left him, nor did I turn to watch when I heard the sound of the key in the lock and the door to the strongroom swinging open. Indeed I made straight for the stairs.

What a strange scene awaited me when I opened the door and entered the kitchen! There sat Annie at the table, her face all but covered by a linen kerchief with which she dabbed at her eyes and into which she honked with her nose. At her knee knelt Clarissa, who murmured words of consolation and comfort. She held Annie's hand in both her own.

As I stepped into the room and closed the door, I felt the eyes of both girls upon me. There could be no doubt that the looks I received from them were of the accusatory sort. I wondered at this, for I could think of naught that I had done to offend either one. I felt a strong impulse to get away as quickly as ever I could. Toward that end, I bobbed my head in greeting and made swiftly for the steps which led to Sir John's bedroom. Thus I hoped to escape whatever trap had been laid for me: Get in and get out quickly, and say as little as possible. But I hesitated at the bottom step. Would Lady Kate be in her bedroom, or . . . ? I decided that I had better ask.

When I put the question to them, I was informed by Clarissa in quite frigid tones that Lady Katherine had been called to the Magdalene Home. Before she could say more, I thanked her and rushed up the stairs and into the bedroom shared by master and mistress, in search of Sir John's sling.

It was, to be honest, an untidy room. Clothes—most of them Lady Kate's—were tossed about on the chairs; a frock hung from the open door of the wardrobe; and the bed was unmade. It was plain that the two in the kitchen, whose duty it was to tend to this room, had so far neglected it. Ah well, it was Sunday; much could be forgiven on a Sunday—though it took a minute or two. I located the makeshift sling that Mr. Donnelly had arranged for Sir John's left arm, the sling which Sir John seldom wore except in the surgeon's presence. I found it hung over the bedpost. With it in hand, I ducked out of the room, careful to close the door behind me, and made my way down to the kitchen. I hoped to get past the two girls before they could engage me in argument, controversy, make accusations, or otherwise impede me on my way back to Sir John.

Vain hope. I had not even reached them at the table when Annie bounded out of her chair and pointed her finger at me. Then, with an angry face and a voice all choked from weeping, she said, "It was *you*, Jeremy!" I stopped. Still she pointed. She was like some storybook witch pronouncing a curse.

"It was I who . . . *what*?" I asked in all innocence.

Clarissa rose to stand beside Annie; I noted that she was near half a head taller. "I think you know very well," said she to me, nodding solemnly.

"I know nothing of the kind," I yelped in frustration. "What is it that you say I've done?"

"It was you led us down Little Jermyn Street so that that horrible fat man might look upon Robert and tell his horrible lies," cried Annie.

"I may have done, but I had no such dark design in mind. I had no design at all!"

"So *you* say," said Clarissa with what seemed suspiciously like a sneer. (Why did she always seem so eager to believe the worst of me?) "Annie swears that your usual route is along Pall Mall, as it is hers."

"Well, there you have the why of it," said I. "I was tired of walking the same old route, bored with it. It's as simple as that."

"It's not simple at all." Annie stamped her foot. "Mr. Burnham may die because you were bored with it."

Then I spoke out stupidly in exasperation: "Well, if he dies, it will be his own fault. It will be a form of self-murder, suicide, if you will."

"Jeremy!" Clarissa squawked, "How can you say such a thing?"

For a moment I wondered at that, too. Nevertheless, I attempted to justify myself: "I say that because he has only to tell Sir John where he was on the night in question to be free of suspicion."

"He has told where he was. Why will you not believe him?"

"Because," said I, "he lied."

"How can you say that?" Annie demanded.

"Because I caught him in the lie."

"So it is your word against his?" said Clarissa. "You wish to see him convicted so that you may shine in Sir John's eyes as having closed this case by yourself. Is that it?"

"No!" I shouted. "I wish him only to tell the truth, as Sir John does. We support him. Yet unless he tells the truth, he will convict himself. And that, to me, is a form of suicide."

Annie raised her hand most dramatically. Then did she speak out in a manner equally dramatic: "That matters naught to me," said she. "I care not that he has lied. It would matter not to me if it were proved that he had truly robbed that disgusting fat man. All that matters to me is my love for him."

Oh dear, thought I, this is sure to be difficult. "If all you suggest were true, he will be convicted," said I, trying to reason with her. "But . . . but . . . well, if he is, Sir John would certainly recommend transportation. The judges usually follow his recommendations in such circumstances."

"Then I shall follow him wherever he is sent—just to be near him." She walked slowly to the steps which led upstairs; to her room, presumably.

"And if—though there is little chance of it—if he is sentenced to death?"

"Then I shall join him in death. I cannot live without him." She started slowly up the steps—a tragic heroine. Or perhaps Ophelia—she was acting a bit mad, or so it seemed to me. As she disappeared, I turned to Clarissa with a look that must have expressed the bewilderment I felt.

Clarissa, for her part, had a tear glistening in each eye. "Did you hear her?" she asked. "Was that not the most beautiful, the most romantic speech ever anyone did speak?"

I sighed. "Yes," said I—for how could I say what I truly thought? "I suppose so." And with that, a deep sigh did escape from me.

I fled the kitchen before Clarissa could comment further, descending the stairs three at a time, and jumping to a halt when I reached the ground floor. I looked about and saw that the strongroom was empty and that Mr. Fuller was nowhere in sight. This meant that Sir John was questioning Mr. Burnham as he might a common criminal—that is, with a guard present. I approached his chambers quietly—yet I needn't have, for Sir John's voice, seldom truly soft, seemed to thunder forth from the room at the end of the hall. I doubt that any of the three men present there could have heard my step had I stamped my feet the entire distance. Yet I did not wish to be heard. I took a place on the bench outside the open door.

It was, after all, Sir John's purpose to intimidate Mr. Burnham, to break down his resistance, to reduce him—if possible—to a quivering mass of porridge. I had heard and seen him do as much to many a footpad and cutthroat. Villains who would fight to the death when cornered would, under his relentless badgering, simply crumble completely; a few of the worst had even burst into tears. I fully expected Sir John to work the same sort of destructive transformation upon Robert Burnham; the only difference I anticipated was that rather than a confession, in this instance, an alibi was sought. I pitied the victim in advance. My regard for Mr. Burnham was such that I had no wish to be physically present at his humiliation; my curiosity, however, forced me to listen.

To my surprise, however, the tutor was made of stronger stuff than ever I had expected. Sir John's usual mode, in situations of this sort, was to begin in a reasonably friendly manner and gradually to grow sterner and more severe, to feign anger, and finally, to rage forth in accusation and demand the truth. Far more often than not, it was given him. Because of my delay upstairs with Annie and Clarissa, I seemed to have missed his opening, for by the time I arrived, he had moved into the second, more severe, phase. Sitting on the bench with no view through the door, I could well imagine his glowering countenance as he asked: "When did you learn to ride?" "Do you enjoy it?" "Have you continued riding while here in London?" "You say you go out 'occasionally,' but surely two or three times a week and *always* on Sunday would be described as more frequent than 'occasionally,' would it not?"

Mr. Burnham had been rather forthcoming up to that point, but when Sir John asked to know where he went on "these occasional rides which took place three, even four times a week and *always* on Sunday," he was answered with absolute silence. "Who do you see?" Silence. "What is the purpose of these rides?" Silence.

Then did Sir John take it upon himself to explain in quite reasonable terms why it was in Mr. Burnham's own interest to answer these questions in order that he might establish an alibi for himself to counter the accusation put against him by Mr. Trezavant.

"You see," said he to him, "we know that your tale of remaining at home that night and running about the house to read bits and pieces of Mr. Goldsmith's book to all who would listen was simply a fabrication got up quickly to satisfy us. You insult us with such poppycock, sir, for you see, we *know* that you went out riding in the late afternoon and did not return until near midnight. That was how you spent the evening in question, was it not? A long ride to some undisclosed location, to visit some undisclosed person for some undisclosed reason. You see, sir, why you must tell us what we wish to know? Without the missing facts, it all sounds a bit like a child's tale, does it not? Tell us what we wish to know, Mr. Burnham. Your very life may—"

Here Sir John had broken off, for he heard the door to Bow Street slam shut and footsteps begin in the hall.

"Uh, that will be all for the time being, sir," said he. "Mr. Fuller, return him to the strongroom, if you will."

"You wish me to persuade him my way?" the jailer asked.

"No, it's a bit early for that. I'm sure he will cooperate before extreme measure need be taken. Jeremy? Are you here? Come in and help me get into that thing, will you?"

It was a long walk from the street door to Sir John's chambers—and a good thing, too, for I had no sooner managed to guide his arm into the sling and get it over his head than did the familiar figure of Mr. Donnelly appear in the doorway, a smile upon his face and his bag in his hand. "Well, Sir John, Jeremy," said he, "I congratulate you. You just did manage to get the thing on, did you not?"

Mr. Gabriel Donnelly's visit to change the dressing was short and unmemorable, except for a warning he issued to Sir John. "Let me tell you, sir," said he, "that if you do not take the wearing of that sling seriously, then that arm will bother you for the rest of your life. There can be no doubt of it." Though Sir John dismissed the notion with a wave of his hand, Mr. Donnelly's words proved prophetic.

When the surgeon had departed, I expected Sir John to send me to Mr. Fuller that he might bring back the prisoner. In fact, I went so far as to suggest it to Sir John. He considered the matter for a moment, then shook his head in the negative, a dour expression upon his face.

"No, I think not," said he. "I've explained his situation to him. And while he showed no willingness to respond to my questions in any substantial way, I think perhaps after he has spent the night in the strong-room, in the company of whatever the night may bring, he may be a bit more talkative."

"But Sir John," said I, "what was this matter that passed between you and Mr. Fuller about 'extreme measure'? Surely you're not—"

"Going to torture Mr. Burnham? No, I daresay we are not. We thought only to put the possibility in his mind. That should give him something to think about, eh?" He pondered the situation further. "No, I believe that what I should most like from you, Jeremy, is a report upon what happened to you in the area of St. James today."

And so I told him, deleting most of what passed between Crocker and me, saying simply that the outing yielded nothing. He responded with a shrug. I told him, however, that I had learned the significance of Mr. Robb's mention of the King's Carabineers."

"Oh? What was that?"

"Well, I found out, to my surprise, that Arthur Robb had served with the regiment some time before."

"Truly? A butler who was once a soldier? That is indeed most singular. Ah, but Jeremy?"

"Yes, Sir John?"

"I fear I must correct you. You said—if I may quote you back to yourself—that you had 'learned the significance of the butler's mention of the King's Carabineers.' But really, you've done no such thing."

"I haven't?"

"Indeed no. All you learned was the regiment's significance to him. What we have yet to discover, and perhaps never will, was why he mentioned it when you asked him what he saw when he opened the door and made it possible for the robbers to enter the Trezavant residence. *Why* did he mention the King's Carabineers? And what *significance* did they have to him in relation to the robbery?" He paused at that point and rubbed his chin. "You see my point? Interesting, eh?"

"Well," said I, "perhaps he saw someone who reminded him of—"

"No," said he, interrupting, "guessing won't do. It simply won't do in this case. But . . . perhaps that bit of information will ultimately be of use. Now, however, Jeremy, I trust you can set me to rights on that question of Frank Barber's escape from the mob which pursued him. I fear he carries with him a reputation for exaggeration and self-promotion."

Needing no more explicit command than this one from Sir John, I set about to do just that. I was determined to tell the whole truth in this instance because Frank had made such a botch of it. This was in spite of my certainty that Sir John would disapprove of the part played by firearms in my tale. And so I told it just as it had happened, pistols and all. Nor did I scant the key role played by Constable Patley in driving away the mob.

"You say that he saved both you and Frank Barber?"

"I would say, Sir John, that that would not be overstating the matter."

"And then he did simply disappear before you could thank him properly?"

"That is correct, sir," said I.

"And you did not see into which house he went?"

"Well, no, but I suppose he could have drifted down to Pall Mall."

"Not likely, though?"

"No, not likely."

"Hmmm. Still, I must say I'm glad to hear a good report on this fellow Patley: something, at any rate, to counter the bad things I have heard up to now. But answer me this, lad."

"Yes sir, whatever you wish to know." (I knew very well what he wished to know, and I dreaded what lay ahead.)

"Are you in the habit of carrying loaded pistols with you wherever you go on the streets of London?"

"Oh, by no means, sir."

"Then how did it come about that you happened to have them with you during the afternoon in one of the grandest sections of London?"

"It was that the night before Mr. Baker had given me pistols for my protection on the way to St. Bartholomew's."

"Ah well, it's true that the area round St. Bart's and the Old Bailey is not a good one. But tell me, why did you not return these firearms upon your return?"

"Because Mr. Baker had gone off duty, sir."

"Ah, so he had. You did not return till morning. Had quite a row with Kate about that, did you not?"

"Well, I . . . I . . ."

"You could have turned them in to Mr. Fuller, could you not?"

This question was perhaps the most difficult of all to answer. Perhaps foolishly, I resorted to evasion. "I could have, yes," said I, "but I feared he might disapprove of my carrying loaded pistols about and lecture me on the matter." (The truth was, reader, that I disliked Mr. Fuller and had decided to have as little as possible to do with him.)

"Well," said Sir John, "perhaps you thought *I* approved of carrying loaded pistols about?"

"No sir, I—"

His voice rose as he plunged ahead: "Indeed, I do *not* approve, though it is true that on certain occasions, when special duties were required of you, I have allowed, even specified, the wearing of pistols that you might frighten away interferers. Do you *need* to be lectured on this subject, Jeremy?"

"No sir."

"Well then, let us consider that you have learned your lesson and taken it to heart, and let us thank God together that you neither killed nor maimed anyone in that unruly crowd. I admit that since you had the pistols at hand, you made good use of them."

"Yes sir." Hearing that, I brightened considerably.

"And Jeremy? One more thing."

"What is that, sir?"

"Do try to get along with Mr. Fuller, won't you? You needn't make a friend of him—just get along with him. That is all that is required of us in our dealings with most of those we see daily."

Having promised Sir John that I would do my best to do just that, I left his chambers and, seeking Mr. Fuller, found Mr. Baker. In the hours that I spent after my time with the magistrate, it had grown dark. Just as Mr. Fuller came earliest in the morning, Mr. Baker was first to arrive at night. And so, as it happened, I returned the pistols to him.

He took them with a smile and a chuckle, and immediately he asked, "Which is the one needs cleaning?"

I looked at him queerly. How could he have known, after all?

Seeing the puzzlement written upon my face, he made the matter clear: "I happened to meet that fellow, Patley, on the way over, and he told me all about what you'd done—holding off a mob with a pair of pistols. I'd say you had some bollocks on you, lad."

I blushed at his obscene flattery, yet I wondered, had he heard the whole story? "Did Mr. Patley tell you his part in it?" I asked.

"Why no, what was that?"

Whereupon I told him all: how, when I was faced with the choice of shooting a woman or being overcome by the mob, Mr. Patley stepped forth and sent her packing along with the whole wild bunch of them; and then, how he disappeared before I could so much as thank him.

"He did all that?"

"He did indeed."

"I'm glad to hear he's up to some good at last. The constables had about decided they'd rather have one-legged Cowley back again. Slow he may have been, but willing he was. This man Patley is about the *un*willingest ever was."

"I've made a promise to myself to judge less severely," said I. "I've no right."

"None of us has, I suppose," said Mr. Baker.

"I regret to say I even put that little prank—locking the cellar door—on Mr. Patley. As it turned out, the guilty party was none other than Mr. Fuller. He owned up earlier today." Then did I add a bit inconsequentially, "He acted a bit odd about it, though."

"Odd?" said Mr. Baker, looking a bit sharp at me. "How odd? What do you mean?"

"Well," said I, "it was the way he apologized — more than was necessary, it seemed to me."

"That's as I thought you meant," said he. "I think I know how that came about. I was off with Mr. Bailey, and Fuller was just leaving, and we were all by the Bow Street door. That was when I first heard you beating on the other side the cellar door. I remember it well, for I was interested in what Bailey was saying. It was about you, so it was. He was talking how Sir John was reading law with you, and he wagered that you would be the next magistrate of the Bow Street Court. That struck me as most interesting, it did — and it must've struck Fuller the same way, given him something to think about on the walk home. Must've decided he did the wrong thing, lockin' you up, don't you think?"

EIGHT

*In which Sir John
puts Mr. Trezavant
to the test*

It has been my observation that one may trudge along for days, even weeks, in a sort of fog—that is, with no real sense of direction, nor any feeling of having accomplished anything. And then one day you wake up, and all that is changed: You know somehow that things are falling into place; the tempo of the day increases; you feel yourself able to make associations and connections which before had been hidden to you.

I felt that change on the following morning, and I'm sure that Sir John felt it, too. Where he had kept largely to himself during previous days, he now strode about meeting the Bow Street Runners as they returned, one by one, from their night duties. He had been up early, earlier than I, and he had found his way downstairs well before his usual time. As soon as I had the fire going in the kitchen and some bread and butter inside me, I was down to see what I might do to help.

Sir John was deep in whispered conversation with Constable Brede and Constable Perkins. Though I wanted greatly to know the subject of their conversation, the three were so absorbed that I simply could not bring myself to eavesdrop in a crude and common way. I kept a respectful distance and simply burned with curiosity. It was only at the end of it all that I managed to hear anything worth hearing.

Mr. Perkins had broken away from the other two and was heading for the street door, when he turned and called back to them: "You may count on me, of course. But sir, tell me, when do you wish me there to start?"

"A little earlier than Mr. Brede, I think," said Sir John. "Perhaps an hour, if you don't mind, Mr. Perkins. I must arrange a few things first."

"I don't mind at all. I live quite near."

"That, of course, is why you were chosen," said Sir John.

"And not my fierce nature? My lion's heart?"

"That, too, certainly."

Both men turned away, laughing. Nor did Mr. Brede stay a moment longer than was necessary. Taciturn by nature, he mumbled no more than a few words, bobbed his head to the magistrate, and headed after Constable Perkins out the door to the street.

"Now you, Jeremy," said Sir John as he waved in my approximate direction.

"I, sir? How did you know I was here?"

"Oh, I had a notion you were about. I hoped you would be, in any case." As I came closer to him, he fumbled down into his voluminous coat pocket and fetched up a letter; sealed tightly it was, so that there seemed little chance of peeking inside. "This is a most important letter," he continued, holding it out to me, "which I dictated to Mr. Marsden when you were out wandering about St. James Park with that chambermaid."

"But sir, I—"

"Oh, never mind. You're being teased, lad. Can't you tell?"

"I suppose so, sir," said I. (Overearnestness was ever a fault of mine.)

"Very well, I wish you to deliver this immediately."

I took the letter and saw that the name writ upon it was that of Lord Mansfield, the Lord Chief Justice.

"You've been there often, and know the way," Sir John continued. "The most important thing, however, is to get this to him swiftly, before he leaves for Old Bailey. But this," said he, drawing out a letter from his other pocket, "may be delivered afterward. It is, as you see, addressed to the provost marshal at the Tower of London. He will not have an immediate reply for you, but Lord Mansfield will—a simple yes or no. All that understood?"

I took the second letter. "Perfectly, Sir John."

"Then off with you, lad."

Indeed I did know the way. I had brought letters so often to the grand house in Bloomsbury Square that I could find my way wearing a blindfold—though I should never make such a claim to Sir John. And though it was quite early, I must say that I enjoyed the brisk walk up

Drury Lane and beyond. I even found myself looking forward to the duel at the door with Lord Mansfield's arrogant butler. Thank God, thought I, that I had had the presence of mind to wear my best coat that morning.

The butler, whose name was Egbert, answered my insistent knock a bit tardily, but answer it he did. He stood in the doorway, blocking my path, as if he feared that my intent was to push past him and into the residence. He was tall, over six feet, and he seemed to enjoy looking down at me.

"You again," said he. There was no evidence of emotion to be seen in his face, certainly no sign of pleasure at my visit.

"Yes, it is I." With a smile upon my face, I responded most pleasantly to his baleful look. "I have a letter for Lord Mansfield from Sir John Fielding, magistrate of the Bow Street Court."

"What does your letter concern?"

"I know not, for I did not take it in dictation, and I would not tell you in any case, for what it concerns comes under the heading of official court business."

"Hmmmph," said he, something in the nature of a belch it was, and yet it sounded, too, like a bit of a cough.

"Is Lord Mansfield still here?" I asked. "Or has he left for court?"

"Oh, he is still here. Give me the letter, and I shall deliver it to him."

"I fear I cannot," said I. "There is an answer requested."

"The usual thing, eh? Well," said he, throwing open the door and stepping aside, "come ahead then. His Lordship is at breakfast for the moment. Do not interrupt him longer than is necessary."

I followed the butler at a respectful distance until a thought occurred to me. Then did I catch him up by moving forward at a jog-trot.

"Sir," said I to him, "may I ask you a question?"

"You may."

"Have you recently added to your staff a maid of the name of Pinkham?"

The butler looked back at me over his shoulder. "I am in charge of the staff," said he. "I do all the hiring. I can assure you that no maid named Pinkham, nor anyone else, has been added to the staff for years."

"Thank you."

He conducted me to a surprisingly small room at the back of the house. It drew light through its eastern-facing windows. It occurred to me that this breakfast room may have been a later addition.

Lord Mansfield, wearing a robe, still in his nightcap, looking for all the world as if he had just staggered from his bed, looked up from a bowl of country porridge and squinted distrustfully at me.

"Ah," said he, "it's you, is it? Sir John's lad. Got a letter for me, have you?"

"Yes sir, I do." Wherewith I produced the letter and presented it to him.

"He wants an answer, does he? He usually does."

"A spoken yes or no will do, he says."

"Hmmm." Only then did he break the seal, open the letter, and start to read. As he did, he began blinking his sleep-weighted eyes and rubbing them vigorously until he had them wide open. At the same time he sat up straight in his chair and shook his head in a gesture of bewildered astonishment. He held the letter open before him for such a length of time that I was sure that he had taken the trouble to read through it twice. At that moment, I would have paid dearly to know the contents of the letter I had given to Lord Mansfield.

When at last he lowered the letter, he looked me straight in the eye and said, "You may tell Sir John, 'yes—emphatically yes.' "

"Thank you, Lord Mansfield, I shall, of course, deliver your message." I bowed and started for the door.

"Joseph," said he to the butler, "show this young man out and return here immediately. We have much to discuss before I leave for court this morning."

My route to the Tower of London took me near the office of Mr. Moses Martinez in Leadenhall Street. Because no limit of time had been put upon me, I thought I might look in on him. There was, after all, a chance that he might have heard something from Amsterdam regarding the jewels stolen from Lady Lilley. Or was I perhaps a bit too optimistic? It was less than a week that I visited him on Sir John's advice to ask his aid in the matter. In any case, I proceeded up the street which led past the imposing home of the East India Company, then beyond to the more modest building wherein Mr. Martinez maintained his chambers, and his living quarters, as well.

Again, I was ushered swiftly into his chambers by a young assistant. (I had but to mention Sir John's name.) Mr. Martinez stood, welcoming me politely, yet he wore on his face a curious and slightly confused expression as he waved me to a chair.

"Was there some other request from Sir John?" he asked in a somewhat tentative manner.

"Uh, no sir," said I, "but I was wondering if any word has come from Amsterdam. I know it hasn't been very long since —"

"*Long*? Young man, two letters were posted only Wednesday. They may not even have arrived yet. I would remind you that Holland is some distance away."

"I . . . I know that, sir. I'm sorry to have troubled you." I rose from the chair where I had sat, feeling quite mortified of a sudden at my own impatience, my inability to allow things to happen in their own time. No doubt I had caught a bit of that same sense of excitement that seemed to have possessed Sir John that very morning. "In truth, Mr. Martinez, Sir John did not send me—not today. Coming here was my own idea. As you may have heard, there has been another robbery, and I simply hoped for the kind of information that might move the investigation along at a swifter pace. Again, forgive me."

By the time I had concluded this speech, I had retreated to the door, bowing frequently, and was about to leave in a great rush before Mr. Martinez could say another word. Yet he spoke out before I could make good my escape.

"Stay! Stay!" said he. "As a lad, I was like you myself. I could not tolerate the pace at which the world went—always too slow, never swift enough to suit me."

He waved a finger in the air rather sententiously; I was reminded of a schoolmaster, or a vicar, perhaps.

"As I say," he continued, "I remember having the same sort of feelings that you have today, and because I remember so well, I will tell you something that may be of interest to you."

"Oh, tell me, please do."

"It was something that happened yesterday which indeed made me wonder. There is a man known to me by reputation—his is a *bad* reputation. He was pointed out to me a year ago on the streets of Rotterdam, and a good many colorful stories were told me of his nefarious enterprise in Europe. It should be said, by the bye, that his criminal pursuits constituted his *second* business, for he presented himself as a successful trader in ordinary goods—compasses, lenses, linens—the sort of thing the Dutch are known for."

"He was Dutch, then?"

"Oh yes, did I not make that clear? He did well enough in his first line of trade that he managed to keep secret his second line."

"Which was . . . ?"

"He dealt in all manner of stolen goods."

"Jewels? Paintings?"

"That and much more."

"And you saw this same man here in London, did you?"

"It was but one day past."

"What is his name, sir?"

"Oh, I could not tell you that."

Why ever could he not? He had good as described Mr. Zondervan of St. James Street to me. And now to withhold his name? That made no sense. Yet I told Mr. Martinez nothing of the kind. I had learned there were subtler ways of handling a reluctant witness.

"Then, sir, you must dictate a letter for Sir John in which you tell him all that you have told me about this man with the addition of his name. I shall wait in the next room, so I shall be none the wiser, and you may double-seal the letter tight so that I may not peek inside."

"That would do no good," said he. "I cannot divulge the name, not even to Sir John."

"I honestly do not understand," said I. "Do you not trust Sir John?"

"Of course I do. And for that matter, I trust you, too."

"Do you fear retribution from this nameless trader?"

"I fear no one."

"Then, sir, please make it clear to me why you refuse."

Mr. Martinez nodded, then said nothing for a good long moment as he considered the next step to take. At last he proceeded.

"Are you a Christian?" he asked me.

"Well, I . . . I try."

"And you know that I am a Jew, and I, too, try. Our two religions have much in common. Among the most important: We worship the same God, and we live by the same rules of life."

That last was a bit obscure to me. "Sir?"

"The Decalogue," he explained.

"Sir?"

"The Ten Commandments."

"Ah yes," said I, "of course."

"One of these Commandments—it is the ninth—prohibits the bearing of false witness. It tells us not to say of another what we know to be false. In commentary, this has been extended to mean not only must we not speak falsehoods, we must also say of another *only* what we know to be the truth. Now, concerning the man of whom I spoke, it may well be that all I told you of him was true, yet I cannot be certain. I do not know it from my own experience, therefore I have withheld his name that I may not bear false witness against him."

I followed his reasoning, and I admitted to myself that it was sound reasoning. Nevertheless, I felt obliged to attack it.

"But sir," said I, "you said that the man in question is Dutch. Surely that provides a considerable hint to his identity."

"Indeed," said he, "but there must be hundreds of Dutchmen in London, perhaps over a thousand."

"Well . . ." said I, grasping for inspiration, "it may interest you to know that what little you have told me has already suggested to me one who fits it in a number of ways."

"Excellent! I had hoped that it might, and that is why I chose to venture as far as I did in this matter."

With that, he clapped his hands together in a gesture which I took to mean my time with him had ended. I could, I suppose, have wheedled and begged, but I was sure that it would have done no good and would have reduced me considerably in his eyes. Having thus made my decision, I thanked Mr. Moses Martinez politely and took my leave of him.

So elated was I at what I had learned from Mr. Martinez (or what I thought I had learned), that upon delivering the letter to the office of the provost marshal at the Tower of London, I charted a course for my return to Bow Street which would take me by Lloyd's Coffee House.

As I had hoped, Mr. Alfred Humber was there at his usual table, sipping the usual strong blend of coffees served there. He was alone, which is to say, his young assistant was absent—off, no doubt, on some errand ordered by his chief. Lloyd's was, as it always was at that time, humming with quiet conversation, with occasional interruptions from the brokers to the clerk at the chalkboard. He saw me enter and immediately signaled the nearest server. Thus the coffee was poured just as I reached the table. Though I was eager to be off to Bow Street, I could hardly decline the steaming cup that awaited me. I was, however, ungracious enough to say to Mr. Humber, as I sat down beside him, that I could not stay long.

"Ah well," said he to me, "I've never known you to turn down a cup of coffee."

"Right enough, sir," I admitted, "and I thank you for it." Then did I add: "I was wondering, sir, if you had any information for Sir John as might pertain to the robberies of the past week."

"Well and good," said he. "Indeed I do have information of a kind that may be helpful to the investigation." He reached deep down into the interior of his coat and into a pocket hidden from plain sight and brought forth a letter of a kind quite like the one I had delivered to the Lord Chief Justice; only the color of the sealing wax differed. "It is all in here."

Thus did he catch me unawares, taking my first gulp of the coffee that he had kindly provided. I swallowed it quickly—too quickly, I fear, for I fell immediately into a fit of coughing.

"You all right?"

I assured him that I was quite well as soon as I had my voice back. Only then did I venture to take a bit more coffee—just a sip this time. After clearing my throat once again, I asked Mr. Humber: "Might *I* know what information you're offering to Sir John?"

He leaned toward me then and, lowering his voice, he said: "I'm afraid not. There are a bit too many about who would be interested in anything I might have to say on this matter."

Looking about, I saw that what he said was no doubt true. Conversation had stopped at a number of tables around us. Two men at the closest were openly staring in our direction.

"I quite understand, sir," said I, concealing my disappointment with another gulp of coffee. "That being the case, I fear that I must be off. Do forgive me, Mr. Humber." I took another swallow of that sublime brew and stood. "Sir John will be eager to have the information you've provided. With your permission, then?" I bowed rather formally and, seeing one last sip left in the cup, I took my leave and that last sip, as well.

.   .   .

Well, of course I *assumed* Sir John would be eager to know what was inside Mr. Humber's letter, but I *knew* I was myself more than eager. Therefore, I hurried the distance to Bow Street that I might have time to give Sir John my report and deliver the letter before his court session. Presumably, of course, I should be the one to read it aloud to him.

Upon my arrival, I saw just ahead of me that a most impressive (and familiar) coach-and-four had pulled up at the door to Number 4. It was unmistakably that of Lord Mansfield, the Lord Chief Justice, to whom I had earlier delivered the letter. Had he come to respond to that message which had disturbed him so in some more personal way?

No, evidently not, for when the footman came round to open the coach door, it was not Lord Mansfield who stepped down, but rather two young ladies of obvious quality. Both were well dressed; neither looked to be any older than I. The only difference I could discern between them (and, oddly, it struck me then as being of little moment) was in their complexion; the second of the two to emerge had face and hands of a rich chocolate hue. I had come to an abrupt halt, expecting Lord Mansfield to emerge and not wishing to get into his path; so I saw the young ladies at a slight remove, and they wasted no time in getting inside. I was nevertheless certain of what I had seen. With them inside, the footman leaned against the coach door, and the driver began his descent. It was evident they meant to stay a good, long while. I saw that it was time to follow those two young ladies inside.

They had not gotten far—no farther, indeed, than the strongroom. There they had taken their places. While the darker of the two posted herself at the bars and talked in earnest whispers to Mr. Burnham, her companion had taken a place behind them. Watchful as a sentry, she guarded them both.

I walked swiftly past them, yet not so swiftly that I failed to notice a few things. Though voices were so hushed I could not make out a word that was whispered, I did see that the darker of the two was standing so close to the prisoner that they were able to clasp hands between the bars; I saw, too, that in spite of her tears, she was quite beautiful. Her skin was a rich, lustrous brown, not quite so dark as Mr. Burnham's. Her facial features seemed also a mixture: She had full lips in the Negro manner, but her nose was as long and narrow as any in the city of London.

Her companion, blond and distinctly pink in complexion, regarded me in a somewhat hostile manner as I passed her by. Nevertheless, I thought her quite comely. Though not as striking as her companion, she was, in a way, prettier, and would, no doubt, be widely regarded as beautiful.

All this I took in with a few furtive glances as I went past. Then, once beyond, the gawking faces of Mr. Fuller and Mr. Marsden took me somewhat by surprise. Yet they, in turn, were surprised, indeed more than surprised, by the two female visitors. It was as if they had never seen such before—and perhaps they never had.

I went quickly to Sir John's chambers. There I found him standing at his desk, his attention fastened upon the open door, whereon I knocked.

"Who is there? Is it you, Jeremy?"

"It is, Sir John."

Proceeding inside, I discovered Clarissa in a far corner applying Sir John's official seal to a letter—apparently one just given her by Sir John. I was shocked. Had she now usurped my position as the magistrate's amanuensis?

"Ah," said she, looking in my direction, "the postman has arrived!" Was that to be my sole function? I thought not!

"Yes, Jeremy, I've just dictated a letter to Clarissa which must be delivered as swiftly as possible. I realize you've just returned from one such errand, but it is really most important to get this into the hands of Mr. Trezavant."

"But Sir John," said I, "Mr. Martinez has told me something which I feel I must convey to you."

"It can wait, can't it?"

"Well . . ." said I, most reluctant, "I suppose so. But I also have a letter for you from Mr. Humber."

"Oh, give it here. We'll get to it later."

I had no choice, of course. I surrendered the letter. Just then, however, a despairing wail sounded from down the long corridor.

"What *is* that?" Sir John asked in a most peevish manner. "Just before you came in, Jeremy, I thought I heard the sound of female weeping. Now *this*."

"You *did* hear a female weeping," said I.

"Oh?"

"Indeed, sir. You recall that you postulated the purpose of Mr. Burnham's long rides? 'Two or three times a week and *always* on Sunday'?"

"Why, yes," said he. "I do recall hazarding a guess of some sort."

"Well, your guess has proven out, sir. She and a friend arrived in Lord Mansfield's coach-and-four."

"Ah, truly, you say? Why not invite them here into my chambers? I should like to meet the young lady who so turned the head of Mr. Burnham that he seems willing to go to the gallows rather than divulge her identity."

"That will not be necessary, Sir John Fielding."

All in the room turned to the sound of that voice—unmistakably female. It was, as I anticipated, the voice of the lighter of the two young ladies. She spoke for them both. Her partner was, at least for the moment, too distraught to express herself with ease; she sniffled into her kerchief and dabbed at her eyes.

"You have the advantage of me," said Sir John. "You know who I am, yet I know not who you are."

"That is easily remedied," said she. "I am Lady Elizabeth Murray, and this is my cousin, Dido Elizabeth Belle."

"Why, if I may ask, have you two young ladies decided to come here? Surely not simply to cheer our prisoner."

"No sir," said Dido, now recovered and speaking for the first time to Sir John.

"Oh?" said he. "What then?"

"My cousin and I are both wards of the Earl of Mansfield, who is the Lord Chief Justice. I believe you know him well."

"Professionally acquainted, let us say, rather."

"As you will," said she. "I meant only to suggest that through him we know something of the law. We are here to make a formal statement."

"One statement for the two of you?"

The two cousins regarded each other, frowning. Then did Lady Murray clear her throat and speak forth: "Two statements, I suppose, would be the proper thing, one from each of us. They will speak in support of Mr. Burnham. We just want them done correctly and according to the rules of law so that they will stand up in court."

"I assure you, young ladies, I shall do my part." Then did he turn away from them and toward us, Clarissa and me. "Will you summon

Mr. Marsden, Clarissa? Tell him to bring pen and paper. And Jeremy, are you still here?"

"I am, sir."

"Whatever for? Did I not tell you that the letter to Mr. Trezavant must be delivered quickly?"

"Uh, yes, Sir John."

"Then off with you, lad. Take a hackney coach, if that will get you there faster. You'll be reimbursed."

I left the room at a jog-trot with Clarissa behind.

"Here, Jeremy," she called after me. "You'll need this, won't you?"

I halted, turned, and saw that she waved at me the letter for Mr. Trezavant she had taken in dictation from Sir John. This was most embarrassing! "Yes, of course I'll need it." And I snatched it from her quite rudely.

"Here now," said she. "I've saved you from making a fool of yourself, you must at least answer a few questions for me."

"Oh, all right, but quickly. You heard what Sir John said."

"What was this mysterious matter between you and him that had to do with Mr. Burnham's long rides?"

I thought about that a moment. There was really no reason why Clarissa should not know. "Well," said I to her, "Sir John guessed at the very beginning that the most likely explanation for Mr. Burnham's frequent rides to the country was that he was courting some woman."

"And you think it was one of those two, do you?"

"Of course—the more beautiful, the darker of the two."

"Oh, but this is terrible!"

"Terrible? Why should it be terrible? She will make a statement which will prove Mr. Burnham's alibi. He will be set free."

"I know," said Clarissa, "but just think of poor Annie! What will she do?"

"What will she do? Why, get on with her life, just as I must now get on to Mr. Trezavant." And with that, I left her where she stood.

A few minutes later, sitting in the back of a hackney, I considered the fatuousness of women. Certainly Clarissa, and perhaps even Annie, would prefer that Mr. Burnham be punished for a crime of which he was innocent so that they might keep alive their foolish fancies. But was Mr. Burnham any less foolish? Had he not put himself in a most perilous position, all because he felt it necessary to protect the good name of a young woman? What romantic rubbish!

Though politely worded and nicely phrased, the letter to Mr. Trezavant was nothing more or less than a summons. Sir John had gone to some pains to explain that, while most impressive, the accusation he had made against Mr. Burnham was of no legal worth unless it were made in court. Therefore, much as Sir John hated to ask, it would be necessary for Mr. Trezavant to come to the magistrate's court at noon that very day and repeat the accusation. Otherwise, Sir John would have to release the prisoner.

Mr. Trezavant made no attempt to hide his displeasure at this turn of events. Indeed quite the opposite was true. He railed against rules and procedures which allowed countless malefactors to go free and commit further crimes. This and other complaints were directed at me, as if I were at fault and had the power to change the situation. But in the end he left off such carping and agreed to do as Sir John had asked. Satisfied, I bade him good day and took my leave of him.

As Arthur had done before him, Mr. Collier accompanied me to the street door. He was, however, far more talkative than his predecessor had been — and far more inquisitive.

"Mossman tells me that you were with Mr. Robb when he died there in St. Bart's," said he to me. "What did he have to say?"

"Oh, nothing of value."

"Surely he said *something*."

Hastily, I attempted to explain that while it was true that I had been with Arthur during the last hours of his life, for most of that time I had been dozing peacefully in the chair beside his bed. The few things he had said before that proved quite worthless.

But still he pressed: "Such as . . . what?"

We stood at the door to Little Jermyn Street; I wished to be through it and away from his prying questions. With that and only that in mind, I said, "Oh, there was something about Crocker, and . . ." And there I halted when about to mention the King's Carabineers. It had suddenly occurred to me that he had no right to know any of this. An alarum sounded within me.

"You mean little Crocker, the chambermaid?" he asked eagerly. "What did he say?"

"That, sir, is none of your affair," said I, drawing myself up and looking him coldly in the eye. "And I must say, Mr. Collier, I wonder at your intense curiosity in this matter, seeing that you were hardly even acquainted with Arthur Robb."

"Oh . . . well, I did know him, you see . . . in a way. I'd seen him every day . . . spoken . . ."

"Goodbye to you," said I to him, and so saying, I grasped the large brass handle and heaved open the door. I did not hear it close behind me, though I'm sure it did.

There was a considerable crowd in court that day. It was unusually large for the magistrate's court, though the number assembled would not in any way have compared with the crowds in attendance in any of the courtrooms at Old Bailey.

In addition to the "regulars"—drabs, women of the street, porters, and layabouts who dropped by Bow Street for their midday's entertainment—there were many more who had come because it was rumored that an arrest had been made in what were then popularly called "the St. James robberies." Some had even heard that the robber in question was a "proper blackie"; they wanted an early look at him before he was sent on to Old Bailey and given his ticket to the crap merchant.

Because so many had come thus to gawk at Mr. Burnham, they grew restive as Sir John heard a pair of lesser matters that had been brought before the magistrate's court in search of settlement. They were of the usual sort: two Covent Garden green merchants who claimed the same choice stall (one of them, it turned out, had simply arrived earlier one morning and claimed the spot as squatter's privilege). The second matter, in its own way just as frivolous, turned upon the discovery in the street of a deal of money by two men who purported to be friends; both claimed to have spied the sack of gold first and fell into a brawl over it; this attracted another, a merchant, who claimed to be the true owner of the sack of money (Sir John awarded the sack to the third man after the latter had correctly given the exact amount therein, but the magistrate then instructed him to given a guinea to each of the other two men in reward for having discovered the fortune in the street).

As they shuffled off, Sir John turned to Mr. Marsden and instructed him to bring on the next case and have the prisoner brought forth.

That Mr. Marsden did, calling out Robert Burnham by name, and turning to the door through which he would be brought by Mr. Fuller. But when the door opened, a great noise was heard from the crowd, for Mr. Fuller herded in not one prisoner, but four. Each of the four was of the same brown hue; each was dressed similarly and was about the same height; and each wore hand irons.

They were directed to the bench off to the right of Sir John where they remained standing.

Sir John spoke out in a voice deep and solemn: "Mr. Burnham, you have been accused of taking active part in the robbery by force and violence of the Trezavant residence in Little Jermyn Street in the city of Westminster three evenings past. How say you, sir—guilty or not guilty?"

Then came a most remarkable occurrence: In response to Sir John's question, all four men spoke together as with one voice, "Not guilty."

They did then sit down upon the bench and listen as Mr. Marsden read forth a description of the robbery, complete with a list of the goods taken—paintings and furniture, table silver, and various objects made of gold. Appended to this was a description of the "apoplectic disorder" of Mr. Arthur Robb, which was occasioned by the robbery and caused his eventual demise a day later in St. Bartholomew's Hospital.

Though seated, the four men gave all this their full attention. It was while they were thus occupied that I, looking upon them, was able to identify two of the four. At the far end I recognized Mr. Burnham; and at the nearest was none other than Dr. Johnson's young charge, Frank Barber. But who the two men were between them, I could not say, though there was something about each which did seem familiar.

Once Mr. Marsden had done, Sir John intoned (again most solemnly): "We have a witness. He is Mr. Thomas Trezavant. Come forward please, sir."

Thus invited, Mr. Trezavant rose from his place in the front row of benches and moved forward as swiftly and resolutely as his great bulk would allow. When he halted, he was directly in front of the magistrate, with Mr. Burnham and his companions a good fifteen feet or more off to his right.

"Will you tell us, Mr. Trezavant," said Sir John, "what you saw on the evening that your residence was robbed in the manner just described by Mr. Marsden?"

"That I shall and gladly, but first let me congratulate you, sir. I thought you had but one of this black-faced crew in captivity, but I see that you have captured all of them."

"That's as may be," said Sir John. "Or perhaps better said, it is neither here nor there, for the task I put before you is to describe what you yourself saw and heard on the evening of the great robbery."

And that Mr. Trezavant attempted to do, yet he lapsed often into hearsay and surmise. Sir John was forced a number of times to remind him of his injunction to report only what had personally been seen or heard.

"I begin to suspect," said the magistrate, "that you were safely sequestered in your study during the entire event."

"Not so, sir. I may have been made a prisoner in my own study, but I was hardly 'safe,' as you assert."

"Oh? What then?"

"I was tortured."

"Yes, I recall you said something about that. In what way were you tortured? And to what purpose?"

"Well . . . they came blustering into my study without so much as knocking. There were but two of them, but frightening they were, and of fearful countenance. They took me quite by surprise."

"Let me interrupt to ask you, sir, were you aware before their appearance that your house had been invaded, so to speak, by this robber band?"

"Uh, no sir, I was not."

"How did they know to find you there?"

"That I cannot say. They seemed, indeed, to know their way about the house. Perhaps one of the servants directed them to me."

"Do you know which one it was?"

"No, but I have my suspicions."

"Keep them to yourself. A magistrate's court is no place to air suspicions." Sir John rubbed his chin in thought, producing a scowl of vague disapproval. "Let us get back to this matter of torture," said he. "What did they wish to know?"

"The location of my wife's jewels."

"And how did they go about torturing you, Mr. Trezavant?"

"Well . . ." He hesitated, looking about the courtroom as if in a state of acute discomfort. "They described to me their intentions."

A low hum of comment swept through the attending crowd. Yet Sir John made no effort to quiet them, so eager was he to understand properly what he had just heard.

"They described to you their intentions?" he repeated. "Was that . . . *all*?"

"Yes," said he, "but I have a most vivid imagination."

The hum in the courtroom rose to a pitch, then exploded into a great gale of laughter. Though Sir John himself smiled broadly at Mr. Trezavant's confession, he must have thought that such unbridled hilarity at the expense of the witness was altogether improper, for he thumped loudly with the mallet which served him for a gavel and called loudly for order.

But damage had been done. Mr. Trezavant turned round and faced the courtroom—and quite charged with indignation was he.

"You would not think it amusing," he shouted out, "if you were to hear in precise detail the steps those black villains meant to take in castrating *you*—now would you?"

The laughter ceased abruptly, except for a few titters and giggles heard from the females at the back of the large room; they, too, quietened as Sir John beat louder still upon the table before him.

"I'm sure we would not think it in the least bit amusing," said he when all was quiet. "I take it, Mr. Trezavant, that you told the robbers what they wished to know."

"No sir, I referred them to one of the servants who had greater knowledge of such matters than I. As it happened, my wife had taken her jewels with her on a visit to her father in Sussex."

"So you might have been gelded to no purpose whatever."

"I had not thought of it quite that way."

"Indeed, sir, you might prefer not to. But let us go now direct to the matter at hand, shall we? You indicated earlier that the man who made those threats to you, who was the leader of the robber band, is in fact here in this courtroom. Is that not so?"

"It is, Sir John." Mr. Trezavant seemed to speak with a confidence that was of a sudden renewed.

"Do you see him here now? You have my word, sir, that he is one of the four you noticed earlier. Can you pick him out from the rest?" He gestured toward the four. "Stand, please, all of you."

"I . . . I am confident that I can identify him."

"Very well, take your time."

He not only took his time, he also took it upon himself to move much closer to the four. Had it been within his power to walk softly, he might have accomplished his purpose—due, that is, to Sir John's blindness. Nevertheless, at a good twenty stone, he would have been utterly incapable of tiptoeing about. An individual large as Mr. Trezavant could only crash about in one compass direction or another.

Thus it was that the witness had not got far ere he was called back by Sir John, who advised him to return to his place.

The witness objected: "How am I to see them clear if not close up?"

"Sir," said the magistrate, "I have it on good authority that on the night in question, you could not see clear at all because of your inebriated state. Since it would be time-consuming and inappropriate to put you again in that state, let distance serve in its stead."

Glowering, Mr. Trezavant returned to the point from which he had started. Though he said nothing more about the matter, it was evident that so far as he was concerned, the matter was not settled.

He did not take long to make his choice. If his confidence had been shaken, there was no sign of it as he stood studying the four men, his right hand at his jowls, his left folded across his great belly.

"It is he who stands second from the right," said he with great certainty.

"That, of course, means little to me," said Sir John. "Since my affliction prevents me from viewing the man you have identified as the leader of the robbers, perhaps he might step forward and give his name."

The man chosen by Mr. Trezavant did as he had been told. "My name," said he, "is Philip Rumford, sir, as you should well know."

"Oh? And why would I know that?"

"Because, sir, you employ me as a constable."

"Ah yes, so I do. Mr. Marsden, will you fetch forth the towel that you brought into court today against such an eventuality?"

The clerk rose from his place at the table next to Sir John with a smile upon his face. In his hand was indeed a towel, which he must have had across his lap during this court session. He simply went to Mr. Rumford and handed it to him.

Mr. Rumford, for his part, took it from him and began rubbing at his face. "Oohs" and "ahhs" of wonder were heard from those in the crowded courtroom, for as he did so, the color of his skin changed from black (or at least the shade of brown that is commonly called that) to white (or the shade of pale yellowish pink that is so called). I knew Constable Rumford, of course, though not so well as some of the rest. He dearly loved a good joke, and one such as this would have greatly pleased him. When he had completed the work of wiping himself clean, the assemblage broke into applause. In response, he bowed left, right, and center.

"All applause is due Mr. Falder who applies cosmetics and paint at Drury Lane," he declared. "He did us up right fair, didn't he, Ben?"

He tossed the towel to him who had stood at his right. And as that one began to change the color of his skin, I saw to my astonishment that the man who caught the towel was none other than Benjamin Bailey, captain of the Bow Street Runners and my close companion for all my years in London. It was amazing to me, as it must also have been to many others in the courtroom, how completely a change of skin color disguised one.

Sir John had been quite lax up to that moment. He had allowed laughter and applause from the benches and permitted saucy comments from Constable Rumford. But the time had come for him to put an end to such frivolity. He beat without mercy upon the table at which he sat and called for "Order! Order!" And at last he was given what he sought: The room went still, and he cleared his throat and made ready to speak.

Before he could do that, however, Mr. Trezavant bellowed forth: "Sir John, I believe you tricked me."

"Nothing of the kind, sir. The man you originally pointed out and declared to be leader of those who robbed your residence is here, right enough. Mr. Burnham, step forward and identify yourself."

That Mr. Burnham did, though somewhat reluctantly (or so it seemed to me); he regarded Mr. Trezavant suspiciously, feeling perhaps that he still had something to fear from him; and if that were what he thought, then he may indeed have been right.

"I identified him correct one time, and one time is all that should be necessary. Send that man on to Old Bailey. I would see him hang yet on Tyburn Hill."

"I cannot do that and would not," said Sir John. "Mr. Burnham is now a free man. He is alibi for the entire evening in which you were robbed. He may walk from this court whenever he chooses to do so."

"In that case, we have nothing more to discuss."

And having said as much, Mr. Trezavant went stamping out of the Bow Street Court—which, technically, put him in contempt.

NINE

*In which a robbery
occurs in an unexpected
manner and place*

There was great rejoicing in Sir John's chambers following that session of his court. Dido and her cousin, Elizabeth, had waited therein
for word of the outcome. (It would have been unseemly for them to
have appeared in a place so rowdy, so *public* as the Bow Street Court.)
When it came—brought to them by Frank Barber, who ran ahead to
tell—they began dancing about in a state of absolute jubilation. That,
in any case, is how it seemed when I entered behind Sir John and Mr.
Burnham. The magistrate smiled indulgently at the display of high
spirits; Mr. Burnham, however, maintained the same somber expression he wore but a short time past in the courtroom when he stepped
forward and identified himself to Mr. Trezavant. No doubt he was
happy—or more than happy—to have the threat of the hangman's
noose removed. Nevertheless, he seemed to have learned a sobering
lesson: that for a black man, no matter how comfortably situated, London was a far more dangerous place than he might ever have previously supposed.

Though I had not been present at their reconciliation, it was evident
that Mr. Burnham had forgiven Frank Barber (though what had he to
forgive?) for taking the initiative and informing Dido of the terrible
predicament that those frequent visits to her had put her suitor in. She
and her cousin had then acted to rescue him from that predicament.
They were sorely disappointed, however, when they learned that the
statements which had been prepared by them with the help of Sir John
had not been read out by him in open court.

"There was no need," said he to them, "for by the time they were pertinent, that fool, Trezavant, had already mistakenly identified Constable Rumford as leader of that band of thieves. When I introduced Mr. Burnham to him as the man he had earlier accused, I was able to say, thanks to you both, that he is alibi for the entire evening in which the Trezavant residence was robbed."

"But couldn't you have *proven* his innocence by reading our declarations aloud to one and all?" asked Dido.

"Yes," said Elizabeth, "couldn't you? Such a shame not to."

"Oh, I suppose I could have read them out, but I fear Lord Mansfield would not approve the association of your two names with this matter, most specially now as he sits in judgment on this Somerset case."

With a sigh, Dido agreed: "I fear you are correct, Sir John." And then to Elizabeth: "I fear also, coz, that we must be on our way back to Kenwood."

"Ah yes, Uncle will need his coach."

The two, who seemed for all the world like visitors from some distant star, called out their goodbyes and farewells, then poised for their flight back through the ether.

"But where is Robert?" asked Dido of the other, as she looked round the room.

"Oh, there he is! See him? Sulking in the corner?"

They ran to Mr. Burnham, who, though not truly sulking, might indeed have looked a bit happier, considering the circumstances.

"Robert!" said Dido. "We have saved you from the hangman. Can you not at least give us a smile and a sweet farewell?"

Though it seemed to take a bit of effort, he managed to provide both. Encouraged, Dido went up on her tiptoes (for Mr. Burnham was quite tall and she was not) and gave him a buss upon the cheek. Then did she and her cousin hasten to the door to the long corridor which led to the street. Yet there, blocking their way, stood Annie and Clarissa. Annie, wide-eyed, looked astonished, hurt, completely crushed. Clarissa simply looked sad. They had seen all. I felt like calling out to them, "Be not so downcast. The cousins may be beautifully dressed, pert, and (within limits) clever, but they are no more than silly girls." Yet even as I imagined that, it did occur to me that it was only a short time ago that I had thought the same of Annie and Clarissa. Station mattered little: There was no end to silliness among girls of that age.

It was not long after their departure that the impromptu celebration in Sir John's chambers came to an end. Frank Barber and Robert Burnham left Number 4 Bow Street together, giving encouraging evidence that all was once again well between them. That left me alone with Sir John and gave me the first opportunity I had had to present my report to him. I reminded him of this.

"Yes, yes, by all means, let us sit down that I may better give it my attention."

"You have read the letter from Mr. Humber, I take it?" I posed it as a question to Sir John, hoping to learn something of its contents.

"Oh certainly," said he. "Clarissa read it me as soon as you set off for Mr. Trezavant's. No doubt you are curious as to what it said. Well, it was precisely the sort of letter one would expect from him—full of facts about ships—departure dates, cargoes, that sort of thing. Indeed, Jeremy, I believe I should perish of ennui if my life were taken up with such tedious matters."

"When I visited him earlier," said I, "he indicated that we might well be suspicious if a ship were insured considerably beyond the value of the vessel and its stated cargo. Was any such discrepancy discovered?"

Sir John did not immediately respond. He pouched his cheeks and hunched his shoulders in such a way that he actually appeared to be pouting—though of course I discounted that possibility immediately.

"Mmm . . . well, he mentioned something about that," said he. "But you, Jeremy, I believe you said that you had information from Mr. Martinez that you thought quite important."

"Well, yes I do have something."

"Tell it to me then, lad. I am eager to hear."

It was clear to me that I would hear no more from Sir John regarding Mr. Humber's letter. And so, for the time being, I put it from my mind and concentrated upon the task of remembering in detail my conversation earlier that day with Moses Martinez. Considering that so much had happened during the intervening hours, I believe I gave a good account of my questions and his answers—up to a point. I reached that point when I repeated to Sir John the reply Mr. Martinez had given me when I asked him the name of the villainous Dutchman. Then did Sir John become the interrogator and I his respondent.

First he asked me to repeat what Mr. Martinez had told me.

"He said, sir, 'Oh, I could not tell you that.' "

"But why? What reason did he give for withholding the name?"

"Well, I asked him a number of things. Did he fear retribution? He said he did not. Did he not trust you or me to keep the name secret? He said that he trusted both of us. But I persisted, and he explained at last that it was his religion prevented him."

"His *religion*?" Sir John seemed truly vexed. "What could he have meant by that?"

"He cited the ninth of the Ten Commandments. And he said that we should understand his reluctance, for Christians and Jews alike did honor the Ten."

"Let me see," said he, "which is the ninth?" And having put the question to himself, he began marking them off on his fingers. " 'No other gods before me'—that is the first. 'No graven image' is the second." And so on. He mumbled on until he came to the ninth, and then did he speak forth in full voice: "Thou shalt not bear false witness against thy neighbor? What could he mean by that? I would not have him bear false witness against anyone, certainly not his neighbor."

"Well, sir, this is how he explained it," said I. "In some way, this had been extended to mean that we ought also to say of someone else only what we know from experience to be the truth—what we ourselves have seen; what we may have heard from the person in question. Since he could not give any such guarantee, he declined to name the individual."

"Hmmm. Did he say who it was gave such a broad interpretation to the ninth? Not that it matters greatly."

"No . . . simply . . . well, he used a phrase. What was it? Something to do with 'commentary.' 'According to commentary,' it may have been."

Sir John gave a dismissive wave of his hand. "Simply a matter of Jewish scruples, I suppose," said he. He thought a moment thereon, then did he surprise me with a chuckle. "Or perhaps God is a better lawyer than ever I had thought. What this amounts to, Jeremy, is a prohibition against speaking hearsay. As a magistrate I must accept that, nor could I contemn Mr. Martinez for abiding by this higher standard."

"That may be," said I to him. "Nevertheless, the man he described fitted to the life one on the periphery of this case. I fear I take it ill that he refused to supply a name."

"Do you mean it?" said Sir John. "To the life, you say?"

"Well, perhaps I overstated a bit. I have never actually seen the individual in question."

"Then how can you make such a claim? In point of fact, if you reported correctly, Mr. Martinez gave no physical description of the man at all. What is the name of your fellow?"

"Zondervan," said I. "What his Christian name is I do not know."

"Oh?" Just that, yet I could tell that the name had struck a chord of some sort. "And what makes you think that the man described by Mr. Martinez is this—what is his name?—Zondervan—is that it?"

"Yes, Zondervan. Well, first of all, he is Dutch. And he is a merchant."

"So are many here in London."

"True enough, but he lives in St. James Street, between the residences of Lord Lilley and Mr. Bilbo."

"Mere coincidence, surely."

"Perhaps, but when Mr. Collier, the butler who had been discharged by Lord Lilley, sought a place to shelter himself, he went direct to the Zondervan residence. And I suspect that Mistress Pinkham, who was herself discharged for divulging the hiding place of Lady Lilley's jewels, has taken shelter there, too."

"But you're not sure of that?"

"Well . . . no."

"Mistress Pinkham is not, in any case, a recent addition to the household staff of Lord Mansfield?"

"No sir, I asked after her, and found she was quite unknown there."

He shrugged. "Who knows where these young women go? No doubt she had a better offer elsewhere. But no, Jeremy, this man, Zondervan, does not—"

"But sir," said I, interrupting in a most insistent manner, "he has in his residence a gallery in which many pictures hang—paintings which I am sure are of great value."

"And what makes you sure of that?"

"That they are kept under lock and key."

"How is it you know all this?"

"I visited it the day I took Mr. Collier to Field Lane to tour the pawnshops. He had been allowed inside that he might view Mr. Zondervan's collection. He is a great fancier of such pictures and gave me to understand that these were of great worth."

"Hmmm, well, that is certainly more interesting. Paintings have also been stolen. But I hardly think that the fact this Dutchman has in his possession a collection of valuable pictures would be reason enough to seek a warrant giving us leave to invade his premises and poke around in search of stolen goods. Nevertheless, all this is of interest, as I said. We might try to learn more about this fellow."

There was then silence from him, the sort of silence that told me that my time with him had run out. Reluctantly, I rose to my feet and made ready to leave. Yet he had something more to say.

"By the bye, Jeremy, I hope you have not forgotten that it is this night that Mr. Johnson visits us to take dinner at our table."

"Oh indeed not, Sir John." (But indeed, reader, I *had* forgotten.)

"Wear your best. Shave yourself, if need be." He then tested his own chin and jowls. "And yes," said he, "I should like you to shave me, as well. Ah, but hold on, lad. You must tell Annie that there will be one more guest for dinner."

"Oh? And who will that be, Sir John?"

"Why, none other than Mr. Burnham," said he. "During those minutes following today's session, I offered him an invitation. I meant it in apology for our treatment of him. And frankly, I believe he would have declined had I not mentioned that Johnson would also be present. That dictionary of Johnson's has made a great celebrity of him. His opinion is sought on every subject. Before, he was naught but a writer—and I needn't tell you in what low esteem they are held."

I felt no necessity to comment upon that. Nevertheless, I had need to pass on to Sir John one last bit of intelligence. And so I turned, halfway to the door, and spoke quickly to him: "One last matter, sir. It has to do with the letter to Lord Mansfield which you charged me to deliver."

"Yes, of course, and did you deliver it?"

"I did," said I, "direct to him."

"And what did he say in response?"

"He said, and I quote, 'Yes, emphatically yes.' "

"Very good," said Sir John. "That is precisely the response I expected."

Much transpired between that moment and the time, some hours later, when we were all situated round the table. It was, however, the sort of mundane work of preparation that deserves no place in a narrative of this sort. Let it stand that all was done as efficiently and gracefully by us three as a dozen or so might have done in one of the grand houses in St. James. And let it be noted, too, that our captain in this endeavor was our dear Annie. No longer the silly girl she had been, talking of suicide or following her loved one into exile, she was the very model of cool mastery; there could be no doubt when the food was brought to the table that she had the situation fully under control. Which is to say, not only Sir John and Lady Katherine, but also Mr. Burnham and Mr. Johnson were so well-pleased with the roast of beef when it was served that they paid it the supreme compliment of silence as they swiftly devoured the first serving.

Not even Mr. Johnson spoke, and he bore the reputation of one who talked during and through dinner—snuffling and snorting, chewing and gulping—all the rude noises of eating. When he had done, he sat for a moment immobile, in a sweat, his knife in his right fist and his fork in his left. Then did he summon forth a great belch, which so surprised Clarissa that her hand flew to her mouth to stifle a giggle; he paid no mind to her.

"I have never eaten a better roast beef better cooked," said he. "Tell me, young lady"—addressing Annie—"there is a different taste, something new to me. What have you done to it?"

Annie reluctantly drew her eyes away from Mr. Burnham and gave a demure smile to Mr. Johnson. "How generous of you to say so, sir," said she. "In answer to your query, I use garlic quite freely. That, no doubt, is the source of the 'different taste' to which you referred."

"Garlic . . ." he mused. "That is a foreign condiment, is it not?"

"Not foreign to *my* kitchen," said she with a bit of a twinkle.

He chuckled appreciatively and Mr. Burnham quite gawked at her, no doubt taken somewhat aback at her choice of words and perfect enunciation. (Neither Clarissa nor I were in the least surprised at Annie, however, for we had often heard her carry on in this way for hours at a time; this was a role she had created for herself.)

"Perhaps you would like Jeremy to carve you another serving," proposed Lady Katherine.

Mr. Johnson agreed that he would and asked that I also give him a bit more pudding and dripping. As I filled his request, he quite gladly accepted the offer of more claret from Sir John. I hastened to pour that, as well.

Once the silence had been broken, conversation began. All that it took was a question, and that was supplied by Mr. Burnham.

"Mr. Johnson," said he, "what think you of the Somerset case, which is now before Lord Mansfield?"

"What do I think? Why, sir, I think a great deal. At the very least it would mean freedom for one black man, and at most it could mean the end of slavery in all our British colonies."

"Indeed?" said Lady Katherine. "As much as that? How do you think it will be decided, Jack?"

"In some way between the least and the most," said Sir John dryly.

Mr. Burnham persisted in his address to Mr. Johnson: "I myself am particularly interested in the case because in some ways it matches my own experience."

"Indeed? How interesting. Tell me more."

(Since you, reader, have already been given to know the circumstances of Mr. Burnham's manumission, it might be more valuable to learn, or be reminded, of the facts of the Somerset case of which they spoke. James Somerset was a black slave, owned by a man named Stewart in residence in Massachusetts. Stewart took Somerset with him to England, and here the slave remained in a state of forced servitude for two years, and then ran away. When he was recaptured, Stewart was angry and vengeful and so did hand over the slave to a sea captain named Knowles, who was to sail to Jamaica and sell Somerset there. Presumably, Knowles and Stewart would split the profits from the sale. But as it happened, there were witnesses to Somerset's recapture, and they signed affidavits to the nature of it; these were used to obtain a habeas corpus, which Lord Mansfield, the Lord Chief Justice, himself issued. Knowles did fight the habeas corpus with an affidavit of his own, which put the blame upon Somerset for seeking his freedom. Lord Mansfield set a court date and vowed to hear the case himself. The matter came to the attention of Granville Sharp, an active abolitionist; he appointed an attorney to represent Somerset in his suit for freedom, and the case went to trial. It was in process at the time of this discussion.)

Having heard Mr. Burnham out, and learned the details of his liberation, Mr. Johnson took a moment to consider. Then did he give it as his opinion that, in all truth, the only connection he could see between the Somerset case and the tale he had just heard was that both had taken advantage of their presence in England to claim their freedom.

"Of course," said Mr. Burnham, "there is the contradiction in English law: How can slavery be prohibited here, while in English colonies it is permitted, though all the other laws of England are there strictly enforced?"

"And how can it be," said Mr. Johnson, "that when a black man or woman travels from, let us say, Jamaica to London, he or she is not, as one might suppose, subject to the laws of England?"

"But in some curious way," said Mr. Burnham, continuing the thought, "remains defined in his state by the laws of the land he left behind. Exactly!"

Samuel Johnson said nothing for a considerable space of time. Rather, he sat masticating with the same deep seriousness that he had shown some minutes before as he chewed his way through his first serving of Annie's roast of beef.

Clarissa, who sat cross the table from me, looked first at him and then at me, signaling to me with her uplifted eyebrows that she feared that something might be amiss with our distinguished guest.

Perhaps fearing the same, Mr. Burnham leaned forward and asked most politely, "What would you be thinking now, sir—that is, if I might ask."

"Oh, you may ask, certainly you may, sir. I am not one who is noted for keeping his thoughts to himself—no indeed." He hesitated but a moment, and then came out with it: "I could not but note among the details of James Somerset's background that he was held as a slave in Massachusetts by that Scotsman who brought him to England."

"And what of that, sir?"

"Why, do you not see the irony in that, however unintended it may be? It is those 'sons of liberty' in the North American colonies who yell loudest for freedom that are most avid in protecting their putative rights to keep slaves."

"Indeed sir," said Mr. Burnham, "your point is well taken. There is, to be sure, a certain inconsistency there, to say the least."

"To say the least," echoed Mr. Johnson in firm agreement. "I read from time to time of the continuing flow of Negroes northward to Canada where slavery is not tolerated, and in truth, I applaud them. I have heard of slave rebellions on various islands in the West Indies. None has succeeded to my knowledge, and I call that a pity."

There came from Lady Katherine the unmistakable sound of a sudden intake of breath, which expressed her shock at Mr. Johnson's declaration. Yet there was an even greater shock to come.

Mr. Johnson rose from his place and lifted his glass to the table.

"I propose a toast," said he, "to the next insurrection of slaves in the West Indies that it may succeed."

Mr. Burnham was on his feet in an instant, as were Annie and Clarissa, their glasses raised high. Only Sir John, Lady Katherine, and I retained our seats and left our glasses on the table. Though she, I think, had made her feelings clear in this matter, I know that I remained seated simply as a gesture of solidarity with Sir John, who would plainly decline to join in the toast offered by his guest. Nevertheless, the toast was drunk, the glasses were returned to the table, and all resumed their places. There were sheepish looks and downcast eyes.

Even Mr. Johnson who, one would guess, had never experienced embarrassment in his life, regarded Sir John with a little uncertainty.

"I hope, Sir John, that I have not offended you," said he.

"Not in the least, Mr. Johnson."

"I could not but notice that you did not join in the toast I offered."

"No, I did not."

"May I ask why, sir? I am eager to know." And indeed, as he thrust his great head forward, he did appear eager. He even laid aside his knife and fork that he might give full attention to Sir John.

"To put it bluntly," said Sir John, "my position as magistrate would not permit it. A magistrate is, in a modest way, a judge, but he is also responsible for keeping order. And let me tell you, Mr. Johnson, and you, Mr. Burnham, that I place great value upon order."

"Ah, Sir John," said Mr. Burnham in a most schoolmasterly manner, "but do you value order over justice?"

"No, I grant you, sir, that with reference to the matter at hand, there can be no doubt that a great wrong has been done to the Africans who have been taken from their homes, transported across the sea, and sold into slavery, and wrong it continues to be. But I believe it will be rectified soon or eventually—though not by revolt, insurrection, nor by rebellion, or other violent means. I am opposed to such. They offend my sense of order. And more important, they have unpredictable results and seldom accomplish the goals intended. More often than not, they lead to chaos and a situation worse than the one which precipitated the violence. In short, I oppose such means because they do not work. They harden the hearts of those in power against the very injustices they were meant to remedy. No, great injustices are best treated by legislation or in the courts. And such benevolent attention is most likely to be given when order prevails. Thus I stand on the side of order."

While I half-expected the table to burst into applause at his concluding words, I heard, rather, a discreet clearing of the throat from Mr. Burnham and light coughs from Mr. Johnson. I wanted dearly to know what, if anything, could be said in rejoinder to such words. Nevertheless, I had to leave the table. From a time just after Mr. Burnham's question to Sir John until that very moment, I had heard a series of knocks upon the kitchen door, insistent yet respectful. I could not further delay responding. Excusing myself hastily, I muttered something about "the door" and ran off to the kitchen.

I threw open the door and found Benjamin Bailey there. He, I knew, would not come knocking with something frivolous to report. (For that matter, none of the Bow Street Runners would have done so — not even the latest, Constable Patley.)

"I'd begun to wonder if there was anyone up here," said he.

"Sorry about that, Mr. Bailey. We've guests. Sir John was addressing the table, and I didn't want to leave whilst he was speaking."

"Oh, I wouldn't've wanted you to do that," said he, clearly appalled at such a notion.

"What have you to report? I'll pass it right on to him."

"A yes, well, it's most peculiar, it is, but there's been another robbery."

"Same district? Same robbers?"

"That's the part that's most peculiar. It's the same house as the last."

"The same house? The Trezavant residence?"

"Yes," said he, "oh yes, but it wasn't the same robbers — not the Africans, anyways. Or at least there wasn't any sign of them this time. No, the lady of the house, she just went to look over her jewels — and they wasn't there where she kept them. They was gone."

"A burglary?"

"I don't know. Nobody seems to know when they were taken — or by whom." He stopped at that point and frowned. "One of the servants is missing, though."

"Which one?"

"I don't know. One of the footmen ran to tell me, then went back to the house before I could get any more from him."

"Well," said I to him, "just give me a moment. I'll tell Sir John, and then get my hat."

As it came about, however, the trip to the Trezavant residence was made in a coach well-packed with passengers. Not only did Mr. Bailey and I sit left and right upon the padded bench in the cab directly behind the driver, but Mr. Burnham sat between us as well, still bitterly complaining that he would not be allowed to accompany all into the Trezavant house. Across from us three sat Mr. Johnson and Sir John, filling their bench seat completely.

Sir John had jumped to his feet when I informed him of the odd circumstance of the theft in Little Jermyn Street and declared himself fit enough to lead the investigation. Then did Mr. Johnson rise and claim a place in our party. Yet when Mr. Burnham attempted to do the same, he met strong resistance from Sir John.

"Do you not see," said the magistrate, "that it would be a slap in the face to bring into Mr. Trezavant's home the very individual who was the cause of his humiliation earlier in the day?"

"It would be a good lesson for him," Mr. Burnham declared.

"It might indeed," said Sir John, "but neither you nor I is the one to teach it to him."

All the way to the hackney coach waiting in Bow Street, he held firm against Mr. Burnham's protests. And even when we reached our destination and dismounted from the coach, there were grumbles still. Then and there Sir John silenced him.

"Mr. Burnham," said he, "please go home. You are but a street and a few houses away from Mr. Bilbo's residence. Is that not so? Sir, I regret that our evening was cut somewhat short. Even more do I regret that it was necessary to detain you in Bow Street for near two days, but had you been more forthcoming . . ."

"I now regret *my* choice of action, sir."

"Good. Then you will be less likely to repeat it." Sir John thrust his hand out in Mr. Burnham's general direction. "Come, let us press flesh and part on the best of terms. You are welcome in Number 4 Bow Street at any time. Visit me next week on some afternoon, and we shall continue our discussions."

Mollified and reconciled, he grasped Sir John's hand and pumped it vigorously. Then, taking his leave of Mr. Johnson, he blessed the occasion that permitted their meeting for this first time. For his part, the lexicographer assured him there would be other such occasions in the future. With that, after exchanging bows all about him, Mr. Burnham headed down Little Jermyn Street toward St. James.

"An odd fellow, don't you think?" commented Mr. Johnson as he watched Mr. Burnham's form dwindling down the street. "A prickly sort, yet at the same time rather unsure of himself."

"Oh, but intelligent," said Sir John. "You have my word on that."

"And a gifted teacher—or so I hear from Frank Barber."

It struck me as strange to hear the two men assess Mr. Burnham so. I wondered what they might say of me if I were absent.

"Well," said Sir John with a sigh, "let's inside, shall we? The sooner we begin, the sooner we'll have done. Give the door a good, stout knock, Mr. Bailey."

That he did, beating a tattoo upon it with his club. None within could have failed to hear.

"Very good of you to allow me to accompany you," said Mr. Johnson. "I have long wondered what transpired at such nocturnal sessions as these."

He seemed ready to go on in this vein, but there came voices behind the door raised in argument. One of them—unmistakably that of Mr. Collier, the butler—objecting sharply to . . . what? Then a stronger, deeper voice, also familiar: "Oh, enough of that!" Locks were thrown; bars were drawn; the door came open at last. And there stood Constable Patley, with Mr. Collier cowering behind.

"Ah, I knew it was you," said the constable, throwing the door wide and stepping back. "This little mousie"—tapping Mr. Collier upon the shoulder—"feared it was the Africans come back, but I was ready for them if it was. He waved his club. "Come along inside. I got the two of them ready to talk to you, Sir John."

Once inside, the door shut behind us, Sir John turned to Mr. Patley. "Two?" said he. "You say two? And who are they?"

"It's the Mister and the Missus."

"Ah, very well. We meet her at last, eh?"

"It's an experience you'll easily survive, sir. But this way, right through here."

Our party moved swiftly down the long hall. I realized before we reached the door that the Trezavants awaited us in the room always referred to as the "library." When at last we reached it, Sir John paused and signaled us to stand close round him.

"Now, Mr. Bailey and Mr. Patley," said he softly, "I should like you to go below stairs and talk with all who will talk to you. Who in particular do you suggest, Jeremy?"

I took a moment to think. "I should say Maude Bleeker, the cook, and Mossman, the porter, would be best."

"Very good. You've got that, have you? Find out which of the servants is missing. Search the room of that person. Meanwhile, one of you look outside the house for anything, anything at all, that may help us along." Then did he pause for a moment, perhaps for effect, though more likely to satisfy himself that he had nothing to add to these, his instructions. "Alright then, off with you."

The two constables started off together, ready to begin their task.

"Mr. Johnson? Shall we see what awaits us? Jeremy, give the door a knock."

Thus bidden, I gave it a few sound thumps and immediately opened the door for Sir John and Mr. Johnson, not wishing them to be beholden to Mr. Trezavant for an invitation to enter. Once both were inside, I pulled the door shut and rushed ahead that Sir John might place his hand upon my arm and thus be led forward through unfamiliar territory.

Only then did I have a proper view of the master and mistress of the house. They were as unlike as they could be. The Mr. I have oft described as fat. Yet indeed those three letters—f, a, t—do no justice to the shape of the man; let us say, rather, elephantine or mountainous and thus begin the proper work of description. As for Mrs. Trezavant, all that I have said of him could be said of her in its antithesis. Where he was fat, she was thin (skinny even); if he was elephantine, she was serpentine; and if he appeared mountainous, then she seemed (what simile here? Perhaps, reader, if you have ever been inside a great cavern, this will do) stalagmitic.

Not that this great contrast was immediately apparent to me, for both were seated behind that grand desk which so dominated its end of the room. Oddly, both were dressed for bed, though it was not near so late in the evening as that might suggest; they wore heavy robes and proper nightcaps.

"Ah yes, Sir John," said Mr. Trezavant, drawling in a most supercilious manner, "you have come, have you? What a pity to have dragged you forth. We have no need in this instance of your investigative powers."

"Oh? And why is that, sir?"

"Why, it is quite obvious who committed the theft. But ah"—he interrupted himself—"I see that you have another with you."

"Well, you've often met Jeremy, of course."

"Of course, but . . ."

"May I present Mr. Samuel Johnson?"

Big as he was, Mr. Johnson could hardly be said to have hidden behind Sir John. He had nevertheless managed somehow to shrink himself in such a way that he had remained, until that moment, an anonymous presence in the room. But then, raising his face to the Trezavants, he bowed—not deep, but in a most proper manner.

"At your service, sir and madame," said he.

The effect upon the couple was altogether remarkable. Both rose quite automatically, a courtesy neither had offered Sir John. For his part, Mr. Trezavant said nothing intelligible and merely stammered awkwardly for near a minute. His wife, however, found a voice within her slender frame (and a very deep, commanding voice it was).

"Samuel Johnson? It is you then who wrote the dictionary?"

"Alas, madame, not exactly so. I am a poor harmless drudge who has written *a* dictionary. Nothing more."

That, however, was sufficient to inspire from her an entire vocabulary of cooing and twittering sounds interspersed with phrases of abject idolatry.

Did Mr. Johnson enjoy this? Was he taken in by it? There was no telling, for his face had become like a mask, one upon which a half-smile was fixed and whose opaque eyes were utterly unreadable. And so his face remained, virtually immobile, as the couple talked on and on, apologizing for their state of deshabille, praising his vast fund of knowledge, asking how he came to know so many words, et cetera. Clearly, they knew little about him—only that he still enjoyed great fame for his dictionary; that he had enjoyed awards, honors, and a pension for his work, even a sobriquet, "Dictionary" Johnson.

Although, through Sir John, I had met a few who had been touched by fame, this was my first opportunity to see the effect of celebrity upon those who lived in awe of the celebrated. Mr. Trezavant, who was said to mingle with eminent politicians, did manage to keep his wits about him. His wife, however, seemed to have gone quite mad. She would immediately improvise a dinner party in his honor—"just a few of our closest, dearest friends"—if Mr. Johnson would but give them a few minutes to dress themselves.

"I am sorry, madame, but I have just dined with Sir John—and quite well, too."

"Oh," said she, "what a pity. It is so seldom our home is visited by literary men. It seems a shame to waste your presence here." Her hand shot to her mouth—a child's guilty gesture. "Oh dear, I fear I didn't phrase that very well, did I?"

"Think nothing of it, madame. Indeed, I'm satisfied that my presence here is not wasted. I am here as an observer."

"An observer?" she echoed.

"Yes, I wish to observe Sir John's methods of investigation."

"Ah well," said Mr. Trezavant, "as I declared earlier, there'll be little need for an investigation."

"Yes, you did say that, didn't you?" said Sir John. "What precisely did you mean?"

"Why, I meant that my wife's jewels have disappeared, and so has one of the servants. You must either find her, or find him to whom she delivered them."

(Let me say at this point, reader, that I liked not the sound of Mr. Trezavant's prattling; I drew inferences from it which made me uncomfortable.)

"Speak plainer, man," said Sir John. "You've no need to withhold names."

"All right then," said Mr. Trezavant, accepting the challenge, "it is Jenny Crocker, the upstairs maid, who is missing. I suspected her the first time the jewels were gone."

"The first time?" I yelped, unable to hold back. "That was when your wife had taken them with her to Sussex!"

He grunted a low grumble. "Well, yes, but she was always about upstairs and no doubt knew right where the jewels were hid."

"But you had made up your mind she was the criminal before ever a crime had been committed!"

"Sir John," said he, "I do object strongly to your lad's tone. He seems to be accusing me of some impropriety."

"But Mr. Trezavant," said the magistrate, "I believe he raised a point worthy of consideration. Why *were* you so sure of her guilt?"

"Why? Why? Well, she seemed the criminal type. As did, let me say, that black fellow whom you dismissed so lightly this very afternoon. She may already have passed the booty on to him. I've no—"

"Ah sir," said Samuel Johnson to him, "there I believe I can put your mind to rest. Robert Burnham, to whom you refer, has been in our company all through this evening. We left him before your door not many minutes past."

"You *what*? You let him get away?"

"Please, sir," said Sir John, "I believe you are not thinking things through properly. Do not speak quite so recklessly. As Mr. Johnson has just explained, Mr. Burnham has been in our company the entire time." He turned then to Mrs. Trezavant. "Madame, do you not have a lady's maid?"

"Yes, yes I do."

"Does she not know where you secrete your pieces?"

"Indeed she does." She hesitated. "Well . . . it was in fact my maid who discovered the jewels were missing."

Mr. Trezavant glared at his spouse in a manner most stern and disapproving. "You didn't tell me that," said he. "I thought it was you found they were gone."

"It matters little," said she to him, "for I trust her completely. And besides, if I *had* told you, you would have paid little heed to me, so certain were you that Crocker was guilty."

"But . . . I . . . I . . ."

Sir John stepped in to put an end to this wrangle. "This is a point of some importance, madame," said he. "When did she report to you that the pieces were missing?"

"Why, I'm not sure. I'd had a rather wearying day, and so I dressed early for bed. What time is it now?"

I glanced at a tall, upright clock in the corner. "Just on ten o'clock," said I.

"About an hour has passed since then, I should say, or perhaps a little less."

"Very well," said Sir John. "Had she some reason for visiting the hiding place? Something that you had worn and wished returned to your collection?"

"Yes, a ring—a ruby ring with quite a large stone."

"And where is she now, this personal maid of yours?"

"Below stairs in her room, I suppose. I sent her off to bed. She was terribly upset."

"We must talk to her," said Sir John firmly. "Jeremy, go below and fetch her. If she lies abed, then roust her out. If she sleeps, then wake her."

"Is this quite necessary?" asked Mrs. Trezavant.

"Quite," said he. "But you must tell us, what is her name?"

"Hulda. She is easily the best servant I have ever had. But she is Dutch, and her family name is quite unpronounceable."

"Hmmm. Dutch, is it? On your way, Jeremy."

I left forthwith. Remembering the way from my earlier visits, it took me but a moment to descend the stairs, yet that gave me time enough to reflect upon the unexpected involvement of the Dutch in this matter. What did it mean? And more important, did the fact that Crocker had apparently fled the residence mean that she had taken with her the jewels of her mistress? I hoped not, indeed I did, for I had thought better of her than that.

Entering the kitchen, I found Constable Bailey at one end of the long table, deep in conversation with Maude Bleeker, the cook. The porter hovered at some distance. Mr. Bailey looked up as I arrived and rightly perceived that I had come on an errand for Sir John. He held up his hand, thus silencing Bleeker who turned about to see the reason for the interruption.

"Yes, Jeremy, what is it?"

"I've been sent down to fetch Hulda," said I to the cook. Then to Mr. Bailey: "She's the one discovered the jewels were gone."

"So I was just told," said he. "Miss Maude, could you rouse her?"

"Oh, I could and I will," said she, rising with a nod to me. "You ask me, and I'll tell you it's time somebody asked her some questions."

Without being specific as to what questions might be asked of Hulda, the cook lumbered through the doorway and into the common room.

Glancing at Mossman in the far corner, I determined that he was at a sufficient distance that I might speak without being overheard. Nevertheless, I lowered my voice to little more than a whisper: "Has the questioning gone well, Mr. Bailey?"

He screwed his face into a rather pained grimace and responded in the same low tone: "So far, nobody saw anything, but they've got lots of ideas about who the thief might be."

"Where's Constable Patley?"

"Outside. He thought it best to leave the interrogation to me."

Then, as if he had been summoned by my inquiry, Mr. Patley appeared in the open back door. He held a lighted lantern in his hand, and upon his face he wore a look of the utmost solemnity; his eyes, though cold, seemed burning with anger. I had never even imagined him in such a state. He said nothing, but took in the room with one great glance.

At last he spoke: "I've something to show you."

Mr. Bailey and I exchanged puzzled looks; he rose, and both of us made for the door; so also did Mr. Mossman.

"Not you," said Constable Patley rudely to the porter. "You stay here."

Mossman did as he was told. We two followed Mr. Patley up the stairs and into the back garden. I had little noted it before, but the space was thickly grown with bushes and flowering plants now beginning to burst into spring blossom. He led us off the path to a corner, which, even in bright moonlight, seemed darker and less open than the rest. We pushed against the bushes. The branches snapped back and punished our thighs and ankles.

"Just a bit more," said Mr. Patley. "Under that tree ahead."

And so it was that at last we came upon that which we had been led out to see. Under the tree, nearly obscured by the bushes at its base, lay a human form, a woman's body clothed in a petticoat.

Mr. Patley knelt down, pushed back the bush, and lowered his lantern so that we might look upon the face. It was Jenny Crocker's face we saw—pale, drained of any hint of life, the color of death. Her eyes were open. She stared back at us coldly, as if accusing us of the brutal deed. Below her chin was the bloody wound that had taken her life. Her throat had been cut from ear to ear.

TEN

*In which Sir John
and Mr. Zondervan
meet at last*

The discovery of Crocker's body put the investigation into a state of absolute turmoil. Should she be moved? Mr. Patley was all for "dusting the dirt off her" and removing the remains to the kitchen. I insisted she be left where she lay, for that was as Sir John would have it. He argued that to leave her thus would be to show disrespect to the dead, and he only gave in when Mr. Bailey came to my side in the matter. The last I heard from them, Mr. Patley was swearing solemnly that he would "catch the whoreson who did this and personally send him straight to hell." What Mr. Bailey said in response was lost to me, however, for when I came crashing down the stairs, I nearly bowled over Mr. Mossman, careened into the cook, and bumped heads with a blonde woman in robe and slippers, whom I took to be the Dutch maid, Hulda.

"All of you, back inside," said I with all the authority that I could muster.

"What is it?" asked the cook.

"What have they found?" the porter asked quite simultaneously.

The Dutch woman said nothing, simply peered suspiciously at me.

"All your questions will be answered soon," said I, "but I must insist that you go back into the kitchen."

Reluctantly, they trooped back inside—except for Hulda. She looked me up and down and liked not what she saw.

"Who are you to tell us what to do?" said she. "You are but a boy."

"That's as may be," said I to her, "but I speak for Sir John Fielding and at his command. If you wish to spend the night in your bed, rather than on the cold floor of the strongroom at Number 4 Bow Street so that he may question you tomorrow at his leisure, then I would advise you to do what he says—and what he would have me say speaking for him."

She said nothing in reply but looked at me critically, then proceeded into the kitchen.

I followed her, closing the door behind us, and headed for the stairs. "Keep her here," said I to the cook and the porter. "Sir John will be down soon." And that was how I left them.

When I returned to the library, I found the interrogation proceeding apace. Mrs. Trezavant was enumerating, describing, and giving an evaluation to each piece of jewelry in her collection, no doubt at Sir John's request. Whether or no he had requested it, he seemed powerfully bored by her recital: He, now seated, moved his head about—right and left, up and down—in an exercise he sometimes used to keep sleep at bay; Mr. Johnson, his chin resting upon his chest, had evidently already succumbed.

I went quickly to Sir John, making no effort to tiptoe or otherwise muffle my footsteps. He turned in my direction as Mrs. Trezavant looked up in annoyance and stopped speaking.

"Yes, Jeremy, what is it?"

I bent to his ear and whispered the news, much abbreviated but accurate so far as it went. He nodded his understanding and rose. "I regret, Mr. and Mrs. Trezavant, that I must leave you and attend to matters below stairs."

"What could you possibly learn from our servants that you cannot know from us?" she demanded.

"A great deal, I fear. You did not know, I'm sure, that a corpus lay in your back garden."

"What's that? What's that? A corpus?" cried Mr. Johnson, suddenly awake and jumping to his feet with surprising agility.

"That is correct, sir," said Sir John to his companion. "Do you wish to accompany us?"

"By all means, let us go then," said Mr. Johnson, most eagerly.

"By all means, we, too, shall come along," said Mr. Trezavant. "We must know who is dead."

"Oh, I think not," said Sir John. "That you will find out soon enough. And it has been my experience that servants are much more likely to talk freely if their masters are not present."

"But may I remind you, sir, that they are *our* servants."

"I'm aware of that, Mr. Trezavant, but if you insist upon interposing yourselves in such a manner, then you will make it necessary for me to bring them to Bow Street one by one that I may talk with them privately. It would likely prove disruptive to your household and troublesome to me." He paused but a moment, then went on to add: "Please, sir, oblige me in this."

A silence of greater duration ensued. Man and wife exchanged looks, then at last he responded to Sir John's plea. "Well, you have bested me in this, sir, as you have often done before. Will you have further need of us?"

"I think not."

"Then Mr. Trezavant and I shall retire. Goodnight to you."

With that, we left. I led the way with Sir John at my side, his hand resting lightly upon my forearm. Samuel Johnson followed close behind; we were, I fear, not quite out of earshot when he pushed forward and said in a loud whisper, "Well done, sir, well done!"

By the time we had reached the kitchen, it had been decided that I must go and fetch Mr. Donnelly, the surgeon, and arrange for a wagon to convey Crocker's corpus to his surgery.

"Do you not wish me to search round the body and describe its condition?"

"No," said Sir John with a sigh, "the three of you have already trampled the area, no doubt. As for describing the body to me, perhaps I shall depend upon Mr. Johnson for that. He is said to have great powers of observation, and since he is with us, he may as well earn his keep." Then did he call out to our guest, who trailed us on the stairway: "I trust you heard that, sir?"

"Oh, I did indeed, and I assure you I am quite ready to do whatever may be required of me."

Having had the matter thus settled, I put Sir John in the charge of Mr. Bailey and made ready to go. As I said my goodbye, Sir John grasped my wrist and brought me closer to him.

"Jeremy," said he, "the girl who lies dead in the garden, she is the one with whom you went out walking Sunday last—is she not?"

"She is, yes sir."

"Well, I know not if you were attracted to her in the way that lads your age often are, but perhaps you were. If it is so, and you feel a sense of loss, I want you to know that you have my sympathy."

"Yes sir," said I obediently. "Thank you, sir."

So troubled was I by his parting words that I pondered them the entire distance to Mr. Donnelly's surgery. How did I feel about Jenny Crocker? Had I fancied her as all the lads in Covent Garden seemed to fancy Annie? Perhaps, for our conversation had touched upon intimate matters I had not discussed with any female; that, I admit, had titillated me somewhat—or perhaps more than somewhat. That she was quite fetching in a saucy and well-favored sort of way, there could be no doubt. She was likeable and responsive. Yet we had parted on bad terms—why was that? As I recalled, she had taken offense at my questions, which had to do with the robbery—quite ordinary questions, they seemed to me. Still, there was something more, was there not? She wanted something from me I was unable to provide—what it was I could not quite understand. Perhaps I was too thick-headed, or simply had not sufficient experience to read the signs.

In fact, I considered the matter even after I arrived at the surgery in Drury Lane. Mr. Donnelly, as it happened, was not present when I came banging upon his door. There was naught to do but wait for him there on his front steps and think more upon this matter of Jenny Crocker.

Had I acted callously toward her? I thought not, though perhaps she would have been of a different opinion. Was I sorry for the awful fate that had taken her? Of course I was, yet I felt sorrow in the manner that anyone might if shown the lifeless body of one who had died so young. And to have died in a manner so squalid! *Why* had she been murdered? What was she doing out there in her petticoat? Did I feel a sense of loss, as Sir John had suggested I might? No, merely a sense of bafflement.

As I posed such questions to myself and attempted to dig deeper that I might solve the mystery surrounding Crocker's death, my eyes registered the curious street life before me there in Drury Lane. Though the theater (across the street and off to the right) had discharged its audience sometime before, there were many pedestrians teeming the walkways on both sides of the street. Most of them gave the impression that they were casual strollers, moving with easy indifference up and down the street. Nevertheless, I, who had by then lived years hard by Covent Garden, knew very well that though they seemed so unconcerned, they were truly a great gang of sharpers, pimps, whores, and pickpockets out on a darkey and on the lookout for flats and cods easily caught. The same faces appeared in the street from night to night; many of them, men and women, had spent nights in the strongroom at Number 4 Bow Street.

And as they sauntered and ambled, all the while the coach horses hurried along, hooves and shoes clip-clopping on the cobblestones. Hackneys and private coaches with teams of two and four pranced smartly up and down the lane. I found the scene before me somewhat hypnotic. As I waited, I continued to watch. And as I watched, my head began to nod, and my eyelids drooped. I might have fallen asleep right there on Mr. Donnelly's doorstep (and had my pocket picked right down to the last farthing as I dozed), but I was fortunate in that Mr. Donnelly chose that moment, when I was about to topple headlong into the arms of Morpheus, to make his return.

And indeed, reader, he made it in style. He arrived in no mean hackney, but rather in a coach-and-four painted black with a great orange-colored device of some sort painted upon the door. Thus I could not be certain that Mr. Donnelly was within until the footman came round the coach and opened the door. And even then there was naught but a leg visible to the eye. Since I had never given particular attention to the shape of Mr. Donnelly's leg, I was no better off than before. Nevertheless, the voice that came to me through the open door was recognizably his own. What the words were I could not be quite certain, yet the laugh that followed them I knew quite well. But whose was the other voice, the one that boomed forth from deep inside the coach? I had never heard a laugh to equal it in volume or grand hilarity. Such a laugh as that would bring a smile to the face of a mourner, or brighten the sour countenance of a Scottish judge.

I rose to make my presence known and advanced toward the coach that I might catch a glimpse of Mr. Donnelly's companion. As it happened, a glimpse was all I could manage, for just as I came near enough to see within, Mr. Donnelly finished with his leave-taking and climbed down; the footman slammed shut the door behind him.

"Jeremy!" he exclaimed. "Is it you? What news do you bring? Nothing dire, I hope."

"Ah well, a body for you to examine, I fear. We must go to the Trezavant residence in Little Jermyn Street."

"The Trezavant residence? Is it my employer who has been killed?"

"No sir—one of the servants, rather."

"Well, just give me a moment. I'll go upstairs and get my bag."

With that, he disappeared into the building. I heard him rushing up the stairs, and not much more than a minute later, I heard him rushing down again.

As I had described earlier, Drury Lane was so lively at that hour that there proved to be no difficulty whatever in finding a hackney coach available. We were thus on our way to the livery stable where I might hire a wagon and a driver, then on to Little Jermyn Street.

Once we were settled in the hackney and bouncing about, Mr. Donnelly remarked to me that it was only by good fortune that he had returned at such an early hour.

"Whose good fortune?" I asked in a bantering mode.

"Why, yours, if you were determined to wait, and mine because I was given the chance to escape from a most dreary dinner party."

"Oh? Whose dreary dinner party was that?"

"Lord Mansfield's."

"Truly? I'd always felt that the Lord Chief Justice was anything but a dreary conversationalist—rude perhaps, even upon occasion dictatorial, but never dreary."

"Oh I know," said Mr. Donnelly, "but he had made his invitations to the party a month ago, and since then he has taken on that blasted Somerset case, which has all London talking. All London, that is, except for Lord Mansfield."

"I don't quite follow," said I.

"Well, since he is the presiding judge, and since the case is still in trial, he absolutely refused to discuss it, nor would he allow it to be discussed at his table."

"But Mr. Donnelly, that is quite customary."

"Well, I know, but the Somerset case is all his guests wished to discuss. Couldn't he have loosened his restrictions for just this one night?"

"I don't think so. It wouldn't have been proper."

"Well, perhaps so," said he, the exasperation he had felt lending a certain tone to his voice, "but really, there must have been twenty of us there, and you've no idea what pathetic attempts were made at table talk. The evening would have been a total loss had it not been for that Dutchman."

"Dutchman?"

"Indeed," said he, "Zondervan is his name. He began telling some of the jolliest and funniest tales that ever I have heard. We were to imagine ourselves in this place—probably of his own invention—there in the lowlands. Oh, what was the name of it? Dingendam, something like that. But he told the stories, and he acted out all the parts, even the women. Oh, he did the women very well indeed, all in falsetto. Dear God, the man was *so* entertaining!"

(This was high praise indeed, considering that it came from Mr. Donnelly, for he himself was one of the most entertaining men at table I have ever known. Many is the evening that he had us all rocking with laughter with his own tales of Dublin, Vienna, and the Royal Navy.)

We were drawing near to the livery stable, but I was determined to pursue the matter that I might have my answer as swiftly as possible.

"Mr. Donnelly," said I, "this name, Zondervan, is it a very common one among the Dutch?"

He took a moment to think before answering. "Why yes, it must be. I've known of a few in my time—one in Vienna, another in New York—used to be New Amsterdam, did you know that? The Dutch had it first. Did you know that, Jeremy?"

"Uh, yes sir, I did, but—"

"Why do you ask?"

"Well, I'd come across the name myself in the course of my investigations in St. James Street. Would it be the same Mr. Zondervan?"

"Oh, I daresay it would. In fact, it was he who took me home."

"The man with the laugh?"

"Indeed he does have a great, booming laugh, does he not? When he rose from Lord Mansfield's table and said that he must be off to the wharves to check the manifest of a ship arrived today, I gave my apologies, as well, saying I must look at a patient of mine in St. Bart's. We were both excused and left together. He offered me a ride to Drury Lane, saying that it was on his way, then he kept me laughing the entire distance with another tale of those fools of Dingendam."

"He's a merchant then?"

"Oh yes, and quite a successful one, too, I'm sure. And indeed, he must be the same man, for I now recall that he did mention that he lived in St. James Street."

The hackney in which we had been riding pulled to a halt. A glance out the window told me that we had reached the stable. I threw open the door and promised Mr. Donnelly that I should only be a moment or two. And as it proved, engaging the wagon, the team, and the driver took less than five minutes in all.

The events of the rest of that long evening hardly warrant description. Even then, it seemed to me that I had spent many times like it before during my years with Sir John Fielding. Nothing conclusive was learned during the magistrate's interrogation of Mrs. Trezavant's maid, Hulda. All that was gained from Mr. Donnelly's preliminary examination of Crocker's body was that she had not been murdered where she lay beneath the tree, but dragged there from a place much nearer to the house. Mr. Patley's lantern revealed blood on the path at a spot much nearer to the back door of the house. When the wagon arrived from the livery stable, Mr. Patley and I carried Crocker's body out to the front and placed it in the conveyance. It seemed to me that every step of the way the constable uttered some new curse or a threat under his breath at those who had done this awful deed. The driver threw a canvas cover over the girl's form and made ready to go. Mr. Donnelly climbed up beside the driver and they set off for his surgery in Drury Lane, where he would conduct a postmortem examination. Only then did our party, which included the two constables and Mr. Johnson, take our leave from the Trezavant residence and venture forth to engage a hackney. The evening was done at last. I was so greatly tired by the long day and the many nights I had recently gone wanting for sleep that, when I climbed up to my little bedroom atop the house, I managed only to kick off my shoes before I collapsed upon the bed and sunk instantly into a sound sleep.

And that, reader, is how Annie found me next morning. She shook me awake. Yet I came to myself only reluctantly, emerging from a dreamless sleep as from some deep, dark forest pool. I sat up, panting and gasping, doing my best to come to terms with the state of wakefulness into which I had been rudely hauled.

"What . . . what . . . I . . ."

I can only guess what I was trying to say to her at that moment, and I would venture that it had to do with the lateness of the hour. There was a sufficiency of light pouring in the two windows, so that the realization eventually came to me that I had overslept. I was, by custom, the first in the household to arise, for it was my duty to kindle the fire so that Annie might get up to a proper blaze and prepare breakfast. That is the way it had been even before Annie came into the household — since the time, that is, when Mrs. Gredge ruled the kitchen. And during all those years — now nearly four — I could number the times I had overslept (and thus failed to do my duty) on the fingers of one hand. This was, I believe, only the third such occasion.

"Do wake up, Jeremy, please," said Annie.

"I . . . I'm awake now," said I. "Truly I am. I'll have a fire for you in no time at all."

I swung my feet out of bed and stood as tall as I might, as if to prove to her that I was fully capable of doing what was required of me.

"Don't be silly, I've got one started. I'm quite capable of laying a fire myself. But I must talk to you now — while it's quiet and everyone's asleep."

"Oh," said I, somewhat puzzled, "all right."

At her direction, I picked up my shoes and carried them down the stairs as I went tiptoeing in my hose. When I came into the kitchen, I found the fire burning bright and the kettle steaming away.

"Would you like a cup of tea, Jeremy?"

"I would, yes," said I. Then, surveying the table as she poured the boiling water into the china teapot, I saw that she had baked scones, as well. "You've been up for well over an hour, haven't you? Scones for breakfast? What's the occasion, Annie?"

"Ah well, I thought I'd give you something to remember me by."

"To remember you by? I don't understand."

"I'm leaving, Jeremy. This will be my last day here at Number 4 Bow Street."

I looked at her, studied her face. I saw that she meant exactly what she said. "But why? What is your reason?"

"Oh," said she a bit sadly, "I think you know my reason well enough — or if not, you can guess it."

"You mean that matter with Mr. Burnham? Why, Annie, that's nothing, nothing at all. Only Clarissa and I were privy to it, and you know that we're your friends. We would say nothing of your embarrassment."

"That's what Clarissa said — and in just about the same words."

"So you've talked with her about this?" In response she nodded, but then did an awful thought cross my mind: "You didn't . . ." — How to put this? — "You're not . . ."

"No, I'm not pregnant," said she. "Nor was Mr. Burnham ever anything but a gentleman toward me. Jeremy, I've given a good deal of thought to this — and to that embarrassing matter these years past with Tom Durham — and it seems to me that both times when I made a fool of myself it was me, not anyone else, who was to blame."

"Well, I see what you mean, but —"

She interrupted: "Let me tell you a story. When I was a girl of twelve in Kent, and my mother was about to give in to my pleading and put me in service in London, she took me aside, she did, and she said to me, 'My girl, let me show you the face of the only one can get you into trouble.' And then from behind her back she pulled a looking glass and held it up to me. And of course it was my face that I saw."

"Well," said I, "I can see the sense of that, I suppose. She must have meant —"

Annie held up her hand and silenced me. "But she wasn't through, for then she said, 'Now let me show you the face of the only one can get you out of trouble.' And again she puts the looking glass before me, and again it's my own face that I saw."

She paused that I might understand the story better. She even took time to pour a cup of tea for me. Only then did she resume. "Now, for years," said she, "I thought that she was telling me that when I left her, she washed her hands of me. But that wasn't it, not really. What she was saying was that when I left, there was little she could do for me, so I would have to take control of myself and be responsible. Well, my first few years, as you know, I was none too responsible and not well-controlled, either. I kept hoping someone would rescue me. First I thought Tom Durham was the one, and then I thought it was Mr. Burnham would be my rescuer. But no, I'm the only one can do that — and by God, I'm going to try. I'll rescue myself."

They were brave words—but then, she was a brave girl. I'd known her long enough that I might attest to that. Still, that did not relieve me of my worries.

"How do you intend to go about rescuing yourself?" I asked.

"Oh, I've a plan. I'd rather not talk about it just now, though."

"You'll need money, won't you? Perhaps I could get some together for you if—"

"Jeremy, you're much too good," said she, laughing as she interrupted me. "But no, I'll not need money, not for a while. Late yesterday, when I'd had a chance to think all this through, I went down to visit Sir John and told him I'd be leaving. It . . . it was good to talk to him. He gave me a bit of money for each year I'd worked here. He promised me a grand character, as well—'the very best,' he declared."

"It seems as if I'm the last to know," said I.

"Oh, but I did not intend it so. You, of all people, have helped me more than I can reckon. You brought me here and convinced Lady Katherine I could cook, even when you did not know that yourself. And all the while I've been here, you've been like a brother to me. And . . . and . . . it's because of you that I've learned to read and write."

"I could not teach you."

"No, but you saw that I went to the one who could."

There we stopped—or paused for a space of time. We looked at each other sadly, but said nothing until Annie flew round the table and embraced me, putting her cheek next to mine.

"I shall miss you terribly," said she to me.

"Well, yes, I shall miss you, too," said I, "particularly at dinnertime." She laughed just as she was meant to.

"But listen, Annie," I continued, "your mother sounds to me like a very sensible woman. Why don't you go down to visit her and ask her advice? Even responsible people sometimes ask advice. I'd be happy to give you the price of the coach ride. That way you could keep what Sir John gave you for later on."

"Ah, that's very kind of you, but did I never tell you? My mother died in the same year I came up to London. A tumor, it was, that killed her. I think she must have known she hadn't long when I left."

"Oh . . . no, I didn't know that."

She stepped away then with a sigh. "I must pack," said she, and started to turn away; then, remembering, she came back to me.

"Jeremy, there is just one more matter."

"And what is that?"

"Clarissa."

"What about her?"

"You should try to be a better friend to her. She quite admires you."

"So I've heard—though I daresay she has an odd way of showing it."

"Oh, that's just her way. Pay no attention."

"What am I to pay attention to then?"

"To her, to her good sense. There's some girls, you know, who want to be known for the brains in their head and not the pretty face outside it. She's one of those."

"I'll remember that."

She shook a finger at me. "See that you do," said she, and laughing, she left me.

Later in the morning, when all had breakfasted and gone their separate ways, I returned with a farewell gift for Annie. It was a collection of verse by Elizabeth Rowe, one of those female poets whom she seemed most to admire; I had rescued it from the bin before a bookshop just east of Grub Street.

Coming into the kitchen, I looked about but saw her not, nor did I receive a response to the call that I gave. Yet just to make certain, I jog-trotted up the stairs and went to the room she shared with Clarissa. Her bed had been stripped and the blankets piled at the foot of it; the doors of the wardrobe stood open, and half of it was empty. I saw that Annie had truly departed.

The errand which took me in the vicinity of Grub Street took me to the Tower of London and the regimental headquarters of the King's Carabineers. I had not visited the Tower so often that I had grown used to the military exercises inside its walls. And because the Carabineers were a mounted regiment, I was especially taken with the display of horsemanship out upon the parade ground. The four-legged members of the regiment were at least as well-drilled as the rest—walking in formation, cantering, wheeling left and right. I could have gawked and ogled at their maneuvers the entire morning, but I had places to go and things to do.

I went directly to regimental headquarters, as I had been instructed to do. There I asked for the colonel but was shunted off to one of his adjutants. He—a Lieutenant Tabor—reminded me a bit of Lieutenant Thomas Churchill of the Guards, with whom Sir John had previously had some dealings; both Tabor and Churchill had the same round, pink cheeks, the same arrogant manner. The adjutant pulled the letter from my hand in a needlessly rough manner when it was offered and ripped it open, destroying the seal altogether. His eyes sped over the page. I had no idea of the letter's contents, for Mr. Marsden had taken it down from Sir John's dictation. I found myself hoping that Lieutenant Tabor were a poor reader that I might catch him muttering the words aloud to himself. But, alas, no: He was as skilled and silent as any—and far better a reader than most.

When he raised his eyes from the letter and began speaking, it was as if he were dictating a reply himself and fully expected me to play the role of amanuensis.

"You may tell your magistrate fella that we are aware of the situation. The colonel gives his assurances that the small force your Sir John requests will be present when and where he wishes them. I shall command it myself."

This was all very interesting to me. I wished greatly I might have the letter back that I might read it and discover what small force Sir John had requested and for what purpose.

"Lieutenant," said I, "there is, I believe, room at the bottom of the letter for you to write your reply. Would you care to do that, sir?"

"By no means. There will eventually be a file begun on this matter— if the provost marshal has not begun one already. I shall need the original that copies may be made." He then gave me a rather doubtful look. "But perhaps you will have some difficulty remembering the reply I have given you. I daresay you don't seem to me to look particularly bright."

His nose seemed to wrinkle a bit as he regarded me, as if he had just noticed what a stupid-looking fellow I was. That irked me somewhat. I had no wish to seem stupid to anyone.

"I believe I shall have no difficulty with it," said I. And so saying, I repeated to him what he had said, word for word.

"Yes, well, that will do, I suppose." He looked me up and down. "You may go now."

That I did—and gladly, executing a volte-face surely as smart as any soldier in his regiment could do—at least to my mind it was so. I marched out of his small office and kept right on marching until I made my exit through the Thames Street gate.

Then, after making my detour toward Grub Street, where I found the book by Elizabeth Rowe, I went as swiftly as those winding streets permitted to Drury Lane and Mr. Donnelly's surgery. Though not early, there were as yet no patients in the waiting room. He, himself, answered my knock upon the door and welcomed me inside.

"You'll not have to wait," said he. "I've just finished writing the report. The apothecary's boy has gone off to fetch the mortuary wagon."

"She will be given a church burial?"

"Sir John said he would get Trezavant to pay for a proper funeral, even if he had to squeeze the price of it from him."

"Surely Trezavant can afford it," said I.

"Living in such a house as that? Of course he can." He hesitated, then asked: "Would you like to see her?"

I gave that only brief consideration. "No, I think not," said I. "You see, sir, I knew her."

"That does make a difference, doesn't it? But . . . well, just give me a moment, I'll bring you my report."

He left me then and passed through the door into the next room. He could not have slept much the previous night; having performed his postmortem examination and written his report would have taken him hours. Yet he looked none the worse for it. I suspected that his years as a surgeon in the Royal Navy had prepared him for work in less-than-ideal situations. He always seemed to have a store of energy upon which to draw in emergencies. And what surprised me far more—he was of a remarkable and consistent good humor.

As he came forth from the next room, I caught a glimpse of a sheet-covered form lying upon the examination table. Poor Jenny Crocker, thought I, life did not offer her many possibilities, nor did she live long enough to pursue even one of them.

Mr. Donnelly waved his report in my direction. "It's all about as you might suppose," said he. "Time of death, approximately ten o'clock. Cause of death, a deep wound to the throat, which severed the jugular vein and the carotid artery. The attack was probably from the rear. Probable weapon, a long knife or short sword. And so on."

"Would there have been much pain?" I asked.

"I doubt it. The shock would have blocked feeling of any kind. Death would not have been instantaneous, though it could not have taken long to come — no, not long at all. Still, it was an ugly sort of death, particularly for one so young and pretty."

I took the report from Mr. Donnelly, tucked it away, and made ready to depart. He put his hand to my shoulder and walked with me the few steps to the door opening onto the hall.

"There was one more thing, Jeremy. It's in the report, so I might just as well mention it."

"Oh? What was that, sir?"

"The girl was pregnant — less than three months gone, I'd say, but pregnant, nevertheless." He looked at me curiously, and then said, "You didn't . . . ? You're not . . . ?"

"Uh, no sir, I had only known her about a week."

"Ah, well then . . ."

"Yes sir, goodbye sir." I left, greatly embarrassed.

And so I returned to Number 4 Bow Street, saw proof of Annie's departure, and then sought out Sir John in his chambers. I told him of my delivery of the letter to the Tower and what had transpired there. In general, he seemed satisfied with Lieutenant Tabor's assurance that a small force of mounted Carabineers would be made available to the magistrate, and that the lieutenant himself would command the force.

"He agreed then to the time and place I stipulated?" Sir John asked me.

"He did, sir."

"Well then, we must put our faith in him. What else have you for me?"

"Mr. Donnelly's postmortem report on Jenny Crocker."

At that, Sir John sighed so deeply that it sounded near to a moan. "Well, read it me. We may as well know all that he can tell us."

I took the report from my pocket and began reading it aloud as Sir John sat at his desk, hands folded before him, giving it his full attention. I had always been impressed by Mr. Donnelly's powers of concision. Though somewhat more detailed in description and presentation, the points he covered in the report were roughly the same ones he had made to me as we talked in his surgery. And just as before, the last of them had to do with Crocker's pregnancy.

Sir John shifted in his seat and leaned forward, indicating to me at least his keen interest in this new matter. When I had done, he leaned back and rubbed his chin a bit in concentration.

"Well," said he at last, "this is quite interesting. This puts a somewhat different complexion on matters, does it not?"

"How is that, sir?"

"Why, the unmarried woman who finds herself with child is, in most cases, simply the victim of him who has put her in that state. There are exceptions, however. When a woman is bold enough, she may seek payments of money for her and for her unborn child from the father — or from the putative father. She threatens him with disclosure should he refuse to pay up. Men who are in a sensitive position — married, members of the clergy, others who do not wish a scandal of that sort for whatever reason — are particularly vulnerable."

"But sir, that is blackmail, plain and simple."

"Indeed it is, Jeremy. In many cases, however, some might say that it is justifiable blackmail, for after all, who will take care of the unwed mother and her babe if she does not take care of herself?"

"Even so," said I.

"Even so," said Sir John, "it is a way fraught with peril. You'll recall that I said that the woman who attempted such a maneuver would have to be bold. That is because there are three courses of action open to the male victim of blackmail."

"Oh? Not merely two?"

"Pay up, you mean, or face disclosure?"

"That's right, sir."

"No, there is a third course. There is always danger that the intended victim may turn on the blackmailer and murder her, or have her murdered."

"Do you believe that to be the case in this instance?"

"Not necessarily. I say merely that it is a possibility we must now consider — one among others. But let me put it to you, Jeremy: Do you think this girl, this Jenny Crocker, would be capable of blackmail?"

I gave that a bit of thought, remembering her rather odd relationship with Arthur Robb, the late butler of the Trezavant house. But after all, I told myself, to go from that relatively innocent practice to blackmail was indeed a very great jump. And so, having thought, I gave Sir John a most judicious answer. "Perhaps," said I.

"Ah, thank you, Jeremy. I *do* like a firm opinion firmly stated."

"Well, I . . . I . . ."

"Never mind. It was wrong of me to ask. I would not want you to cast a stone at one who could not defend herself."

Not wishing to end our interview on that rather sour note, I ransacked my brain for some bit of information which might interest him, some triviality to do with the continuing investigation, but all that occurred to me was what I had heard the night before from Mr. Donnelly regarding Zondervan, the Dutch trader.

I put it to him rather casually, for that, no doubt, was all that it deserved. "Oh, by the bye, Sir John," said I, rising to leave, "did Mr. Donnelly tell you of his dinner at Lord Mansfield's residence and who it was he met there?"

"No, who was it, pray tell?" He seemed to have little interest in the matter. "Some duke or earl, I presume."

"By no means. It was that man Zondervan, who lives in St. James Street."

The change in Sir John was immediate and most impressive. He threw himself forward with such force that he seemed almost to be jumping across the desk at me.

"Tell me that again, Jeremy. Zondervan was at Lord Mansfield's last night?"

"Well, yes sir, but . . ."

"Perhaps you'd better give me the entire story."

Since I knew not what part of it he was interested in, I was obliged to do as he suggested and tell it all, as Mr. Donnelly had told me. And so that is what I did.

When I had done, Sir John sat thinking for a good long moment, saying nothing, merely fidgeting with the wedding ring on his finger. I thought, perhaps, that I had bored him so with my inexpert telling, that his mind had wandered off to more engaging matters. In that case, I decided it might be best to beat a hasty retreat.

"Will that be all, sir?" I asked.

"All for the present," said he, "but I should like to meet your Mr. Zondervan. He might have some interesting things to tell us. Why don't you call upon him and invite him here that I might speak with him."

"What if he does not wish to come, or puts me off to another day?"

"Then you must do as you did with Mr. Burnham."

"And what did I with him, sir?"

"You persuaded him."

Having no idea how I might go about that and feeling a certain trepidation, I brought myself to the Zondervan residence in St. James Street early in the afternoon; Sir John had requested that I bring him by just following that day's session of his Magistrate's Court. What was I to do? How was I to persuade him?

I thumped upon the door with the great hammer-shaped door-knocker hung in the very middle of it. The butler came — the same butler who had twice admitted me when I had come in search of Collier. He frowned at me, not inhospitably, but as one might frown in concentration. Then, of a sudden, did he smile in recognition.

"Now I remember you," said he. "You're the young fellow came investigating for the Bow Street Court, are you not?"

"So I am," said I. "And I've need to talk with your master today."

"My master? You mean, Mr. Zondervan? Why, he has just returned from Holland. He was not even present at the time of that robbery."

"There has been another since then," said I, "and in any case, I am not come to interrogate him, nor would I presume to."

"Oh," said the butler. "What then?"

"I have an invitation to offer him."

"Give it me, and I shall deliver it."

(All butlers are the same.)

"I am to present it in person."

"Yes . . . well . . . indeed." At least I had succeeded in perplexing the fellow. "All right, come inside and stay here at the door. I shall go and discuss the matter with Mr. Zondervan."

I did as he said and saw him disappear down the long central corridor. As I did, I became aware of a hum of activity throughout the house. Voices, footsteps, even a bit of hammering and sawing sounded from deep within the place. Might it have been upstairs or down? In truth, I could not tell.

I had not long to wait, for the butler quickly reappeared. I could not tell from his expression if I were to leave or be conducted into his master's exalted presence, for he wore, as near as I could tell, no expression whatsoever. He stopped a modest distance from me.

"If you will follow me, please."

That I did, and gladly. He moved along at a good pace, yet I had no real difficulty in keeping up. Remaining a few steps behind as I did, I was able to look right and left into the rooms as we passed them by. I know not quite how to express this, but an air of departure, of sudden change, seemed to have settled over the place. At first it seemed that there was naught which seemed truly different, except for cloths thrown over the damask-covered furniture in one room. But in another, there was something truly astonishing: that was the room wherein Mr. Zondervan's collection of paintings had been hung. The door stood open (which, I had been given to understand, was quite rare), and the afternoon sun poured in through the windows, lighting walls that were altogether empty. The room, which but a week ago was crowded with canvases, was now quite bare of them.

Could it be? I wished to stop and go inside the room to give it a thorough examination—but of course, I could not. I glanced back over my shoulder and gave a swift count to the rooms we had passed—yes, as I thought, there were three that side of the hall, which made this the fourth, which fitted my memory exactly. Yet perhaps my memory played me false.

"Young man, this way please." It was the butler, standing before the door opposite the empty picture gallery. I had wandered past him as I stared.

This was quite embarrassing. Nevertheless, I was determined to find out more.

"The paintings," I whispered to the butler, as I pointed at the room across the hall, "what happened to them?"

"They've been moved," said he, his face quite like that of a statue. "Spring cleaning, you know." And then, with a slight bow—hardly more than a nod of his head—he indicated the open door, and I proceeded into the room.

Mr. Zondervan was not quite what I expected. Mr. Gabriel Donnelly had told me what a remarkably entertaining man he was, and I had heard his great booming laugh, and so I believe that I thought to find a proper Dutchman of the sort frequently caricatured; which is to say, I looked for one who was fat, blustering, and jolly. What I found instead was a man of near six feet in height, slender, and handsome both in his features and in his bearing. He looked, in short, as every Englishman hopes to look. He stood next the fireplace, his elbow upon the mantelpiece, examining a vase of delicate porcelain, which, to me at least, appeared to be of Chinese origin. It looked quite like that one which Thomas Roundtree had stolen from Lord Mansfield's house and thereby brought such misery upon himself.

Mr. Zondervan looked up, took my measure, and surprised me by offering me a bow of an impressive depth; I could do naught but return the salutation.

"I like your manners, young sir," said he intelligibly enough, though with a bit of an accent. "Come over here, let me show you this vase."

I came forward (noticing as I did that the butler remained standing in the doorway) and looked with some interest at the object in Mr. Zondervan's hands. He surprised me a second time by handing it to me.

"You will be careful of it, of course," said he. It was in the nature of an order. "You are no doubt surprised at its lightness."

And indeed I was careful, though I was not surprised at its negligible weight. In that way, as in nearly every other, it was a duplicate of that which belonged to Lord Mansfield. It differed only in the design or picture which it bore upon its side. Whereas the one I held presented a noblewoman gesturing in a pacifying manner, the other, as I recalled, offered a dragon in an unusual pacified posture — head down, its scaly feet stretched out before it in an attitude of obeisance. No doubt it illustrated some tale well-known to the Chinese.

"Yes," said I, "it is wonderfully light. Even more impressive is its beauty." I offered the vase back to him.

"Ah, a true connoisseur," said he, taking it.

"I am flattered."

"You should be. I am the greatest of connoisseurs. For me to name you as one also puts you in truly exalted company."

At that, he erupted into laughter. I do not believe that he thought it such a *great* witticism. Perhaps he wished only to signal to me that it was indeed a witticism and not spoken in earnest. When at last his fit of laughter subsided, he placed the revered object upon the mantel and studied it for a moment.

"This vase has a mate. Did you know that?"

I had vowed to myself that I would plead ignorance in this matter — and I kept my pledge. "Why no," said I, "have you seen it? How do you know that this mate exists?"

"I held it in my hands last night." He shrugged. "But even before that, I knew that this mate existed, that it *had* to exist."

"Oh? How is that, sir?"

"Well, you see, there is a Chinese proverb—is that the word, 'proverb'?"

I nodded reassuringly.

"And the proverb says something like this, 'Even the fury of the dragon can be stilled by words of comfort from a beautiful woman.'"

"You have the beautiful woman, and so the mate to your vase must picture . . ."

"The dragon, yes," said he, "exactly so. It is a most unusual sort of dragon, for he grovels before her. In every other way the vase is exactly like the one here on my fireplace. Same size exactly, same shape . . . *Och*, I would love to own it!"

"Well, why don't you buy it? Make an offer?"

My questions were left unanswered. Of a sudden, he turned round and looked sharply at me. "Charles says you are from the Bow Street Court, and you wish to offer an invitation." Then did he shift his gaze beyond me and call out, "Is that correct, Charles?"

"That is correct, sir," said the butler.

"And so, young sir," said Mr. Zondervan, "what sort of invitation is it? To dinner? To coffee? To Newgate?"

He caught me with that. "Newgate, sir?" I laughed. "Oh no, not to Newgate. It is my understanding Sir John wants merely to meet you."

"To *meet* me? Has my fame spread so far? How would he hear of a simple Dutch trading man like me?"

"Why, from Mr. Gabriel Donnelly, sir. I believe you met him last night, did you not? It was at some dinner or other."

Then a look of realization appeared upon his face. "*Och, ja!* The Irish doctor! I brought him last night to his home."

"And I brought him away again."

"*You?* I don't understand."

"Simple enough," said I. "There was a murder last night, and I was sent by Sir John to fetch Mr. Donnelly to the location of the crime. He is, though you may not know this, the medical examiner for the coroner."

"Ah," said Mr. Zondervan, "I do believe I heard that."

"Yes sir, well, coming from this dinner party, he was full of your stories and talking of how well you told them. I believe they were tales of some town in Holland, one with a rather comical name. I can't quite . . ."

"*Ja, ja, Dingendam!*"

"That's it, of course. But Mr. Donnelly could not remember them properly, nor could he do them justice in the telling."

"I daresay," said he, puffing up a bit.

"But Sir John heard enough so that he was eager to meet you."

"To tell him the stories?"

"Oh, perhaps one or two, but just to meet you, sir. He leads a rather humdrum life, poor man. We're after him constantly to expand his circle of acquaintance, but he is shy of it—his affliction, you know."

"Affliction?"

"Perhaps you didn't know, sir, but he is blind."

"Yes, yes, I heard something of that." He fell silent then, considering the matter. Then, rousing himself: "Charles, have we any reason to doubt this young man is who he says he is?"

"None that I know, sir," came the response of the butler from behind me.

"Well then, I believe that we can spare Sir John Fielding an hour or two, don't you?"

"As you say, sir."

"Have the coach brought round. I must attend to something before we go." And then to me: "You will accept a ride in my coach back to Bow Street, I assume?"

"With pleasure, sir," said I to him.

"Good. If you will wait for me at the door, I shall join you there."

With that, Charles, the butler, ushered me out into the corridor and we began our march to the street entrance. As we set out, I could not but notice that the door to the room across the hall—the former picture gallery—had mysteriously (and noiselessly) been closed. Then did I note that all the doors along the way, some of which had earlier stood open, were now likewise shut.

The butler left me at the vestibule, promising that the master would be along shortly. "I must go summon the coach, or you and he will both be kept waiting." Then, turning, he left me.

When I stood at that same place a few minutes before, I had heard sounds of considerable activity from a place or places in the depths of the house. So was it again. The hammering, the sound of heavy objects pushed across the floor, all of it heard, but dimly, suggested to me that preparations were underway to move Mr. Zondervan's entire household a considerable distance. There were voices, too, of course, yet so muffled and indistinct that it was impossible to make sense of what they were saying. Yet as I listened, I remembered that Sir John had often said that each voice had its own song, its own pitch, and its own key. And it seemed to me that I knew the song one of those voices was singing. It was a song I had heard before. This one, it seemed to me, came from somewhere below stairs, and though I could understand little or nothing of what it said, I sensed the emotion it expressed: It was anger, no mistaking that—and this, too, seemed right. Where had I heard it? Who was it? Whence such anger?

I know not how long I stood there, deep in concentration, trying to answer those questions. Yet when I heard footsteps down the hall, I looked up, smiling, to greet Mr. Zondervan. He stepped briskly into my sight, the very picture of male elegance in dress; he wore a cape about his shoulders, and in his hand he carried his tricorn and his gloves.

Though the butler was absent, I saw no need to wait for him to open the door for his master. I hauled it open and pulled it back. Quite heavy it was, too.

"Good God, where *is* Charles?" asked Mr. Zondervan more or less rhetorically.

As if in answer came the sound of running feet, then appeared the butler, jog-trotting for all he was worth.

"Too late, Charles, this young man has usurped your position, I fear. He opens the door with great authority."

"Sorry, sir, I was delayed in back there with the porters."

"Ah well, the coach will no doubt soon appear."

"At any moment, sir."

And indeed in the very next moment it did come, rattling, rumbling, clop-clop-clopping into view. The driver reined in the four horses before the house, and the footman was down in a trice to throw open the door to the carriage. Mr. Zondervan strode past me and was already down the steps before he turned round to look for me.

"Come along, young man—unless it is that you would prefer to walk."

"By no means, sir," said I and ran in pursuit.

I have no idea how at that moment I happened to remember, nor what trick of the mind then came into play, but it was precisely then, as I scrambled up and into the interior of the coach that I realized whose voice I had heard in the vestibule. It belonged to none other than Constable Will Patley, the most recently recruited of the Bow Street Runners.

In the event, the meeting between Sir John and Mr. Zondervan was something of a disappointment—or so it seemed to me. The two got on famously. Whereas I expected Sir John to launch into a merciless interrogation of the Dutchman, all I heard from the magistrate's chambers was the sound of laughter. How could he be taken in by him in such a way?

Later it occurred to me that my expectations were rather unrealistic. After all, what more had he to rely upon than my suspicions that Mr. Zondervan was indeed the ruthless Dutch trader that Moses Martinez had described to me in such peculiar fashion? (And later, much later, I discovered that he had a good deal more than that to rely upon—but I anticipate somewhat.) Leave it that having done my part in persuading Mr. Zondervan to visit Sir John, I expected for insufficient reason that some great result would come from the meeting. And so in my frustrated state, I felt relieved when at last I detected sounds indicating the Dutchman's imminent departure; chairs scraped across the floor as their occupants rose; the laughter ceased; their voices deepened in cordial farewell.

As both men appeared at the door to the magistrate's chambers, I rose from the bench nearby. Sir John summoned me to them.

"Jeremy," said he, "would you accompany this gentleman to his coach?"

Then did the gentleman in question make his final farewell in phrases so fawning and insincere that I now find that I have expunged them totally from my memory. All I can now recall is that I suddenly experienced a profound wish to gag.

I fought it off, however, and in respectful silence conveyed our guest to the door, and through it to the street. There he paused before his waiting coach and offered me a smile.

"I wish to thank you, young sir. I spent a very pleasant hour with your Sir John Fielding. I found him a charming old character, not in the least impeded by—how did you call it?—his affliction."

We said our goodbyes, and I, once more feeling my gorge rising, retreated swiftly through the door. When I reached Sir John, I found him once more at his desk and chuckling still.

"Jeremy, come in, come in," said he. "What did you think of him — this fellow Zondervan? Very amusing, very entertaining, couldn't you say?"

Well, you certainly seemed to find him so," said I, a bit cross. "I've seldom heard such laughter come from this room."

"I believe I laughed as much at our situation as what was said."

"And what was the situation?"

"Each of us was trying to convince the other that he was different from what he might seem."

"I don't quite follow," said I.

"Quite simple. He seemed to me to be rather large — at least tall. Have I got him right so far?"

"You do, yes."

"And there was a bit of vanity crept into his voice, in spite of himself. And so I should say he is rather handsome, or fancies himself so. Altogether, he thinks himself superior to the rest of us. Did you see some of that?"

"I did," I said. "I'd say you have him to the life."

"And yet that tall, handsome fellow who believes he is one of nature's noblemen comes before me and seeks to convince me that he is nothing more or less than a jolly Dutchman. And I, at the same time, do my best to convince him that I am naught but a . . . a . . ."

"A charming old character?"

"Right you are! A codger, an eccentric, a . . ." He stopped. "But whence came that 'charming old character' phrase?"

"Where indeed!" said I. "From Mr. Zondervan, just as he departed."

"Perfect!" he gloated, all but rubbing his hands with glee. "But I bested him! He let drop a few things he would not have said to one he held less in contempt."

I judged from this that Sir John held him seriously suspect. This, then, was the time to bring forth the observations I had made while in the house in St. James Street. I proceeded to do so, describing the empty picture gallery and the cloth covers thrown over the furniture, the general air of a household in transition.

"There was a good deal of hammering and sawing, and the sound of boxes dragged about," said I. "The butler claimed that it was no more than spring housecleaning. Nevertheless, I am certain that they were preparing to make a move."

"Yes, well, most interesting, I must admit." He said it in that musing, dismissive manner that quite drove me mad.

And so I vowed that I would present the next bit of news I had for him in such a way that he would be unable to dismiss it in his usual manner. I thought how I might engage his interest.

"Sir John," said I then in a tone of great importance, "you will never guess who was there at Zondervan's residence."

"You are right, Jeremy, I will never guess that, for as you know—or should know by now—I do not indulge in such childish practices as guessing. Now, if you have something to tell me, by all means do so. You have my complete attention."

"Do you wish me to tell you, or no?" I fear I sounded quite petulant, for I was rather distressed at that moment.

"I have said so, have I not?"

Having gone thus far, there was naught for me to do but continue. And so I described to him where I was when I heard Constable Patley's voice, and how I heard it; which is to say, as a song without words. Sir John did indeed listen carefully, and when I had done, he seemed for a few moments to be at a loss for words. On such rare occasions, it was difficult to divine just what he might be thinking.

But then he shrugged rather grandly, and I could tell that he had decided to deal with it as lightly as possible. "Ah well, those old houses, you know," said he, "they play tricks upon your ears. If you had stood in some other spot, the same voice might have sounded exactly like Clarissa's or even mine." At that he laughed abruptly, as if the very idea were so outlandish that it amused him greatly.

"I do not believe, sir, that Mr. Zondervan's house is particularly old."

"Ah well, some of the new ones also have such faults. But let us get on to more serious matters, shall we? I have here a letter that must go out by today's post. In your absence, Mr. Marsden took it in dictation for me. Will you take it to the post coach house, Jeremy?"

We had done with our sparring. "Of course I will, sir."

He pushed it from its corner across the desk toward me. I reached over and took it, turned it over, and saw that it was addressed to the chief customs officer, Gravesend, Kent. Below that, written in red, as Mr. Marsden so often liked, was the single word, "urgent." I could not suppose, nor even imagine, what matter Sir John might have with the chief of customs down at the mouth of the Thames. But I would ask no more questions. I would simply go where I was sent, and do what I was told, like a good errand boy.

I said my goodbye and started for the door, only to be called back.

"By the bye, Jeremy, you did not happen to mention to Mr. Zonder-van—or to anyone else, for that matter—that you believed you had heard Constable Patley's voice in the house, did you?"

What was he getting at now? "No sir, I told only you."

"That's as it should be," said he. "Keep it so."

Like many an errand boy before me, I sulked the distance to my destination and dawdled all the way back. I dawdled willfully and skillfully, investigating streets and shops that had not, until then, received proper attention from me. So much time did I waste that before I knew it, dark had fallen without my notice. When at last it did come to my attention, I thought it likely that I was late for dinner. But then, with Annie gone, would there be any dinner?

In any case, I hastened home to Number 4 Bow Street and arrived in time to see the last few of the constables disappearing into Sir John's chambers at the end of the long hall. An operation of some size was under way.

Jog-trotting down the hall, I was stopped by Mr. Baker, who was checking his armory.

"What's afoot?" I asked him.

"Something big," said he. "Pistols and cutlasses for all, and I've been invited along. He's been asking for you, Jeremy. Better get inside."

As I stepped into the magistrate's chambers, I did a swift survey of the Bow Street Runners in the room and counted but nine present. Constable Perkins, Brede, and Patley were missing.

Sir John stood before them. ". . . and much as I dislike it, it will be necessary to divide our meager force . . ."

ELEVEN

*In which matters
are brought to a
startling finish*

There would be little point in presenting to you, reader, only what I saw and heard on that decisive night, for though I saw much in the company of Sir John, I did not see all. This was, I daresay, the most far-reaching and ambitious undertaking ever attempted by the magistrate and his Bow Street Runners. In fact, so bold was it that the assistance of both the Army and the Coast Guard was required.

As Sir John explained his plan to the listening constables at the start of the evening, it was necessary to divide his force into three much smaller groups. There had to be Bow Street Runners at the residence of Lord Mansfield in Bloomsbury Square, at the Zondervan house in St. James Street, and at the dock in Bermondsey, where a Dutch ship by the name of *Dingendam* prepared for departure—and all parts of the divided force had to be in place more or less simultaneously.

"It would not do," Sir John explained, "if one or more should escape our net and run to tell his fellows at another location before our net has closed upon them. Now, you all have timepieces, do you not?"

There was a general sound of assent throughout the room in response to his question. Perhaps only I was without one of my own.

"Be in place by eight. Wait in concealment until you have action from the two houses of the sort I have described. Those of you who are assigned to the dock in Southwark, simply wait, but if they should try to take the tide and slip out, stop them. You may not be able to do that, but if you can't, the final move will be out of our hands. Mr. Bailey will be in charge of the Bermondsey group, and he will make all decisions of that sort. If you have questions, ask them quickly and ask them now."

There were a few. The most fateful of them came from Mr. Bailey himself: "Just how much force are we permitted to use, sir?"

"As much as is necessary," responded Sir John. "If there be any casualties this evening, let them not be constables. That is as clear as I can be on that question. Pistols and cutlasses. Do with them what must be done."

It was well over an hour afterward that Sir John and I sat in the coach loaned us by Black Jack Bilbo. The coach sat some houses down from Lord Mansfield's grand place in Bloomsbury Square. With the door to the coach open, I had a good view of the house. Mr. Rumford sat next to me, as did Constable Queenan, and across from us, altogether relaxed, sat Sir John, curled comfortably within the generous space of the coach interior. He had a smile upon his face. It was as if, having planned this undertaking as precisely as he had, he was certain that it had already taken place and had come to a good conclusion. Nevertheless, the event had not yet taken place, and the conclusion to which it might come was still open to doubt. All we could do was wait and see.

"Do you see anything?" asked Constable Rumford; it was, in fact, the third time that he had put that question to me.

And again I responded, "Nothing yet."

Mr. Bilbo's driver and footman seemed to be getting restless, as was the team of four horses. I knew those animals. They were rather high-strung. When they were in harness, they wanted to be off and running. Such inactivity as was not their lot made them fractious and nervous.

It was now well after dark, of course, and though the square was well-lit with streetlamps, there was no moon at this hour of the night. There were dark corners and spaces enough to hide a good many. I paid particular attention to those places, looking for movement. At last I saw a bit of it, as a figure in black emerged from a passageway which seemed to run beside the house just beyond Lord Mansfield's. As the figure moved closer to the nearest streetlamp, I saw better; it was a woman, one wearing a voluminous skirt, a shawl, and a prim little kerchief upon her head. She looked familiar.

Of course she did! I had indeed forgotten that the last such robbery had begun with a woman seeking refuge from an attacker. That was how the robbers had cozened Arthur, Mr. Trezavant's butler, into opening the door to them. This was doubtless the woman. Further, she looked at a distance quite like Mary Pinkham, formerly Lady Lilley's personal maid. I had come to suspect that she had played this role earlier. She looked the street up and down, paying little mind to Mr. Bilbo's coach, for the driver had pulled up in such a way that it faced away from her; in appearance, it seemed simply to be waiting for a passenger to emerge from the house. Having satisfied herself, the woman removed her shawl and waved it several times in the direction of Great Russell Street. From where I sat, it was impossible to see who or what she waved at without dismounting from the coach. I had no intention of doing that.

Before I saw their wagon, I heard the sound of horses' hooves and the squeak of the wheels. Then at last it appeared. The wagon was an unusual covered sort, so that quite a number of men could be carried in back without being seen.

"They're here," said I very quietly.

Constable Queenan shuffled and stamped, collecting himself, and was near out of the coach before Constable Rumford grabbed him and pulled him back.

"Don't jump out just yet," said he to him. "They're not supposed to know we're here."

"Oh . . . oh yes, sorry," said Mr. Queenan.

"The idea," said Sir John, "is to catch them between you two on the outside and Mr. Perkins and Mr. Brede on the inside. You see the sense of that, don't you, Mr. Queenan?"

"Yes sir, I do sir."

"Just be careful not to shoot or slice any of our fellows, won't you?"

"Oh, I will, sir."

As this whispered discussion continued, I kept my eyes upon the odd-looking wagon as it pulled up before Lord Mansfield's residence. Five men jumped out the back, well-armed, dressed in black, and all likely wearing black face paint as well. One, whom I took to be the leader, held a hurried conversation with the woman — Mistress Pinkham? They parted, nodding in seeming agreement, and the leader beckoned the others to follow.

"They're about to go inside," said I, sotto voce.

Once more, Constable Queenan shifted his feet nervously.

"How many are there?" Constable Rumford asked.

"Five of them," said I.

I could see her talking through the door. Was she weeping? Could Pinkham have done that? Whoever she was, she was quite an actress. The robbers were lined up behind her on either side of the door; they leaned forward in their eagerness to be inside.

Then, of a sudden, the door came open just a bit. The woman remained a moment, but was swept aside in the concerted dash of her five companions. The door slammed shut behind them, and she went to the wagon.

"They're in," said I, excitedly, all but shouting it.

"All right, gentlemen, take your places before Lord Mansfield's door."

There was a great scramble to leave the coach. I threw open the door on my side and jumped out to allow Constable Rumford an easy passage to the pavement. Constable Queenan was already out and running for the wagon, a pistol in his hand. Rumford took a place directly before Lord Mansfield's door. While standing on the walkway, I had a better view of the situation, and saw a flaw that had developed in the plan due to the positioning of the robbers' wagon. It had pulled up a bit shy of the door of the house, thereby making it quite impossible for Queenan to cover both the door and the wagon at the same time.

"Sir John," said I, leaning back into the coach, "I see something that must be done! Don't worry. I'll be careful."

Running to relieve Mr. Queenan, I heard Sir John call after me twice, yet I continued, sure that had he eyes as I had to see things plain, he would no doubt have sent me out himself.

(Have no fear, reader, I was armed. Though I had no cutlass at my side, Mr. Baker had buckled round me a brace of pistols. He would not allow me to venture forth at night unarmed, and on that night in particular, he thought it my duty to serve as Sir John's guard. I hoped that in lending a hand to the constables, I was not neglecting their chief.)

By the time I reached Mr. Queenan, he had ordered the driver and the woman down out of the wagon; they were slow to move, angry, desperate; they seemed ready to bolt at the first opportunity. I explained my intrusion to Queenan, and he assured me he was grateful for my aid. Then did he join Rumford at the door.

I saw that indeed I was correct: The woman in black, who had played out the drama at the door, was indeed Mistress Pinkham. Her eyes widened in recognition as I pulled out both pistols and cocked them. The driver, an old teamster, hard-faced and silent, looked to be one who had driven many an illegal mile in his life.

No more than a minute had elapsed in all this.

Shots were fired inside the house. Though they sounded no more lethal than those of a child's pop gun, the sound of them had penetrated an oaken door: The skirmish had truly begun.

Then, just moments later, that oak door flew open, and out tumbled the robbers. There were just four of them; one of their number had fallen inside the house. And after them, in noisy pursuit, came Constable Perkins, a pistol in his hand, and a knife clenched between his teeth, and Constable Brede, waving a cutlass about, shouting, aiming his pistol in a most threatening manner at the nearest of the villains.

Reader, you cannot imagine the look of consternation upon the black-painted faces of those in that robber band when, as they emerged from the house, they beheld four pistols, loaded and cocked, aimed at their hearts by Rumford and Queenan. The trouble was, you see, that I myself did not imagine that look of consternation, I saw it. In so doing, I took my attention away from my two prisoners for no more than the length of a glance. Yet that was time enough for them to wreak havoc upon us.

First of all, I had made an error in allowing Mistress Pinkham and the driver to stand but six feet away, which was much too close. ("Jeremy," Mr. Perkins lectured me afterward, "you must never allow them to get that close unless you intend to shoot them on the spot"— and such was not my intention.) In that brief space of time, Pinkham leapt across that short distance, grabbed me by the back of the neck with one hand, and with the other grasped my right wrist and attempted unsuccessfully to wrestle the pistol from my hand. Unable to do more than hang on, she settled for that and hung on to me like a lamprey. And then did she begin screaming, rending the night with fearful wails.

Meantime, the driver slipped from my view and made for his seat on the wagon box, and one of the four on the steps broke away from the others and ran to follow.

What I did then, no gentleman would have done, but I was not then a gentleman, nor have I become one: I clubbed Mistress Mary Pinkham upon the head with the pistol in my free hand. I delivered a sharp whack with the barrel, which quite surprised her, but did nothing more. It took two more stiff blows and a bleeding pate to render her unconscious. She slipped with a bump down to the pavement, giving me the first full picture I had had of the situation since her assault upon me.

The driver urged the restive horses forward just as he who had leaped aboard behind him raised a pistol to shoot at us. Seeing that, I raised my own and fired at him. I did not know then whether I had hit him, but he pulled back, leaving the driver exposed. I set myself to fire again with my second pistol just as the horses pulled the wagon past me, removing the driver from my sight. But then, from behind me, was a final shot discharged. I looked round me and saw that it had come from Constable Perkins, who stood coolly, his arm still outstretched, the pistol in his hand still smoking.

We waited, holding our breath as one for a long moment as the horses plunged onward past Mr. Bilbo's coach and toward Hart Street. We knew that if it made the turn in good order, then it was under control. If, on the other hand, it did not, then whoever held the reins was badly wounded, dead, or dying. And as one, we heaved a sigh of disappointment as it sailed round the corner like a frigate on wheels.

Though Sir John was reasonably pleased to have four of the robber band (including the now-conscious Pinkham) under guard, and a fifth wounded on Lord Mansfield's floor, he had little time for his constables' reports on how it had all been accomplished. I, however, did welcome Constable Rumford's call; he had wiped the faces of the prisoners with a towel and all proved to be white, except the wounded fellow in the house. Once Sir John had me in the coach, he signaled Mr. Bilbo's driver that it was time to move on to the next stop of our itinerary. As the coach began to roll, I was caught in the midst of reloading the pistol I had discharged. It was a ticklish job at best—to attempt it as we bumped over cobblestones and as he berated me for what he called my "childish propensity for getting in the worst sort of trouble."

He continued: "And what good did you do? One in your charge escaped. The other—a woman, if you will!—you had to beat senseless to bring under restraint. How much help did you, in truth, provide?"

Continuing in that vein, he filled the time it took to drive from Bloomsbury Square to St. James Street—not a great distance. I made no effort to defend myself, simply let him talk on—for what, after all, could I say in my defense?

At last, as we pulled up before the Zondervan residence, I said to Sir John: "You cannot say anything to me in criticism, sir, that I have not already said to myself a dozen times over." And indeed it was so.

(I did manage to get the pistol reloaded, however.)

As we climbed from the coach, Mr. Bilbo's driver called down to us, asking if we would be needing him further. "We're right close to home here," said he.

"I know that, driver," said Sir John, "but I fear that we have one more stop to make this evening, and that will take us all the way to Bermondsey."

"Ah well, sir, not that we mind. We was quite entertained by that show your lads put on back in Bloomsbury." He cackled at his little witticism. "Ain't that so, Charlie?"

"Aw, ain't it!" the footman agreed. "I ain't seen such fireworks since the king's birthday. I swear I ain't."

Sir John did not respond. He was not amused. Instead, he turned to me. "Well," said he in little more than a whisper, "how does it look hereabouts?"

"What do you mean, sir?" I was honestly puzzled.

"I *mean*," said he, "do you see any villains lurking about? Any of our fellows?"

"No villains, sir, but I see Constable Sheedy posted at the door of the Zondervan house."

"Then that means they have it secured. Come along, Jeremy, take me to him."

With that, he pawed the air with his right hand, indicating that he wished to be assisted to the door. I put my left arm out, and he placed his hand upon it. Thus we proceeded through the open gate and up two shallow stairs, where Constable Sheedy greeted us enthusiastically.

"Welcome to your new home, Sir John," said he.

"Whatever could you mean, Mr. Sheedy?"

"I mean, sir, it's been emptied out clean as a whistle, and it's for you, if you want it. Whoever moves in first can claim it."

"Hmmm," said Sir John, giving a vigorous rub to his chin. "You followed my instructions, did you?"

"Oh, yes sir, we waited till that black-faced crew was out of the house and away in that wagon."

"And you waited till Zondervan had left, as well?"

"The big, tall Dutchman? Oh yes, sir, but that was earlier. His coach pulled up at the door, and he come out, and without a word to the driver or the footman, he got in and they took off—like it was all worked out beforehand."

"I'm sure it was," said Sir John. "But tell me, did Constable Patley follow close behind?"

"Oh, yes sir, just like he was supposed to. I don't know where he got his horse, but he sure knew how to ride it."

I was quite baffled by this. I had, of course, noticed that Mr. Patley was absent from the assembly of the Bow Street Runners in the magistrate's chambers, just as constables Perkins and Brede were; but I half-suspected that he had gone over to the other side, for I was sure that it was Patley's voice I had heard during my last visit to this house. Could he have been a turncoat, a spy for the Dutchman? Could such things be?

"He got his horse, Mr. Sheedy, at the same place we got our coach— on loan from Mr. John Bilbo, down the street a few houses. But is that the full schedule of events?"

"Uh, no sir, it's not. Just before you came along, that same wagon came back, the one that left with all that black-faced crew about half an hour ago."

"Oh? Who was driving it?"

"Not the one who drove it out of here. That one was an old fella, kind of hard-looking, if you know the sort."

"Yes, I do, I certainly do," said Sir John. "But the old fellow was *not* the driver?"

"No sir, it was a much younger one—not one of the blackies, you understand. This man was just as white as you or me."

"And what happened? Were you at the door then? Did he see you?"

"Yes, I was at the door, sir, and he did see me. And when he did, he just whipped those horses and took right off again."

"You're sure he saw you, your red waistcoat? And that's why he ran?"

(The red waistcoat, reader, was all that the Bow Street Runners had in common as a uniform.)

"As sure as I can be about anything."

"Very well, Mr. Sheedy. I'd call that an excellent report. Now where are Mr. Baker and Mr. Kelly?"

"Oh, they could be almost anyplace," said the constable. "They were going to go through the house room by room to make sure it was just as empty as we thought."

"All right," said Sir John, "we'll find them. Come along, Jeremy."

Eventually, we did, though not before we had searched through many an empty room, calling for them, hearing nothing in return but the echo of our own footsteps. I had never been in a house so big that was so empty.

"It's a bit like walking through a haunted house, isn't it, sir?" said I.

"I was just thinking something like that myself," said he. "Ghosts, however, are not quite in my line."

It was not until we reached the rear of the ground floor, and the stairs which led to the kitchen, that we heard voices; I recognized Mr. Baker's, and with a bit of difficulty, Mr. Kelly's as well; but the third, though familiar, eluded me completely.

Sir John and I descended the narrow stairway in the usual way: he with one hand upon my shoulder, and the other touching the walls as we circled downward. The voices ceased as we neared the bottom of the stairs. I must have taken that as a menacing development, for I suddenly found my hand upon the butt of the pistol I had just loaded. Yet I removed it when I saw that the voice I had failed to identify belonged to Mr. Collier, once the butler in the Lilley house and now the same in the Trezavant residence.

"Well, it's you, Sir John," said Mr. Baker. "I've got a fellow here you may know."

"His name is Collier," said the magistrate. "I met him at Lord Lilley's, who discharged him following the first robbery. Jeremy met him again on numerous occasions, lately at Trezavants."

"I guess I was right. You do know him."

"His voice is quite distinctive—whinging, most irritating. I identified him immediately when I had heard it."

"We found him hiding in the kitchen pantry," said Constable Kelly. "There's some food in there still—potatoes, apples, and the like. Maybe he got hungry."

"Maybe he did. What about that, Mr. Collier? What were you doing in the pantry?"

The butler glanced left and right, first at Sir John, then at me, then back to Sir John. "Hiding," said he at last.

"Come now, Mr. Collier, I remember you as much more forthcoming than that. Hiding from what? Hiding from whom? Surely you can do better than that, sir!"

"Well . . . I would, sir, but to answer as frankly as you wish me to would involve me in matters I do not wish to discuss. They are far too personal."

"Too personal?" said Sir John rather skeptically. "Or might it be that in discussing those matters frankly you would incriminate yourself?"

Mr. Collier presented to us an expression of wounded innocence. "Why, sir," said he, "I do not know what you might mean by that!"

"Why, sir, I believe you do," said Sir John, thrusting himself toward the butler with such force that he came within an inch of butting him in the head. "I believe it was you who stole Lady Trezavant's jewels."

"That's . . . that's wrong. I did not even know where they were hid. How could I know such secrets of the household when I had been there but a day or two?"

"Because you went there *knowing* that secret of the household. It was all too convenient, your arrival just after Trezavant's former butler had been felled by an apoplectic stroke—and so early, too."

"I told you—" Then did Mr. Collier realize his error and point at me, "no, I told him that I had heard the news on the street. Such matters are much discussed from house to house."

"Mr. Collier, from whom did you hear it?"

"As I say, I heard it on the street."

"*From whom did you hear it?*" Sir John's tone was most severe.

The poor fellow—in spite of myself, I felt pity for him. He looked all about the room: at me, at the two constables, everywhere but at Sir John. The smell of fear was upon him.

Finally, he said, "I heard it from Charles, who was the butler here."

"And perhaps not then, but eventually, you heard—from Mr. John Abernathy, whom you may know as Johnny Skylark, or more likely from Mr. Zondervan himself—the location of the jewels, your best opportunity for removing them, and the nature of your payment." At that, Sir John paused. "What *was* the nature of the payment, Mr. Collier? I believe you came here to collect it."

No response came.

"Constable Baker, did you search this man? You had the right, you know."

"I did, sir. I found naught but a few odd pence and shillings, a linen kerchief, some bits of string, and some keys."

"No bag of sovereigns?"

"No sir."

"Well, the keys may prove of some value. Have you encountered any locked doors?"

"Not as yet. We found the front door wide open, but we've not been through the servants' rooms."

"Well, let us do that now, shall we?" Then to Mr. Collier: "What say you to that, sir?"

He had naught to say, but went along willingly enough. Yet I, on the other hand, wished to stay, for I had an idea all of a sudden—one which made perfect sense, at least to me.

"Sir John," said I, "might I remain and search a bit on my own?"

"Certainly you may," said he. "If you've an inspiration, by all means pursue it."

I took an unlit candle in a single holder and lit it from the candelabrum in Mr. Kelly's hand. As they marched off together, Mr. Collier threw me a look of concern, while at the same time Sir John began discoursing on just how it was the location of the hiding place had come to the butler.

"It was that poor child Crocker who divulged the secret to Abernathy, chief of the robbers, on their visit. They threatened Crocker, and she quite rightly gave it up. But Mrs. Trezavant had then taken the jewels away with her. It was a stupid place to hide valuables, anyway. After all, just above the cistern in the water closet—people in and out all day long. You cannot expect . . ." And so on.

Sir John continued, yet I, though interested, set out upon my search—not for gold or paper money, but rather for a painting. That, it seemed to me, was the payment that Mr. Collier would have begged from Zondervan. He might steal for something from Zondervan's collection.

In truth, I believed that Sir John was wrong. It seemed to me that just above the cistern in the water closet would have made an excellent hiding place—though it should have been altered after Jenny Crocker had told of it. Had she also told her master? Had she confessed to her mistress? Had she breathed a word of her betrayal of the secret to the rude Dutch woman who served as Mrs. Trezavant's personal maid? Perhaps not. Perhaps only to me. And Mrs. Trezavant had doubtless told Sir John.

Furthermore, I believed above the cistern to be a good spot to hide such grand items as jewels because it was commonplace and indecorous. And so I resolved to look for the painting, if it be a painting with which Collier was paid, in the most ordinary places. I reasoned that the butler had not been long in the house when Constables Baker and Kelly came down the stairs. He had been found in the pantry, and so that was where I began my search.

Looking round it, I saw that there were not many places in the pantry where one might tuck away a good-sized painting in its frame — and all the paintings I had seen in Mr. Zondervan's gallery had been rather large. I looked behind the two barrels (one of apples and the other of potatoes), but there was no such object hidden away there. I clambered up upon the apple barrel and looked on every shelf, feeling a bit foolish as I did so, for there was not room enough upon them to accommodate any package so large. I left the pantry.

Perhaps he had been longer in the house than I supposed. Why, then it could be anywhere. Perhaps I was wrong about the mode of payment. It might indeed be a bag of sovereigns that I should seek. In that case, he could have dropped it in with the apples or the potatoes. In annoyance, I began roaming the kitchen, throwing open drawers, looking behind doors, looking into every dark corner, even in such places as a framed picture such as I envisioned could not possibly be hidden.

Then came to me an impulsive notion which struck me as fitting, but a bit unreasonable. Feeding the sink where dishes, pots, and pans were washed was a capacious and, no doubt, efficient lead cistern. What if payment had been left for Mr. Collier atop the cistern, just as the jewels had been left atop the cistern in the Trezavant water closet? What if, indeed? Well, were that the case, then the payment, if a picture, would have to be very much smaller than any I had in mind — but no matter, I thought it worth a try.

I found a wooden bucket under the sink and pushed it over to what seemed a good vantage point, then upended it, making it an excellent stool. I stepped upon it and looked at what was there. Initially, I was disappointed, for there was no such object as a framed picture upon the cistern, neither wrapped nor unwrapped.

But there was something there—rolled up—at the very farthest reach there at the top of the cistern. I stepped off and pushed the bucket still closer, then stretched to the utmost and managed to get a tentative grip upon it and pulled it off. I stepped down and examined what I had.

It was indeed a large piece of canvas, but unframed and rolled up and secured by three separate bands of string. It was a good two-and-a-half or perhaps three feet high. And there was no telling just how much had been rolled up within, or what it might contain—but I was eager to find out.

As in so many of these kitchens below the stairs, there was a great deal table set back a bit from the cooking space. It ran nearly the length of the room. It was here that I might unroll the canvas and see what it contained. I worked excitedly to remove those lengths of string which secured the roll. I had one off and was working on the second when I heard the voice of Sir John hectoring Mr. Collier as the four approached the open door.

"Sir John," I called out, "I've something here will interest you."

Just as he was asking what that something might be, Mr. Collier came crashing through the doorway, wide-eyed, angered, and expecting the worst.

"How dare you!" he shouted. "That is not your property. I advise you to take your hands from it this very moment."

With that, he flew to me and attempted to grab the rolled canvas from me. Quite taking me by surprise as he did, he almost succeeded. Though a moment later, the constables were there pulling him away, there was no silencing him.

"You've no right," said he most petulantly. "That painting belongs to me and to no other."

"Just what is this painting?" asked Sir John. "Is it one of great beauty? Of great worth?"

"Sir," said I, "it is one of those I described to you that hung in the gallery in the floor above." (I had unrolled enough of it to recognize the peasants at play.) "I believe this is what served as payment between Zondervan and Mr. Collier."

"A painting?" said the magistrate, surprised near to disbelief.

"Mr. Collier values it highly."

"You understand only its worth in pounds and shillings," said the butler contemptuously. "There are other, higher modes of valuation."

"Why, I suppose there are," said Sir John, "just as there are other modes of valuating the worth of a human life. To most of us, the life of another would be worth a great deal, and to Jenny Crocker, her own life was of inestimable worth. But you took it, as if it were a paltry thing, did you not? You stole her life from her, just as you stole the diamonds, pearls, and rubies from the Trezavants."

"You accuse me of murder?"

"What else am I to think? She ran out after you, suspecting what you had done, and you simply killed her in order to cover your crime."

"Where is your proof?"

"Oh, we shall find a blood-stained knife in the garden that someone will identify as your own. Perhaps there is blood upon some item of your clothing. It could be, too, that one of the servants other than Crocker saw you depart for the back garden, may even be aware that the girl followed you. We have barely begun our investigation. There is no telling what we shall turn up."

Mr. Collier fearfully considered what Sir John had just said. He seemed about to speak when the magistrate himself resumed his reasoned accusation.

"You should be aware, sir—though you may not be—that we successfully laid a trap for the robber band at the home of the Lord Chief Justice. We pulled in four of them—perhaps five, if another of them survives his wounds. Now, Lord Mansfield is unlikely to show them any mercy, since it was his home they attacked, but if one of these can give witness against the rest, he might be given transportation, rather than the rope. But you, sir, you are in a position worse than any of those, for you committed murder to cover your theft. I see little possibility of leniency for you."

Now Mr. Collier seemed so wracked by emotion that he appeared near tears. Again, he seemed about to speak when Sir John spoke up.

"Unless . . ."

That single word gave him reason to hope. He clasped his hands tightly together and uttered a heartfelt response: "Yes?"

"Unless you were to admit your part in the theft, convince me that you did not murder Crocker, and bear witness against him who did. If you do, then I may be able to save your life."

"I . . . I believe I can do all that, but . . ."

"But what, man?" Sir John's patience was near exhausted.

"Can you save the painting for me, too?"

"I can try."

"Well . . . alright."

And so saying, he told the tale of what had happened the night before. Sir John, it seems, was quite right: Mr. Zondervan and John Abernathy, alias Johnny Skylark, had informed him of the hiding place and had agreed upon the mode of payment, even told him when best to attempt the theft—that last because Abernathy would be waiting in the back garden. All that Mr. Collier actually had to do was remove the jewels from the upstairs water closet and bring them outside to hand over to John Abernathy.

In the event, however, Maude Bleeker, the cook, caught a glimpse of Collier as he went out the door to the back garden, and she ran to tell Crocker, for she was aware, as were all the servants, that if the mistress's jewels were stolen, Crocker would be blamed. That was why, when Crocker was found, she wore only her petticoat and shift. She had run out after Collier without so much as bothering to dress herself. There she saw Collier with the case containing the jewels. She did not, however, see John Abernathy come up behind her. He grabbed her, put a hand over her mouth, and then cut her throat.

Collier's voice shook as he described the horror he felt when he saw the deed done. I believed him, and I believed he did feel horror. He was not a violent man. Nevertheless, when the body was found, and Maude Bleeker threatened him with what she had seen, he told her to beware, or she herself would likely get the same as Crocker; that was sufficient to silence her for the nonce.

"And did you mean by that you yourself would murder her if she were to inform of what she had seen?"

"No sir," said he to Sir John, "I meant it as a warning that Abernathy might have the same done to her."

"Did she realize this?"

He sighed deeply. "Probably not. She may have thought that I murdered Crocker."

"But you are willing to testify that it was Abernathy murdered the girl?"

"I suppose so . . . yes." Then, realizing that might not suffice, he declared forthrightly, "Yes, I am willing to testify to that."

"All right, Mr. Baker, you may take him away," said Sir John. "Lock him in the strongroom with the others from Bloomsbury Square. Leave constables Sheedy and Kelly here to secure this place. Jeremy and I must get on across the river to Bermondsey."

"But . . . what about the painting?" wailed Mr. Collier.

"Ah well," said Sir John, "you really ought not to bring it with you into that band of thieves. We shall keep it for you, sir, until your future be more certain."

It did not take near so long to reach Bermondsey as I supposed it would. This was due partly to the lateness of the hour, and partly due to the speed with which we were conveyed there by Mr. Bilbo's men. Though he did not resort to the whip, the driver did not spare the horses. He simply seemed to know how to get the most from them. And bouncing about as we were, there was little chance to talk, but what little Sir John said surprised me no end.

"It was you, Jeremy, who caused all that to happen."

"Oh?" said I. "What do you mean, sir?"

"He would not have given forth as he did, if you had not discovered that painting. How did you know to look for it?"

"An informed guess, sir. He revered the paintings in that gallery of Zondervan's, treated them almost as sacred objects."

"Indeed he seemed to care more for it than he did for his own life. Who painted it, do you know? Who was the artist?"

"I've no idea, sir."

"Ah well, it would mean little to me, in any case."

When we came to the wharf, I saw a considerable crowd of people — and horses — gathered round an empty berth. There were five Bow Street Runners, a whole squad of the King's Carabineers — standing at attention by their horses — a few longshoremen, urchins, and assorted dockside layabouts who had come out of curiosity. I described the confused scene to Sir John as we stepped down from the coach. Mr. Bailey spied us and hurried over, giving a greeting that was in itself not the least encouraging.

"Ah sir," said he, offering a casual salute, "we've a great mess on our hands, I fear. I only hope that Baker and Perkins did better than we've done here."

"They did quite well, thank you," Sir John replied. "But what is the trouble here?"

The trouble was this: Upon the arrival of the constables from Bow Street, the captain of the *Dingendam* quickly assessed the situation, sent off the last of the stevedores, and pulled in the landing plank. Mr. Bailey, as head of the detachment, was forced to negotiate for permission to come aboard. It became evident to him that negotiation was no more than a means of delay. The captain was waiting for something or someone, insisting that because the ship was Dutch, English peace officers had no right to come aboard and inspect the cargo.

"That, Mr. Bailey," Sir John commented, "is pure humbug."

"Just as I believed, sir, and I told him so in so many words — though my words was a bit rougher."

Nevertheless, the captain of the *Dingendam*, Van Cleef by name, continued to argue long past the point of good sense — until he heard something that caused him considerable alarm. Mr. Bailey heard it, too, and at first believed the noise to come from a coach, then a whole procession of coaches, for the sound of a goodly number of horses, their hooves striking against the cobblestones. It was the squad of the mounted King's Carabineers with Lieutenant Tabor riding at the head. Whereas Captain Van Cleef had managed to hold out against Mr. Bailey and his handful of constables, just the sight of the contingent of mounted troops was sufficient to send him to the main deck, where he began shouting orders to the crew (which were, of course, in Dutch and therefore quite incomprehensible to all but them). He attempted to parley with the lieutenant, but Tabor would have none of it. The young officer simply assembled his men along the wharf opposite the ship, whipped a document from his high boot, and read it forth from astride his horse. It was, in effect, a threat in support of the constables from Bow Street; if cooperation were not given by the captain and crew of the *Dingendam*, then the squad was given permission to blow the ship out of the water (though how this was to be accomplished with carabins was not said). The order was signed impressively by Colonel William Trotter, Comm., Sixth Dragoon Guards (King's Carabineers) and countersigned by Major Francis Hughes, Provost Marshal, The Tower.

The Dutch captain's response was to call out further orders (in Dutch) and to make ready for a swift departure. The hawsers were cut; the anchor weighed; they began to ease away from the wharf. Lieutenant Tabor ordered his men to dismount. Then did he instruct them to pull their carabins from their saddle scabbards, which they did. They aimed, and they fired at the downward flash of the lieutenant's sword.

Truly, not much damage was done to the *Dingendam* by the volley. The crew had the good sense to duck, and their captain took his ship just out into the current. They might have escaped altogether, had they taken the tide, but once some distance from the wharf, he ordered them again to drop anchor. So there they sat in near darkness, not truly out of range of the carabins, but perhaps out of effective range.

"How long has it been at such an impasse?" Sir John asked Mr. Bailey.

"Too long," he replied. "They'll lose the tide if they wait much longer."

"It must be Zondervan who's keeping them. I wonder where he could be."

"And where, for that matter, has Constable Patley got to?"

"I ordered him not to let the Dutchman out of his sight," said Sir John.

"You don't suppose he could have been bribed off, do you?"

"No." It was said with a certain air of assurance. "I don't."

My own eyes, I believe, were sharper than Mr. Bailey's. They may certainly have been keener than Lieutenant Tabor's. With them, I spied movement out there upon the river. It was not the *Dingendam* that moved, except for a gentle bobbing as it rode at anchor. No, it was a waterman's small boat, which made its way slowly but stealthily to the big ship. I walked out onto the wharf and stared into the gloom and was able, after a moment, to see that there were three men there in the boat—the oarsman and his two passengers. Then did I turn back to Sir John to inform him of what I had seen.

He was not, however, where I had left him. I looked about, altogether unsure of where he might have gone, then saw he had been taken by Mr. Bailey to talk with the lieutenant and another man—not in uniform—who, even with his back to me, looked somewhat familiar. Indeed, he turned out to be none other than Constable Patley, who was offering his apologies and excuses for having lost Mr. Zondervan in the great crush of carriages and hackneys in Drury Lane outside the theater.

"I do believe Zondervan hopped out whilst my horse was trapped among the coaches at the theater and unable to move, for when I came up to the coach, stopped the driver, and looked inside, he just plain wasn't inside."

Then, before I could get so much as a word in, Lieutenant Tabor made a remark which puzzled me greatly.

"You were never good in pursuit, were you Patley?" said he with a sneer. "As I recall, you eventually lost the track of those escaping prisoners even before it was properly laid down."

What prisoners? How could you lose a track before it was left? What history did they share?

"To put it simple, Sir John," said Mr. Patley, ignoring the lieutenant completely, "I lost that man Zondervan."

I could hold back no longer: "Sir, I believe I know where he is."

All four faces turned toward me. Patley grasped me by the arm.

"Where? Tell me where."

"Just about to the ship by now," said I. "If you —"

Patley released me suddenly with such force that he near threw me down. Then did he leap beyond the lieutenant and grab away the carabin from one of the troopers, who was too surprised to respond.

He shouted at me: "Come along! Show me!"

Having made the sighting and announced it, I felt I could do naught but show him what I had seen. We ran out to the end of the wharf together, with the lieutenant, the trooper, and Mr. Bailey calling after us.

"There," said I, pointing out across the water at the *Dingendam*. "You see? They've already thrown the ladder down."

And it was indeed true: A rope ladder dangled over the side of the ship. It appeared to me that one of the waterman's passengers had already climbed aboard, since only one remained in the boat, and he now prepared to ascend the ladder.

I attempted to call this to the attention of Constable Patley, but he paid no attention whatsoever to me. He was setting up to take his shot, dropping down into a kneeling posture, resting an elbow upon his knee that his hand might support and steady the barrel. He seemed so completely prepared to shoot that I was quite taken by surprise when he bellowed forth a warning: "Stop or I shall shoot!"

Indeed the man on the ladder did not stop. He began, rather, to scramble up the ladder so recklessly that it began swinging wildly back and forth against the hull of the ship, making it an apparently impossible shot.

Or so I thought. Mr. Patley thumbed back the hammer on the carabin, took the slack from the trigger, and then squeezed. The man upon the ladder halted, simultaneous with the shot. For a long moment he simply hung onto the wooden rung above him. Then his grip relaxed, and he fell back into the river. He made no motion to attempt to swim, nor to float. He simply sank.

Mr. Patley rose and turned, just as a crowd of troopers, constables, and the principals of the earlier drama gathered round him. He handed the carabin to its owner, thanking him somewhat ironically for the use of it. And to the lieutenant he said: "Maybe I were not much at soldierin', but I could always shoot."

There was no reply.

Sir John, there with the rest, declared that he could hear the sound of the capstan turning. "The anchor is aweigh. They will be off and down the river before you know it, Lieutenant Tabor. I advise you and your men to mount up and be off. You've a long ride ahead of you."

"Yes sir, I agree," said the lieutenant, and with a shouted order, he sent the troopers back to their horses. Then, about to depart, he offered his hand to Constable Patley. "Good shooting, Corporal. I was always certain of your skill."

Then, at another command, the squad mounted in unison, and Tabor led them away in a brisk canter.

"Where are they off to?" asked Mr. Bailey.

"To the Gravesend Customs Station," said Sir John. "I put them on notice that a Dutch ship full of contraband goods might be coming their way tonight. The lieutenant and his men are riding on ahead to inform customs that they might send a Coast Guard vessel to blockade their way at the mouth of the Thames."

"You've thought of everything, haven't you, sir?"

"I've tried," said Sir John. "Indeed I have tried. But Mr. Patley, I do wish you had exercised a bit of restraint."

"Oh? How was that, sir? I shouted a warning."

"I heard you, and that was as it should have been, but it would have been so much easier to sort all this out if I had Mr. Zondervan to question."

"Oh, you may have him yet, sir. That weren't Zondervan I shot out there."

"It wasn't?"

"Ah, no sir. It was John Abernathy."

"You're sure of that, Mr. Patley?"

"I'm sure."

TWELVE

In which matters
are explained and
Annie brings good news

"Didn't you realize the nature of the situation, Jeremy? I thought that you did. Mr. Patley was my spy. Indeed, yes, right there in that den of thieves."

"Why, then I was of no use to you at all, was I? That is to say, all that running round St. James Street, questioning witnesses at Trezavant's, I might just as well have gone out instead and picked daisies in the park."

"Oh, by no means," said Sir John to me. "You brought me an abundance of good information from your investigations."

It was one day past that great evening on which so many prisoners were taken and so much evidence gathered. Mr. Zondervan and Captain Van Cleef had been brought back from Gravesend by Lieutenant Tabor and his men. The *Dingendam* was in quarantine and its crew held in detention. Sir John had emptied the strongroom at his court session and sent Mr. Collier and the captain to the Fleet Prison, and the rest off to Newgate. ("Good enough for them," he declared.) Trials at Old Bailey would take place as soon as dates could be set.

As for myself, I rejoiced less about this outcome than I should have. I sulked and skulked around Number 4 Bow Street through the day, thinking that all had been accomplished without my help. Late that afternoon, Sir John, as he did so often, correctly perceived my state of mind, called me into his chambers, and went directly to the point.

Yet I had still to be convinced. "Could you be more specific?" I asked him. "If there was such an abundance of good information, it should be easy to supply an example or two." (Perhaps since Sir John forgave me these occasional bouts of priggish self-conceit, you, reader, can also find it in your heart to do so.)

"I can do that easily," said he. "Let us take as an instance the trap we were able to lay for the robbers at Lord Mansfield's residence. That was done largely through information you provided."

"Oh? How . . . how was that, sir?"

"You will recall that when you went off to Mr. Bilbo's to check Mr. Burnham's story with residents of the house, you were discouraged because you felt it was quite inevitable that they would lie to protect him. Do you remember what I told you then?"

"Well . . . yes. I believe you advised me to pay strict attention to them, because it is often only through the lies that we can get to the truth — or words to that effect."

"Very good," said he. "I'd no idea you listened to me so closely. Now think, Jeremy, who did you run into there, evidently quite unexpectedly?"

"Why, it was Mary Pinkham," said I, surprised at the memory.

"Indeed, and what did she tell you?"

"That she was going to seek employment."

"Where?"

"Why, of course! How could it have slipped my mind? At Lord Mansfield's in Bloomsbury Square."

"And next time you saw her, that's where she was."

"Acting as one of the robber band."

"Right you are! But you checked her story later, and found she was not employed there and had not even applied. I foresaw that and reasoned that since she was under suspicion as the distressed female who persuaded the butler to open Trezavant's door, she had likely heard Lord Mansfield's residence in Bloomsbury Square mentioned as the next place to be robbed. That was enough for me to seek Lord Mansfield's permission to place two men in his house to guard it."

"Constables Perkins and Brede."

"Exactly! You took the letter to Lord Mansfield yourself. I couldn't allow the Lord Chief Justice himself to be robbed so rudely. If I had done, it would have been an insult to the entire legal system. So I posted Perkins and Brede there, even though I had no proper idea of when the attack might come. Yet you helped supply information there, too."

"I did?"

"Certainly. Do you recall when you went off to fetch Mr. Donnelly to look at the girl's body out in back of Trezavant's?"

"Yes, of course I do. I had to wait, for he had been at a dinner party at Lord Mansfield's home." Then, remembering, I added excitedly: "Mr. Zondervan was there, too. In fact, he drove Mr. Donnelly home in his coach. When I told you about it the next day, you became quite interested and sent me to invite him here for a talk."

"Ah yes, and while you were there, you noted the intense activity in the house, which seemed to you quite like preparations to move the household—and householder. And you thought the move would be very soon, that very evening perhaps. You also heard Mr. Patley somewhere in the house, and that frighted me a bit. But he, by the bye, had confirmed your suspicions and believed that an early departure was planned."

"Why 'early,' Sir John?" I asked.

"Well, yes, why indeed? Because, you see, that letter you brought me from Mr. Humber contained some very interesting information. First of all, it told me that there was indeed a ship which seemed too heavily insured for the cargo that it carried—at least that which was listed upon its manifest. It was a ship of Dutch registry, the *Dingendam*, which was to sail on the 21st for some part in the North American colonies—Boston, I believe it was." He smiled broadly just then. "That's right, Jeremy, that is today's date. In other words, taking the tide, as they did last night, put them out of port a day earlier than the time of departure they had registered with the London port authority. Oh, and yes, perhaps most interesting of all, the owner of the *Dingendam* was listed as a Mr. Hans Zondervan. That confirmed your guess from Mr. Martinez's clews—a very clever guess, I might add.

"Let me see, now, where was I? Ah yes, when Zondervan arrived— you know, I never did find out how you persuaded him to come."

"I described you to him as a rather pathetic sort, one who would be happy to have a visit from one in the great world."

"Excellent! We were then wonderfully in harmony," said he, "for I, in my role as an eccentric old codger, drew from him the names of a few of those in the great world at whose grand houses he had dined—how he was received with his silly Dutch tales, et cetera. And among those who entertained him thus were Lord Lilley and our friend, the coroner, Mr. Trezavant. In other words, he had scouted these houses and decided what they might have that would be worth stealing. Since he had just visited Lord Mansfield and charmed the great company present, and since both you and Mr. Patley agreed that Zondervan was preparing to leave a day earlier than we had been advised, I decided that the raid upon the home of the Lord Chief Justice had to be that very evening—and it was."

This was, I admitted to myself, a very full accounting. And it was apparent that indeed I had played an important part in the gathering of information, but nevertheless . . .

"Now, that is but one instance. There were others," said Sir John. "Do you wish to hear more?"

"Well . . . no," said I hesitantly. "I wonder only why you did not apprise me of the importance of these bits of information when I brought them to you? In short, why did you not keep me better informed?"

He fell into a troubled silence. I could tell that there was something he wished to say, but could not quite put into words. Yet I would hear it from him, and so I pressed him on the matter.

"Do you not trust me, sir, to keep your confidence?"

"Oh, but of course I do," he declared hastily. "It is just . . . well, let me tell you a story." Then, taking a breath, he began: "It was when I was about your age and a midshipman in the Navy. We were part of a squadron sailing about the Mediterranean showing the colors. We put in at Naples which, traditionally, has been a friend to England. To demonstrate this, the Duke of Naples sent to us a troop of entertainers who performed right there aboard ship. There were acrobats and jugglers, all of them most expert in their skills. Yet none could be called a true artist, except for one: a magician. Now, I know not why it should be—perhaps it may have something to do with the Neapolitans' talent for thievery—but it is said that they produce the very best magicians in the world, though one does hear tales of great wonders done in the Orient. I am well aware that there is no such thing as true magic. It is all illusion and sleight of hand. Still, when it is done with great knowledge, talent, and ability, it does approach true artistry. And the magician who entertained us that day in Naples possessed all those qualities: He was a true artist. He spoke not a word during his performance, which made it all the more mysterious. The man may have been mute for all I know. Yet I had no trouble understanding when he pointed to me, seated in the front row, and beckoned me up there beside him before them all, captain and crew. He brought forth a broad-brimmed hat and gestured that I might put it on. That I did, and found it was much too large. It covered my eyes completely, and there was much jollity at my expense, but I minded not a whit, for it was just such a happy occasion. In any case, he showed me and showed all the rest that apart from its size, it was a perfectly ordinary hat. Then, sent back to my seat by him, I sat and watched him do something quite marvelous. He turned the hat upside down and covered it with a cloth. Then, after making a few passes over it, he removed the cloth, reached into the hat, and pulled out . . . a *rabbit!*"

(Reader, I myself had by that time seen the same trick performed two or three times on a Sunday in Covent Garden, yet it was the first and last time Sir John had witnessed it, and even as he spoke of it, he seemed rather awestruck by the memory.)

"Jeremy," said he, resuming upon a lighter note, "I have told you that story for a reason, for ever afterward I have attempted to astound others as that Neapolitan magus astounded me. To put it another way, I love to pull rabbits from a hat! I love to gather all the bits of information, to shift them about, reorder them, and so on until I come up with an astounding solution, the proper solution, the *only* solution. But to astound, I need an audience—and you, Jeremy, are my audience. If I kept you informed every step of the way, there would be no surprise, no astonishment, no rabbit out of the hat. Or far worse, if you knew all, then you might reach the solution before me; then I would be the one astounded. Not only would I then lose the pleasure of pulling the rabbit from the hat, I would also be embarrassed in the bargain.

"Then . . ." I hesitated, "then I would say that it is all something of a game to you. Is that not so, sir?"

He thought hard upon that and seemed about to deny the conclusion I had drawn from what he had said. In fact, he did begin to shake his head from side to side, but then he stopped, pursed his lips judiciously, and said: "Perhaps *like* a game, though not really quite that. Let us call it, rather, a very serious game."

I was not altogether sure what he meant by that, but I did not think that this was the proper time to ask him. It would be best, I thought, to remove myself that I might consider the matter by myself. I rose from the chair where I had sat during our long conversation and made ready to depart. Then did one last question occur to me.

"Sir," said I, "if Constable Patley was your spy there in the enemy camp, how did he manage to ingratiate himself to such a gang of cutthroats?" Then, remembering poor Crocker, I added, "Yes, literally that: cutthroats."

"He did that by convincing them he would be *their* spy in *our* camp," said he. "But it is a good deal more complicated than that, and thereby hangs a fascinating tale. You would do better to ask him yourself."

I climbed the stairway to our kitchen, aware that it was late enough that I must stoke the fire for Lady Katherine. She, of course, had taken Annie's place as cook until such time as another could be found. The idea of replacing Annie gave me a heavy heart indeed. How could she be replaced? She had become as one of the family—and a more important member than either Clarissa or I, for she fulfilled a far more fundamental function. What could Lady Kate's secretary or Sir John's assistant do that could match cooking, baking, and filling bellies with good things to eat? A well-fed family is a happy one.

As I came to the top of the stairs, I heard voices, women's voices, from beyond the door. Thinking them to be Clarissa's and Lady Kate's, I saw no need to knock. I threw open the door and walked right in. What I saw made me believe for an instant that I had somehow stepped back a day, a week, or even a year in time, for there at the kitchen table, laughing and chattering as sisters will, sat Clarissa and Annie. They turned to me.

"Annie," I shouted. "You've come back!" She jumped from her chair and embraced me, and even went so far as to plant a kiss upon my cheek.

"Yes," said she, "but only for just this one evening."

"Oh Jeremy," sang Clarissa, now also upon her feet, "you've no idea what wonderful news she has. Tell him, Annie, tell him!"

"Yes," said I, "by all means, do tell me. You must!"

"Well, you, of all people, will remember what sent me to school to learn to read."

"Of course, it was that performance of *Othello* at the Drury Lane. I remember well how we all trooped down afterward to congratulate Mr. Garrick."

"Then I," said she, "made bold to tell him that he would one day welcome me in his company." She paused—for dramatic effect, I suppose—then did she sing out most gleefully: "And that is what he has done!"

It took me a moment to grasp fully what she had said. "Oh, Annie, can you mean it? Is it true?"

And then, with help from Clarissa in the form of interruptions, reminders, and comments, Annie began her story. She had taken herself in hand the evening of the dinner at which Mr. Johnson and Mr. Burnham were present. She lay awake that night lecturing herself regarding Mr. Burnham. Had he led her on? No, he had held himself within the limits proper to a teacher and his student. Had she then deceived herself? Yes, indeed she had, just as she had done early on with Tom Durham, Lady Katherine's son. She was embarrassed, ashamed, and humiliated even to think upon the circumstances which had brought her to this state.

But then did she take heart, remembering the joy of her first night at the theater—and the promise she had made to herself and to David Garrick. She had given it all up for some daft child's dream of eternal love with Mr. Burnham. Why, you would think that she had been inspired in it by one of Clarissa's romances! Annie cursed herself for having put aside her ambition so cheaply. But then did she recall that Mr. Burnham had called to her attention a notice upon the door of the Drury Lane Theatre to the effect that Mr. Garrick would audition candidates for the Drury Lane apprenticeships by appointment during this month. And below this a warning: "Many are called, but few are chosen." Mr. Burnham assured her that she was ready and would be chosen. By that time, she was indifferent to all but him, and promptly put thoughts of Drury Lane and David Garrick out of her mind. But now they were back.

Next morning, she went off to the theater to ask for an appointment and was promptly brought into the presence of Mr. Garrick himself. He had looked her up and down and said, "There is no time like the present." And with that, he brought her up to the empty stage of the deserted theater.

"Have you prepared something?" he asked her.

She nodded, and he retired to a chair placed in the wings. He gave her a wave, signaling she might begin.

Annie knew a good deal of Shakespeare by heart, and there was no question in her mind but that Ophelia's soliloquy from Act Three of *Hamlet* (which begins, "O, what a noble mind is here o'erthrown!") was the one that was best for her. She did not recite it, she acted it with gestures and a bit of movement, ignoring Mr. Garrick and playing to the empty, darkened theater.

When she had done, she turned and found him close by, staring at her quite intently. He asked if she knew the song in Act Four. When she said that she did, he told her to sing it. That she did, putting it to a tune she had adapted from "Lord Randall," to which it fitted quite well. Once through it, he asked her to sing it again, which she did to his satisfaction. He then asked her to walk across the stage and return to him, which she did, pleasing him less. He told her that she needed to work on movement, but then he went on to inform her of the terms of the apprenticeship, which were made to sound quite harsh, though they did not seem so to Annie. He asked her for her full name and told her that papers would be drawn up immediately and she was to come in next day to sign them.

"Does that mean . . . ?"

"That means that you will be a lowly apprentice, nothing more—but nevertheless, a member of our company."

The story that Annie told set Clarissa and I burbling once again with excitement. It seemed near impossible that she had triumphed so signally over circumstance and chance, and over herself—but she had. And there were none more happy for her than we two, unless it be Sir John and Lady Katherine, who joined us in little more than an hour. They found a grand celebratory meal prepared for them by Annie and Clarissa. Sir John called for a bottle of claret, and toasts were drunk that Annie might prosper in her new career. (And as you may know, reader, she did.) It was a most happy occasion, yet at the same time a sad one, for it was the last time we five gathered together there at Number 4 Bow Street, and I believe that we all had some presentiment of that.

It was a number of days before I was able to make more than fleeting contact with Constable Will Patley. Mr. Bailey had taken him under his charge and was teaching him all that could be known about being a Bow Street Runner. Patley was well-liked by Mr. Bailey and the other constables. The only area in which his performance was in any way disappointing continued to be his written reports. And at last, I was called in, as I knew I would be eventually, to help him with those. He learned quickly enough, but he had little knowledge of English orthography and usage to build upon. As for orthography, I secured enough from Mr. Marsden from our ready-cash fund to purchase Samuel Johnson's dictionary and for usage, a copy of *Robinson Crusoe*, both well-worn but readable. These I presented to him with a bit of pomp and ceremony, telling him that I had never heard of the man who could read through Defoe's greatest work and remain indifferent to it. It was a grand story, said I, and it was also written so well that if he read it through, it could not but improve his manner of writing. And the dictionary would provide meaning and the correct spelling of every word of Defoe's that gave him the slightest bit of trouble. He took all this with equanimity, saying little of anything that could be interpreted as a promise that he would read the one and use the other to help him to do it.

Therefore was I somewhat surprised when, after a week or so had passed by, he engaged me in a conversation which, if not about the book directly, was at least more or less inspired by it.

"You know," said he, "I been readin' that book you gave me, and I will say it ain't dull. But it put me in mind of my time on the island."

"What island?" I asked, having heard nothing of this before. "Were you shipwrecked, as he was?"

"Oh no, nothin' like that, though I come to feel like I was marooned there for fair. The island was Jamaica. And they had our regiment there—that's the King's Carabineers, otherwise known as the Sixth Dragoon Guards—to keep order generally and to put down any rebellion amongst the slaves, should one arise."

"So you were in the Carabineers, were you? That's how you and Lieutenant Tabor came to be on such familiar terms."

"Familiar maybe, but not friendly," said he. "But indeed we was there for three years, and I don't mind tellin' you that they was the worst three years of my life. They put me in such a state, I wanted out of the regiment soon as I come back."

Much was coming clear; the more he told, the more I wished to know. "What affected you so deeply, Mr. Patley?"

"You mean what stuck in my craw so bad about the place? Well, it wasn't the look of it. It fair took your breath away, some parts were so pretty. That was what was so strange—seeing that kind of cruelty where everything was flowers and green and the sky so blue you'd swear it couldn't be the same one as is up above us here."

He hesitated then for a good long moment, but I had the sense that he would continue, so I said nothing. With a sharp glance at me then, as if assessing my capacity as a listener, he resumed his tale.

"It was the slaves," said he, "the way they was treated—just like animals. Or worse, really, 'cause the planters treated their cattle and horses better. I couldn't quite believe it when first we come. They told me I'd get used to it—but I never did. It only got worse. The last year was worst of all."

"Why was that?" I asked.

"Well, there was a lot of what they called 'unrest' there amongst the slaves then—which was just last year, come to think of it, though it seems much longer ago than that. Anyways, things was specially bad at three of the plantations, so the colonel let himself get talked into putting a platoon at each of them—just living right there on the plantations. As it happened, Tabor was our platoon commander. Now, neither the planter, or his family, or the overseer and his family, none of the whites who ran the place, would have anything to do with us troopers—only with Tabor. So we had nobody to talk to except ourselves or the slaves. We got pretty close to them that way. And we saw that the reason why this plantation had more 'unrest' than the others was because the slaves there got treated worse. Any fool could see that.

"So, like I said, we got pretty close to them, and we were even what you might call friendly. You might not realize it—or maybe you would, working for the magistrate and all—but not all the slaves was black Africans. A number were white Englishmen, just like you and me, who was convicted and given transportation, instead of the rope. Glad they were to get it at the time, but afterwards, I just wonder if they were. There were more of them on this partic'lar plantation than on most, but they didn't get treated any better than the Africans—if anything, they got treated worse. Anyways, I got pretty thick with one of them, called himself Johnny Skylark. He was a Londoner and a thief—he made no bones about that—but a very entertaining fellow, he was. I asked him how he managed to keep his spirits up in this awful place. And he said that he was going to escape some day. He was sure of it, and it was knowing that kept him going. I remember I told him then that if he was going to do a scarper, then he'd better do it after I'd left, 'cause I didn't want to be the one brought him back. He just sort of smiled at that and nodded, and we let it go. Or I did, anyways.

"So it wasn't long, o'course, before he made his run for it, and he weren't alone. He took all the healthiest blacks and a few whites who was working in the south field right along with him when he did. There were four troopers riding inspection through the coffee plants. One of them saw the other three get pulled off their horses, and he turned round and rode like the devil was after him for the rest of the platoon. The slaves, all of them, might have made it to the mountains where the maroons hid themselves, if he hadn't made it back and put the lieutenant on notice what was happening. As it was, we rounded up most of them, but not all. The leaders were all up front, and just us few—the lieutenant, me, and maybe six more. I'm out in front because I was the best tracker in the platoon. Tabor was right behind me, though. We come upon them on an uphill. They was right close to the crest. We had a good look at them, and they wasn't so far away, so Tabor yells to me that I should stop and take the shot at one of them. So I had no choice. I reins in, dismounts, pulls the carabin out of the saddle scabbard, and made ready to fire from a kneel. The lieutenant was down off his horse, and the rest of the troopers was pulling up—lot of noise and confusion just then. I take aim at one of them on the hill, but Tabor's right behind me, sighting up my barrel. And he yells at me, he said, 'No, get the white man. He's the leader. They'll all turn back if you get him.' He meant Johnny Skylark, of course, so I took aim at him. It wasn't really a hard shot, but he was pretty close to the top of the hill, so I'd only have the one chance at him—but after all, I was regimental champion, the king of the sharpshooters, weren't I?

"So I aimed, I shot, and I missed. The lieutenant called for a volley from the rest of the troopers, and they let go on command. Two or three of the blacks dropped, but two or three more, as well as Johnny, made it over the hill and down into the bush where our horses couldn't go, and our carabins wouldn't do us no good. I lost their tracks, anyways. The lieutenant claimed I'd missed Johnny on purpose, brought me up on charges before the colonel. I just denied and denied and denied. 'Course it didn't help that Johnny turned and waved just before he disappeared. He knew it was me shot at him and missed. Still, there was so much going on behind me—the lieutenant yelling in my ear, the troopers reining up and dismounting—that who could say that I hadn't missed fair and square?"

"And did you?" I put in quickly.

"No, I missed on purpose. The lieutenant was right. But the colonel said it was impossible to court-martial a man for missing a target, else three-quarters of the regiment would be up for it. So I would be permitted to resign as soon as we were back in Britain."

"Well, that's . . . that's quite a story," said I.

"Wait, I ain't done yet," said he, catching a deep breath or two. "Anyways, I resigned. Ben Bailey and Sir John took me on here, and I wasn't working this job more than a month when the Lord Lilley house was robbed, and about two days after that, who should I run into drinking away on Bedford Street but Johnny Skylark, who now wants to be known as John Abernathy, which he swears is his rightful name. I can't say as I was surprised to see him. First of all, he was a Londoner, and a thief must know a city well to work in it proper. And there was this about that raid on the Lilley house. It was exactly like the ones he and his crew carried out some years before when he was caught and given transportation for the term of his natural life."

"Except for one thing," said I. "There was a man murdered."

"So there was, and I'll talk about that in just a bit. So, as I say, I wasn't so surprised when I met him right there. I was surprised, though, that he knew so much about what had happened to me—that I'd been more or less drummed out of the regiment, and that I was now a constable with the Bow Street Runners—but he did. He as good as admitted that it was him and four of his chums, including one from the Burnham plantation, who did the robbery at Lord Lilley's. And he wound up asking me if I had a good place to dorse. 'Why don't you come live with us in the Dutchman's castle?' he asked me, and I told him I'd have to think about that, might get in the way of my work as a constable. But he said no. 'The two might go right well together. Meet me here tomorrow.'

"So I went to Sir John with it, and he said that I ought to go and be his spy. That didn't appeal to me much until he reminded me of the porter who'd been shot dead without a plea."

"And he, himself, was wounded that night in St. James Street," said I. "It must have been Abernathy."

"Oh, it was," said Constable Patley. "You damn near scared him to death shootin' back. He didn't expect that. And then there was the three troopers who was pulled off their horses. I knew all those boys. I should have. They was in my platoon. They got their throats cut. If it wasn't him did it, it was him ordered it. So you can see, I didn't have much of an argument with myself on this question of spying for the law. The funny thing was, Johnny never had a doubt I was with him, because I'd had a shot at him and missed out of friendship back there in Jamaica. He even explained away the murder of the porter at Lord Lilley's. He told me that just by luck that fella turned out to be one of his old robbery gang, the one who bore witness against him and sent him off to Jamaica. Just settling old scores, he said. For some reason, it was important to him that I think well of him.

"I don't know how much good I was as a spy. You seemed to get more information than I did. About all I could do was say yea or nay to what you'd dug up. But Zondervan paid me in sovereigns, and there were things that the Dutchman wanted to know, like how many constables there were at Bow Street, who was in charge. Y'see, he couldn't really believe that a blind man could run things the way Sir John did. What they really wanted to know was who and how many they might meet in the neighborhood of Bloomsbury Square. So, naturally, we knew that the next house they raided would be in Bloomsbury. Sir John told me what to tell them, so it was just a matter of waiting them out.

"But I'll tell you, young sir, I might still have had a bit of feeling for John Abernathy left in me, for I knew what he'd escaped from, and I knew what such mistreatment can do to a man. But when I found out he'd killed that poor pregnant girl, that ended it between me and him. I saw he'd become like a mad dog, and so like a mad dog, he was shot down."

"I have a pair of questions," said I.

"Ask them," said he.

"Why did Abernathy's robber gang always do their work in blackface?"

"Because Johnny said one thing he learned working on the plantation was that whites can't tell one black man from another. All they see is the color of the skin. And besides, one of the gang really was an African; Osili was his name. He angered me by wearing my Dragoon's coat on that second raid. Had a fondness for it, he did. He used to study himself in the looking glass wearing it, when he could."

"He was the one died of his wounds there at Lord Mansfield's?"

"He was the one."

"Just one more question. Did I hear you aright when you gave the name of the plantation where you were that last year as 'the Burnham plantation?' "

"That's the one. That's the name. It was a Welshman, getting on in years, who owned it and operated it. But he married a widow with four children. I heard his own son was living in London. You don't, by any chance, know him, do you?"

I never gave Mr. Patley's question a frank answer. Indeed, whether out of consideration or cowardice, I never mentioned to Robert Burnham what I had learned from the constable. As for what became of those taken into custody on that grand night, all were hanged for theft, with the exception of Mistress Pinkham, who was given transportation to the North American colonies, and Mr. Collier, who in return for his testimony against Mr. Zondervan was generously given but a year in Newgate Gaol. The captain and crew of the *Dingendam* were held for near a month while the ship was searched thoroughly, and all but Lady Lilley's jewels were found aboard the vessel. The maritime court tried to decide what laws had been broken, but finally, after repeated protests by the Dutch ambassador, the captain and crew were allowed to depart in their vessel. I happened to hear that John Abernathy's body, pulled from the Thames, was claimed by a woman for burial. Though I have no certainty of it, I have always assumed that it was Maude Bleeker who saw him to his last resting place.

Thus do things change, lives end, people come and go. Only, it seems, do the laws of our country and colonies remain static. The contradiction as regards slavery remains unchanged. The Somerset case was continued until autumn as the Lord Chief Justice wrestled with it. In the end, it bested him. Though Mr. Somerset, the former slave, was given his freedom, the decision came in such a way that it changed naught but that. It remains for Parliament to remove that cancer upon the body politic.